D0387935

THE MENTOR

Also by Lee Matthew Goldberg

Slow Down

THE MENTOR

A THRILLER

Lee Matthew Goldberg

A Thomas Dunne Book
St. Martin's Press New York

This is a work of fiction. All of the characters, organizations, and events portrayed in this novel are either products of the author's imagination or are used fictitiously.

THOMAS DUNNE BOOKS.
An imprint of St. Martin's Press.

www.thomasdunnebooks.com
www.stmartins.com

The Library of Congress Cataloging-in-Publication Data is available upon request.

ISBN 978-1-250-08354-8 (hardcover)
ISBN 978-1-250-08355-5 (e-book)

First Edition: June 2017

10 9 8 7 6 5 4 3 2 1

For MOM and DAD,
two great mentors

Poor is the pupil that doesn't surpass his master.

—Leonardo da Vinci

THE MENTOR

1

FROM FAR AWAY the trees at Bentley College appeared as if on fire, crowns of nuclear leaves dotting the skyline. Professor William Lansing knew it meant that fall had firmly arrived. Once October hit, the Connecticut campus became festooned with brilliant yellows, deep reds, and Sunkist orange nature. People traveled for miles to witness the foliage, rubbernecking up I-95 and flocking to nearby Devil's Hopyard, a giant park where the students might perform Shakespeare, or enter its forest gates at nighttime to get high and wild. William had taken a meandering hike through its labyrinthine trails that morning before his seminar on Existential Ethics in Literature. It had been more than a decade since he'd entered its tree-lined arms, but today, the very day he was reaching the part in his long-gestating novel that took place in Devil's Hopyard, seemed like a fitting time to return.

His wife, Laura, hadn't stirred when he left at dawn. He slipped out of bed and closed the mystery novel propped open on her snoring chest. He often wrote early in the mornings. Before the world awoke, he'd arm himself with a steaming coffee and a buzzing laptop, the wind from off the Connecticut River pinching his cheeks. His chirping backyard would become a den of inspiration, or he'd luxuriate in the silence of Bentley at six o'clock when the only sound might be a student or two trundling down the Green to sleep off a fueled night of debauchery.

He'd been at Bentley for more than twenty years, tenured and always next in line to be department chair. He refused even the notion of the position for fear it might eat into time spent writing his opus. His colleagues understood this mad devotion. They too had their sights set on publications, most of them well regarded in journals, only a few of them renowned beyond Bentley's walls like William dreamed to be. Notoriety had dazzled him since he was a child—a time when his world seemed small and lifeless, and dreams of fame were his only escape.

His colleagues often questioned him about this elusive manuscript he'd been toiling on for years, but he found it best to remain tight-lipped, to entice mystery. It was how he ran his classroom as well, letting only a few chosen students get close, keeping the rest at enough of a distance to regard him as tough and impenetrable but fair. Maybe he'd made a few students cry when a paper they stayed up all night to finish received a failing grade, or when his slashes of red pen seemed to consume one of their essays on Sartre's *Nausea,* which he found *trite* and *pedestrian,* but that only made them want to do better the next time. They understood that he wanted his kingdom to be based on fear, for creativity soared in times of distress.

William's legs were sore after his hike that morning through Devil's Hopyard. The terrain was hilly and its jagged trails would challenge even a younger man, but he kept fit, wearing his fifty-five-year-old frame well. He had been an athlete back in school, a runner and a boxer who still kept a punching bag in the basement and ended his day with a brisk run through his town of Killingworth, a blue-collar suburban enclave surrounding Bentley's college-on-a-hill. He had all his hair, which was more than he could say for most of his peers, even though silver streaks now cut through the brown. He secretly believed this made him more dashing than during his youth. Women twenty years younger still gave him a second glance, and he often found Laura taking his hand at department functions and squeezing it tight, as if to indicate that *she* fully claimed him and there'd be no chance for even the most innocent of flirtations. He had a closet full of blazers with elbow patches and never wore ties so he could keep his collar open and expose his chest hair, which hadn't turned white yet. He had a handsome and regal face, well proportioned, and although his eyes drooped some due to a lifetime of battling insomnia, it gave him the well-worn look of being entirely too busy to sleep. People often spoke of him as a soul who never enjoyed being idle, someone who was always moving, expounding, and expanding.

"Hi, Professor Lansing," said Nathaniel, a tall and gangly freshman, who after three weeks into the semester had yet to look William in the eye. Nathaniel's legs twisted over one another with each step. William guessed that the boy had recently grown into his pole-like body and his brain now struggled with how to move it properly.

"Nathaniel," William said, wiping the sweat mustache from his top lip. He could smell his own lemony perspiration from the intense jaunt through Devil's Hopyard. "How did your paper on *The Stranger* turn out?"

Nathaniel's eyes seemed to avoid him even more. They became intent on taking in the colorful foliage, as if it had sprouted overnight.

"Well . . ." the boy began, still a hair away from puberty, his voice hitting a high octave, "I'm not totally sure what you meant about Meursault meeting his end because he didn't 'play the game.' "

William responded with a throaty laugh and a shake of his head. He placed a palm on Nathaniel's shoulder.

"Society's game, Nathaniel, the dos and don'ts we all must ascribe to. How, even if we slip on occasion, we're not supposed to admit what we did for fear of being condemned. Right?"

Nathaniel nodded, his rather large Adam's apple bobbing up and down in agreement too. He stuffed a bitten-down nail between his chapped lips and chewed away like a rat, leaving William to wonder if the boy was on some newfangled type of speed. He liked Nathaniel, who barely spoke in class but once in a while would give a nervous peep filled with promise. The students he paid the most attention to weren't the heads of the lacrosse team or the stars of the theater productions; those students would have a million other mentors fawning over them. He looked for the hidden jewels, the ones who were waiting for that extra push, who'd been passed over their whole lives but would someday excel past their peers. Then they would thank him wholeheartedly for igniting a spark.

"Is that why Camus didn't personalize the victim that Meursault killed?" Nathaniel asked, wary at first, as the two entered the doors of Fanning Hall past a swirl of other students. "So we sympathize with him despite his crime?"

William stopped at the door of his classroom, its cloudy window offering a view of a haze of students settling into their desks. He stood blocking the door so Nathaniel had no choice but to look in his eyes.

"Did you sympathize with him?"

"Yes . . . umm, it's hard to penalize someone for one mistake," Nathaniel said. "I know he shot the Arab guy, but . . . I don't know, sometimes things just happen. I guess that makes me callous."

"Or human."

William stared at Nathaniel for an uncomfortable extra few seconds before Kelsey, a pretty sorority girl with canary yellow hair, fluttered past them.

"Hey, Professor," Kelsey said, without looking Nathaniel's way. William could feel the boy's sigh crowding the hallway.

"Come, Nathaniel, we'll continue this debate in class."

William led the boy into the room. The students immediately became hushed and rigid.

Nathaniel slumped into a chair in the back while Kelsey cut off another girl to get a prime seat up front.

William placed his leather satchel on the table, took out a red marker, and scribbled on the board, *I didn't know what a sin was.* The handwriting looked like chicken scratch and the students had to squint a bit to decipher it, but eventually the entire class of twenty managed to correctly jot down the quote. They had gotten used to his idiosyncrasies.

"At the end of the novel, Meursault ponders that he didn't know what a sin was," William said. "What does that mean?"

A quarter of the class raised their hands, each one eager to be noticed. Kelsey clicked her tongue for attention, as if her desperation wasn't obvious enough. She looked like she had to pee. In the back, Nathaniel was fully absorbed in a doodle that resembled Piglet from *Winnie-the-Pooh.*

"Nathaniel," William barked, sending the pen flying out of the boy's hand. Nathaniel weaved his long arms around the desk to pick up the pen and then gave a slack-jawed expression as a response.

"Why does Meursault insist to the chaplain that he didn't know what a sin was?" William asked again.

Nathaniel silently pleaded for William to call on someone else. He let out an "uuuhhhhhhh" that lasted through endless awkward seconds.

Kelsey took it upon herself to chime in. "Professor, while Meursault understands he's been found guilty for his crime, he doesn't truly see that what he did was wrong."

William turned toward Kelsey to admonish her for speaking without being called on, a nasty habit that happened more and more with this ADD-addled generation than the prior one, but a red-leaf tree outside the window captured his attention instead, its color so unreal, so absorbing. The red, so vibrant like its leaves, had been painted with blood.

"Professor . . . *Professor.*"

The sound came from far away, as if hidden under the earth, screaming to be acknowledged.

"Professor Lansing?"

Kelsey waved her arm in his direction, grounding him. She gave a pout.

"Like, am I right, or what, Professor? He doesn't truly *see* that what he did was wrong."

William cleared his throat, maintaining control over the room. He smiled at them the same way he would for a photograph.

"Yes, that's true, Kelsey. Expressing remorse would constitute his actions as wrong. He knows his views make him a stranger to society, and he is content with this judgment. He accepts death and looks forward to it with peace. The crowds will cheer hatefully at his beheading, but they *will* be cheering. This is what captivates the readers seventy years after the book's publication. What keeps it and Camus eternal, immortal."

Kelsey beamed at the class, her grin smug as ever.

William went to the board, erased the quote, and replaced it with the word *IMMORTAL* in big block letters, this time written with the utmost perfect penmanship.

THE REST OF William's day included a creative writing class that he'd had to beg the department chair, Dr. Joyce Yancey, to give him, and an independent study on Edgar Allan Poe, which two seniors took. Mondays were his busiest, since he booked all his classes that day and then took the rest of the week for writing and office hours. Dr. Yancey had been hesitant about offering him a creative writing class, simply because he hadn't had a novel published yet and prospective students might want a "bigger name." Brooks Jessup, a newer hire, had a lockdown on the creative writing seminars after publishing a literary thriller to some acclaim that he liked to obnoxiously describe as a "modern Faulkner-esque journey." But this semester, Brooks had gotten a nice deal for his second novel, so a freshman seminar opened up. Unfortunately, the class was available for anyone to take, and most of the students were just there to express themselves or fulfill a requirement rather than actually displaying talent.

When William returned home, his house was eerily still. His twin children, Alicia and Bill Jr., had lived there while going to Bentley, so it'd been only a few years since they moved out. He hadn't entirely gotten used to their absence yet. They'd purchased a ramshackle bar in the next town over and chose to room together in the apartment above. Laura thought it best that they stayed at home to save money in case the bar went belly-up, but William advocated for their independence. Ideally, he wanted them to live apart and forge separate lives, but they always had a close symbiotic relationship he assumed one could have only from sharing a womb. As an only child, he had to admit being jealous. He couldn't think of anyone he was that close to besides Laura, and he was twenty-five when he met her. Twenty-five years of experiences that she'd never be able to share in so they could fully understand each other like twins would.

The glass door to the backyard slid open and Laura entered with a basket of squash blossoms. She wore heavy gardening gloves and had a swatch of dirt across her forehead, often from combing her hair out of her face after digging into the ground. Four years older than him and pushing sixty, she was beginning to slow down but she still had a youthful face. The long New England winters kept her away from any excess sun exposure and her skin was porcelain smooth, the color of pearls. Her light blond hair had thinned out some and turned off-white, but she maintained it with weekly trips to a salon in Old Saybrook. She'd always been a nervously thin woman, prone to being spooked, and her gray eyes took on whatever color she wore. She dressed simply, matronly, but no one would ever say she didn't have style. Sweaters were tied around her neck, a cross necklace often sat above her heart, and white gold bracelets usually jangled from her wrists. She might be described as quiet, which William liked. The two of them never worried about lulls in conversations. Dinners were sometimes spent silently reading the papers, occasionally remarking on the news of the day. She was a loving and doting woman, and after all these years the couple still appeared drawn to each other.

Laura was humming an indecipherable song as she stepped inside, likely from her church choir. The choir took classic songs and updated them by inserting *the Lord* for *baby, love,* or *honey.* She leaned forward and squinted at William before a warm smile broke out. She fumbled with her glasses and hung them low on her nose.

"Oh, William, I didn't even see you. Been home long?"

William pointed to his leather satchel, still in hand. "Just got in."

She fixed the basket of squashes on her knee to get a better grip and then hoisted it onto the dining room table.

"Cabbage worms have been gobbling these up," she said. "Hit them with the Spinosad but had to spend the day watching over them like a hawk."

He never envied her days. It seemed as if she spent too much time finding ways to fill up her time. She had the church and did charity work for it, lunched with a smattering of friends, and of course her bookcases were full of mystery novels, but William always felt he was the most exciting part of her life, which saddened him. They'd met studying literature in grad school, and he'd tried to get her to start writing her own novel too. She gave the excuse that she could only write what she knew, and few would want to read what she knew these days.

"I was thinking spaghetti squash with marinara sauce, maybe some turkey meatballs to cut down on your red meat intake like the doctor suggested."

William frowned. Besides his opus, red meat was one of his other true passions. He liked it as rare as possible, practically raw.

"I'm reaching a major part in my novel tonight, so I might just eat in the study."

She clapped her hands and gave him a peck on the cheek.

"Oh, William, how exciting. I'll cook up some mixed beef and pork meatballs, then."

She gave him a pat on the butt. "Well, go now, scoot up there and get to finishing."

He kissed her on the lips and wiped away the smear of dirt on her forehead. Her cheeks reddened.

"The novel's really good, Laura. I mean . . . I feel like I've finally figured out the snags."

She fiddled with her cross necklace.

"Of course you have. I married you for your brain, not your body."

She gave a harder pat on his butt, shooing him away and humming louder than before as she removed the squash from the basket.

He retreated upstairs.

That night, he furiously typed for hours, demented in his strokes. He had devoted more than ten years to these words, and tears crinkled at the edges of his eyes as he reached the midpoint of the novel. A melancholic aura filtered through the room, the frightening notion of what might come next when the project was done. He assumed that this was what all novelists wrestled with, the desire to elongate their works to avoid saying farewell to the characters. Saying good-bye meant killing them; it meant finality, and this weighed heavy on his heart.

The next morning, the sun baked through the window as he reveled in the solitary bliss of a creation born from his mind alone. This meditation was interrupted by a *thwack* against the front door. He cocooned himself in a bathrobe, slid on slippers, and headed downstairs. Opening the front door, he swiped the *Times* and the local paper, the *Killingworth*

Gazette. A biting breeze rustled his bones as he closed the door. Winter would be arriving soon. He tossed the two bound-up papers on the dining room table and brewed a pot of coffee. Sitting down, he picked up the *Gazette* and read the article on the front page: "Former Bentley College Student Strikes Gold as an NYC Editor."

A massive picture of Kyle Broder, handsome and chiseled with stylishly messy dirty-blond hair and sea blue eyes, stared back at him. William was shocked to see his former student, one he knew well. At thirty, Kyle had just brokered a megadeal at Burke & Burke Publishing for his debut author, Sierra Raven. Beyond being Sierra's first novel, this was her agent's first client and Kyle's first acquisition as an editor. The book had gone to auction and ultimately Sierra got an unreal $500,000 advance before the novel had even been finished. Film rights had already sold to a major movie studio for another $500,000.

Wonderful fate had delivered this news to William's door. If this girl could get a deal with Kyle before completing her novel, then he certainly had a shot too, especially since he already had an in.

He sat back with his hands laced behind his head and couldn't help but smile.

2

MORNING SEX HAD become a regular occurrence for Kyle and Jamie, at least on the nights she stayed over at his place in Brooklyn. Their relationship was inching up on six months, new enough to still discover fresh maneuvers to get each other off. Both were overachievers and brought this competitive drive straight into the bedroom. While his nights these last few weeks had been full of potential manuscripts and author or agent dinners with bottomless gin drinks, and she was in the throes of starting an interior design business, the alarm was permanently set for five to ensure a full hour of sweaty fucking before they continued their workouts at the gym and then parted ways for the rest of the day.

This morning was truly one for the ages, and why shouldn't it be? Kyle had just closed the deal of the year with his new author, Sierra Raven, after she finished only a hundred pages of a manuscript now primed to be a sensational literary debut. The mind-boggling insanity of this deal was compounded by the fact that (a) this was Sierra's first book and (b) she'd been the first author he nabbed on his own besides the difficult ones tossed to rookies by the company's publisher, Carter

Burke. Within a day, the movie rights had been snapped up, and the name Kyle Broder no longer evoked the dreaded response, *Who?* Now the words fluttering from everyone's lips in the biz were more like, *Ah, yes, Kyle Broder, that young rising star.*

All these career-excelling thoughts flooded Kyle's mind while he thrust into Jamie with one of her ample breasts in his mouth. The headboard slammed into the wall, practically knocking off his Wisconsin Badgers banner—its gruff mascot, Bucky Badger, sternly trying to remain intact. Jamie slapped his firm backside, her favorite part of him. *Hey, I'm an ass woman,* she'd say, *so sue me.* She wailed loud enough for the alley cat to scratch at the window. Kyle had dubbed the cat Capone due to its ugly mug. Capone's heated mimicry caused them to burst into fits of laughter as they got each other off. And all of this before five thirty, plenty of time left to spoon.

"I think Capone's jealous," Kyle said, scooping his arm under Jamie's head so she could nestle into his chest. She played with a patch of his light brown chest hair.

"Jealous of you or me?"

"Maybe he was looking for a three-way?"

She hit him with a pillow. He kept his smirk, her second favorite physical attribute of his. Delivered properly, it made it hard for her to ever stay mad for long.

Kyle, however, was pretty much smitten with everything about Jamie. Her athletic body she worked hard for. Tan skin no matter what the season. Sandy blond hair always coolly slicked back. Electric blue eyes with flecks of brown and green. Jamie was chic and fashionable without being high maintenance, but, equally important, chill enough to throw back beers at a sports bar like she was one of the boys. In fact, they had met at Kettle of Fish down in the West Village, a Wisconsin Sconnie bar, since they both hailed from that state, him from Sheboygan, her from Kewaunee. In a sea of failed relationships with jaded New Yorkers, their

Midwestern states of mind had been exactly what the other was looking for. And while they wore their tough New Yorker masks throughout most of the day, in private they'd sing praises for fried cheese curds and use 'Scansin slang like *dem, dat, dis,* and *dere* without any worry of being looked at strangely.

Capone was now humping the window, his furry stomach splayed against the glass.

"He's hungry," Jamie said, heading over to open the window.

Capone leaped at the chance for some indoor living and darted inside, flying past Jamie and already trotting out of the bedroom in search for scraps in the kitchen.

A gust of wind sent a chill through Jamie. She picked up one of Kyle's button-downs and put it on.

"Why don't you just go ahead and adopt him?" she asked, smelling Kyle's musky cologne that remained on the collar, a mix of vanilla and forest.

"Yeah, I don't think I'm ready for that type of commitment . . ."

He stopped himself, the words trailing off his tongue, already floating in the air between them. He had never lived with a girlfriend before, usually ending a relationship after six or so months when the inevitable inkling of antsiness would seep in. Granted, no one else had maintained his interest like Jamie so far, but it was still too early to get real and hand over a spare key, especially with the life-changing last few weeks he'd had.

Jamie looked like she wanted to give a clever retort about his fear of cat commitment, but she chose to touch her tongue to her top lip instead. In her mind, it wasn't worth ruining the bliss of the morning. The two of them also had the tendency to let a casual remark spiral into a full-blown fight. Both were hotheads, and while their arguments never lasted long, to someone listening beyond the walls, those fights could read as intense.

Jamie wasn't one hundred percent ready to move in either. She enjoyed her space, her separate life. The only true issue she had with their situation was the "long-distance" aspect of it. She lived on the upper Upper West Side, two trains and more than an hour from his Cobble Hill apartment. Also, she had a Craigslist roommate named Sybil who was a messy drunk but paid her rent on time and worked from home selling items on eBay. How Sybil managed to make her share of their $4,000 rent baffled Jamie, but what pissed her off the most about Sybil was that Kyle never stayed over because of the girl's slovenly ways. Sometimes, if Jamie took a step back and looked at their relationship with fresh eyes, it seemed like she was the one really putting in the work while Kyle just reaped the benefits.

She glanced at the clock, 5:45, fifteen minutes left to spoon. He was giving her that slick grin, which admittedly made her wet, so she slid back into his arms and tickled his stubble.

"I'm so proud of you," she said, kissing his soft lips.

"Thanks, baby."

He spun on top of her, hard once again. Maybe her third favorite quality of his was his impressive libido. Before she knew it, her legs were wrapped around his neck and the headboard slammed into the wall hard enough for the Bucky Badgers banner to become dislodged this time.

RIDING TO ROCKEFELLER Center on the F train, Kyle read through the unchecked e-mails on his cell. Like every rush-hour train in New York, getting a seat was a pipe dream, so he hovered over a lady who wore what looked to be Santería garb. Since the Sierra Raven deal, every top agent in the biz had a "hot" new book for him. This meant he needed to read everything, because an editor's worst nightmare is to overlook a gold mine. He knew how many of his peers were kicking themselves for passing on *Girls Without Hope,* Sierra's heartbreaking tale of four sisters in the Ozarks dragged through the foster system, a dark *Little Women* for the times. In fact, it had first crossed Brett Swenson's desk, the editor at Burke & Burke who had taken Kyle under his wing when Kyle was still just an associate editor. Kyle often got the scraps no one else wanted, but when an e-mail from Brett came through with the subject *Girls Without Hope—Hell NOPE!,* Kyle felt a stirring in his heart before seeing any pages. He pictured the book on a shelf at Barnes & Noble. Its title would be in the bold pink of a little girl's diary against the stark blackness of a night sky with a lone tire swing dead center. Brett's e-mail lambasted this "chick-lit disaster-in-the-making," with a series of other digs, although Brett hadn't even opened the attached manuscript. At the time, Kyle had mostly been after boilerplate thrillers and mysteries but found it tough to break in new crime writers in an oversaturated market. After the success of a slew of bestsellers with *Girl* in the title, he figured he'd give this one a chance. He took the first hundred pages—which turned out to be all Sierra had written—to Bouchon Bakery, and over a raspberry jam donut became mesmerized. The initial pages showed the promise of winning some literary awards. Once other publishers started biting, Carter Burke agreed to fork over a serious amount of dough. Because Kyle made the discovery and closed the deal, he got a promotion to editor.

The F train halted while he was in the middle of reading a pitch about a dystopian future after a nuclear fallout where robots try to recreate humankind with disastrous results. He spun around, practically landing in Santería Woman's lap. She was dressed in white with a spherical white headpiece and colorful jewelry. Her plastic bag full of hair and shells fell to the floor. She clicked her tongue at Kyle as she scooped up the bag, her eyes like lumps of coal. She hissed in an indecipherable language that he could only imagine was some type of voodoo curse. The train moved forward once again and stopped at Rockefeller Center.

He sandwiched his way out of the doors. On the platform, the woman's coal eyes turned toward him with a shake of her head before the train zoomed into the tunnel.

"*Fucking* New York," he murmured out loud, sometimes enthralled by its eclectic mix of people, other times longing for a quiet Wisconsin lake with only his thoughts as company—far from a rush-hour morning full of chaos and voodoo spells.

BURKE & BURKE'S offices were styled with a retro 1960s *Mad Men* ambiance. Carter's father had started the company with his uncle in '62, and his will stipulated that the look of the company remain intact. So each office was fitted with Saarinen glass tulip tables and Artemide Nesso lamps that resembled mushrooms. Clean-lined sofas bordered the walls in signature burnt orange. Plastic Eames armchairs and dazzling wall sculptures had been placed in the waiting area.

Amanda, who sat at the front desk, gave Kyle a wave upon entering, each of her fingers painted in a different color nail polish.

"Sierra is waiting in your office," she said, choosing turquoise for her thumb.

Down the hallway, Brett Swenson sipped an espresso over his assistant, Darcy's, desk, his tie tossed over his shoulder. He wore a blue pinstriped suit with a cornflower pocket square. He had the slightest hint of a paunch despite an hour on the treadmill every day. Just a few years older than Kyle, Brett's hair was still more pepper than salt, but the tiniest moon had begun to surface in the center of his head. Kyle had the kind of hair that would be described as golden in Roman times, swept back with only a dab of gel, good to go until his head hit the pillow at night. Sometimes he noticed Brett staring at his hair in conversations and at meetings, as if Brett was desperately searching for any type of thinning or stray grays.

"*GQ*'s Man of the Year," Brett said, shooting back the espresso and raising his hand for a high five. Kyle grudgingly complied. Brett rubbed at his nose. One time at a Kentucky Derby party, Brett confessed to Kyle about losing all the cartilage in his nose from doing too much blow at Duke.

"GQ?" Kyle smirked.

"Let me amend that to GQ dot com's Man of the Year."

This was a common joke at Burke & Burke, the death of print, and more specifically, the death of literature. It was why Kyle had aimed for a career in genre books, worrying that there was no longer a place for beautiful sentences in today's market. Well, at least until *Girls Without Hope* hit the stands.

"Your ingénue is looking on point today," Brett said, rubbing his hands together and sucking at his teeth. Darcy looked up from typing to frown. "She's in this baby doll dress." Brett's voice dropped to sotto voce. "I need more talent like *that* around here." He eyed Darcy, who was taller than them all but managed to sink low in her seat.

"Sierra could've been yours, Brett."

"Don't remind me about the e-mail of my nightmares," Brett said, "when I let that sweet fish slip away."

Brett was showing all of his teeth to Kyle, bleached to the point of absurdity. The man drank too much coffee for his enamel to be anything but a tinted brown. He slapped Kyle on the back, harder than the average bro pat, enough to make Kyle pivot in place. Kyle made sure not to look like it affected him in the least.

"Guess you're just becoming careless in your old age," Kyle said, keeping his tone as light as possible. The two of them often sparred like this over their first coffees.

"Up yours, you towheaded son of a bitch," Brett cackled, as Kyle continued on his way and threw up his middle finger in response.

In his office, Sierra was tucking her short brown hair behind her ear and scrolling through a series of pictures on her phone. The photos were of the Ozarks near her hometown, a meth-ridden landscape of burned-out houses and double-wide trailers, the bleak setting for *Girls Without Hope*. Kyle knocked on his door so he wouldn't startle her and then felt foolish for doing so.

"I hope I haven't kept you waiting long, the F train was slow," he said, easing into his desk chair. Behind him stood Rockefeller Center in all its glory. He hoped he would eventually have a view of its famous Christmas tree. His last office didn't even have a window.

"You're lucky," Sierra said. "I have to rely on the M train. Short for my miserable commute."

"You're in Bushwick, right?" He remembered how she spoke of her up-and-coming neighborhood that now attracted a hipster spillover from pricey Williamsburg.

She nodded and shifted in place to cross her legs. Kyle noticed the dress Brett had described as baby doll, a cutesy pink that he could picture Jamie wearing.

"Yup, fellow Brooklynite here," Sierra said. "I'm surprised you don't live in Manhattan. Somehow I picture every editor in town living here. Like all of them together in a giant apartment building off Central Park, quoting Salinger."

"You try affording that on an editor's salary. On *any* salary!"

Kyle laughed and she did too. *Was he flirting?* Admittedly, he flirted with everyone, girls and guys, cats and dogs; he was a charmer.

"Well," he began, "you could actually afford Central Park views with your new advance and movie money."

"I'm not spending any of it until the book is finished. Except for this dress." She felt its fabric and then lifted her leg into the air, showing off her ankle-strap high heels. "And these Jimmy Choos. My first pair of heels outside of Payless."

"You deserve it, Sierra." He clapped his hands together to avoid staring at her leg. She lowered it with a smile. "So, do you have some new pages for me?"

She took a sharp breath and scrunched up her face. She had the tiniest nose, what could truly be described as a button.

"I've only finished one more chapter."

She eased a few pages out of her bag and handed over chapter 5. Her fang tooth picked at her bottom lip and her butt hung on the edge of the chair. These were the first pages she'd given him since the deal had closed. He could tell she was nervous.

"You could've e-mailed me this, you didn't have to come all the way here."

"I wanted to personally give it to you. I wanted to thank you for changing my life."

"I could say the same to you."

His office phone rang, loud and disruptive. He almost didn't acknowledge it, but then looked down and saw a Connecticut area code. He wondered if it was someone from college who'd heard about his success.

"Take it," Sierra said. "I don't mind."

"Okay." He answered the phone. "Hello?"

"Kyle? This is your old mentor, William Lansing."

"Professor!" Kyle said. *Ho-lee shit,* he mouthed to Sierra.

"I hope I'm not disturbing your workday."

"Not at all. Hey, what a great surprise."

Kyle immediately pictured Professor Lansing in his classroom staring out at an Ultimate Frisbee game on the Green: a little older, a little grayer and stooped, but still dignified. He held up a finger to Sierra to indicate that this would take a minute. She had already gone back to scrolling through her Ozark photos.

"I saw the article on you in the *Killingworth Gazette* this morning," William said.

"Oh, right. Right."

"How exciting, Kyle. Burke & Burke is a very reputable house. How long have you been there? The last we spoke, you were getting an MFA after I wrote you a rec."

Kyle had gone straight to an MFA program at U. of Wisconsin after graduating from Bentley. He had illusions of being a writer back then. It had been a tough time, since he was so near to his hometown while his mom was going through terminal cancer. They had never been close and by then he'd become numb to the idea of death. He wound up workshopping the same story over and over, realizing he was better at giving critiques than fixing his own maudlin prose.

"I moved to New York after grad school," Kyle said. "I was an editorial assistant at Macmillan before coming to Burke & Burke."

"And now this huge deal. Kyle. My boy. It is truly outstanding. It was the front page of the *Gazette.*"

"I guess in Killingworth it's top news."

William responded with something between a chuckle and a cough. Instantly, Kyle regretted the comment. Professors spent their whole lives in small towns while students just passed through and often went onto bigger and better places. It had to have stung once in a while.

"It's not like any other publications really wrote about the deal," Kyle said. "Besides *Publishers Weekly.*"

Kyle knew this was a lie. Just Google his name and you'd find a flood of articles now—albeit, not the front page like the *Gazette*; there were wars going on. He didn't know why he felt the need to act so humble.

A break in the conversation seemed to stretch and stretch. Something about his former mentor always made Kyle tongue-tied. William finally broke the lull.

"So I'm calling because I was planning on being in New York for a conference this week."

"Oh, yeah?"

"I know it's last minute, but I thought we could get together."

"Absolutely. It'd be great to see you."

"As long as you're not too busy—"

"No," Kyle said. "I mean, I am, but I'll make the time. How about dinner one night? I'm in Cobble Hill. My girlfriend and I could cook for you."

"I'd love that. Let me check my schedule."

Kyle heard the sound of pages being flipped. He was glad to know that Professor Lansing kept things old school with a print calendar.

"Is tomorrow all right?"

Kyle scanned his mind for any possible hurdles on Tuesday. He had a thousand manuscripts to get through, but he figured he deserved a night off.

"Yeah, Tuesday works. Seven thirty? I'll e-mail you the address. Still have the same e-mail at Bentley?"

"I do. I'll bring the wine. I have a 2010 Sequoia Grove Cambium I've been saving for a special occasion. I'm looking forward to it, Kyle."

"Me too. Thanks for calling."

"My pleasure. I always like to see how my best students have excelled."

Kyle couldn't help but beam.

"Cool, I'll see you tomorrow, Professor."

"I haven't been your professor in a while." He laughed. "Please, call me William."

"Sure. William. Okay."

The name felt awkward on Kyle's tongue. He traveled back ten years ago to when he was just a skinny kid in the back of the classroom. Professor Lansing had seemed so much grander, so much more refined than he ever thought he could be. He never imagined he'd be calling the professor *William.* That they'd be on the same level as peers.

"Timshel!" William said.

"What's that?" Kyle asked. For a moment, he thought William had hung up.

"Quick, what great novel ends with the word *Timshel*?"

Kyle chuckled. This was a game he remembered playing with the professor at Bentley. The final novel they had read in his Spirituality in Literature class was *East of Eden,* a book he devoured and then flipped right back to its opening page to read again. It was one of the first novels that truly excited him.

"East of Eden," Kyle said. "I reread it every few years. Except after Adam Trask says *'Timshel,'* Steinbeck wrote, *'His eyes closed and he slept.'* That's how the book ends. With him dying."

"Ah," William replied, like he had just tasted a great sip of scotch. "The pupil surpasses the master."

Another pause lingered.

"E-mail me your cell number as well and I'll see you soon, Kyle. Till then."

William ended the call.

"Till then," Kyle said, to an empty line.

"Aren't you glad you picked up the phone?" Sierra asked. She already had her coat on and was hanging by the door. He hadn't even realized she was still there. He must have looked bemused.

"I am."

"Let me know what you think of those new pages," she said. "And I'll have to read *East of Eden* if you love it so much."

"I do," he said, finally lowering the phone. "Although now you know the ending."

She put the back of her hand to her forehead, as if she felt faint.

"That someone dies?" she said. "*Oooh,* big spoiler. Isn't that how all great novels usually end?"

She walked away, her high heels clacking down the hallway. He turned on the computer and e-mailed William all his info, his fingertips buzzing in anticipation of Tuesday night.

3

THE REST OF the day and Tuesday passed in a mad rush. Kyle devoted his time to reading Sierra's pages. He really had only one note for her to fix. The *Girls Without Hope* sisters had spent the first four chapters fighting to stay together after their freebasing father overdosed and their bipolar mother went AWOL. Now chapter 5 began with a brutal foster parent named Biggie who forced himself on the oldest girl, Alexandra. The chapter ended with Alexandra obtaining a gun from a boy who was a local meth dealer and shooting Biggie in the arm. Then the sisters all fled in the middle of a cold January night. Kyle's suggestion was simply to stretch out the drama, since it all felt a little rushed. He guessed that Sierra wanted to have a *big moment* happen already, but a better way to create suspense would be for Alexandra to purchase the gun and enter Biggie's bedroom, setting up a cliffhanger and having the readers wonder if she might kill him.

Kyle e-mailed Sierra these notes and she wholeheartedly agreed, praising his ideas as *genius.* The day, however, fell away from him, and he hadn't gotten around to reading a manuscript about a future of robots that decide to recreate humankind after it's wiped out. Sure enough, the book sold to an editor at Simon & Schuster in a *very nice* preemptive deal. *Eh,* he figured, sci-fi wasn't really his bag. He'd discover his next big success soon enough.

Kyle also found himself preoccupied with thinking about Professor Lansing or, rather, William. The name seemed like it belonged to someone else, a man he'd never met before, not the guide who had made sure he stayed on a sound path during those dark times when he started to sway. His dad had died freshman year, not that he ever had a relationship with the guy. His father might have joined the circus for all he knew after checking out when Kyle was a little kid. But the finality of his father's death, of *never* being able to rekindle a relationship, had really set him off.

He'd told Jamie snippets of his troubled freshman year, but he hadn't gone very deep into the specifics. He could sense it made her uncomfortable to hear about those days and he worried she might see him in a different light, so he never brought it up again. In fact, he hadn't thought about those disastrous months in a long time, not until Professor Lansing's—*William's*—call.

"How should we cook the skirt steak?" Jamie asked, shortly before William was supposed to arrive. Kyle had to admit feeling anxious about seeing him again.

"I remember he likes his steak really rare," he said, adding homemade dressing to a bowl of greens.

Jamie made a face to that request. She liked her meat to be the consistency of shoe leather while Kyle was more in the bloody raw camp.

"So he just called you out of the blue?" she asked. She was wearing sweats and a Badgers T, her hair in a ponytail.

"I think you should change," he said, worrying that William might show up early and Midwestern Jamie would open the door instead of Cosmopolitan Knockout Jamie dressed to impress.

"I'm not gonna risk getting meat grease on my clothes," she said. "I'll change when we're done cooking."

"It's seven o'clock already!"

"Kyle, you need to calm down," she said slowly.

"Professing Lansing—*William*—he . . . I just feel like I owe so much of my success to him. I was really in a bad place until—"

"I know," Jamie said. She left the steak to go over and run her hand in a circle around his back. He found it immediately reassuring. "With your dad dying so young—I get it, Kyle. I went through the same thing."

Their respective tragedies helped them bond on Date #2. Date #1 had been a wild, drunken whirl, practically fucking in the cab up to her apartment and then sealing the deal on the floor of the foyer once they got inside, pants around their ankles, a hiccupped shrug coming from him when she mentioned using a condom. Date #2 was their first real one. He learned that her father had died when she was in high school. He'd had a love of boating and one night took a solo trip out into Lake Michigan, to return only when a fisherman hooked his bloated body out of the water. She never knew if he drowned by accident or on purpose. Even now, Kyle could tell it still pained her to think about it. A solitary tear lingered at the corner of her eye. She brushed it away with her sleeve.

"I didn't have someone like that," Jamie said. "To guide me. Mom had my younger brothers to worry about. And at the University of Wisconsin? It's not like Bentley. Classes with over a hundred students. The professors barely knew my name."

"I bet you were something in college, with a line of boys waiting at your feet," he said, steering the conversation into better territory.

She managed to smile wide enough to show the dimple in her cheek. He kissed it.

"I had my nose in fashion magazines," she said. "I didn't notice any boys waiting."

"All the better for me. Some quarterback would've snapped you up and married you right after graduation."

He took her in his arms. She rested her chin on his shoulder.

"Those quarterback types do nothing for me," she said. "I like a man who can quote Proust."

" *'Our shadows, now parallel, now close together and joined, traced an exquisite pattern at our feet,'* " Kyle said, his foot hooked under hers, their shadows lit on the far wall, entwined.

"I love you," she whispered.

"Love you too," he said. They had said it before to each other, but only recently.

"I'm gonna go change into a little number." She grinned. "Something that will let your old professor know just how well you're killing it at life."

She glided her fingers through his hair, left a kiss on his lips, and sashayed into the bedroom.

If he had enough time to follow her inside before William arrived, he'd already be in bed, pants around his ankles.

THE SLICED STEAK dripped blood on a wooden platter along with grilled heirloom mushrooms doused in balsamic and Caesar salad with freshly grated Parmesan and anchovies. Jamie had changed into a cream-colored dress, her left shoulder strap hanging on the groove of her arm. She wore silver earrings in a lightning bolt pattern and lipstick as red as the steak. Kyle donned a blue pinstriped jacket and a periwinkle tie, managing to finish grooming his beard with clippers before the doorbell rang.

Jamie rubbed a circle into Kyle's back one last time before answering the door. A hand reached inside the apartment with a bottle of wine as Jamie said hello. She and William did an awkward dance that began with a handshake and ended with a hug, and then William fully stepped inside.

"Kyle," William said after a breath. He wore a brown blazer with elbow patches—*so professorial.* His silvery hair had been slicked back, thick as ever, and smile lines ate at the edges of his eyes and lips. He seemed tired or, rather, more tired than Kyle remembered. Kyle wondered if that was just an inevitable product of age.

"So great to see you!" Kyle said, and the two gave each other a solid man hug, slaps on the back and a patting of shoulders. William had to put down the large satchel he was carrying.

"Notes from your conference?" Kyle asked, pointing at the satchel placed on a side table.

"It smells wonderful in here," William said, all smiles.

"Jamie's a fantastic cook," Kyle said, standing beside her. "William, this is my girlfriend Jamie. Jamie this is my . . . well, my mentor—William."

The two of them exchanged hellos again.

William's eyes roamed around the apartment. "Great place you have here."

"We can give you a tour!" Kyle said, realizing that he was speaking too loudly. He cautioned himself to simmer down a bit. "Although it's a brief tour, the apartment isn't too big."

"New York City living," William said, still all smiles.

Kyle took William around the living area that Jamie had helped style. White oak flooring. An alcove kitchen with stainless steel appliances. A coffee table that looked like it was cut and stained straight from a giant tree trunk. A sleek television mounted to the wall. Above the couch, a painting of a skeletal man played the trumpet, his face appearing as if it was melting into the notes flowing from the bell. They stepped into the bedroom next.

"I see you have a Wisconsin banner but not a Bentley one," William said, arching his chin at Bucky Badger.

"Yeah, the aardvark doesn't really inspire too much rah-rah."

William nudged him the ribs. "I think they'd just run out of mascot options by the time Bentley was founded."

Jamie came up behind them. "Ready to eat?" she asked. "I stuck the steak back in the oven for a quick hit of heat, but I heard you like it rare, William."

William placed his hand over his chest. "A woman after my own heart. Let's feast."

They made their way to the "dining room," an alcove nook that fit a small table. Jamie had lit candles, the wax dripping into the holders. William opened the Sequoia Grove Cambium, a rich red.

"It smells like chocolate," Jamie said after William poured them all a glass.

"Yes, it has hints of mocha," William said. "Shall we toast?"

They raised their glasses.

"To this wonderful meal you've prepared," William said. "And to the start of an illustrious editorial career. Chin chin." He clinked each of their glasses and everyone took a sip.

The meal proceeded pleasantly. Jamie really did have a knack for cooking. The bottle of wine was quickly finished and Jamie opened a second one. William asked her what she did for work, and she talked about the interior design business she was trying to get off the ground.

"It's amazing what people in New York will pay for you to hang their curtains in a certain way," she told him.

"She's being modest," Kyle said, his hand massaging her neck. "She has an eye for design."

"I'm not saving lives or anything," she said, slightly slurred, her teeth stained wine dark.

"None of us are," William said.

"And how is your wife doing?" Kyle asked. "And your kids? They were only a few years younger than me, right?"

"Yes, they're bartenders now. Took over the Royal Wee on the outskirts of Killingworth."

"I remember having a rough night there once," Kyle said. "Too many fireballs."

"Plus some other things," William added, tracing the top of his wineglass and letting it sing. "I recall having to drive you back to campus that night."

"Do tell," Jamie said, leaning forward.

Kyle waved his hand. "We don't need to get into it—"

"I was a chauffeur a few times during Kyle's freshman year," William said. "I will say I wouldn't have done it for just any student."

"He told me he had a tough go of it that year," Jamie said.

William gave her a look, which clearly said that *a tough go of it* was a nice way of saying *complete disaster.*

"An addictive personality is in my genes," Kyle said, chewing at his cheek. "Not alcohol, but . . . other substances seemed to take hold."

"Bentley was different back then." William cleared his throat. "Killingworth was in shambles. Drugs were readily available."

"Of which I partook," Kyle said.

William shook his finger in admonishment. "Of which you got clean."

"You got me clean," Kyle said, staring at William, feeling the utmost sense of gratitude swelling. Sometimes fate drops certain people in your life at the right time—*guardians*—and that was what William had been.

"What I did was stop enabling him," William said.

"And I'm thankful you did. There were a few days back then that I lost completely, like they'd been scooped from my mind."

"It's great that you would do so much for one of your students," Jamie said.

"I saw bits of myself in Kyle," William said. "I was lost when I was younger. Where I came from . . ."

Kyle could see William almost shudder at the thought.

"Well," William continued, "I had to get far away from there to survive." He took a sip, sloshed the wine around his palate and relished in its mocha hints. "But there was something special about Kyle in the way he analyzed text. I remember when reading Camus' *The Stranger,* his empathy for its tragic main character was wildly divergent from the rest of the students' opinions. So mature for an eighteen-year-old."

Kyle could feel his face heating up. He didn't know if it was due to the wine or if he was blushing. Or both. Jamie laced her fingers in his.

"I'm glad he had you to look after him." Jamie picked up the second bottle of wine and saw it was empty. "Looks like we need a third. You boys up for it?"

"This night is just getting started," William said.

Jamie rose on drunken legs. "Yes!" She shuffled out of the dining room. "I'll be right back with the vino."

"She's really lovely," William said, raising an eyebrow.

"She's amazing," Kyle said, a little drunk. He hadn't allowed himself a true celebration since the Sierra Raven deal, too focused on every new manuscript coming his way. He couldn't get past the nagging fear that his newfound success might just suddenly dry up.

"I didn't mean to bring up the past," William said.

Kyle shook his head. "No, no, it's all right. She knows about my dad, about my state of mind then."

"You were running with a bad crowd."

"I still might be if you hadn't helped me break away," Kyle said, his words slurring. "Selling drugs with Stoolie and Rocco, the townie hoodlums—I think those were their names—and that girl, Mia . . . *Mia . . .*" Kyle let the name dance on his tongue. He puckered his lips. "Whatever happened to Mia?"

William shrugged.

"It's good to see you, Professor . . . William," Kyle said, a grin tucked into his cheek. "Real good."

"We won't let this many years pass again."

"Definitely not."

"Oh, yeah," William said, snapping his fingers. He got up and walked to the foyer and fetched the large satchel left on the side table. Kyle could see it was heavy.

"So, I'm writing a novel," William said nonchalantly, as if he wrote one every day.

"Really?" Kyle said. "I would love to read it."

"I know you're a big shot now and all . . ."

"Hey, it would be *awesome* to be your editor."

William opened the satchel and pulled out what looked to be about five hundred pages.

"Holy shit," Kyle said. "That's a thick manuscript."

"It's only about half finished."

"A thousand pages?"

William placed it in Kyle's hands. The cover page said **DEVIL'S HOPYARD**.

"Devil's Hopyard?" Kyle said with a laugh. "No way."

"Yeah, the park inspired me. I found it a fitting title."

Kyle flipped through the pages, his brain too drunk to really take in the words.

"How long did this take you to write? Five hundred pages so far, *Je-sus*."

"Over a decade. I started it . . . well, right after your freshman year, I believe."

"A lifetime ago," Kyle mumbled.

"I know the book will be really long," William said, frowning. "Don't feel like you have to read it."

"William," Kyle said. "William, I would be honored. Really, this is so cool. And imagine if it sold to Burke & Burke and we could work together?"

"That would be a dream," William said, retracing a finger across his wineglass, creating a sharply pitched hum.

Jamie returned with another bottle. She had taken off her high heels and neither Kyle nor William heard her approach.

"Oh, Jamie," Kyle said, beckoning her to come into his arms. "Look what William wrote. A novel! What'll be a one-thousand-page opus. *Devil's Hopyard*. Devil's *Fucking* Hopyard."

Jamie popped the cork. "To Devil's *Fucking* Hopyard."

William's eyes had glazed over, sentimental tears emerging. He finished his glass and held it out for more red.

They all heard a scratching sound of claws coming from the bedroom.

"What's that?" William asked.

"That's just our resident alley cat at the window." Kyle spun out of his seat and headed into the bedroom. He returned with the cat and brought him over to William. "I kind of watch over him. Capone, say hi to William."

William reached out a hand. "Hello, Capone—"

Capone hissed and batted William's hand away, baring its claws. The cat leaped out of Kyle's arms and darted away.

"You're bleeding," Jamie said.

"It's the tiniest nick," William said, sucking on his wounded finger. Capone now watched him from the kitchen counter, its tail swinging back and forth like a pendulum.

"Capone is super temperamental from growing up in the wild Brooklyn streets," Kyle said, and then swiped the bottle from Jamie and poured three more generous glasses. "I'm sure he'll warm up to you soon."

IN BED LATER that night, Kyle and Jamie's pores oozed wine. They fumbled through a drunken attempt at sex before giving up. Both were too sloshed to go to sleep yet so they just held each other.

"I could use a giant plate of fried cheese curds right now," Jamie said. "To soak up all *dis* alcohol."

"I would chop off my pinkie for *dat,*" he said.

"So William was really great," she said, curling toward him until their noses touched. "I can see why you looked up to him."

"And then the guy goes and writes a novel. Out of nowhere. Is there anything he can't do? He's so damn brilliant, it's sickening."

"You think the book will be any good?"

"How could it not be? I can't see him spending ten years on something that's dog shit."

"Teaching literature and writing it are two very different things."

"Ha, and you always say *I'm* the negative one."

"You usually are. This is a new bright and shiny Kyle that William has unearthed."

"Hey, I have a knack for spotting raw talent. First Sierra Raven, and I gotta tell you, her book is so good. Like this last chapter she gave me—*damn*—and she's so young too. Like, who at twenty-two can be that much of a literary rock star?"

"Hmmm," Jamie said, squeezing her eyes shut. She rolled over on her back.

"That'll be my thing," Kyle said. "Plucking these diamonds out of obscurity."

Jamie bolted upright, her cheeks puffed out.

"Shit," she murmured, and dashed into the bathroom.

Kyle heard her vomiting; she hadn't closed the door fully.

"Baby, do you need help . . . ?" he asked as his eyes closed and darkness eclipsed the room. Before he knew it, Jamie's gagging sounded like it was a million miles away and sleep took over, engulfing him in its deadening embrace.

4

KYLE NURSED A particularly unsettling hangover the next morning. He would've gone the hair-of-the-dog route if not for a ten o'clock meeting with Carter Burke. At least he was able to snooze until about eight. Jamie had fallen asleep with her arms wrapped around the toilet, and when he found her, she went right to bed and enveloped herself in his comforter. She had the luxury of sleeping away the day and taking a break from conquering the interior design world.

On the way out of his apartment, he spied *Devil's Hopyard* sitting on the dining room table. For a second, he'd forgotten that it was William's novel—the title alone sent an icy chill down his back. One of the last times he'd entered Devil's Hopyard, he'd done enough drugs to think he was a wolf and found himself howling at a family of hikers, only to come down sometime around midnight, naked and covered in dirt, soon to be hospitalized for pneumonia.

"Devil's *Fucking* Hopyard," he said, shaking his head. He grabbed his keys and headed out.

At Burke & Burke, he kept his aviators on in the elevator, dreading the moment he'd fully be exposed to light. Three extra-strength Tylenols and an Alka-Seltzer had barely done their jobs. Amanda, the front desk girl, wagged a neon green fingernail as the elevator doors opened.

"It's ten ten," she said, pointing at the wall clock in case he didn't believe her. Carter Burke was a stickler for being on time. The boss came from Swiss stock and had a mantra that efficiency—*like clockwork*—relied on being precise.

"How are my eyes?" Kyle asked, lowering his shades.

Amanda winced. "Bloodshot and ghoulish." She reached into her desk and pulled out some Visine. "You're lucky I'm so into 420."

He squeezed some into his eyes.

"Hold on," she said, grabbing his arm and pulling him down to her level. She licked her fingers and dabbed at an unruly patch of hair that curled away from the rest of the brood. "Cowlick."

"You're a lifesaver," he said, and headed in.

THE BUDGET FOR Carter Burke's office could rival that of a small nation. When Kyle entered, his boss was sitting behind a Parnian desk custom-made with six kinds of exotic wood. In back of him, multiple windows overlooked Rockefeller Center. A small Rothko, black on gray, hung on the far wall. Carter's white hair was always combed to the right with a part on the left, a nod to an antiquated era. His tiny eyes looked out through thick black frames. A bow tie cinched his neck. Brett was already sitting in the Eames chair closest to Carter. Kyle had to make do with the couch off to the side.

"Nice of you to join us, Kyle," Carter said, his thin lips pressed tightly together.

Brett, in true dick fashion, made a point to look at his watch.

"I apologize," Kyle said. "The train sat at Borough Hall for what felt like forever."

Carter gave no response to this excuse.

"Where are we with Tucker Noley?" Carter asked, linking his fingers together and leaning forward in menacing fashion.

Shit, Kyle thought. Tucker Noley had been Carter's author back in the '80s when Carter took over the company from his declining father, Carter Sr. Tucker had made a lot of money for the company back then, churning out a series of spy thrillers about a CIA operative named Gregor Spade who had some Russian in his blood and used his extended family back in the Motherland to out KGB threats. Then the cold war ended and Tucker's output became less and less. For a while, Gregor Spade tussled with Middle Eastern terrorists and Tucker had Brett as his editor. Now it had been five years since Tucker's last book, which flopped. Carter decided to pass him over to the new kid, but any profits wouldn't go on Kyle's P&L. To add insult to injury, besides being a notoriously slow writer in his advanced age, Tucker was a pompous, bloated, racist d-bag.

"He's still working on the new Spade book," Kyle said, although since the Sierra deal, he hadn't checked up on the old bastard at all.

"What's the premise?" Carter asked, taking off his glasses to pinch the bridge of his nose.

"Spade goes after ISIS?" Brett chuckled.

Carter gave a solitary bark of a laugh. Kyle didn't laugh at all.

"Is that seriously the premise?" Carter asked. "Spade is what, a hundred and sixty-five now? Those kinds of spy books need a heavy dose of techspeak. ISIS is recruiting people over Twitter for Christ's sake. Does Noley even know how to use a computer?"

"I've set him up with a social-media major from NYU as an intern," Kyle said.

"That's a major these days?" Carter said. "These millennials and their lunacy. Our future is doomed."

"Speaking of a doomed future," Brett added. "I heard that Lo Bowles at the Hershen Agency sent you *First Human*."

"What's *First Human*?" Kyle asked, the pounding in his head taking a sharp turn to an all-out assault.

Carter and Brett gave each other a look that made Kyle feel small.

"Simon & Schuster's latest preempt," Brett said. "The book about robots that start a new race of humans after a nuclear fallout wipes out the entire planet. Six-figure advance."

"Kyle, you need to be spreading the wealth," Carter said. "With your name in the papers, agents are feeding the hottest books to you now."

"I will," Kyle said. "I'll cc you on everything."

"Copy me only on the good shit." Carter frowned.

Kyle rose and extended his hand. "Of course, sir."

Carter waited a moment before shaking it. "Land that next great gold mine," he said. "And get some pages from Tucker that aren't utter crap."

Brett nodded along, cosigning the boss's every move.

"And get the door on your way out," Carter said.

Kyle left Carter's office and closed the door slowly, seeing Brett speaking in a hushed tone toward Carter—*clearly* about Kyle. He would've worried about this more, except his stomach was churning and he burped up an acidic glob of wine-tinted bile. Luckily, he made it to the bathroom before he upchucked a flood of red.

AFTER A NAP as soon as he got home, Kyle woke up around nine feeling refreshed. Jamie had left a note for him on the fridge with a basket of fried cheese curds. She'd picked up the curds from Stinky Bklyn LLC, and then fried them with milk, flour, beer, salt, and eggs—her specialty. He devoured the fried curds, since he had skipped dinner. With greasy hands, he fumbled a text to her.

Thnx for the curds. Perfect cure for my hangover. You are the best ;)

He wiped the crumbs from his lips as his phone beeped. He wondered if it was Jamie texting back, wanting to come over. She could probably make it to him by ten thirty. He looked at his phone and saw a message from William.

Had a wonderful time at dinner. No rush to start Devil's Hopyard, but I'm definitely curious to hear your thoughts!!!

Kyle had a pet peeve about people using multiple exclamation points to express excitement. It made him feel as if he had to respond in the same fashion or the other party would think he didn't really care. He went to the fridge and poured a glass of club soda, debating whether to add a shot of bourbon and then tapped in some Bulleit since it was easier than having the debate. When he went back to his phone, Jamie hadn't responded—she was usually quick with texts—so he decided he'd dig into *Devil's Hopyard*. It was probably too late for her to trek over from the other end of the world anyway. He jotted a quick text back to William first.

Had a wonderful night too. So great to catch up!! Got a bourbon in hand and I'm ready to dive into Devil's Hopyard. Can't wait!

He was about to put down the phone when William wrote:

Fantastic, Kyle. Hope it's up to snuff!

Kyle grinned at this. He enjoyed having William back in his life, unsure why the two had lost touch. He had a quick fantasy of reading the acknowledgments page in William's book after it was released to much acclaim.

And to my brilliant editor, Kyle Broder. Once was my student, but who now has taught me so much more.

Kyle picked up the hefty manuscript and flipped to the dedication page.

To Laura and the twins. And to the one who got away. *La Vita Nuova*.

An odd dedication, but Kyle didn't spend too much time thinking about it. Maybe Laura had a stillborn pregnancy, or possibly the twins were initially triplets. It didn't pay to assume. He also didn't know Italian. He turned to page 1 with a pen in hand and read the first few lines.

> This is my story about the secret to immortality. Read carefully and let me teach you. Take notes, my friend. Welcome to DEVIL'S HOPYARD.

An interesting opening, Kyle thought. At least it pulled the reader in and left room for speculation. He twirled the pen between his fingers as he read on. Unfortunately, the next few pages weren't on a par with those opening lines. The novel began in a college professor's classroom as he was giving a lecture on Camus' *The Stranger.* Kyle immediately recognized some similarities to William's own lectures. This would have been a fine way to open a novel, but then the narrative jumped into the professor's head and stayed there for ten illogical pages while he obsessed over a girl in his class. She was unnamed, described only as "withdrawn." William wrote about all of the things the professor wanted to do to her, disturbing things. The professor started describing her heart and his *need* for it.

> I think about the heart that pumps in her chest. Pumps for me, possibly? But I doubt that. Even if she says she wants me, even when I'm devouring her in the shack in Devil's Hopyard where we have our trysts, and she says she loves it, she does not. My bones are old and she thirsts for the young. For a peer. So sometimes I think about taking a knife and cutting out that heart. Feeling it BEAT in my hand as I BEAT my meat to its pumps until it pumps no more. And then I will put butter in a pan and watch her heart SIZZLE. Cut it up with a fork and a knife and let it sit

on my taste buds. Swallow it whole as her eyes close for good and it is the last thing she sees. Wash it down with a bottle of red, red wine, the REDDER and bloodier, the BETTER.

Kyle put the manuscript down. The fried curds were gurgling in his stomach. Reading about cannibalism certainly didn't help. He stared at *Devil's Hopyard,* wondering if it was a joke, although he didn't remember William having a weird sense of humor like that. He also wasn't sure why William would go to the trouble of pranking him, since he seemed genuinely proud and eager for Kyle to read his book. Maybe just the first few pages were wonky and then the real story would begin? Kyle decided to flip to a passage toward the end.

And taste the FLESH and the FLESH tastes like love and the heart has been digested and beats inside of ME now. It gives me power. I am powerful with her organ. And the body has been discarded and left to rot, and sometimes I dig it up for more, more, MORE!!! And then I shit her out of me until her FLESH stinks up the bathroom.

Kyle dropped the pages onto the table. He had a terrible taste on the back of his tongue.

"What the fuck . . . ?" he said. He tossed back the bourbon and soda, got up, and poured another glass.

His cell rang, spooking him. He wondered if it was William, and he had no idea what he'd say. *Oh, sure, I'm reading your book, which is pretty fucking sick and twisted so far. Will the whole thing be about eating a girl's heart? All one thousand pages?*

He inched toward the phone and saw Jamie was calling. *Thank God.*

"Hey," he said, picking up.

"So you liked the curds?" Jamie said coyly.

"The what? Oh, yeah, they were really good."

"You don't sound so convincing." She seemed a little disappointed.

"No, no. They were great. It's just that . . . I started reading *Devil's Hopyard*. William's book."

"And?"

"Like, it's really fucked-up. Really, *really* fucked-up. And not even well written, which makes it even worse."

"How much did you read?"

"I dunno, like ten or so pages."

"*Ten* pages? Kyle, you have to give it more of a chance than that."

"Ten really bad pages."

"Kyle, he was your favorite professor. You need to read the whole thing."

"I don't know if I can."

"Well, then, you shouldn't have told him you would," Jamie said. "You're stuck now."

"He's writing about eating a girl's heart."

Jamie responded, but it sounded like static.

"Jamie, you're breaking up."

"I just got home, Kyle. I'm headed into the elevator."

"Okay, well, I'll call you—"

"Read his book," Jamie said. "That's your homework for tonight." He could tell from her tone that there'd be no swaying how she felt. "I'll talk to you tomorrow," she said.

The call ended. Kyle looked at the scattered pages on the table. He started gathering them up. There was a possibility that only the beginning and the part he turned to were the truly fucked-up parts, but he had an uncomfortable premonition that the rest would be even worse. Still, Jamie was right. He had told William he'd read the manuscript, and he owed it to him to give it more than a few minutes of his time.

Once the pages had all been sorted back together, he retreated to his bed, the manuscript like a heavy brick. He turned to where he'd left off.

And then I will put butter in a pan and watch her heart SIZZLE. Cut it up with a fork and a knife and let it sit on my taste buds.

It was going to be a long night.

5

THE GIRL TRIED to stand up in the shack, but she was chained to the floor. A broken wooden slat allowed a slice of moonlight to pierce through the darkness. Only her eyes could be seen, the blood vessels popped from gagging. The welts on her face had opened up and started to ooze. She could taste blood seeping through the muzzle. Her dress was soiled and glued to her skin. She'd given up shivering from the cold and now had gone numb. She gave standing one more try, only to collapse to the floor in exhaustion. The blood on the ground from the slaughtered animals had mixed with her own and smelled of corroded loose change.

She heard the jingle of the padlock being tampered with and thought for a moment it could be a savior. But from the way it jingled she knew. *Him.* And not just him—the violent side of his personality that resembled the villains in horror novels she used to love. She could never imagine reading them again.

The door swung open and moonlight flooded inside, revealing every deplorable nook of the prison she'd lived in for the last few weeks. She was embarrassed by the fetid stench. It seemed as if thousands of days had passed since he'd cleaned the shack. She hated the bugs crawling on her legs and the way they'd wormed into her skin, or even worse, that she'd gone insane and was imagining those bugs. And there he stood, panting and sopping with sweat, rubbing the elbow patch on his blazer that had caught on a branch and torn a gaping hole.

She screamed as loud as she could through the muzzle, but it was tied too tight. He hated when she screamed and would punish her for this, but the punishments would happen regardless, and it made her feel good to piss him off. He balled up the chain that attached her to the floor and whipped her across the face. An old welt opened and the blood poured over her eyes until everything was bathed in red.

She felt herself being turned around as he groped her, a daily tradition. His thumb traced the small tattoo on her butt. She could feel his thumbnail digging into her flesh and heard the sound of him sucking. His hand grabbed at her left breast, but she knew he cared less about that part of her flesh. It was her heart he hungered for. With his fingers, he kept in time to her heartbeats as he entered her from behind. The worst thing was his delicate nature once he was inside her. She'd rather be impaled, not made love to, which she knew was how he'd describe it. Her heartbeat sped up along with his thrusts, and he let out a cry of release that shook the foundations. She had the ominous sensation of the two of them being the only people left in the world. No savior would ever find this camouflaged shack and her hidden existence. She'd do her nightly dance with him until one of them perished.

The weight of him on her back got lighter as he finished. Tonight he decided to sob, his weeping becoming softer as he backed up toward the door. She turned around to see his face, to torture herself even more so she could visualize all the ways she'd kill him. The two locked eyes. His were tired and ringed with circles. Hers were reddened and a poor reflection of her former self. Did he say he was sorry, or did her demented mind just imagine that? Each night, it got harder and harder to tell.

"You know I do this because I love you," he said, gripping the doorknob.

She gave a solemn nod.

"Ours will be a story for the ages," he said again, and then shut the door.

She heard the jingle of the padlock. In the darkness, she conjured him up again. In this vision, she'd become unchained and given a sharp knife by the gods, which she plunged into his chest and twisted around until she scooped out his heart and held it beating in her hand.

"Fuck you," she said, as his dripping heart slid from her fingers and the shack's broken slat revealed her moonlit smile.

KYLE SHOT OUT of bed, drenched in night sweats. He instinctively reached for Jamie and then realized she wasn't there, her pillow a cruel replacement. *Devil's Hopyard* sat on the nightstand, responsible for his heart slamming into his chest. He gulped to catch his breath and shut his eyes only to see the girl in the shack, reaching out toward him as if he could stop the madness.

Save me, she said in his mind. He opened his eyes to make her go away.

He gulped another breath and chased it with a swallow of water. Finally, his heartbeat slowed to a normal thump. He unstuck the drenched shirt from his body and swung himself out of bed, planting his legs on solid ground. He eyed the *Devil's Hopyard* manuscript with disdain.

His phone rang and the caller ID said William. Kyle chewed on a nail, wondering if this was still a part of his dream. The pages he'd read during the night were even more depraved than the earlier ones. He tried to rationalize why William would choose to enter the mind of such a sick and twisted character, especially for ten long years. The writing was god-awful, nonsensical in parts and obsessively repetitive. He kept reading, hoping to see a purpose, a shift in the narrative that might reveal its brilliance. He didn't remember falling asleep, the manuscript's words bleeding into a nightmare.

The phone stopped ringing and he heard the beep of a voice mail. He had no desire to hear it now. He spied the clock, 8:00—*way* past his usual wake-up hour. He rushed into the shower and turned on the water to full blast, no time to process the horrific night he had experienced.

In his office at Burke & Burke, after a double espresso shot and a round of e-mails, he finally got around to listening to William's message.

Mornin' Kyle! It's William. Just thought I'd see how far you got with Devil's Hopyard. My stomach's been doing flips all night in anticipation. Let me know if my baby has potential. Ciao.

The most disturbing part of the message was the fact that William called it his *baby,* as if the manuscript were a real living thing. Kyle had tried to block it out all morning, purposefully leaving *Devil's Hopyard* at home, but it had crept into his consciousness. To distract himself, he read the first twenty-five pages of a just submitted thriller called *The Dead Can't Hunt You Down,* about an ex–hit man who tries to leave his former organization only to become hunted by them. Its opening in Marrakesh was taut and suspenseful enough to keep him invested, and he found himself wishing William had written this book instead.

His phone buzzed with a text. Instinctively, he knew who it was.

Hey Kyle! Just wanted to see if you made any more headway with Devil's Hopyard? If I don't hear back, I might have to give my exclusive to someone else. Ha!!!

Normally Kyle would've grinned at that joke, but he was in no mood. Breakfast wasn't sitting well. He also had no idea how to respond, not wanting to hurt his professor's feelings, but William needed to know that

Devil's Hopyard was one of the vilest things he ever set eyes on. He couldn't stop thinking about the poor girl in the shack because it seemed like William was writing out some dark fantasy.

Kyle texted back: *Slammed from work, but will get to Devil's Hop soon.*

His phone immediately buzzed with William's reply: *Don't keep me hanging!!!!!*

Kyle typed a response, cracking his neck in annoyance. *I promise I'll call you when I can.*

His phone buzzed again, but he shoved it in a drawer without even looking at what William wrote. He resolved to spend the rest of the day reading about the ex–hit man gone rogue so the gruesome images from *Devil's Hopyard* might slowly fade away. Hours later, he found himself plunged into a gripping cat-and-mouse tale until he had finished half of *The Dead Can't Hunt You Down* and it was time to meet Jamie for dinner.

KYLE HAD MADE reservations at ABC Kitchen, a trendy restaurant in the Flatiron District with a chic laid-back California vibe. When he entered, Jamie was already seated and nursing a margarita. She wore a dress with a plunging neckline and had a thin teal sweater hanging from her shoulders. She stood and kissed him on the lips, tasting of pomegranate.

"I ordered some calamari to start," she said.

A waitress came over, and Kyle immediately asked for a glass of Four Roses Single Barrel. Jamie scooped up his hand in her own.

"I have some news," she said, clearly excited. "I've got a lot of interest from that investor in Sweden, Elka. She'll be here next week to see some of my work."

"That's fantastic."

"It's a start. She's looking for foreign businesses as a way to expand her brand. She's loaded, though. I think Ingvar Kamprad is a close relative."

"Who's that?"

"The founder of IKEA."

Jamie followed Kyle's eyes, which were drifting away from her.

"Kyle?"

"What? I'm sorry. I'm distracted."

Jamie cinched her thin sweater at her neck, as if she'd gotten cold.

"I could tell," she said, twirling the straw in her drink.

The waitress brought Kyle's bourbon.

"This is fabulous news," he said, raising his glass. "I know you've worked hard."

"I have," she said softly.

"My day was just crazy," he said, after taking a stiff sip.

She crossed her arms. "I know. I'm getting used to that."

"It's just . . ." he stammered. "Well, what did you think of William?"

"Your professor? He was lovely. I could tell how close the two of you were—"

"I read more of his manuscript."

"And?"

Kyle traced a finger around the edge of the glass.

"Jamie, it was so fucked-up. Like, really dark and disturbing."

"Isn't that good? Aren't you in the market for thrills and chills?"

"Yes, but . . . this had no point. Its just page after page of a madman babbling."

"It has to have some plot."

"I mean, the narrator is a professor, just like William, and he fixates on this student in his class. He dreams of cutting out her heart—"

Jamie laughed and then covered her mouth. "I'm sorry, I wasn't expecting you to say that."

"And then he has this fantasy where he chains her up in a shack and abuses her. It's brutal. I had nightmares all night."

"Doesn't that mean it affected you? You always complained about the queries you used to get. That the writing wasn't real enough."

"William's writing is *terrible,*" he said, lowering his voice. He didn't know why he felt the need to be quiet, as if someone could be listening.

"Are you more upset about the subpar writing or the fact that it's disturbing?"

Jamie often liked to play devil's advocate, a trait Kyle found frustrating. She'd been a prelaw major before making the switch to design.

"Who spends five hundred pages writing about eating a girl's heart?" he said, throwing up his hands.

"So you finished the pages?"

"Well . . . no."

Jamie gave a self-satisfied grin as their calamari arrived, pretzel-dusted and with marinara and mustard aioli. She popped one in her mouth.

"These are *soooo* good, Kyle, you have to try."

She held out a dripping piece of squid, but he was more interested in making his point.

"If a book is going to be seriously depraved, it has to be well written."

Jamie ate his piece of calamari, a dot of mustard lingering on the corner of her mouth.

"So that means if William's book had amazing prose, you'd be fine with it?"

Kyle ate some calamari to avoid an answer he didn't want to give.

"Listen," he said, after he swallowed, "today I read this thriller about an ex–hit man hunted down by his former organization. Exceedingly violent, half the characters die in a vicious way, but—"

"It was well written?"

"Yeah, the author has actual talent and the violence felt organic. I was at a literary panel once where a crime writer spoke about how every time you kill a character, you have to take into account the weight of that death, their families—"

"But it's just fiction," Jamie said, exasperated. She could discuss books for only so long before her eyes began to glaze over.

"But fiction is a mirror for reality," he said. "*That's* what's so fucked-up about William's book. It felt real."

Jamie finished the last bite of calamari and pursed her lips. "Again, you could make an argument for that being a good thing."

"Like with Sierra Raven," he began, not noticing Jamie's eyes roll slightly to the left. "Her writing is haunting but beautiful. It's clear she lived through a tragic childhood being bounced around foster homes, and she was able to infuse that into her work."

"Well, not *everyone* is as brilliant as Sierra Raven," Jamie said, knocking back a big gulp of her margarita.

"Where's that tone coming from?"

Jamie blew the bangs away from her eyes. "It's the way you talk about her."

"Sierra's amazing. She netted a million-dollar deal in one day. Jamie, she changed my life."

"Have you ever spoken about me that way to someone?"

"What's that supposed to mean?"

Jamie spoke slowly. "Have. You. Ever. Spoken. About. Me. That. Way?"

"Of course!"

"Sometimes, Kyle," she began, and stared at a twinkling chandelier to get her thoughts right, "I don't know, you *light up* when you mention Sierra, and I get it—I know how much your career means, we've always connected because of that, but I don't think I've ever seen you look at me that same way."

The waitress came over to take away the plate of calamari. She asked if they were ready to order an entrée, but neither responded. The waitress backed away, clearly wanting no part of their tension.

"Why would you want to start something tonight, Jamie?"

"Why would *you*?"

"I just mentioned what a shitty day I had after getting no sleep."

"And I just mentioned what a wonderful day I had after getting a possible investor, but that doesn't warrant more than a minute of interest from you before your problems become front and center."

"Now you're just being silly."

Jamie raised her hand in the air to signal for the waitress.

"I'm not ready to order yet," Kyle said.

"I'm getting the check."

The waitress came over and Jamie asked for the bill.

"Come on, let's talk this out," he said. "Don't be like that."

"I'm not hungry anymore."

He tried to grab her hand, but she slid it under the table.

"I'm just gonna go home," she said.

She rose and he knew it was best to let her go. When Jamie made up her mind, there was no changing it. She pushed her chair into the table.

I'm sorry, he mouthed to her, pressing his hands together in the form of prayer. "Please don't be mad."

"I'm just tired," she said. "I have to get things ready for Elka this week."

"Okay."

He stood to embrace her and was glad that she accepted it, meaning she was mad but it would pass. She even allowed him to kiss her on the cheek. He hated his impulsive mouth, wishing he could take back calling her silly.

"Let me know you got home okay," he said, and sat back down as she left. A moment later, his phone vibrated, and he anticipated it being a text from her. He frowned when he saw William's number.

So what's the news, Kyle? Should I be making room for a Pulitzer on my mantel???!!!

Kyle texted right back, his fingers typing at an angry pace.

Got through some pages. Yes, we definitely need to talk tomorrow. Will call. Night.

He thrust the phone in his jacket pocket but could still hear it incessantly buzzing as reply after reply came through.

Each one caused a minor twitch in his eye before he silenced the cell for good.

6

WILLIAM BARELY SLEPT during the night. Sometimes his mind ran at such an accelerated rate that nothing could quiet it down. Instead of counting sheep, he took himself on a tour of *Devil's Hopyard,* running through sentences in his head and making sure they were shaped with utmost accuracy. He envisioned Kyle reading the manuscript and cringed at the thought that it might not be perfect. Kyle's last texts had been abrupt, which was surprising after the great dinner they'd had. He reasoned that Kyle was a busy man now, no longer that kid in the back of the class he knew from Bentley. It irked him a little to think how the power had shifted.

In the hour before sunrise, he watched Laura sleep. She was positioned like she was dead, hands folded across her chest. She never made a sound while sleeping, her flaring nostrils the only sign of life. He curled a strand of her hair around his finger, tying it tighter and tighter till it cut off his circulation. This occupied him until the sun finally came up and he slid out of bed.

He had an early-morning meeting with his student Nathaniel, whose essay on *The Stranger* was a sorry affair. With a red pen, William had drawn a giant F on the cover page and didn't leave any comments. He had plugged some of it into Google and a few identical papers came up. The protocol would be to inform the administration, but he wanted to deal with Nathaniel first. Since he'd been at Bentley for so long, he justified that he had the right to do what he wanted.

In his office, he reread Edgar Allan Poe's short story "The Cask of Amontillado," since his independent study class would be covering it this week. He reached the end.

I forced the last stone into its position; I plastered it up. Against the new masonry I re-erected the old rampart of bones. For the half of a century no mortal has disturbed them. In pace requiescat!

There was a knock on the door as Nathaniel peered inside. The kid hadn't combed his nest of red hair and was wearing sweatpants. William became instantly annoyed. He placed Poe down.

"Shut the door and take a seat."

Nathaniel slunk into a chair, chewing on his lip.

"You know how serious plagiarism is, don't you?"

Nathaniel started to cry, his face turning pink.

"College is just so *hard,* Professor," he said, using his arm to mop up the tears. "Like, sometimes I sit in class and everyone has these great ideas and I have nothing."

"Stop crying, Nathaniel."

"And my parents, my dad, he's this businessman and he wants me to be one too and they tell me how much money they've spent on my education, and, like, if I got kicked out . . . !"

"You're not getting kicked out."

Nathaniel gave a hard sniff. "No?"

"I want to know why you tried to plagiarize in such an obvious way." William held up Nathaniel's essay with the big red F. "This whole paper was literally cut and pasted."

"I know, it's just, I have *so* many classes. And, like, I had a chemistry test and then these guys in my dorm were being loud—"

William held up his hand. "Stop."

Nathaniel shoved a fingernail in his mouth.

"You will rewrite this paper. *And* I want you to research why Camus wrote *The Stranger.* Tell me what inspired him and if you can spot any similarities to Meursault."

Nathaniel let out an audible breath. "Thank you for not turning me in."

William wasn't listening, caught up in his own tangent.

"Also, I want to make you my personal research assistant."

"Uh . . . why?"

"This isn't a punishment; it's an opportunity. A way to prove yourself. I haven't shared this with the class, but there's an editor at a big publishing house reading a manuscript of mine."

He waited for Nathaniel to show some type of enthusiasm. The kid just sat there.

"Anyway, since the book is only half done, I have a lot of research left to do. I can't just *wait* for the editor to get back to me, I have to keep writing, stay in the groove, you know? Can I count on you, Nathaniel?"

Nathaniel nodded and tossed his eyes at the door.

"Can I go now, Professor? I was up all night worrying about this and need to sleep."

William shooed him away. As Nathaniel approached the door, William rapped his knuckles against the desk.

"By Monday I want both essays," he said. "So get some sleep and then start when you wake."

"Okay," Nathaniel said. "Thanks again."

After Nathaniel left, William checked his phone to see if Kyle had contacted him. He had been itching to do so for the past few minutes. The most recent text Kyle sent was from last night and said he'd call tomorrow. William had sent a few texts afterward, asking for some initial thoughts on *Devil's Hopyard,* but Kyle never responded. He didn't like when people left him hanging. When he asked a question in his classroom, he expected an answer. He had *earned* the right to an answer.

He checked his watch and saw it was only eight in the morning, and he figured Kyle hadn't gone to his office yet. He had the sudden urge to drive down to Burke & Burke, now dissatisfied with a conversation over the phone. After ten years of slaving over his opus, he felt he warranted a face-to-face. Maybe Kyle would see how hungry he was to get *Devil's Hopyard* published, that it was more than just a novel, that it could be the kind of book studied in advanced college English classes years from now: picked apart, lauded, ripe for discussion.

Before he knew it, his car keys were jingling in his hand and he was bounding down the stairs toward his car.

AFTER A BURGER at Bill's Bar & Burger, Kyle returned the office ready to finish *The Dead Can't Hunt You Down* and bring it up at the editorial meeting that afternoon. It was the perfect mix of literary fiction and thriller, and had series potential as well as a sympathetic female lead, crucial for sales. He was confident Carter would throw money at it.

When the elevator doors opened, Kyle saw a circle of people by Amanda's desk. She had dyed her hair aqua, and he figured the discussion centered around that. Brett was there, obnoxiously laughing at something, and even Brett's assistant, Darcy, had managed to giggle, a rare occurrence.

The circle opened up to reveal William in the center, wearing khakis and his signature blazer with elbow patches.

". . . Dickens walks into a bar and asks for a martini," William was saying. "The bartender responds, *olive* or *twist*?"

Darcy let out a rapid-fire laugh. It was the loudest noise Kyle had ever heard her make. He approached the circle.

"Kyle," Brett said, slapping him on the back. "Your old professor is *killing* it over here with these literary jokes." He turned to William. "Tell him the other one."

William caught Kyle's eye to gauge if it was okay to proceed. Kyle nodded and gave William a wide grin that felt phony, but he couldn't muster up the energy to make it appear genuine.

"Who's the biggest motherfucker in literature?" William asked. He let the joke hang in the air. Brett and Darcy leaned in; only Amanda was more amused by her fingernail polish. "Oedipus!"

This elicited a roar from Brett, whose face turned red. Kyle wondered if the guy was on coke.

"Ha, *motherfucker,*" Brett repeated. "'Cause Oedipus actually wanted to fuck his mother. I know you can relate, Kyle."

"Cute," Kyle said, the grin still plastered on his face.

"Evidently, "Brett continued, "your old professor has been writing a novel for a decade that you're reading now." He faced William. "Don't sign anything yet with this douche bag before a more experienced pair of eyes has a look."

Brett shadowboxed with Kyle before summoning Darcy, who slinked down the hallway after him.

Kyle finally dropped his shit-eating grin.

"What are you doing here, William?"

If William sensed Kyle's displeasure, he didn't let on.

"I had a business meeting nearby this morning and figured I'd stop by. I hope I'm not interrupting."

"Yeah, I'm slammed today," Kyle said, starting to walk past William. "We have an editorial meeting."

"It's just a rare opportunity I'm in the city," William said, stepping to the side so he was practically blocking Kyle. Now Amanda looked up from her fingernails.

"The editorial meeting isn't until four," Amanda said midyawn.

"Thank you, Amanda," Kyle responded, gritting his molars.

"There you go," William said. "It's only past one now. I promise I won't overstay my welcome. You can show me your office."

Amanda pressed the button on her desk so the door opened, leaving Kyle no chance to worm his way out.

"Après vous," William said, extending his hand as Kyle walked past.

Neither spoke as they headed down the hallway. William was taking in the décor, primed to impress by Carter Sr.: sleek and mod inspired with swirls of book spines stacked to the ceiling. Kyle's office was at the end.

"They really put you in the back of the bus," William said as he entered. Kyle stepped in and closed the door.

"Have a seat, William." Kyle indicated a chair as he went behind his desk. He couldn't help recalling the countless times William had brought him into *his* office at Bentley and the two faced each other in reverse.

William rooted around in his pocket. Kyle expected him to pull out something, but he only removed his hand. A moment of silence passed between them.

"So dinner was really fantastic," William said. He rubbed his left eye that was full of bloodshot veins.

"Yeah, it was great to have you over," Kyle said, busying himself with turning on his computer. He really did want to get back to *The Dead Can't Hunt You Down,* refusing to let another big deal like *First Human* pass him by.

"And Jamie is such a talented chef," William said. "Don't let that one get away, she's a keeper."

"We had a little tiff last night," Kyle said, not even realizing he said it out loud. He immediately wanted to take it back.

"Oh?"

Kyle opened the *Dead* doc. "Yeah, just stupid stuff. We're fine. So what are you in the city for?"

William's eyes glanced to the right. "A follow-up from the conference. A meeting with someone I'd met."

"An editor?"

"Would that make you jealous?"

Kyle leaned back in his chair, caught off guard. He picked up the handball on his desk and squeezed it for stress relief.

"Jealous?"

"I'm kidding," William said, chuckling. Kyle remembered his mentor's chuckle, soft at first as if it was barely there, as if you were imagining it, and then overpowering until it took up the entire room.

"I want you to have an exclusive for *Devil's Hopyard,*" William continued. "No one else has seen it yet. I wouldn't show it to your colleague Brett, he was just kidding about reading it."

"I don't know about that. Brett has a talent for poaching clients rather than finding them on his own. I wouldn't be surprised if his ear was up against the door right now."

"Oh?"

"It's just his shark-like nature. He's chastised me for not having enough of one. It's the good boy Wisconsonite in me."

"Well . . ." William rubbed his elbow patches a little obsessively. Round and round Kyle watched his hands go. "So how far did you get?"

"With what?" Kyle had started to scroll through *The Dead Can't Hunt You Down,* looking for where he left off.

William's bass chuckle echoed in the small office space. "With *Devil's Hopyard,* of course. I have to admit not sleeping last night in expectation."

Kyle looked away from the computer at William. His mentor seemed sad and crumpled, his face morphing from handsome to toad-like.

"Oh, William, I apologize, really. It's just been one of those weeks, one of those months, actually."

William ran his fingers through his hair. "I've been an insomniac for some time."

"I remember that."

"You were too, Kyle."

Kyle cocked his head to one side. That had been such a small sliver of his life. The speed continuously flowing through his body at the time certainly didn't help. But he couldn't recall sharing that with William.

"Anyway," Kyle said, his smile becoming a flat line, "I made it through about forty or so pages of your book."

"Only forty?"

Kyle ignored that comment. He had sort of prepared what he'd say to William and was formulating the precise way to begin.

"You definitely have a voice," Kyle said, starting with a positive. That was how his MFA instructors had always opened before the criticism came. "But I worry that the plot is too . . . elusive?"

"You sound as if that's not the word you wanted to use." William had straightened up in his seat—no longer toad-like, now rigid instead like a hawk.

"What is the book really about?" Kyle asked.

"What do you think it's about?"

"Well, if I had to go on what I read, it's about a professor fixated on a girl in his class who fantasizes about eating her heart."

"And?"

"That's not a plot."

"What would you call it?"

"Very disturbing."

"Can't a plot be *very disturbing*?"

"Not if you want readers to buy it," Kyle said. He saw William's ear twitch, clearly not pleased with his response.

"I don't know how forty pages is enough to make a claim like that," William said. He was fidgeting with the paper clips on Kyle's desk.

"A lot of editors only give a manuscript the first chapter to get a sense," Kyle said. "Readers are even more picky. If the opening paragraph doesn't grab them, they won't buy it."

"Have you ever heard of a cult classic?" William asked, slightly raising his voice. "Literature meant for the fringes instead of the masses? Nothing worthwhile was ever truly appreciated in its time."

"I don't know about that," Kyle said, looking back at his computer, wanting to get this over with. "William, fiction is very personal. What one editor loves another might hate."

William slowly cracked his knuckles, one at a time. "So you hated *Devil's Hopyard*?"

"I didn't say that."

"Do you not want to read any more?"

"It just made me uncomfortable." Kyle looked William in the eye again, fixating on the red veins. "You have to understand that. Maybe it's because I know you, and the narrator kind of . . . resembled you, and he's talking about doing some really fucked-up shit."

William bowed his head, staring at his hands in his lap. He stayed in that position long enough for Kyle to feel awkward.

"Sometimes a writer needs an outsider's perspective," Kyle said, trying to hold back a sigh. "You can't see what's not working because you're too close to it."

"*Devil's Hopyard* is everything to me," William whispered.

Kyle went to respond but stopped, cautioning himself to proceed more gently. He needed to take off his editor's cap and just be a friend.

"All first drafts have kinks," he said. "Donna Tartt takes more than a decade to write each of her books, and look at *The Goldfinch*—it won the Pulitzer."

"I've already spent ten years," William said, still so quiet that Kyle could barely hear him.

"But it's your first. Now if you just work on more of a cohesive plot—"

"I don't want to make any major edits. In my eyes, it's perfect."

"You have to be open to criticism."

William shook his head back and forth like a child.

"*Look*," Kyle said, dragging out the word. "I need to get ready for that editorial meeting. I'd be willing to discuss some plot beats . . ."

William slapped his knee. "You're right."

"Come again?"

"*You* are the professional, Kyle. I came here today telling myself I'd be flexible, and now look at me, I'm stuck in mud. I apologize."

Kyle squeezed the handball and it almost popped out of his hand. He couldn't recall William's personality back at Bentley changing so haphazardly from moment to moment.

William spread out his arms. "I am open to being molded," he said. "I am clay."

"O-kay," Kyle said. "Well, good. Good."

"How about we go over it right after your meeting?" William asked, blinking wildly.

"I have drinks with my author Sierra Raven afterward."

"Look at you, fancy pants. Author drinks, an office in Rockefeller Center, the power to crush a writer's spirit with just a squeeze."

The handball popped out of Kyle's hand and bounced across the room.

"I'm kidding," William said.

"I'll call you, William, and we'll set up a time."

William stood, forcing Kyle to rise as well. He extended his hand and they shook.

"Thank you for your candor, Kyle."

"Thank—"

William turned on his heels and headed for the door, scratching at his ear. Kyle wondered if the guy was shielding his face because tears were emerging. He felt terrible. This hadn't gone how he planned. But once William left, he reasoned it was probably better to tear off that Band-Aid in one fell swoop so the wound of rejection could begin to heal.

He went back to reading *The Dead Can't Hunt You Down,* reaching the part in the novel where the ex–hit man's former boss shows up to silence him for good.

7

WILLIAM PURCHASED A Yankees cap and stood across the street from Burke & Burke's offices all afternoon waiting for Kyle to emerge. He kept the cap low over his eyes. Rockefeller Center was a busy mix of tourists and suits, and he blended in with the rush of people speeding by.

After a while, his leg began to cramp up, an injury from the army when he fell from a high wall in an obstacle course. The army was a solution to get him away from his father's farm in upstate New York and his only chance at a scholarship for college; he found the experience invaluable. Discipline was what he craved, and he embraced it wholeheartedly. He was a good solider too, never tested in battle but obedient, strategic, and focused, traits he'd built on in his adult life.

He spied a young woman standing at the Burke & Burke entrance. She was wearing a vintage sweater too large for her frame and her short hair was tucked behind her ear with a barrette in the shape of a bookmark. *Sierra Raven.* He had done his homework and looked up her Facebook profile. She had more than a thousand friends who liked to respond to posts with emojis. The past month, her feeds were devoted to gushing comments about the book deal.

Soooo coooooooooolll, Sierra ;)

Girl, you rock, yer famous ☺

Don't forget us lil' people when you're climbing the bestseller charts :P

It hurt William to read any more. This fetus had achieved the kind of success she couldn't possibly appreciate. And Kyle probably signed her because he wanted to fuck her. William figured it was a lot easier for a cute girl to get a big contract than it was for an over-the-hill professor. He wondered if publishing had become a pretty person's game now that social media was such a necessary part of sales. Would grizzly Dostoevsky have had a shot in today's market? Not likely.

The sun was flirting with setting when Kyle finally stepped out of the building. William noticed a jaunt in Kyle's step, which made William feel like he'd been punched in the stomach. He tried to recall the last time he walked so sprightly; it had been one night about a decade ago. He'd practically skipped up the stairs and made love to Laura all night as if he was discovering the pleasure of flesh for the first time. At Kyle's apartment after dinner, he'd felt a similar swell from the thought of *Devil's Hopyard* getting out there in the world, but now that joy had shrunk to the size of pebble, a puny reminder of pure bliss.

He watched Kyle hug Sierra, which lasted for seconds longer than a causal embrace. He couldn't hear what they were saying, but Kyle made a gesture to head down the street and the two walked away. Making sure he stayed three people behind, William followed them into an Irish pub off Fifth Avenue, its interior dimly lit. They nabbed a booth with Sierra facing the front door, and William slithered into the adjacent booth so his back was against Kyle's. He took out one of Laura's compact mirrors so he'd see them if he angled it properly. Some hits from the 1980s played over the jukebox, but it was at a low enough volume that he could hear their conversation. A petite waitress came over, and he ordered a Manhattan and settled in.

KYLE HAD BEEN looking forward to drinks with Sierra after his long day. The surprise of William showing up at the office had left him flustered. He kept wavering between feeling bad for being honest and pissed off for being put on the spot like that. He resolved to give *Devil's Hopyard* another look to see if there was anything redeemable worth rewriting. Unfortunately, he never got a chance to finish *The Dead* before the editorial meeting. Since Carter liked an entire manuscript to be read, Kyle remained mute at the meeting except when asked about any progress with Tucker Noley. He had completely forgotten about getting on Tucker's ass to put out the next Gregor Spade novel, so he lied and said Tucker had finally gotten back to work. When the meeting ended, it was already six o'clock and time to meet Sierra.

"ID?" the waitress asked, when Sierra ordered.

"It happens all the time." Sierra removed her ID from her wallet and handed it over. The waitress looked up and down a few times before accepting.

"So today was my last day at work," Sierra said, taking off her roomy sweater. Underneath she wore a T-shirt that said WHAT FRESH HELL IS THIS?—DOROTHY PARKER.

"You were a nanny, right?"

"Yes, to Satan's offspring. I swear I once saw this kid's head spin during a tantrum."

The waitress came over with a bourbon on the rocks for Kyle and a tall beer for Sierra.

"To bigger and better things," Kyle said, clinking her glass and swallowing half of his drink. "Now you have all the time to write."

Sierra seemed to shrivel up. "How do you know when you might have writer's block?"

"What do you mean?" Kyle asked. "You just gave me some amazing pages."

"But since then I've written nothing. And I was working on those pages before I got the deal. Now I sit in front of the screen and want to slit my wrists with a razor blade."

"Have you outlined the next few chapters?"

"I can't work like that, I wish I could." She tapped at her front teeth. "Like the story doesn't feel real unless it unfolds as I type."

"But you lived through some of it, didn't you?"

"Everything I wrote so far, except that's where the truth ends. Should I not be telling you this?"

"Yeah, the deal is canceled now."

Her eyes bugged.

"I'm kidding, Sierra," he said, knocking back the rest of his bourbon and signaling the waitress for another. Usually by his second bourbon, he felt at ease. He figured he'd have his forties to sober up.

"It's just the pressure," she said, her fingers tracing over her eyebrows. "I've started picking at my eyebrows recently. I'm a mess."

"You're a working writer, welcome to the club."

The waitress brought his bourbon.

"Look, you are *brilliant* and everyone at Burke & Burke is so excited that you're part of our team."

She managed to half smile. "Really?"

"Do you know the kind of publicity you've brought us? Do you realize the magnitude of what you're about to become?"

"I *know.* That's what fucking with me."

Kyle placed his hand on top of hers. She seemed to relax a little.

"I'll be your cheerleader," he said. "I played football in high school, and I watched the girls' pep squad closely." At this close distance, he could smell her perfume, lush and floral. "Give me an S . . ."

"Stop," she said, with her hand over her face.

"Give me an I . . ."

Sierra finally laughed. "You're such a goof."

"And you're such a wonderful find. Really."

"Shouldn't you reserve statements like that for your girlfriend?"

Kyle inched away from her, as if he just realized how close they were sitting.

"Wow, I'm sorry," Sierra said, hands running through her hair, shaking her head. "*Inappropriate,* table for one over here. I guess I was just curious if you had a girlfriend . . . I mean, you must . . . I mean, how could you not?"

Kyle took a stiff sip. "I do. Her name is Jamie."

"What does she do?"

"She's an interior designer."

"Oh, cool. Yeah, I pictured her being creative . . . I mean, I never really pictured her, it's just . . . I'm sure you'd be into creative girls 'cause you're so creative." She lunged for the beer and saved herself by taking a long foamy swig. "Does she work for a company or on her own?"

"She's starting her own business and just rented an office that faces the Astor Place cube. She says it inspires her."

Talking about Jamie reminded Kyle that he needed to call her when he got home. They hadn't spoken all day since their minifight, not abnormal, but usually one of them checked in with the other.

"I'm not seeing anyone now," Sierra said. "There was a guy when I first moved, but he got in the way of my writing, like he devalued it and made me unmotivated."

"That's no good."

"I need another artist or someone creative too. So we can feed off of each other, y'know?"

"Once *Girls Without Hope* is published, they'll be lining up."

"That could be like two years from now."

"Well, maybe you're just meant to focus on writing now, to put all that angst on paper."

He opened his J.W. Hulme executive leather briefcase. He'd purchased it right after Sierra's deal went through, the first recklessly expensive gift he'd ever given himself. He removed a notepad and pen and jotted YOU ARE ______________________________. He looked up at her and then, in the blank space, he wrote AMAZINGLY AND WILDLY TALENTED. He ripped off the piece of paper and handed it to her.

"Each day I want you to write one great thing about yourself before you begin working," he said. "If you can't think of something, e-mail me and I'll have a spare ready."

"Thank you, Kyle." She held the paper close to her chest. "I'm glad I can talk to you about this stuff."

"Anytime."

"Enough about me and my neuroses. So is there another great talent you're about to sign?"

"Yeah, there's something new I'm digging," he said, stroking his stubble. "A fantastic new thriller with a lot of potential. It's about a guy who gets his eye gouged out as a sniper in Iraq. He winds up working for a hit man organization until he decides to leave and is hunted down by them."

"You're a modern-day Max Perkins."

"That's the plan." Kyle finished his drink and gestured to the waitress for the bill. "Shall we?" He paid and they both stood. "I hope you feel better about your book."

"I do," Sierra said. "Good pep talk, head cheerleader."

Kyle put his arm around her in a friendly way as the two walked past William. If they'd been paying better attention, they would've seen the man in the Yankees cap digging his nails into the wooden table with such force that his fingers were bleeding.

8

WILLIAM WOKE UP especially early the next morning. It was still dark outside when he drove down to the city, and he made it in record time without any traffic. He put the car in a garage and positioned himself at the Astor Place cube, facing west toward the two buildings that looked like possible offices. The sun rose, NYU students milled about, and he kept his eyes on the nearby subway station, munching on an egg and cheese sandwich he'd picked up at a nearby deli. He wore gloves since his fingers hadn't healed from scratching into the wooden table at the bar the night before. The conversation he'd overheard between Kyle and Sierra had proved that Kyle had no interest in *Devil's Hopyard.* When Sierra asked Kyle if he was excited about any new authors, Kyle spoke of an asinine novel about an ex-sniper who becomes a hit man. Sure, it had the possibility of being adapted into a film that would probably mint money, but what about books that had meaning, like William's? Books that would inspire. Books that would be remembered.

After an hour of silent patience, Jamie popped up out of the train station. She was typing on her phone and looking a little frazzled. Her blond hair had been thrown into a ponytail and she wore sweats and sneakers, apparently coming from the gym. In her other hand were a pair of high heels and a dry cleaning bag. He swallowed his last bite of egg and made his move.

JAMIE WAS TYPING an e-mail to her possible investor, Elka, and hesitated. She hated the notion of business e-mails, since they could show every misspelled word or wrong turn of phrase until the end of time. She needed to explain to Elka about the style of the model room she was showcasing in her office. She had crafted the e-mail last night and spent the train ride editing. Finally, she hit Send.

"Jamie?"

The voice seemed to come from inside her head, as if it was double-checking to make sure she described the colorful archival-based patterns conveying the legacy of iconic French design in the right way.

"Jamie, right?"

She practically ran into the man in front of her and slowed so as not to collide. One high heel slipped from her finger and fell to the sidewalk. The man bent down and held it up for her.

"You dropped this," he said. He had tired eyes, well-groomed hair, and jowls that made his smile appear as a sad affair. "It's William."

She'd been so absorbed in the e-mail that she would've walked right by her own mother.

"Oh, William," she said, accepting the high heel. "Hi!"

He went in for a quick hug. She patted his back with the hand holding the dry cleaning bag.

"I didn't even see you," she said. "I always seem to have my blinders on when I'm out in the city."

"I'm the opposite," William said, steering her away from a swarm of people coming up the stairs. "I'm so rarely here that I must look like a wide-eyed tourist."

"No, not at all," she said, and glanced toward her office building as if it was calling her. "What are you doing in town?"

"I have a meeting in the Village this afternoon and thought I'd get in a little early."

"It was really great to meet you the other night," she said, making a move toward Starbucks.

He followed her lead. "Yes, I agree. I was about to get a coffee as well."

"Is it terrible that I basically need it to open my eyes?"

"My wife has tried a coffee intervention on me with little success."

They entered the Starbucks, already busy at this early hour. She saw him scanning for seats.

"Students stake their claim by sunup at this one," Jamie said, heading toward the line. "I usually get mine to go."

"Busy day?"

"Yes, I'm getting a showroom ready for a possible investor coming in from Sweden."

"*Grattis,*" he said, winking.

"You know Swedish?"

"I'm a lover of all languages, meaning I know at least five words or phrases in most."

They reached the front of the line.

"I'll have an iced caffè latte," Jamie told the barista.

"I'll have the same," William said, taking out his Starbucks card. "It's on me. To thank you for the lovely dinner."

"I accept."

While waiting for their coffees, Jamie observed how attractive she found William, in a fatherly way, of course. She often noticed guys on the street who were almost twice her age and knew the psychological reasons why. In fact, Kyle was the youngest guy she'd ever seriously dated, and she wondered if Kyle's lack of maturity was the main cause of the friction between them. She knew he couldn't help his age and it was unfair to expect him to behave like someone much older, but she often found herself dreaming about them twenty or thirty years from now and how he would look and act. She liked having this fantasy.

"You seem to be in deep thought," William said. Their lattes waited on the counter and he handed hers over.

"Would you like to see my showroom?" Jamie asked, the words flowing from her mouth before she could take them back.

"*Efter dig,*" he said. "Lead the way."

ENTERING HER SHOWROOM/OFFICE, Jamie regretted inviting William. First off, no one else had seen the room yet and she didn't know if it was ready. Second, she realized she invited him as a way to make Kyle jealous and instantly felt shitty. Kyle had left her a genuine—*albeit drunken*—message of apologies, to which she responded with a brief text saying that she'd come over the next night to discuss things. She realized their fight had started because he'd been so adamant about his displeasure with William's manuscript. She chalked that up to simple envy. Here William had gone ahead and created five hundred pages of an actual book while Kyle had never come close to finishing one of his own projects. Even though he was achieving a lot of success as an editor, she knew that part of him probably wanted adulation as a writer too. She felt he deserved to know that she'd still be kind to William no matter what. She'd behave exactly how she wanted to without needing Kyle's approval.

As William stepped inside, Jamie was nervous to see how he'd initially respond to her work and was delighted to see his eyes go wide. The style she was going for was classic and subdued, not out of place in an elegant château.

"I feel like I stepped into Paris," he said.

She couldn't mask her grin. "Good, oh good. That's what I was hoping."

He ran a finger across a nineteenth-century desk that she had restained. "You're very talented."

"It's not like I wrote a novel."

"That's just manipulating words in the right way." William stood at the window and watched two skateboarders rolling around the Astor Place cube.

"It's very impressive nonetheless," she said.

"Kyle doesn't think so."

He looked less attractive to her when he said this, as if all the handsome parts of his face had turned against each other. His hair seemed finer and more unruly, white as opposed to silver, and his mouth sloped into a frown that made him appear older and forlorn.

"I don't think Kyle hates your book," she said, stepping closer to place a friendly hand on his shoulder.

"He's definitely not impressed."

"Did he tell you that?"

William gave a solitary nod, which upset her. Kyle was always brutally honest, a quality that obviously made him successful but how difficult would it have been to say some nice things about William's manuscript, just to give the guy some hope? After all that William had done for Kyle back at college—which she'd probably never know the extent of—would it have killed him to think of someone else's feelings more than his own personal drive? Just because William's novel wasn't at the level Burke & Burke published, it still had to have some value and could certainly be improved. Jamie decided then that she'd make sure Kyle gave *Devil's Hopyard* a fair shot and would urge him to do anything in his power to nurture its success.

"Kyle isn't always the easiest person to get along with," she said.

William gave a solitary laugh, which said, *Tell me about it.*

"The two of us got into it the other night," Jamie said. "Even though he was in the wrong, I'm trying to give him some slack because of these intense few weeks at work."

"He was having cozy drinks last night at a bar with his author. The young girl."

"Sierra? What do you mean, *cozy drinks*?"

"I passed by and the two were sitting in a booth side by side. They just seemed to be enjoying each other's company."

Jamie pretended not to hear this. She had a busy day planned and knew that the minute any kind of suspicions entered her mind they would fester and spread.

"You don't know what I did for that kid back in school," William said.

"He knows, trust me, William. He told me all about it."

"They were ready to expel him, and I went to bat—"

"Expel him over what?"

"I guess he hasn't told you everything."

"If he didn't tell me, then he probably wasn't ready to yet," Jamie said, trying to be diplomatic despite being curious as hell.

"He got caught selling drugs and not just *college kid* drugs, bad shit that he was hooked on too."

"Oh."

"Want to know more?" William asked, facing her. She hadn't noticed how red one of his eyes was, and she couldn't help staring. He cupped a palm over it. "It's from not sleeping."

"What else was Kyle involved in?" Jamie hated herself for probing, but she was also a tad hurt that her boyfriend hadn't been as forthcoming about his past as she'd thought.

"No, it's really not my place to say."

Jamie waved her hands in front of her face. "You're right, don't tell me. I can't believe I asked. I would never want to be in a relationship that wasn't based on trust."

"He's very lucky to have you," William said, licking his lips. Jamie became lost in the swirl of his tongue before she came back down to earth, as if momentarily hypnotized.

"We're lucky to have each other," she stated.

"My wife always says the same thing."

"I'm going to have a talk with Kyle about your manuscript," Jamie said.

"Please don't."

"No, for whatever reason, he's not giving you a fair shake, and that's not right."

"I don't want pity."

"But you deserve respect, and I'll be sure he understands that."

William placed his hand over his heart. "Thank you."

"Think nothing of it." She glanced at her watch. It was way later than she'd intended to start her day. She made a face and he automatically understood.

"I'll let you get back to your work," he said, cupping his red eye again, a source of embarrassment.

"We should have you for dinner again, William. And your wife. I'd love to meet her."

"It's a date."

"And I'm glad you liked the showroom," she said. "You were the first to see it."

"I'm honored," he said, and left her office after saying good-bye. When the door shut, Jamie had the impulse to run outside and probe his mind about Kyle's mysterious past, but she latched onto the antique desk to keep her in place. She was certain that Kyle would eventually feel close enough to her to reveal those dark secrets. But if that didn't happen soon, she swore she'd find a way to pull them out of him.

9

KYLE SPENT THE day finishing *The Dead Can't Hunt You Down,* a pulse-pounding mix of Elmore Leonard with a Quentin Tarantino edge. He contacted the writer, Shane Matthews, who hadn't published anything other than a few short stories in noir journals. Shane had sent the manuscript after reading about Kyle in the *Times* and had been blown away to hear back so quickly. Kyle gushed about the novel but wasn't ready to offer a deal until Carter signed off. He shot Carter an e-mail about its prospects and forwarded the manuscript for him to read over the weekend.

On the way home, he picked up a dozen blue roses and a bucket of Buffalo wings, extra spicy the way Jamie liked them. He also stopped at the liquor store and bought a twelve-year-old Macallan that he opened as soon as he entered his apartment. While getting out two whiskey glasses, he heard scratching against his bedroom window and let Capone inside. The cat seemed to have gotten in a scuffle, so with a glass in hand, Kyle placed Capone in the sink and gave him a good washing. After drying the cat with a towel, Kyle even let Capone lick some scotch off his finger. The doorbell rang, and he opened the front door with the cat tucked in his arm.

"There's my two favorite men," Jamie said, kissing Capone and scratching Kyle's head.

"No kiss for me?" he asked as she walked inside.

She dropped her bags and fell into the couch. "Let's see how you behave tonight."

"It'll be worth striving for," Kyle said, putting the cat to the side and sitting on the couch too. He had told himself to focus on Jamie tonight, especially about her work. "Making headway with the showroom?" he asked.

"Yes. In fact, a mutual friend of ours gave it a glowing review."

"Oh, yeah, who?"

"William."

Kyle didn't know if he'd heard her right. William was the last person he wanted to talk about now that the weekend was here. In fact, he had sworn he wouldn't so much as think of *Devil's Hopyard* or its creator until he was back in the office on Monday.

He had a hard time swallowing. "Did you say William?"

"I ran into him near my office and invited him to come up," Jamie said, shrugging her shoulders as if it was nothing.

"What was he doing around Astor Place?"

"I don't know. He had a meeting—"

Kyle jumped to his feet, spooking Capone, who darted away.

"That's the same excuse he gave me when he showed up uninvited at my office."

"He's a renowned professor. Is it so crazy he might have *two* meetings?"

Jamie got up and went over to the bouquet of blue roses still wrapped in paper.

"These need to be put in water," she said, and whisked them into the kitchen.

Kyle followed her. "Don't you find it strange that William has popped up in our lives for the past three days in a row?"

She turned on the water at full force. "Not everything is a conspiracy." She jammed the flowers into a vase and took a deep, meditative breath. "They're beautiful."

"I know you love blue roses."

She rubbed a petal between two fingers. "I don't want to fight, Kyle."

He opened the fridge and took out the bucket of wings.

"Let get some wings and booze in us," he said, nabbing a wing and hovering it over her lips.

"Damn, you know my weakness." She took a bite, then left a saucy kiss on his cheek.

WITH BELLIES FULL of wings and scotch, Kyle and Jamie retreated back to the couch. They'd managed not to bring up William, Sierra, or any other sore spots between them throughout dinner. She placed her feet in his lap and he gave them a good rub. She was a little drunk because she was hiccupping. Kyle thought she had the cutest hiccups, which sounded like a bird's chirps.

"Hold your breath and stick your head in water," he said.

"No, my grandmother used to say to put sugar on the back of your tongue." She held up her half-full glass of Macallan and took a swig. "Well, this has sugar in it."

"I'm sorry," he said. "If that helps."

"For what?"

"You ready for a grocery list of reasons?"

"Just give me the highlights."

"I haven't been making you a priority," he said.

She made her hand into the shape of a gun and shot him. "Bingo."

"I'm learning how to balance it all. You and work."

"Listen." She hiccupped. "I am so happy for everything that's happening to you right now with . . . *Sierra* . . ."

She couldn't help rolling her eyes when she said Sierra's name.

"I apologize. That eye roll was just a knee-jerk reaction," she said. "An *eye*-jerk reaction, I swear."

"You've never even met her," he said, and stopped rubbing her foot. "You don't have to feel threatened."

She swung her feet off of his lap.

"Kyle, I'm not threatened. It's just"—she hiccupped again—"I hear about the two of you having cozy drinks in a bar—"

"Wait, what? Who told you that?"

"I won't reveal my sources."

"Did William . . . ?" Kyle saw Jamie avert her eyes when he mentioned William's name. "He *did* say something to you. What the fuck is his game?"

"First off, he doesn't have a *game.* This isn't the . . . plot of some mystery."

"Yes, I had a drink with Sierra, and I've had many drinks with authors before. I like to drink. Writers like to drink."

Jamie inspected her glass, found it was empty, and poured another thumbful.

"All I'm saying is that you have a teeny, tiny crush on this girl, and if you just admitted it, we could move the fuck on," she said.

"This is ridiculous. When did you become so insecure?"

She pointed at him with the glass, spilling some liquid on the couch. "You're the insecure one."

He went into the kitchen, returning with a paper towel. He proceeded to mop up the spill.

"Kyle, the couch is dark gray, you can't even see the stain."

"How am I insecure?"

She blew the bangs from her eyes. "Because of the way you're threatened by William."

"And why would I be threatened by William?"

"You're not gonna want to hear this."

"Haven't we already taken off the gloves here?"

"Fine. Because William is working on a manuscript that he's proud of and he believes in, and you gave up on your own writing."

"I have a high-pressure job, Jamie, and I don't have the time to tinker all day on some piece of shit opus about a sicko professor who wants to eat one of his students' *hearts*!"

Jamie put her head in her hands. Her body was lightly shaking, and Kyle had worried he'd gone too far. He hated the tone of his voice when he yelled. He placed his hand on her back and rubbed in a circle, just like she'd do to soothe him. When Jamie looked up, she was laughing so hard her face was stained with tears.

"Are you crying or laughing right now?" he asked. "Tell me how I'm supposed to react."

She threw up her hands, hiccupping again. "I don't know . . . Goddamn it!" She shot off the couch and made a beeline for the bathroom.

Kyle could hear the water running. He couldn't decide what made him angrier: William inserting himself into their lives, or Jamie bringing up his inability to write, which—*years ago*—he swore he wouldn't let bother him anymore. Sure, there were a few unfinished novels left to pasture in the far reaches of his closet, but if he had to choose between that and editing now, it was an easy decision.

Jamie emerged from the bathroom, her face dripping with water.

"I dunked my head in the sink and now my hiccups are gone," she said, and sat back on the couch. "Thank you for that." She took his hands in hers, as if she was about to reveal some awful tragedy.

"Kyle, you can get obsessive about things."

"What?"

"I've wanted to say this to you before because it's not healthy, but you get your mind fixated on something and then obsess over it."

"Like what?"

"Like your job. Ever since I met you, getting ahead at Burke & Burke is all you've talked about."

"I'm driven."

She patted his hand, as if to a child. "And now it's William."

"*He's* the obsessed one."

Jamie shook her head. "From your reaction right now, it's clear that you are too. Wouldn't it be easier to just read his manuscript and give him some helpful edits?"

Kyle snatched his hands away from her and got up to bring over *Devil's Hopyard.* He shoved it in her lap.

"You read it. It's filth."

"You don't have to be so negative."

"It's misogynistic, senseless, offensive, and—"

"Maybe it's ahead of its time?"

"Look, we think about literature in two very different ways. It's *everything* to me while it's a way to pass the time for you."

She shook a finger at him. "You always say that fiction is subjective. And I don't have the time to read Proust like I used to. Half my day is spent shuttling back and forth on the train between your apartment and mine. And I don't want to read Proust while being sandwiched in a crowd of bitter rush-hour commuters."

"That's what this is all about, isn't it?"

"What?"

"Our situation. You living in another country practically on the Upper West Side and me in Brooklyn."

"Let me ask you, Kyle, do you ever come to my place?"

"Your roommate is a drunk—"

"So are *we.* I'm sopping wet right now and you're half-a-bottle wasted.

We are thirty-year-old New Yorkers just like Sybil. Can you tell me one other professional person our age in this city whose life doesn't revolve around cocktails?"

"So you want me to come uptown more? You have a cramped apartment on the first floor—"

"It shouldn't matter. If I was living in a box in a ditch, you should want to come. It's indicative."

"Indicative of what?"

"Of the fact that this—you and me—where are we honestly headed?"

The fight had escalated beyond Kyle's comprehension, and he was having trouble focusing on all her grievances.

"Your silence tells me all I need to know," Jamie said, darting for her coat.

"Wait, you're going to leave? It's late, it's Friday."

He grabbed her, but she wasn't having it.

"I want stability, Kyle, okay? I want a place we can call ours."

"We've only been dating six months."

"Which is exactly when you told me you've ended *all* of your other relationships."

"So that's what this is about? I'm not going anywhere."

"But neither are we." She took a moment to compose herself. "I'm gonna leave before I say anything more I regret."

"No, no, no," he said, chasing after her when she made a move for the door. "Let's just go to bed."

"You think I want to sleep with you tonight?"

"Of course not. I mean, we're pickled, we're tired, and we're lousy when we're like that. We should drink less and listen better to each other."

He embraced her from behind as she put her hand on the doorknob.

“I’ll just leave in the morning, then.”

“That’s fair,” he said, kissing her neck. “God, this was *not* the way I wanted tonight to go.” He let go of her to swipe a blue rose from the vase, which he placed in her hand. “I do have a tendency to obsess over things.”

“And be negative,” she said.

“Yes,” he said, “and be negative. I think in doomsday terms, I can’t help it.”

“Will you be nicer to William?”

“Is that really what’s bothering you the most?”

She gave a little shrug.

“Okay,” he said, eyeing *Devil’s Hopyard,* which had fallen off the couch onto the floor.

“You’ll read the entire manuscript and give him good advice about it?” she asked.

He frowned at *Devil’s Hopyard,* but she couldn’t see. He nodded with his nose tickling her earlobe.

“I promise.”

She rested her head on his arm. He ran his fingers through her hair.

“Are we good?” he asked, but she was already snoring. She had the ability to fall asleep anywhere, anytime. “Jamie?”

She snored back in response. Her eyes were closed, so he picked her up and carried her to bed, taking off her high heels and tucking her in. He shut off the light and meandered back into the living room, grabbing *Devil’s Hopyard* and turning to where he left off.

“This is for you, baby,” he said, and plunged back into its nightmarish prose.

And in the shack that is our world, I clean her till she’s pure again, filling her with my seed and getting her ready till I make that final incision and cut out her beating heart so it can dance on my TONGUE. And then I chew, chew, chew until it's ingested and beats beside my own. Two hearts beating as ONE, my lovely, lovely . . .

That was as far as Kyle got before his head tipped back and he was snoring his own dirge at the ceiling.

10

KYLE WOKE UP on the couch, *Devil's Hopyard* heavy in his lap. His legs had fallen asleep from its weight. He pushed it aside, groggy, and felt his way to the kitchen, turning on the coffeemaker. "Jamie?" he shouted. "You wanna cup?" He made one for her anyway and brought it steaming into the bedroom, but she wasn't there. A note left on the bedstand said, *Have to get ready for Elka, xoxo.* Kyle was having a hard time remembering exactly what they'd said to each other last night and if it had ended okay.

His phone buzzed and he picked it up without looking at the caller ID, assuming it was Jamie.

"Hey, baby, you didn't have to run out."

"Kyle?" The voice was decidedly male. Kyle knew right away who it was. "It's William, did I catch you at a bad time?"

"What time is it?" Kyle asked, annoyed. He glanced at the microwave clock and saw it was noon. He couldn't recall the last time he'd slept so late, but it had been a long week.

"Did I wake you?" William asked, and gave his standard chuckle. "You keeping college hours there?"

Kyle kept his tone cold, so William might get the hint. "You didn't wake me, I was working."

"You editors never stop, do you?"

"So I should be getting back to it—"

"Were you serious about helping me fix some of the kinks in *Devil's Hopyard*?"

Kinks? Kyle wanted to say. *The whole fucking book is a kink.*

"I didn't mean over the weekend," Kyle said.

"It's just that I'm in Brooklyn now."

"Let me guess, you have a meeting?"

"No, I was visiting family in Carroll Gardens and thought I'd pop in a little early."

"You've certainly been coming into the city a lot."

William laughed, a slightly deranged cackle.

"You'd find Killingworth tough to be in all the time too. Sleepy is an understatement."

"I really have a busy day ahead—"

"It's funny," William said. "I've been thinking about that night I bailed you out of jail."

"Why were you thinking about that?" Kyle was clutching the cell phone tightly. He could feel it digging into his palm.

"I guess because we've been reunited. You know that was one of the only times in my life that I've lied?"

"William, do you have something you want to say?" Kyle was losing his patience and thought about hanging up. But then he imagined the phone ringing and ringing again, forever.

"Do you know Ground Up Café?" William asked.

"Yeah, it's a few blocks down."

"Can I buy you a coffee? I feel like we've gotten off on the wrong foot."

"It's just been a hectic week and you've been . . ."

"Persistent?"

"Yeah, you have."

"Laura tells me that all the time. My kids too. I have this drive, and when I want to make something happen, I can be a little obsessive. I'm working on it."

Kyle stroked his chin, not expecting this apology of sorts. He felt bad. Maybe he hadn't given William a fair shot? Maybe he *was* a little jealous that the guy had written more than he ever had? He eyed *Devil's Hopyard,* propped up on the couch. He thought back to the first paper he stayed up all night to write for Professor Lansing's class. This was after his time in jail and after the charges were dropped. He'd given up consuming every bad drug out there. He found literature and let it become his savior, underlining passages of Steinbeck's *East of Eden* that mirrored his own life. He put everything into a paper on spirituality in the novel and freaked out while waiting for the professor's response. He wanted more than anything to do well, to prove that he'd been worthy of saving. He would've been destroyed if Professor Lansing had demolished his paper. He couldn't imagine what William must be feeling right now.

"I can meet you at Ground Up," Kyle said.

"Well, good. I was hoping you'd say that, Kyle. I'm there right now."

"Let me jump in the shower first."

"Don't forget *Devil's Hopyard.*"

Click.

WILLIAM LEFT A voice mail for Laura while he waited for Kyle. He hadn't returned home last night, instead wandering around the city, soaking in its flavor. A drink began downtown at McSorley's after leaving Jamie's office, and then he headed over to the Whitney Museum and up the High Line with a ham and butter baguette in hand. It was nighttime when he reached Central Park and sat in Sheep Meadow, tucking his jacket under his head as a pillow. He slept better than he had in months, awakening to a fireball sunrise off Fifth Avenue. Its warmth caressed his face and he felt refreshed. He got on the train and made his way down to Cobble Hill. One luxuriating cup of coffee later, he called Kyle.

Laura understood his strange habits and didn't think it abnormal when he occasionally stayed out all night. *Walkabouts,* he called them, not for six months in the wilderness like the Aborigines but a night of entering the "forest of his mind," without any distractions. This was essential for creating *Devil's Hopyard,* and Laura never objected, greeting him with a thousand kisses when he returned, as if he'd been gone as long as a true walkabout.

Kyle entered the café with the manuscript tucked under his arm. Immediately, William didn't like the way Kyle was holding it, as if the manuscript was a nuisance, a dead weight. He'd imagined Kyle walking in with it pressed against his heart, since he loved it so much that he wanted to keep it close, for fear another editor might snatch it away.

Kyle waved and then headed to the counter first to order, which William found rude. If *Devil's Hopyard* had been so amazing, Kyle wouldn't even be thinking about coffee. Earlier, William had a shred of hope that Kyle didn't tell Sierra about the manuscript because it was so fantastic he wanted to keep it under wraps. But now William knew the truth. It was nothing more than a submission quickly shuttled to the rejection pile. He gnawed at a scone that tasted like Styrofoam, and Kyle finally came over.

"Hey, William," Kyle said, extending his hand to shake. William complied and the two battled it out for a second, each one gripping hard, until Kyle slid his hand away. William was satisfied that he hadn't given in first.

Kyle sat and placed *Devil's Hopyard* on the table between them.

"So I've written more," William said.

"You *should* keep writing," Kyle said. "Don't be waiting on me."

William took another bite of the scone, practically chipping a tooth. "I'm not."

"I heard you ran into Jamie by her office and saw her showroom."

"I did."

"It seems like you've been running into us by accident a lot this week," Kyle said.

William could sense frustration in Kyle's tone. "They say Manhattan is like a small town."

"Who says that?"

William placed his hand on top of his manuscript and lovingly caressed the cover. Doing so made him feel bolder, more self-assured.

"I worry that you've misinterpreted my intention with this book."

"I think the issue is that I don't understand your intention at all."

Kyle glanced out the window; William could tell he was avoiding him. A blond girl had removed her bike from against a tree. Seeing this made William's bones ache, as if death grew nearer. This young girl and Kyle still had an endless future ahead of them; William knew his would be limited.

"Are you all right?" Kyle asked, looking directly at William now.

William wondered if he'd been the one staring obsessively at the young blond girl instead of Kyle. Sometimes his mind played tricks. More and more that was happening.

"Don't you believe that the publishing industry needs a wake-up call?" William asked, spearing his tongue with his fang tooth and swallowing a drop of blood. "Look at your bestseller lists—you're fifty shades of *who the fuck cares?* Fiction used to be daring and prose used to be meaty. Hemingway would weep at what is marketed as a novel today."

"Hemingway was probably certifiable," Kyle said.

"Maybe that's what it takes."

"To do what?"

"To reach such great heights," William said. His tongue was still bleeding, the taste metallic and comforting. He patted the manuscript. "That's what I'm after."

"William," Kyle began, in a tone that William already found condescending, "I think it's a little early to talk about Hemingway comparisons. Your prose couldn't be more different. Hemingway was precise; he never wasted a word."

"Forget Hemingway," William said with a flick of his wrist.

"Your prose is loose, disjointed, and angry. Really, *really* angry, like you're writing about something terrible you've experienced before."

William sat back and linked his hands behind his head with a grin. "So you believed it?"

Kyle took a sip of coffee. "I don't know what I believe."

"Are you a Bret Easton Ellis fan?"

"Yeah, love the guy . . ." Kyle stopped himself, realizing the point William was trying to make.

"Would you ever question Ellis's sanity after reading *American Psycho*?" William was getting amped up. "Did you believe that he wanted to chop people up like Patrick Bateman? But see, that's what I'm going for—writing so real that the reader might wonder if the author is letting fact bleed into fiction. That's the hook!"

William could see the young girl out the window getting on her bike. On her T-shirt was a design of a small rainbow situated over her heart.

"Like *Naked Lunch* by William S. Burroughs," William said, snapping his fingers. "You read that in a senior seminar with me."

"I've never been a Burroughs fan."

"But you don't think he should've been locked up, do you? Even though no one can argue he had a depraved mind. In the 1966 trial that cleared the book of obscenity, Norman Mailer argued, 'Just as Hieronymus Bosch set down the most diabolical and blood-curdling details with a delicacy of line and a Puckish humor that left one with a sense of the mansions of horror attendant upon Hell, so, too, does Burroughs leave you with an intimate, detailed vision of what Hell might be like, a Hell which may be waiting as the culmination, the final product, of the scientific revolution.' "

"So you're aiming to show us hell on earth with *Devil's Hopyard*?"

William shook his head. "No, I'm aiming for so much more. And an audience *will* see it someday, whether or not you want to be a part of it, Kyle."

"It sounds like I don't have an exclusive anymore."

"That's entirely up to you. All I want is a chance. Pretend you don't know me. Pretend that manuscript showed up at your door without a clue who wrote it."

"I wouldn't have gotten past the first few pages then."

"So I should be honored you made it to page forty? Or did you even make it *that* far?"

William could see Kyle was losing patience from the way he squirmed in his seat.

"What was the last part you read?" William asked, sneering. He could feel the heat spilling from his nostrils as he breathed in and out.

"The professor is carrying on about eating the unnamed girl's *heart,*" Kyle said, raising his voice. An older couple at the next table glanced over.

"See," William said, clapping his hands. "That's proves you didn't read that far. She has a name, Kyle, even before page forty."

"Fine, maybe it was page thirty that I got to. I don't know, William. But that's my point. Your pages aren't distinct from one another. The whole thing is the same insanity over and over. What's the obsession with this girl's heart?"

"You'll have to reach the end to find out," William said with a wink.

"All right, fine. I'll read every page you gave me. But if I do, I'm gonna be brutally honest with what I thought."

"Because you're sugarcoating so much right now . . ."

"In my MFA program, they said that three percent of us will actually publish and go on to successful careers."

"I *will* be part of that three percent."

Kyle murmured something under his breath that William couldn't hear.

"You would make a poor professor, Kyle," William said, and sighed. "You don't know how to build people up."

"I build up talent. That's what a good editor does. That was how I discovered Sierra Raven when no one else was bothering to look."

"Yeah, Sierra Raven. What a surprise that someone young and pretty caught your eye."

"And speaking of Sierra," Kyle said, getting more heated. William could sense the blood boiling in the boy's veins. "Why would you tell Jamie about me having *cozy* drinks with her? Are you trying to fuck up my relationship?"

"Are *you*?"

"Am I . . . ?" Kyle stammered. "Of course not. Sierra is purely business."

"You can keep telling yourself that—"

Kyle grabbed his coffee in an attempt to leave. "I don't know what you're after, William."

"You were always so sensitive, even at school. Calm down."

"Your book is on another kind of level of *fucked-up-ness* and you are *sick* if you think it's actually written well and has meaning."

William began cackling, softly at first, and then building in intensity.

"But it evoked a response in you. Don't you see that gives it merit? Love me or hate me, it's still an obsession."

"I'm not obsessed!"

Kyle's cheeks were flushed and he was breathing heavily. He was clutching his cup of coffee so hard it looked as if was about to crush it.

"I don't understand why you're getting so worked up," William said. "I'm not a psychologist, but this does seem like displaced anger. Or did you always feel this way toward me?"

Kyle simmered down, trying to regain his cool. He took a long, slow sip of coffee.

"You know that isn't true," he replied, as if he was suddenly ashamed of his behavior.

"You have a funny way of showing it. Back at Bentley, you were a lot more thankful."

"That was a long time ago."

"But then years passed without so much as a word," William said. "I wrote that recommendation letter for you to get into Wisconsin, and then *poof,* never an e-mail telling me how the program went, or that you became an editor in New York City."

Kyle picked at a sugar packet. He crumpled it in his fist. "Maybe I didn't want to relive my time at Bentley."

At this, William gave a stern nod. "Do I represent those dark times for you?"

Kyle stared to the ceiling. "I haven't thought about back then . . . in a long, long time."

"I wasn't responsible for the choices you made," William said in a soothing, hypnotic tone, one he had practiced, which often subdued the other party.

"I know," Kyle whispered.

"I was the one who saw your potential and rescued you from a life of drugs and crime . . ."

"Not so loud, William."

William locked eyes with the elderly couple at the next table. They both looked away, alarmed.

"I helped you when you needed it most," William said. "And now I ask that you help me."

"I can't just publish your book, it doesn't work like that. I have to present it at the editorial meeting, and then it's ultimately up to Carter Burke . . ."

William pushed *Devil's Hopyard* across the table.

"Finish the manuscript before you give up on it."

"It's never gonna be accepted." Kyle took a deep breath. "I'm sorry."

"Are you?"

"Yes, I am. Truly."

William stood and leaned over Kyle. He felt like a giant looming over a lesser creature. He got in Kyle's face.

"*Devil's Hopyard* will be published."

"Not by us."

William pushed the manuscript until it fell with a *thud* into Kyle's lap. "That's very troubling to hear. That could bring about a lot of trouble."

Kyle flinched. "Are you . . . *threatening* me?"

"Don't look at this as a punishment. Look at this as an opportunity. This will take your career into the stratosphere. Trust me."

Before Kyle had a chance to respond, William headed out of the café. He believed he was a soothsayer and had made a prophecy. Kyle would be stupid not to listen. The future would have both of their names flashing in lights. It would occur whether or not Kyle was complicit in making it happen. Otherwise, William would just have to do all of the legwork on his own for both of them.

William felt his heart swell. He finally had that extra jaunt in his step he'd been waiting for.

11

SUNDAY PASSED IN a haze for Kyle. He didn't want to bother Jamie, since she'd be preparing the showroom for her new investor. He decided to get stoned and see if that might help him unlock whatever potential existed in *Devil's Hopyard.* Pot had been the heaviest thing he'd ingested since Bentley, and only occasionally. He'd returned from coffee yesterday with William a little shaken, not knowing how much of a threat had been made. William couldn't be so crazy to assume that Kyle had any pull at Burke & Burke with a stinker of a novel. If this round of pages didn't hold his interest, he'd tell William once and for all to let the manuscript die.

Halfway through a blunt, he took out William's opus. The pages had begun to fray, as if it'd been well read. He flipped to a passage later in the novel.

> This story I tell is a reminder of how far a soul will go to accomplish what it desires. For me, I crave infamy, my name in lights. Her HEART will take me there. We will be talked about for

some time, anointed in history. She has no idea about the part she plays. Reality and fiction WILL combine in a delicious . . .

A piece of lit ash fell from Kyle's blunt, igniting page 279. If he wasn't so stoned he would've caught it earlier, but his clogged mind was a few seconds behind. A small flame, about twenty pages deep, ate through the manuscript. When he finally fanned it out, it had created a hole. He took this as a sign and placed *Devil's Hopyard* in a drawer, where he vowed to leave it for good, and then he smoked some more and watched two of his favorite movies, *Die Hard* and *Die Hard 2: Die Harder,* figuring he deserved the rest of the night off.

ON MONDAY MORNING, Kyle was getting ready for work when he noticed *Devil's Hopyard* on the bedside table. He could've sworn he'd shoved it in a drawer, but he was so stoned last night that either he had imagined doing so, or he'd taken the manuscript out again right before bed. Capone scratched at the window, and he let the cat inside and left it some food. Capone wasn't satisfied by the leftover Chinese and hissed, darting back into the bedroom. Kyle found the cat seated on top of the manuscript, his eyes judging Kyle, seemingly for not giving the book one last chance. So he grabbed it to show Carter. This way he could at least use the excuse that he tried everything he could. His boss also had such a twisted sense of humor that he might even be amused by the story behind *Devil's Hopyard.*

Sitting in Carter's office later, Kyle wished he hadn't smoked so much last night. Pot was a rare release for him, mostly because it made him spacey the next day. Bourbon always seemed to make him just right.

"So I got through that *Dead* submission over the weekend," Carter said, chewing on the earpiece of his glasses. Kyle already knew that action didn't bode well for what was to come. He'd seen Carter slay other editors while chewing on his earpiece.

"Shane has a great voice," Kyle said, already in defense mode. "I'm surprised he hasn't been snapped up."

Carter put his glasses back on, letting them rest on the beak of his nose. "First off, how is Sierra Raven coming along with her book?"

"Well, she's been slower with the next few chapters than the earlier ones."

"Slower?" Carter shook his head. "We're not paying half a million dollars to a turtle."

"I think the size of the deal is messing with her."

"That's a bullshit problem if I ever heard one. Should we take the money back so I can see some pages?"

Carter stood and stretched. He patted his breast pocket and removed a crushed pack of Gauloises.

"Don't tell my wife or I'll have you hunted down like that poor schmuck in the ex–hit man tale."

They heard a knock on the door.

"Fuck, is that Corrine having me followed?" Carter laughed, striking a match and lighting his cigarette. Brett peeked his head through the crack.

"Oh, good, Brett, come in."

"Sir," Brett said, snagging the seat next to Kyle.

"So Brett had a look-see at *The Dead Can't Hunt You Down* too and we agreed on making an offer. We'll change the title, of course, it's too much of a tongue twister."

"That's great," Kyle said.

"But we agreed for *me* to take it on," Carter said, a cloud of smoke obscuring his face. "Between Sierra Raven and Tucker Noley, you have your plate full right now."

Brett cosigned the decision with a sharp nod.

"But I discovered Shane."

Carter's face emerged from the smoke, dissatisfied. "That's not how we speak of our authors here."

"*Burke & Burke* discovered Shane Matthews," Brett chimed in. "Just like *Burke & Burke* discovered Sierra Raven, not *you*."

Kyle told himself not to object, even though he wanted to punch Brett right between the eyes.

"Now, you said you had something else to show me?" Carter said, snapping his fingers.

Kyle removed *Devil's Hopyard* from his leather bag.

"What the fuck happened to this?" Carter said, flipping to the middle where a hole the size of a half-dollar had burned through.

"This is your old professor's book?" Brett asked.

"Is it any good?" Carter asked, meaning, *Is this even worth discussing if it's a pile of shit?*

"It's unlike anything I've read before," Kyle said, as Carter and Brett looked up excitedly. "But not in a good way," he added.

Kyle proceeded to tell them the highlights of what had transpired with William over the course of the week. How the guy had been his mentor, a brilliant professor, but that his book was the most shocking pile of garbage ever put to paper. And worse, that William had become stalkerish and even threatening when Kyle wouldn't agree to publish the manuscript.

"So what do you want me to do with this turd?" Carter asked.

"I need to know if it's as terrible as I think it is," Kyle said. "He's *so* convinced he's written the next Great American Novel."

Carter and Brett exchanged wary looks.

"What if it's stupendous?" Brett asked, rubbing at a stain on his tie. "Should we call your ability as an editor into question?"

"I brought in Shane Matthews," Kyle said. "And Sierra too. I'm having a pretty good month, aren't I, Brett?"

Brett's nostrils flared as if he already knew where Kyle was going with this.

"Who've you brought in recently?" Kyle continued.

Carter let out a carefully concealed smirk; he liked it when his employees tussled.

"I have a long list and I'm not necessarily after new blood," Brett said.

"You should always be after new blood," Carter said. "Writers get old and dry up or die. Some of the best works are made by the young."

"Speaking of ancient," Brett said with a whistle. "How's Tucker Noley's new Spade saga coming along?"

"He's finally back to writing it," Kyle lied.

"Really?" Brett asked, elongating the word in a comical fashion. "Because I had to call Tucker this weekend about a foreign offer for one of his earlier books, and he told me he hadn't started his new one, that the *well* was—to use his exact phrasing—empty."

Carter stubbed out his cigarette angrily. "Is this true?"

Kyle coughed into his fist. "It's taken longer than expected to get him going."

"Kyle," Carter said, "I think you've been spending too much time getting sucked into your own personal thriller and not enough time living in reality."

"I think you're right, sir," Brett agreed.

Of course you think he's right, you kiss-ass fuck, Kyle thought.

"Brett, you give the beginning of this . . ." Carter said, running his finger under the title. "*Devil's Hopyard,* what the sweet Christ does that mean?"

"It's a park in Connecticut—" Kyle began, but Carter held up a fist, a sign he often gave at meetings when he wanted absolute silence.

"Like I said, Brett, you peruse the first chapter," Carter continued. "But if it's utter dreck I don't want to hear one more word about your psycho professor, Kyle. He's obviously getting in the way of you taking care of business with the few authors you have."

Carter chucked the manuscript in Brett's lap, whose butterfingers let it fall to the floor. Brett picked it up and apologized to Carter.

"Now make yourselves scarce while I give Shane Matthews the call that will change his life. The kid doesn't even have an agent."

Carter picked up the phone. Both Kyle and Brett just stood there.

"Go on," Carter said.

Outside their boss's office, Brett jabbed Kyle in the spleen.

"Fuck you for trying to throw me under the bus," Brett said, his breath garlicky.

"You drew first blood," Kyle said, pleased to see *Devil's Hopyard* tucked under Brett's arm, finally giving him a break by torturing someone else.

"I see you, you sneaky son of a bitch," Brett said, halfway down the hall already.

"We see each other, buddy."

"I saw your mother on my dick last night," Brett called out at the door to his office.

"Yeah, well, she's dead, you necrophiliac asshole."

Brett's door slammed, and Darcy's shocked expression told Kyle that he'd probably gone too far there. He reasoned that an outburst like that came from this last week of strange occurrences with William, who'd affected him more than he initially thought.

WHEN KYLE GOT home after stopping in a bar for one, two, *well, maybe three* bourbons, he decided to call William, knowing that Brett would absolutely lambaste *Devil's Hopyard* to Carter, especially after what had transpired between them. This would be the final nail in the manuscript's coffin. Then he'd need to cut off the twisted relationship with his mentor because it was becoming a distraction and harming his career. He didn't want to chicken out, so he made up his mind to dial and got William's voice mail.

"Hey, William. Kyle here. So I gave *Devil's Hop* to another editor and I'm afraid it's a no-go. They found it obscene and wondered if it was some kind of joke. After our meeting the other day, I also think it's best if we keep away from each other, at least for the time being. I'm super busy and can't have any other . . . stresses. So, you know, I wish you best and . . . yeah . . . that's it, that's all I got. Take care of yourself, William. Okay, bye."

He ended the call and stared at the phone. The words seemed to flow out of him without any censoring. He winced at the thought of William listening, thinking that the message might be hopeful, and then having his heart broken by the end. He debated leaving another message to apologize, but he knew there'd be no going back. This was what had to be done before things got worse. The tie was severed and he could resume his life as a rising editor with the talent to wring a bestseller out of Sierra Raven and soon have the kind of sway at Burke & Burke to keep every author he found. He reasoned that if he hadn't left this message, a poison like William would have wormed its way into his veins. He was certain of that and gave himself a mental pat on the back for taking charge of the situation before it spiraled too far out of control.

12

LAURA HAD BEEN preparing dinner all afternoon, since Alicia and Bill were coming over. Mondays were William's full days at Bentley, so she had the house to herself. If William were around, he'd be sure to have to an opinion on what she planned to make. She decided on a buttery roast chicken with yams and parsnips grown in the garden. This season's parsnips had been exceptionally plentiful and she'd been hoping to cook a dish for a while that highlighted their beauty. Surprisingly, she'd spent much of last week eating dinner by herself. William had meetings in the city, all centering around *the book*. She sometimes joked that for the past decade she'd been in a marriage with *the book* as well, but William didn't like when she poked fun. She used to ask to read a few chapters, but that was shot down quickly. He wanted professional eyes on it first, and she couldn't argue with that.

After playing some Joni Mitchell and getting the bird in the oven, she picked some marigolds from the garden and set them in a vase at the dining room table. With winter coming, it'd be too cold to grow any more flowers, and this change in seasons often made her melancholy.

Hours spent cultivating her flowers and vegetables would be traded for soap operas and mystery novels and a shade of loneliness. Even with William home over winter break, he still went into Bentley to work on his novel or retired up to his office, which was off-limits to her. Sometimes she stood in front of his closed office door when he wasn't home with the urge to twist the doorknob and snoop around inside. But she never did, mostly out of respect for his space. She also had the inkling that somehow he would know if she'd been spying. He had the uncanny ability to sense things—she'd *never* try to keep a secret. When her hair first starting going gray she lied to him that she hadn't colored it and was met with a fistful of receipts from Annie's Hair Salon in Old Saybrook that he'd found in her purse. He wasn't angry, just disappointed because he didn't like lying. She knew this stemmed from his relationship with his mother, and she tried to be understanding. His mother had left when he was about seven years old and promised she would return, that she needed a break from his controlling father and would come back and take him with her once she set up a new life; but she never did. Laura pictured little William waiting at the window until he started to lose her face, her smell, her mannerisms, since he'd been too young for those memories to truly stick.

It was tough for Laura to relate, since she'd had a wonderful relationship with both of her parents. They had passed some time ago, but she'd had an idyllic childhood in Darien, Connecticut, living in a home with a literal white picket fence, a dog named Lady, a father who drove his Cadillac into the city every day for his advertising job, and a mother who nurtured the most plentiful garden, a warm woman who always wore chunky knit sweaters and passed down her green thumb. Sometimes Laura missed her terribly, but she could never talk to William about that for fear it would bring up his own dark childhood, which he struggled so hard to forget.

She'd lost herself in the garden for the rest of that afternoon and almost forgot about the roast chicken, rushing inside and removing it from the oven just before it was about to burn.

WILLIAM'S MONDAY HAD been jam-packed, as per usual. He'd delivered his final lesson on *The Stranger,* reaching the end of the book, where Meursault meets with a chaplain while waiting for his death sentence by guillotine. Meursault rejects the chaplain's proffered opportunity of turning to God, explaining that God is a waste of his time. In a rage, he mocks the absurdity of the human condition and conveys his personal anguish at the meaninglessness of his existence. He states that no one has the right to judge him for his actions of murder or who he is. He ultimately grasps the universe's indifference toward humankind, which finally allows him to come to terms with his own execution.

This year's class didn't offer anything new in terms of a discussion, rehashing the same boilerplate SparkNotes drivel that William had come to hate. When he first began teaching, the Internet wasn't a resource, forcing students to form their own opinions. It upset him that he could never return to those days, that the idea of an English professor had lost some clout. The majority of students who took his 100-level classes were required to do so, and his senior seminars had turned into independent studies due to a lack of enrollment. Brooks Jessup, the new literary wunderkind busy at work on his second novel, never had a problem filling up his classes after publishing his much-lauded *The Long and Winding Road,* and garnering comparisons to Faulkner and Cormac McCarthy, which couldn't be more off base. William had forced himself to slog through the guy's novel, a coming-of-age bore about a poor white boy growing up in a heavily black Mississippi town. William almost gave up after each chapter and debated among tearing it to shreds, throwing it in the fire, or shoving it in the toilet (after he finished, he finally chose the fire). The problem was that Dr. Joyce Yancey, the department chair, sang the book's praises to such an extent that no accomplishment from any other professor could quite match up. She barely blinked when he had discussed *Devil's Hopyard* as the kind of work that could be nominated for awards and bring respect to Bentley's English program. When he gave a dig about Brooks, she cautioned him not to be the kind of writer prone to jealousy.

"We should want to uplift our peers' success and have it drive us to reach such great heights," she had said, scurrying away from him and feigning interest in anyone else, like he usually found her doing at parties.

After his independent study on Edgar Allan Poe with two students ended for the day, he returned home to the smell of buttery chicken in the air. Laura opened the door wearing oven mitts.

"The chicken didn't burn," she said, flapping her hands as if the room was smoky. "It's just a little dry."

"I'm sure it's fine," William said, wishing to have a moment of silence before she engulfed him. Sometimes he wondered if she sat poised at the front door, waiting for the lock to turn.

"I also made yams and those parsnips I showed you growing in the garden. One was as thick as a baseball bat!"

"Okay," he said, practically peeling her off of him like a dog that had latched on to his leg. "Just give me a second, Laura."

She scooted away, humming a Joni Mitchell song, and he found solace in the bathroom. He locked the door and turned the water on, staring at himself in the mirror. He'd been feeling out of sorts ever since his final lecture on *The Stranger.* Saying good-bye to Meursault until next semester was never easy—the book was one of his favorites. His eyes clouded over with the tiniest trace of tears, but he splashed water on his face to keep them at bay. In the mirror, he had a vision of a corpse that resembled him. This doppelgänger was feeble and skeletal, left to pasture for the worms and the bugs. He touched the mirror as the corpse touched back, whispering "soon" to him through its dried lips. William nodded, understanding this foreboding premonition, and left the bathroom.

WILLIAM WAS SIPPING his second rye neat of the night when Alicia and Bill Jr. arrived. Laura was fussing over the flowers, the candles, and any other busy work she occupied her time with, so he got the door. Alicia and Bill were leaning on each other, as if each sibling needed the other one to keep them propped up. Alicia wore a belly-bearing Sex Pistols shirt, which bared too much of a stomach that had seemingly grown larger since he saw her last. Her hair was dyed white with the roots showing, giving her appearance a ghostly pallor.

"Daddy-O," she said, disentangling from her brother to throw her arm around William's neck. An array of her bracelets jangled.

"Kitten," William said, and pecked her on the cheek. She flew inside, stomping around. Ever since she was a little girl, she always liked to make her presence known.

Conversely, Bill gave a tired wave, unable to look William in the eyes. While his sister had gotten larger in the few years since Bentley, Bill seemed to shrink until he was barely a presence at all. He had a goatee, a receding hairline that always puzzled William since there was no DNA evidence explaining it, and wore oversized clothes, making him resemble a coat hanger.

"Hey, Billy," William said, forcing the kid to give him a hug. "How's the bar?"

"People seem to always need drinks," Bill replied, without an ounce of humor. From an early age, Bill had been a frighteningly serious child, prone to conspiracies, secrecy, and sulking. William and Laura had thought he was on hard drugs as a teenager, and William even demanded he get a blood test to prove it, but the test came up negative for any toxins, depressing William even more. His son was simply a humorless cipher.

"Your mother made roast chicken," William said. "Your favorite."

Bill had already shuffled inside without a response.

When they sat down to eat, Alicia and Bill were, as usual, next to each other, leaving Laura happily beside William. She scooped up his hand in her own.

"Your father has some news," Laura said, clinking her glass of sherry.

William looked at her sideways.

"Go on," she gushed. "Tell them what you told me about the manuscript."

"The one you've been working on since we were teens?" Alicia asked, placing a napkin over her lap. "Does it finally have a title?"

"Yes, *Devil's Hopyard*."

Bill had been taking a sip of wine and choked, sending a shower of red spittle onto the tablecloth.

"Sorry," he gulped.

"Think nothing of it, honey," Laura said, and patted William's hand. "Tell them about your former student."

"Yes, a former student of mine has become a big editor in New York City at Burke & Burke Publishing, a very reputable house."

"And . . . ?" Laura said, singing.

"And he's very interested in *Devil's Hopyard.* Of course, the publisher needs to get on board too, but it looks very promising. And once they buy it, who knows? Maybe a movie deal in the future?"

"My Mr. Hollywood," Laura said with a big smile.

"I still need to finish it," William added.

"So cool, Dad," Alicia said. "Rock on."

Bill picked at a parsnip. "Yes, congratulations, Father."

"It just goes to show you," Laura began, "that if you set your mind to something and really, really work, anything could happen."

She leaned in to William and puckered her lips for a kiss. William complied.

"I love you, Frankenstein," Laura cooed. This had been her pet name for him when they were grad students, since William was so much taller than her.

"To *Devil's Hopyard,*" Alicia said, holding up her glass of red wine. "Man, I haven't been in *that* park in forever. Used to be such a druggie hangout."

"I was there the other day," William said. "It's really been cleaned up. The whole area too. It's almost as if its past is unrecognizable."

"Billy boy, when was the last time you were in Devil's Hopyard?" Alicia asked, jabbing her brother in the shoulder.

Bill was concentrating on cutting up his oversize parsnip. "Uhh . . . long time, long time."

"Yeah, it has been a *long* time," Alicia agreed, and clicked her tongue. "Maybe a decade for me too." She looked her father square in the eye. "Maybe I should check it out again soon?"

William raised his own glass in response. "Maybe you should."

In his pocket, William could feel his phone vibrating. He went to answer it, but it was deep down and difficult to grab. By the time he was able to locate it, the call had already gone to voice mail. He could see that it had been Kyle who called, maybe with some stellar news that he actually liked *Devil's Hopyard* now?

"William, you know I don't like cell phones at dinner," Laura said, cocking her head to the side in disappointment. "Whoever it is can wait until we're done."

"Of course," William replied, his heart pounding. He could feel it stretching against his chest cavity, the anticipation of the voice mail message making him excited beyond words. He rationalized that he needed to be cool. Even if it was good news, Kyle should have to wait for a response after his reprehensible behavior over the last week. If they wanted

William so badly now, it would have to be on his own time. With the magic that he had written, he'd earned this right.

"Let's dig in," he said, spearing the chicken with a sharp knife as the buttery juices flowed out.

AFTER ALICIA AND Bill left, William retreated to his study and listened to Kyle's message. After it ended, the cell phone slipped from William's hands, crashing to the floor as the battery fell out. He was trembling, balling his fingers into a fist to stop them from quaking. He'd thought Kyle might be calling because he finally saw the genius in *Devil's Hopyard,* its pieces linking together with a greater purpose. Flashes of the thousands upon thousands of hours he spent writing ran through his brain. The solitary days and nights passed entirely in his head. The *devotion.* Most people would've given up long ago after the first sign of difficulty, but he knew a novel must be nurtured, so it could form, and shape, and become more than carefully organized words, so its truth would shine through.

He stomped on his cell until it was crushed to bits. With each blow he imagined Kyle's smug face, or his girlfriend Jamie, or his protégée Sierra Raven, or any other part of Kyle's life that the boy deemed a success. When William was thirty, he'd had to take a job at a local community college to help support his newborn twins. He'd been writing a book then too, which he gave up in the hopes that the teaching job might lead to a full-time position. On his first day, he spent his free period crying in the bathroom, unable to stop. Finally, he refused to keep weeping. He stood at the grimy mirror and slapped his face until not a tear remained. He licked his lips over and over until every ounce of frustration had left his body. He'd recently taken a hypnotist's class and learned certain repetitive motions that he could use on himself and others. He believed this ability to control his emotions was now his best quality.

It angered William that at thirty Kyle was already editing a book likely to become a bestseller. Until the end of time, that book would exist. And what did William have? A handful of students who called him a mentor but would forget him over the years, just like Kyle had. Maybe they'd bring up his name in a passing conversation and talk of what a great professor he was, but eventually they would die, and then who'd speak of him anymore? Once Laura and his children died as well, his name would never be brought up again.

But not if he could help it.

He got on his knees and moved aside the three-by-four rug under his desk chair to reveal a tiny silver keyhole. Using a strange-looking key, he opened a hidden compartment under the floor. A black box sat there and he stared at it for a second before removing the lid. Inside was a gray heart-shaped rock the size of a softball. He held the rock in his lap, caressing its surface as if it were a pet. Then he smashed it into his forehead until he had broken through skin. He smoothed his blood around, his palms dripping, deadly still. He felt at ease one again, his own way of replacing the pain of rejection with a physical sting.

"*William,*" a muffled voice called out.

He put the rock back inside the box.

"William, are you up there?"

He identified the voice as Laura's and it centered him. He floated back into his body. He put the lid on the box, locked it, and placed the rug over his secret. He got out some Kleenex and mopped his brow. When he opened his office door to Laura's scared expression, the blood had clouded his eyes, tinting her red.

"*William!* What happened?" she shrieked.

"I must have fallen," he said, in a detached manner, licking his lips over and over.

"Just an accident," he continued, with a finger to his lips. "*Sssssh-hhhhh.*"

13

TO CELEBRATE HER good news, Jamie got a table at the most expensive restaurant in Brooklyn. She'd briefly dated its owner, Vin Alleghetti, when she first moved to the city and still kept in good contact through design jobs he sent her way. Vin was in his fifties but built like a marine with guns the size of Kyle's legs. He insisted on a secret tasting menu for her and Kyle with crazy concoctions like sea urchin with peanut butter foam and Japanese flower mushrooms with sea cucumber and huan ham. He personally came over at the end of the meal with a cupcake made from rare cocoa beans and the frosting covered in gold flakes.

"Stunning," Vin said.

"It is," Jamie replied, dipping a finger into the icing.

"I was speaking of you." Vin laughed and kissed her on the cheek. "Don't worry, Kyle," he said, massaging Kyle's shoulders. "I gave up pining over this one a long time ago."

Jamie enjoyed the perturbed look on Kyle's face. She figured he should feel threatened after how he'd acted recently, but she wouldn't let the torture go on for too long. She moved toward him for a kiss.

"You lost me to a better man," she said.

"That I did." Vin winked. "All right, you kids, enjoy."

Vin left them to schmooze at the next table over. Jamie heard his powerful laugh. She found herself briefly missing it, since there'd been many laughs with Vin.

"Seems like we've come to Vinyard every time we have a major fight," Kyle said. "Are you trying to show me how easily I could lose you?"

She touched her finger to her nose. "Bingo, Sherlock."

"Mission accomplished." He nervously drummed his fingers on the table. "I need to really apologize. You've been waiting for this all night, haven't you?"

"I figured I was due."

"You're right that I can obsess over things, be it with my job or what happened with William."

"I saw a side of you I didn't like."

"I didn't like it either. It reminded me of when I was younger."

"At Bentley?"

He nodded, almost ashamed.

"Kyle, you don't have to tell me—"

"I want to. I've wanted to tell you this for some time."

Jamie took a sip of water, steeling herself for whatever the outcome.

"So I was on a scholarship and working two campus jobs with no time to do anything else. I'd been hanging around with bad influences, these thug townies. We started selling pot to kids on campus. The townies supplied the schwag, I had the connections. Then there was this girl. She went to Bentley and hung out with us too. We were like a foursome against the world, for about a month or so. She had a relationship with all three of us at the same time. She also knew these other local dealers who could get us coke, speed, crystal, anything we wanted for cheap."

He nibbled on his fingernail. "I'm not proud of this, Jamie."

"I don't care what you did," she said, hoping she sounded genuine because she really was being truthful. "Whatever it is, we'll work through it."

He took a deep breath, relieved. "So we'd buy loads of stuff from these guys. We bought whatever they had and then sold it to rich Bentley kids at ten times the cost. And soon we were controlling like all the drugs on campus, it just happened so fast. But the townies were morons and got busted one day. Of course they only ratted *me* out, both of them were in love with the girl. William knew I dealt, I'd even sold him some pills before, occasionally he needed them to help him sleep or something—anyway, I called him from jail."

Kyle was getting worked up so Jamie took his hand, rubbing a soothing circle into his palm.

"I didn't even ask him to do this, but he went into my dorm room and removed all the drugs, some really bad shit. One minute I'm sitting in jail and then suddenly I'm free. The next day he told me what he did and that he'd convinced the administration it was all a misunderstanding. I couldn't believe it."

"Whoa."

"I quit right after . . . selling, doing, *everything.* Those townies, I have no idea what happened to them—nothing good, I imagine. And the girl, she vanished soon after, like she even made the papers, vanished completely. I don't know if the townies were involved, probably somehow. I just pretended like it was all a dream, a horrible dream. But then I got my shit together. I started really studying, fell in love with literature. I even pulled an A by the end of the semester. So now you know."

Jamie had been holding her breath. In her mind, she'd conjured up something way worse. He'd been young and dumb, and a bit of a bad boy. This she could work with.

"I'm glad you told me," she said. "I know that wasn't easy."

"And with William appearing again—it's been stuff I haven't dealt with in a long freaking time. And with him being so intense, it wasn't a good mix."

"I understand."

"He thinks I owe him, and I do—I'm grateful—but his manuscript is awful. There's no chance it'll be published as is and he's refusing to believe it."

"I'm sorry I pushed you so much with him," Jamie said. "I was letting our problems—"

"You did nothing wrong. Anyway, I told him I couldn't see him for a while, since I'm too busy with work and you. That I'm burning the candle at both ends."

"How did he take it?"

Kyle avoided looking at her.

"He . . . was upset but ultimately understood. He wished me the best and I said the same. I promised him when he finishes *Devil's Hopyard* and really rewrites it, I'd give it another look. It's just a bad time now."

"I didn't realize the kind of history you two had."

"It's not healthy for me to be thinking about my freshman year, too much is at stake with the Sierra deal . . ."

Jamie picked up her knife and cut into the cupcake. Melted chocolate oozed out.

"I'm ready to eat this dessert and start celebrating," she said.

"So am I forgiven?"

She picked up a piece of cake and fed him. "You are."

"I feel lighter after telling you all that," he said.

"Good."

She kissed his chocolate lips, actually feeling lighter as well. She almost used the opportunity to bring up moving in together, casually, of course, to see how he'd respond, but she didn't want to push it. The fact that he finally shared the troubling times from his past was enough for now. They were closer than ever because of this.

• • •

AFTER LEAVING THE restaurant, they hailed a taxi. Kyle offered to stay at Jamie's place, knowing how much that meant to her, but she refused.

"I wouldn't want my roommate to get in the way of what I plan to do to you tonight," she said, sticking her hand down his pants.

"Okay, this is happening." He smiled.

In the darkness of his apartment, he kicked aside a fruit basket left outside the front door and pressed her up against the wall, kissed her lips, her neck.

"I've missed you," he said into her ear.

"I've missed you too."

She broke away with a giggle and turned on the lights, heading into the kitchen. She brought back a bottle of rosé and two glasses.

"I'm trying to drink less," he said.

She scrunched up her face. "Really?"

"I realize I rely on it too much to destress. This last week with William—"

"Uh-uh, no, no." She shook her head. "No more talking about William *at all.* We've devoted enough time tonight to him, to the past. This is my night. We are celebrating Elka being the first investor for Camden Designs."

"Okay, pour me a glass," Kyle said. "I want to make a toast."

She poured him a generous amount and cuddled under his arm.

"Here's to Jamie Camden, a beautiful and talented designer who's on her way to being the next Martha Stewart."

"Without the prison time," she said, clinking his glass.

"And to the best girlfriend a guy could ask for. Seriously, how did I get so fucking lucky?"

"Beats me. But you're about to get even luckier."

She knocked back the glass of rosé and removed her bra without taking off her dress. "I'm slipping into the shower. Meet me in the bedroom."

She disappeared into the bathroom. Soon steam wafted out from under the door. He swore to himself that he wouldn't bring up William again, under any circumstances. He'd been able to pretend his strange year at Bentley was a dream, and he'd do the same with his former professor. This past week would become nothing more than a joke he'd tell at a party one day, the time his old mentor went cuckoo. Although he had to admit, it did feel as if he'd entered his own personal thriller: jarringly insane for sure, but a tad exciting too.

He began stripping down to his boxer briefs as he headed toward the bedroom, leaving his clothes in a pool in the hallway. Upon entering, he saw the window had been left opened wide, *way* too wide for this time of the year. He often left it ajar for Capone to slip through, but never more than a few inches. A chilling breeze rushed in that sent gooseflesh up and down his arms. He went over to the window and forced himself to look out.

In the alleyway below, Capone lay splayed, the cat's front sliced open, its organs scattered.

"What the f—"

A sharp ache throbbed between his eyes as he leaned farther out and saw a wadded-up ball of undergarments stuffed where the cat's heart used to be. He recognized it immediately as Jamie's, since she often left a spare set of panties in case she stayed the weekend.

"I'm ready," Jamie called, stepping out of the shower, the smell of her shampoo in the air.

He took one more look at Capone's mutilated body and mourned the loss of his furry friend before slamming the window shut. He had to lock his fingers together to keep from trembling. When he turned around, Jamie was standing there in a Badgers towel.

"Are you okay?" she asked. "You look like you've seen a ghost."

He couldn't tell her, not after how far they'd come tonight. William must have done this to Capone—what other logical explanation could there be? But to mention him would only cause disaster. And besides, how could he even begin to put what he just saw into words?

She unknotted the towel and let it slide to the floor. She beckoned him to come closer, and he fell into her arms. She led him over to the bed and wasn't wasting any time, pushing him inside her before he had the chance to compartmentalize what had just occurred.

William had invaded his home. William was intent on starting a war.

"Oh, God, yes," Jamie moaned, squeezing her eyes shut.

Kyle thrust into her, but he was still thinking of William, his anger increasing as he simmered with rage. A wild spirit had entered his body and he couldn't deny its intoxication. Jamie was screaming now, but he wouldn't let up. He was possessed, as if William's dark presence had entered the room and taken hold.

Afterward, Jamie slept soundly and Kyle held her tightly, afraid but exhilarated, figuring out what his next step would be in this cat-and-mouse game William was so intent on playing.

14

WILLIAM HADN'T SLEPT all night, but he reasoned it was a good kind of tired. He'd felt energized and stayed up writing, slamming out thirty pages of prose. This was how he worked best, in fits and spurts. At one point, he'd been so engrossed in his art that he didn't notice that the bandage over his forehead had slipped and fallen onto his computer, leaving a bloody streak across the keys. He used that image to inspire the scene he was writing—where the professor came home from Devil's Hopyard with a gash on his face that dripped blood onto his journal. Then the professor stayed up all night to write what had occurred in the park, his blood mixing with the ink.

Midmorning, he met with Nathaniel in his office at Bentley. Having the boy become his personal research assistant was working out well so far. It was amazing what a desperate student would do for a chance at a better grade. The two had spent the other day in the city, and William was beginning to grow fond of him. Each year he devoted himself to one chosen pupil—the needier the better—and Nathaniel was begging for attention from anyone. So he listened to the boy's heartache, how Nathaniel pined for that girl Kelsey in his class, and he promised he'd do what he could to help. Then he got Nathaniel to agree to help him.

"I want to thank you for the other day," William said when Nathaniel finally showed up for their meeting. He was glad to see the boy hadn't come in sweatpants. He'd given him a lecture about respectable dress code.

"Yeah . . . sure," Nathaniel said, munching the hell out of a fingernail, only a nub left. He took a folder out of his backpack and passed it to William.

"Is that your research on Camus?"

"Yes, sir."

William made sure to give Nathaniel a wide smile. He reminded himself to treat the kid with positive reinforcement.

"This is really excellent. You've done a one-eighty in my class."

Nathaniel stopped biting his fingernail. He nodded shyly, ran his fingers through his hair and let it fall over his eyes.

"How did he like it, by the way?" Nathaniel asked.

"What do you mean?"

"The gift we left your friend in Brooklyn. The fruit basket?"

William's smile grew even wider. He chuckled, barely audible at first, but then it became louder, echoing throughout his tiny office.

"Oh, I'm sure he was surprised."

KYLE CALLED THE police when he got home from Burke & Burke. He couldn't do it in the morning, since Jamie stayed over and he didn't want to be late for work. He worried Jamie wouldn't be able to deal with the fact that William had somehow managed to break in and kill Capone, and he doubted Carter would be sympathetic. Carter was interested only in the novels he published, not Kyle's saga with his demented professor.

A detective and his assistant showed up at Kyle's apartment, since he told the police an animal was killed in the break-in. The detective, Tomás Ruiz, had light skin, a pug nose, and a skeptical left eyebrow that seemed to rise every time he asked a question. His assistant, referred to only as Jones, was an African American woman whose hair was pulled back into a serious ponytail and spoke without ever showing her teeth.

"Was this your cat?" Detective Ruiz asked, peering out the window at the alleyway below and cringing at the sight of Capone's disfigured body.

"It was an alley cat, but I took care of it and fed it sometimes. I let it come and go."

Jones looked out the window too, no emotion on her face at the gruesome death scene below.

"Animal control is on its way," Jones said. "Mr. Broder, since it was an alley cat, isn't there a chance that something in the streets might've caused this? A rabid raccoon?"

"I know who did this," Kyle said. "Professor William Lansing in Killingworth, Connecticut."

"Is this from him?" Jones asked, holding up a basket of fruit with a tiny note. Kyle swiped it and noticed William's handwriting.

Kyle, so sorry about what's happened between us.
No reason to let business get in the way of a friendship.
No worries about Devil's Hopyard*, I'll find it another home.*
—William

Kyle let out a huff and flicked the note from his hand. "That's bullshit. He doesn't mean it."

"Now, why would this man want to kill the alley cat that hangs around your house?" Detective Ruiz asked, his left eyebrow floating up to his hairline.

Kyle broke down the highlights of everything that had happened over the past week. The book. The stalking. The thinly veiled threat. And finally Jamie's undergarments stuffed where the cat's heart used to be.

"We see no signs of forced entry," the detective added.

"I leave this window slightly ajar sometimes, for Capone, the cat."

Ruiz and Jones gave each other a look that clearly said *dumb ass.*

"I will remind you, Mr. Broder," Ruiz began, "that you live in a first-floor New York City apartment facing a back alleyway. It probably isn't the smartest idea to leave a window open for burglars."

Jones crossed her arms. "This girlfriend of yours, can we talk to her? Was she also here when you found the cat's body?"

"No . . ." Kyle said, immediately lying. He didn't want Jamie involved at all. He figured it wouldn't be good for the police to know that he kept this from her and they had sex after he discovered the massacre. By morning light, Kyle felt pretty grimy about not telling her. But it was as if he'd been possessed by what he'd seen, with no control over his actions.

"If you read the book this guy is writing . . ." Kyle said. Both cops were inching toward the bedroom door, and he could feel he was losing them. "Real sick and disturbing stuff."

"Do you have this book?" Jones asked, exhaling through her nostrils. It was clear both of them had bigger crimes on their plates to worry about.

"A coworker of mine has it now, but I can get it to you—"

"That's unnecessary for now," Ruiz said, a meaty hand on Kyle's shoulder. "We'll contact the local sheriff's station in Killingworth, and they'll stop over to have a talk with your former professor."

"I don't know what he's capable of," Kyle said, his teeth chattering. The window was still open and the October air had gotten bitter and cold.

"We'll keep you posted," Ruiz said, "but usually these things have a logical explanation to them. The cat probably took your girlfriend's underwear and met with a rabid raccoon outside." He moved toward the door, but Kyle grabbed his arm. This surprised both of them.

"I'm sorry, sir," Kyle said, and let go. Jones was looking at him screwy, her hand resting on top of her holstered gun. Did they think he was crazy? Or that—God forbid—*he* killed the cat? Ruiz's raised eyebrow seemed to verify this. "I have a really bad feeling."

Ruiz rubbed his nose. "Look, it sounds like you and this guy got into it with each other. If you have clear evidence that he's come after you, you contact us right away. But right now, man, what happened ain't enough to do anything more than what we're doing. And trust me, sometimes we create scenarios to be worse than they actually are."

"I'm not creating this—"

Jones had already left the room, uninterested in Kyle's pleas anymore.

"I ain't saying you're making shit up. There is clearly a dead cat in your alley and it's clear you cared for this cat, but that your old professor cut out its heart as a warning for not publishing his book? Man, that's a new one for me."

Ruiz tucked his notebook back in his front pocket and gave Kyle a pat on his arm. "We'll show ourselves out," he said. "We'll be in touch if the police in Connecticut are suspicious in any way."

Kyle heard the front door slam. He walked over to the window and took a final look into the alleyway. Animal control had arrived and was inserting Capone into a plastic hazard bag and the blood-soaked panties into another one.

He shut the window so hard that the animal control guy gazed up in fright.

WILLIAM DECIDED TO jog home from Bentley College that afternoon. He left his clothes in a day bag in his office, changed into shorts, sneakers, and a T, and cut through the backwoods trails. He fought through the pain in his bum leg, actually enjoying its sharp burn. Halfway there, he passed by Devil's Hopyard with the soul-stirring urge for a detour. So he went inside.

A sliver of sun remained along the horizon when he entered, the place pretty empty. Instinctively he knew exactly where he wanted to go, heading into the park's heart in its upper left region. The area hadn't been kept up for years, the weeds growing tall and unruly. A dilapidated shack tilted into the wind, barely accessible because of a surrounding obstacle course of fallen trees and overgrown vegetation. He'd written about it recently, a crucial part of the text. He'd spent some time there again to get the description just right. After drilling the sight of it into his mind, he backed away and ran at top speed for the last few miles home.

Reaching his block, he intended to head into the basement to do some boxing but felt his cell vibrating.

"Hello?" he said, out of breath, clutching his heart as sweat pooled from his face.

"William?" The voice sounded abrupt and demanding.

Kyle? He almost asked, steeling himself for whatever Kyle's response might be.

"This is Brett Swenson at Burke & Burke. We met when you stopped by the office the other day."

"Yes?" William asked, swallowing a lump of phlegm that had been building in his throat.

"Kyle gave me your manuscript, and I have to say it's pretty brilliant."

"*Yes?*" William said again, choking now. He held the phone away from his mouth and got himself together. His heart was beating so fast it felt like his body was glowing, that he could just take off and fly away.

"What a literary voice you have!" Brett said. "This professor is a sadistic motherfucker, but a villain for the ages. Stephen King would be proud."

"Stephen King read it?" William gulped, sitting down in the middle of the street, the world spinning around him.

"What? No, he didn't—well, maybe he will, who knows? Could you come down tomorrow to talk in person? Nine in the morning works for me. Do you have any more pages?"

"I do. Many."

"Bring me whatever you have because I really like what I've read so far. I think I might be a better fit than Kyle for *Devil's Hopyard.* He's overloaded right now anyway."

William couldn't see anything because of the tears blurring his vision.

"Thank you," he said, his voice shaking.

"Truly impressed, my man. See you tomorrow."

Brett hung up. William lay back on the street, the pavement cold underneath his head. He stared at the sky, an iridescent purple with clouds like thin bands of cotton and a moon on the rise. He let out a howl loud enough to cause a dog in the distance to bark along with him. He knew *Devil's Hopyard* was something special and magical, and *FUCK KYLE* for ever making him doubt that. To be a writer meant learning what criticism to take and what to shrug off. Clearly Brett—who was higher up than Kyle—understood the book's promise where a more inexperienced pair of eyes had been unable to see its genius.

William sat up, feeling invincible, and that was when he noticed the sheriff's car parked in his driveway.

ENTERING HIS HOME, William spied Sheriff Morris Pealey sitting on his couch with a cup of tea in hand. The sheriff had scraggily whitish gray hair, a handlebar mustache, and ice blue eyes. William had dealt with Pealey over a matter a decade ago, and the two maintained a polite small talk relationship, usually running into each other at Gussie's General Store, which both tended to prefer to the giant Stop and Shop.

Sheriff Pealey had aged since William ran into him last, probably pushing close to seventy years, a hair away from retirement, but he'd always said that would be his death. His wife, Ann-Marie, had passed some years back, and the town was his family, being responsible for cleaning up its undesirables and helping it become a destination for commuters. New York City prices kept skyrocketing, and people were becoming open to a two-hour commute if it meant they could have a nice backyard for their kids. Pealey had enjoyed seeing his town's expansion and the fact that he'd be busier than ever thanks to its influx of new residents.

"Sheriff Pealey, to what do I owe this visit?" William asked as he stepped into the living room. Laura caught his eye, seated on the couch next to Pealey, a cup of tea jittering in one hand while the other fiddled nervously with her cross necklace.

"Sheriff Pealey wants to talk to you about what you were doing on Sunday," Laura said, her voice shrill.

"Sunday?" William asked, clicking his tongue.

"I told him we were in the garden the whole day!" Laura said, placing her tea down to remove a wet tissue from her sleeve and giving her nose a good blow. "Sheriff, it's probably the last chance we have for my squash blossoms before the season ends. William was putting his green thumb to use all day."

She took a deep breath, pleased with what she had said, and gave another blow.

"I might have to have you come by my place this spring," the sheriff said to him, stroking his mustache. "Ever since Ann-Marie . . ." He stopped, his clear blue eyes misting over.

"I remember the creamed spinach that she'd bring to pot luck luncheons at the church," Laura said. "Everyone always wanted more."

"Yep, gardening was her specialty," Pealey said, his head hanging low.

"What's this about, Sheriff?" William asked, wanting to get this over with so he could dash upstairs to write, the glorious phone call from Brett still swirling in his mind.

"Oh, probably nothing," Pealey said. "Seems like you pissed off an old student of yours and he thinks you had something to do with his cat dying."

William let out a bark of a laugh, loud enough to startle Laura.

"I'm sorry," William said. "Did you say his cat?"

"Well," Pealey began, removing a notepad from his front pocket. He licked a finger and turned a page, grimacing from the rheumatism in his joints. "Apparently, Mr. Broder in Cobble Hill, Brooklyn, is accusing you of breaking in and harming the cat that lives in his alleyway."

"Absurd," Laura said, squeezing at her wet tissue. "Just absurd."

William nodded patiently. "Ah, I know who that is. *Kyle* Broder, right?"

Pealey glanced at his notepad. "That would be the one."

"A disturbed boy," he said to Laura, who nodded in sync. "He was a student of mine ten years ago and got into drugs at the time. He was even arrested for it. You can check his records."

"I will," Pealey said. "Name doesn't ring a bell, but there's certainly been a couple of Bentley students who caught the wrong side of the law over the years."

"Anyway, we've been in touch recently," William began. "I was the boy's mentor. Anyway, it's clear he's not healthy. But accusing me of killing a cat? And an alley cat, did you say? That's ludicrous."

"That's what I thought when the call came through, just wanted to stop by and get your side of it."

"We were in the garden *all* Sunday," Laura added. "I can show you the squash; in fact, I could give you some leftovers mashed with cinnamon. We had it for dinner yesterday."

"That would be lovely, Laura, really."

"One moment," Laura said, and darted into the kitchen.

"Sorry about this, William," the sheriff said.

"Not a worry, Morris. I just hope the boy is all right. He seemed in a really dark place when we last spoke. If there's anything I can do?"

Pealey shook his head. "I find it's best to steer clear of these types. Sometimes helping out can be the worst thing. You know the saying: We bite the hand that feeds us."

"Sure do," William said, forcing a smile.

Laura returned with a Tupperware container full of orange mush.

"Now, stick this in the oven," she said, handing it over. "Nuking will dry it out."

"Aye, aye," Sheriff Pealey said, standing. "Sorry to bother you, folks. You have a good night."

William walked him to the front door. "You too, Sheriff."

Pealey headed to his car, gave a salute good-bye, and drove off. When the car rolled out of sight, William dropped his smile and swallowed the ball of bloody spit that had collected in his mouth from gnawing on his tongue like it was a piece of meat.

Kyle had struck a counterattack by contacting the police, even after William had apologized by leaving a lovely fruit basket from Zabar's. This just meant that he couldn't play nice anymore.

15

WILLIAM STAYED UP writing for the second night in a row and dashed out forty more pages, his personal best. This was a crucial part of his novel—where a big reveal happened—and he was glad he was able to finish it for Brett by the morning. At sunrise, Laura politely knocked on his office door asking if he wanted a fresh fruit smoothie. For a second, he didn't recognize who was speaking or where he was. That often occurred when he was in the thick of a spell. He'd left his body many times before and returned momentarily out of sorts. He gripped his desk table as a feeling akin to the spins tossed him around before he finally became still. He shut down his computer and managed to croak, "Make it strawberry." He heard Laura's feet scurrying away.

He entered Burke & Burke emboldened. When he said his name to the front desk girl, she responded that Brett would see him right away, always a good sign. He walked down the '60s-inspired hallways, checking out the book spines and imagining *Devil's Hopyard* gracing the shelves soon. Brett was on the phone when he stepped into his office. Brett held up a finger and William sat down, the thick manuscript resting on his knees.

"Gotta go," Brett said into the phone. "An important author I'm looking to sign just walked in." He hung up.

"Important author, huh?" William said. "I could get used to hearing that."

Brett picked up his copy of *Devil's Hopyard* and did some curls as if it was a dumbbell.

"I am so *into* this, William. Couldn't put it down."

William told himself to play it cool, but inside he was exploding. "I've written another hundred or so pages."

"Since we spoke?"

William nodded. "Well, forty since then. Your call really inspired me. Everything just flowed once I knew I had a shot at being published. Especially after the last week of Kyle hating it."

Brett blew a raspberry. "Kyle has a lot to learn. He's not always able to see a book's true potential." He leaned in closer. "If you ask me, he got lucky with Sierra Raven."

William chuckled at that.

"But with *Devil's Hopyard* . . ." Brett crumpled up some stray pieces of paper into a ball and tossed it at the garbage can, missing. "I can't say I've ever read anything like it before. It has the chance to really break out."

"I always thought so. I'm aiming for a bestseller with this."

"Oh, yeah, bestseller, definitely. Let me ask you, William, where did the idea come from?"

William cleared his throat. He'd prepared this speech before, revealing only what was necessary, for now.

"I wanted to write the diary of a madman. But over the course of the book, I want the readers to begin to understand his madness and sympathize with his struggle because we're all a little mad, are we not? We're all so close to slipping, to acting out our most debased fantasies, but we stay grounded for fear that society will condemn us. Well, I am not afraid to show what we are capable of."

Brett was nodding like a bobblehead. "So true, so fucking true."

"We never really know what's going on in someone's else head. We are all enigmas. For example . . ." William removed his cell phone and placed it on the desk. "This is what your coworker has been saying behind your back."

He pushed Play. They heard Kyle's voice say, *Brett has a talent for poaching clients rather than finding them on his own.*

William hit Stop and placed the cell phone back in his blazer pocket. "It's been bothering me that Kyle was saying such degrading things about you. That was just the tip of the iceberg, by the way."

"I see," Brett said, sucking at his teeth. "Thank you for sharing this."

"You're giving me such a great opportunity. I couldn't in good conscience keep it to myself. Kyle is not the same person I once knew. I think this early success has gone to his head."

From the way Brett scowled, William knew he was not the type to let things slide. It was obvious Brett and Kyle had a tense work relationship that he could use to his advantage. Burke & Burke was too small a place for all three to coexist; one of them would eventually have to go. William knew which target he had in his sights, a justification for the way he'd been treated.

"So what happens next with the manuscript?" William asked. He had to ask twice, since Brett was unresponsive, probably caught up in plotting Kyle's demise.

"What was that? Oh, yes. I have to get the big boss to sign off, but this is a done deal, William. Mr. Burke has been waiting for exactly what you just brought me."

"Do you want the new pages?"

"Hit me with them."

William passed over his manuscript. "I should be finished with the entire book soon. And the ending . . . let me tell you, the ending is going to be spectacular."

KYLE SHOWED UP to work a few minutes late, the F train once again fucking him over. He stopped at the front desk, waiting for Amanda to look up from painting her nails, today seaweed green.

"You really express yourself through your nails, don't you?" he asked.

She reached out and took his hand. "You have very nice cuticles for a dude."

"I get manicures."

"Why am I not surprised? Care to let me give you one sometime?"

Amanda sat upright in her seat, pushing her cleavage toward him. She had flirted with him in the past, always very chaste, but today she seemed to be upping her game.

"I'll let you know when I'm due next," he said, enjoying their repartee, a haven in the midst of these draining last few days.

"You seem weighed down," Amanda said, letting go of his hand. She ran her palm along the newly shaved side of her head. "I'm an empath, did you know? We have the ability to intuitively feel other people's energies."

"I'm just dealing with a lot of shit."

"The doctor is in if you want to talk," Amanda said.

Kyle hunched over her desk. She smelled like watermelon from the gum she was snapping.

"Have you ever felt like you were losing control?" he said quietly, and then shook his head. "Never mind."

She grabbed his hand again and looked him dead in the eyes. "Always, Kyle. *Always.*"

The door to the hallway opened. The hairs on the back of Kyle's neck rose from a bad energy invading the space. He swiveled around, unsurprised to see who it was, as if they had symbiotically become in sync.

"William," he said, wanting to tackle his former mentor to the ground and smash his face in until the guy's nose spouted blood and he begged for mercy. He held onto Amanda's hand, his life preserver.

"How did your meeting with Brett turn out?" Amanda asked as William walked over. "Kyle, this is your old professor, right?"

"What meeting with Brett?" Kyle asked her.

The front desk phone rang and Amanda answered.

"It looks like I'll be signing with Burke & Burke," William said smugly.

"What the fuck is that supposed to mean?" Kyle asked.

"Your colleague Brett is a fan of *Devil's Hopyard.* He says it has a shot at being a bestseller."

Kyle felt his legs go weak. "That's impossible."

"Why? Because you were too self-involved to see its potential?"

William got in Kyle's face. He was close enough for Kyle to smell the guy's breath, putrid as if he was rotting from within.

"You are not god of the publishing world, Kyle. You can't keep me from my destiny."

"The police are getting involved, just so you know." Kyle was doing everything in his power to restrain himself. In an alternate reality, his fists would be covered in blood and William would be on a stretcher.

"That was a real low blow sending them to my house. After the Zabar's basket I left you to apologize—"

Kyle's eye was twitching. "I know what you did, you son of a bitch. You twisted nut job, you fucking killed that cat."

"I worry about you," William said, his tone softer than before. "I remember when you had a breakdown—"

"I never had a *breakdown,*" Kyle said, his voice raised.

Amanda looked up from the phone and shooed them both away. They reconvened by the elevators.

"What I saw that one time when you were in the hospital, Kyle—"

"I had pneumonia from falling asleep outside in the dead of winter."

"Which was brought on by a psychotic breakdown. The doctors wanted to hold you for psychiatric testing until I talked them out of it."

"That's not true."

"I know it's easier to forget, but these episodes can return."

Kyle put a finger in his mentor's face. "You stay the fuck away from me."

"We want to bite the hand that feeds us," William said, shaking his head. "You're lashing out at me because we used to be so close."

"I don't know what you're trying to accomplish, William, but if you come near me again, I'm gonna have you arrested."

"Arrested for what?"

"For ripping out a cat's heart and stuffing my girlfriend's panties in its place!"

Kyle glanced around the office. People were watching now: coworkers, authors, all of them judging, all of them seeing him as the unhinged one.

"I suggest you get yourself together. You're not even making any sense." William put his hand on Kyle's shoulder, but Kyle smacked it away. "Kyle," he said, in a condescending tone and replaced his hand on Kyle's shoulder only to have it swatted away again.

"Whatever you're attempting to pull, it *won't* work," Kyle said.

William got as close to him as possible, his lips hovering over Kyle's ear. "But look, I'm getting signed at Burke & Burke. It already *is* working."

Kyle closed his eyes to make William go away. His body was quaking. He clenched his fists in anticipation of delivering a beatdown; he thirsted for the feel of causing William an immense amount of pain. He counted to ten, and when he opened his eyes, William was in the elevator. The doors closed as William gave a slow wave good-bye, the sound of his laughter echoing from the floors below until it disappeared . . . but remained louder than ever, rattling around in Kyle's skull.

16

NAÏVE SIERRA RAVEN, who between Facebook, Twitter, and Instagram had mapped out her entire plans for the day for the world to know. So William headed over to Maria Hernandez Park in Bushwick, Brooklyn, where she had promised all her followers that she'd be on a bench working on *Girls Without Hope.* Sure enough, he found her bundled up in a heavy sweater and a scarf staring at her laptop in deep thought.

He hadn't decided yet what he wanted to happen with this interaction. While the girl hadn't done anything to him personally, she did represent Kyle's success, which William believed his *former* protégé no longer deserved. He'd learned from doing a little bit of hardcore snooping that without Sierra's book, Kyle would be left with only one difficult author whose output had become nonexistent. Surely not enough to keep him employed at Burke & Burke. William pictured Kyle begging him for another chance with *Devil's Hopyard.* It was obvious he was jealous after he found out about Brett's interest. It delighted William to know how fast the power had changed in his favor once again.

As he got closer, he took a moment to study Sierra. She was a pixie, all right, tiny and sprite-like, bookish and awkward. He usually noticed sultry types, bad girls who sought out danger, but Sierra appealed to him in a different way. She was a writer, a like-minded soul who'd understand the dedication of tackling a novel and who also dreamed of making it her career. They could discuss their respective works along with other great literature and go on book tours together and make love in fancy hotel rooms and order up room service while watching the sunrise. Sure, Laura loved literature too, her nose was always in a mystery novel, but she didn't get any satisfaction from analyzing it. She was no longer a scholar. Thirty years of home life had left her simple, obedient, and far from a thrill. He longed to be thrilled.

"Excuse me? Sierra?" he asked, removing his wedding ring, as he crept closer.

SIERRA LIKED TO change her surroundings daily, fearing that staying in the same place two days in a row might zap her creativity. Today she chose Maria Hernandez Park for its array of benches and its liveliness. It was less cold out than yesterday and little kids were playing all around her. She had tried to work in her apartment, but the appeal of binge watching television was too dangerous. She even attempted the quiet room at the main library in Midtown with the lion statues, but the silence had been too overwhelming. In silence, there were only the words in her head, and they all felt false. To be outside in the animated city, she hoped that its spirit, its realness, would sink into her book as well.

She had reached a difficult part in *Girls Without Hope*—now the rest of it needed to be fabricated. Her past had been juicy and heartbreaking enough for the first hundred pages, but then she wound up with a great and loving foster family who took her in, bandaged up her bruises, and raised her till she left for college. Certainly not interesting enough for the whole plot of a book, more like just the ending.

The last thing she'd written was the scene where Alexandra and her younger sisters shot their evil foster parent Biggie and fled into the cold January night. In truth, she had shot the real "Biggie" with a hunting rifle that he'd drunkenly left loaded on the dresser. She got him in the shoulder and then took off while his stupid girlfriend, Annalee, wailed into her crack pipe. There were no sisters to follow her out into the snow, and a neighbor instantly called the cops. She was eventually sent to the Dussens, an elderly couple in Arbyrd, Missouri, who cared for her as if she were their own.

But now she had to visualize what it'd be like with three younger sisters in tow, trekking through the stark Missouri woods in the middle of winter. She wanted this portion of the novel to take place solely in the forest, where the girls would come across a cabin and fight for their survival in subzero temperatures. She'd been influenced by the story of the Brontë sisters, who spent a lot of time as shut-ins but still managed to write some of the most brilliant novels of the past few centuries, including *Jane Eyre* and *Wuthering Heights.* Since all four *Girls Without Hope* sisters were basically amalgamations of herself, she envisioned them escaping their harsh surroundings by writing a book about a fantastical kingdom they ruled, one where their lives were better, until big bad Biggie and Annalee finally tracked them down.

But how to start? she asked herself, looking up at the sky, overcast and uninspiringly bleak. Should the sisters come across the cabin right away? Should they starve for days first? What could they eat if the entire ground was frosted over? *Gah!* It was all too much. Looking at the screen, she saw she had only written *Chapter 6* after an entire morning of contemplation.

Time to be a little social, she thought, logging on to all her networks and scrolling through new status updates, commenting on a few, and typing her own, which fit under 140 characters and summed up her dour mood: "*I* care for myself. The more solitary, the more friendless, the more unsustained I am, the more I will respect myself."—Charlotte Brontë, *Jane Eyre.*

Truth was, her real life could use a little more excitement, and she figured it was why she'd been creatively blocked. She hadn't met many people since moving to New York. Her roommate was never home and barely wanted anything to do with her, and she hadn't been with a guy since she broke it off with her boyfriend Jonathan months ago. She found herself thinking about Kyle. She knew he had a girlfriend and would never want to come between them, but she couldn't help fantasizing. They could read through her prose every day in the bath. They could debate for hours about their top ten books. Besides being exactly her type—a literary jock—she felt he'd been coming on to her the other day at the Irish bar. She saw him around the office flirting with the weird girl at the front desk, so she figured it might just be in his nature, but at the bar he had said the sweetest things. She imagined them giving an interview about *Girls Without Hope* and that somewhere in the middle of creating this bestseller they both fell in love.

"Excuse me? Sierra?"

She heard her name being called. Because she'd been thinking about Kyle, she innocently assumed it was his voice. She looked up, expecting to see his sly grin, but an older man was coming toward her instead.

"Sierra Raven?" the older man asked, standing over her. He had a smile that she found sort of sad, as if it took a great deal of concentration to produce. She went through the Rolodex in her head of any older men she knew and came up empty. It wasn't as if she had parents with an array of friends, since none the Dussens ever left Missouri.

"Hi," she said, scrunching up her nose. "Do I know you?" She wondered if he had seen something about her book deal. Her stomach flipped at the thought that this could be her first fan.

"I don't think we've met yet," he said, indicating the spot next to her to sit down.

She shrugged, secretly longing for *anything* to break up the monotony of her day.

"I'm William Lansing. I just signed with Burke & Burke for my first novel too. Forgive me, but Kyle has said such good things about you and I saw your picture in the *Times* article."

"Oh, cool, congrats on your deal too." She was beaming now. "And you're working with Kyle as well? He's great, isn't he?"

"The best," William said, whistling through a pause in the conversation. "Actually, I'm signing with Brett Swenson, just a better fit for my book. But I've known Kyle a long time, he was a student of mine in college."

"I bet he was a really great student," she said, and then realized how dumb it sounded. Sometimes she fluctuated between acting like a little girl and trying to be more grown up.

"He was one of my best pupils," William said.

Sierra saw that William was really trying to keep his smile going, but it sagged a little. She could sympathize. When she was younger, she used to plant herself in front of a mirror and physically shape her mouth into a smile, since it was sometimes too difficult to attempt hands free.

"Are you working on your new book?" William asked.

"I'm trying but not getting very far." She laughed. "Writer's block."

"Ah, the scourge of our existence." William mimed shooting himself in the temple.

Sierra closed her laptop, glad to be free from it, and tucked her legs up to her chest. "So you've had writer's block too."

"Why do you think I'm wandering around Brooklyn right now?"

"Most people don't understand," Sierra said. "Like friends from college with office jobs will ask how many pages I've written today, and when I tell them nothing, they're like, well what did you do all day, then? I'm like, it takes a day of staring at a blank screen to figure out what I'm gonna write the next time."

"We are mad to choose this as a career, the worst kind of masochists."

"Sometimes I'd rather spend the day being whipped—"

She bit her lip to stop babbling. *God,* sometimes she said the stupidest things. She reasoned that happened when you spent the entire day in your head without speaking to anyone else.

"I didn't mean that," she said, covering her face. "I don't like to be whipped, just so you know."

"I wouldn't have presumed," he said. "What part of writing are you finding difficult?"

"This might sound so annoying, but getting this huge deal has made me feel like I'm not worthy. I almost wish it were a tiny amount of money. I would've been happy with just being published."

"Then pretend it was a small amount. Or even better, pretend you don't have a book deal."

"I was getting so much more done before."

"Then there's your answer."

Such simple advice, she thought, but maybe he was right. She had been a lot more productive before all those zeros entered her bank account.

"So is that your strategy too?" she asked.

"I don't have a deal yet, but I'll let you know."

"I didn't mean to come off conceited—"

"No, you're adorable," he said, and then fixed the small bandage on his forehead. She could see a glimpse of what looked like a nasty gash. "I apologize for saying that, I'm going through a separation at the moment. It's been awhile since . . . well, since I've engaged in stimulating conversation. Or was able to avoid walking into walls." He pointed to the bandage.

She liked the way he spoke, erudite and mature. All Jonathan had talked about were video games and RPGs and other uninteresting ways to pass the time. When she bought him an old edition of *Wuthering Heights* on their six-month anniversary with the thought that they could read it together, he picked it up as if it was a dirty diaper.

"I don't read," he'd said. "You know that. Words just take too much concentration."

"What about my book when I finish it?" she asked, but he just chose not to answer. She felt her heart crumble. For days she didn't even want to look at *Girls Without Hope,* surmising that if her boyfriend wasn't interested in it, who would be?

"What do you think of *Wuthering Heights*?" she asked William. She had just started reading it again. She was over the fact that it represented the souring of her last relationship.

William gave a quiet chuckle. "'*I lingered round them, under that benign sky; watched the moths fluttering among the heath, and hare-bells; listened to the soft wind breathing through the grass; and wondered how anyone could ever imagine unquiet slumbers, for the sleepers in that quiet earth.*'"

Sierra mouthed the last part of the sentence along with him. Her eyes grew wide. "How did you know that off the top of your head . . . ?"

"I'm a literature professor. I often play this game with my students where they have to say the last lines of a famous novel."

"I love *Wuthering Heights* because it has a happy ending after so much death," Sierra said. "Evil has been removed once Heathcliff is gone and Hareton and young Catherine no longer need to live in fear of what he might do next."

"Do you like a happy ending?" he asked, and she noticed his reddened eye now that he was facing her entirely. Bloodshot, giving him a wounded glare. She swore not to be rude and look directly at it. His separation from his wife had clearly been hard on him.

"*Girls Without Hope,* my novel, will have a happy ending," she said. "I might not know what'll happen throughout, but I know that. What about yours?"

He took a beat to consider this.

"Depends on your definition of a happy ending. Happy for some, brutal for others."

A gust of wind made her reach for her laptop, almost knocking it off the bench. William saved it with his quick reflexes.

"Oh, shit, thanks," she gushed. "A cracked computer would cause me to procrastinate even worse."

Another burst of wind sent the fallen leaves swirling around them.

"I think Mother Nature is telling me to call it a day," Sierra said.

"It was lovely running into you, Sierra. We should talk literature again sometime."

"My agent is throwing me a party tomorrow." She opened her purse and handed him an invitation. "It's at a lounge in Williamsburg, you should come. Kyle will be there. I don't know too many people in New York, so I'm really trying to spread the word."

"That sounds great." He tucked the card into his blazer pocket. "*Timshel!*"

"What's that?"

"Quick, what great novel ends with '*Timshel*'?"

"I know it means 'thou mayest' from the biblical translation, as in 'thou mayest triumph over sin.' I was a religious studies minor at Grinnell College as well as an English major."

"Then you should know."

"I do. It's from *East of Eden,* but that's not the last line. '*His eyes closed and he slept.*' That's how it ends."

"Very good, Sierra. Very good."

She could tell she'd really impressed him. His eyes seemed to light up—at least the one that wasn't bloodshot and gnarly. Truthfully, she had just read *East of Eden* for the first time after Kyle had mentioned his love for the book, making sure to analyze every sentence in case he brought it up again.

She realized that was why William had felt so familiar. She'd been in Kyle's office that one day when she urged Kyle to take William's call. He had referred to the man as his mentor. She figured it would certainly help her earn points with Kyle if he saw how well she and William were already getting along.

17

JAMIE PUT HER arm around Kyle as they headed downstairs at the Library for Sierra's party. They'd been to the Library before—a trendy spot in East Williamsburg with bookshelves for walls and drinks that referenced old literary titles. They were in a better place than they'd had been in a long time, at least thanks to the other night. Besides being so attentive, Kyle had finally revealed the piece of his past that had been nagging her ever since William brought it up. The fact that he trusted her enough meant their relationship was finally moving to the next step. And after they'd gotten back from dinner at Vinyard, he was an animal in bed. She could barely even move the next day, happily sore. While she was a tad on edge about meeting Sierra for the first time, she resolved to let go of any jealousy toward the girl and not only enjoy the party but maybe snag a new client out of it too.

"There's Sierra," Kyle said.

Even in the dim lighting, Sierra looked radiant. She wore an oversize white floral lace tunic dress that Jamie recalled seeing on the rack at a Cynthia Rowley store. An older lady with red glasses hovered close by. Jamie figured it was her agent.

Seeing Kyle, Sierra skipped over. Jamie linked her fingers with Kyle's before Sierra had a chance to go in for a hug.

"Hi, you must be Jamie!" Sierra said, full of energy. Jamie already pegged her as the kind of girl who never stopped smiling.

"I've heard so much about you," they both said at the same time. Jamie let go of Kyle to shake Sierra's hand.

"So, are you excited?" Kyle asked, surveying the party of about twenty people.

"I hope more people will show up," Sierra said.

"Everyone probably wants to be fashionably late," Jamie said.

The agent poked her head into the conversation. She had an ultra-long neck and a tiny head with a bowl haircut, resembling a periscope.

"Delia Edgecomb," she said, offering a veiny hand to Jamie quickly and then holding on to Kyle's. "Kyle, darling!" She gave him three kisses on his cheeks.

Since Delia wasn't letting go of Kyle anytime soon, Jamie was forced to make conversation with Sierra. She debated excusing herself to get a much-needed drink.

"So Kyle told me you have your own design company?" Sierra said.

Jamie noticed that Sierra barely wore any makeup. It made her question if she had caked too much on herself.

"Yes, I just got my first investor."

"Cool. You and Kyle are like a power couple."

Jamie could tell Sierra felt dumb for saying that. She glanced around the party for anyone she knew, itching to talk to Kyle's boss since he certainly had an eye for design and might want to update Burke & Burke's look. She'd been waiting for the right time so Kyle could make the introduction.

"I hate all this attention," Sierra said.

"Soak it up," Jamie said. "You never know when it'll come around again."

"Did Kyle tell you I was having trouble writing recently?"

Jamie flipped her hair over her shoulder. "Kyle doesn't really talk about you."

"Oh," Sierra said, like she'd swallowed too much water.

"He doesn't talk about work often," Jamie added, realizing she was being cruel. "After a long day, who really wants to?"

"All I want to do is talk about my book because I'm by myself with it all day."

"So much time spent in your head, I don't know how you writers do it."

"I've been wondering that too. How'd you get into interior design?"

"I was studying prelaw in college, leaning toward corporate law, but I realized I'd rather make things look beautiful than help wealthy companies get wealthier."

"I think the only thing I'm good at is writing a novel, and I'm not even close to finishing it."

"Just think, someone will be picking up your book in a store soon and then spend hours reading something you've created. It's rewarding."

"It is. Thank you."

"To be able to do what you're passionate about as a career, it can be rare. You're lucky."

Jamie felt Delia Edgecomb peering around her shoulder. Delia pursed her lips. "Ladies, a drink?"

"Just a seltzer for me," Sierra said.

Jamie shook her head. "No way, you need to enjoy yourself."

"I don't want to get drunk tonight."

"One drink won't put you on the floor," Jamie said, and then turned to the periscope woman. "Two martinis, up."

Delia nodded and made her way to the bar.

"Shit, I see Brett," Kyle said, and left the two of them alone.

Brett had arrived in a sharp navy suit and cuff links in the shape of an A and a Z. He didn't look pleased that Kyle was walking over. Now Jamie would be stuck with Sierra even longer, at least until the martinis arrived. She'd make sure to bring up her design business again once Delia Edgecomb returned. The woman had just made a good chunk of money off Sierra, perfect time for some new home decoration.

KYLE NOTICED BRETT'S ridiculous A and Z cuff links and hated them immediately. It bothered him that Brett had probably picked them out at Saks or somewhere, thinking they'd be conversation-worthy. The guy tried *way* too hard.

"Kyle," Brett said, as if his name was a tart piece of lemon. He wouldn't even look Kyle in the eye. "Don't you think the Library is a little too on the nose for a book party?"

"Sierra's agent chose it."

"She has no other clients, right?"

"Been Google-stalking her?"

"Just a word of advice," Brett said. "An agent with no other clients means she has nothing else to send to editors. Meaning if you're looking to discover a new author from her—"

"Yeah, I get it, Brett."

Brett rubbed his butt chin, as if in deep thought. Kyle could tell he'd recently been self-tanning, his face and neck almost two different shades.

"What I don't get, Kyle, is why you'd say such untrue things behind my back after I was the one who showed you the ropes at Burke & Burke."

"*What?* I should be the one pissed at you right now. You offered to sign William? *Really,* dude?"

"I see talent and I pounce. Besides, you didn't want to have anything to do with his book."

"Because it's garbage."

"*Au contraire, mon frère.* How far did you read?"

"Enough."

"Obviously not. You have a personal vendetta against the guy that's clouding your judgment."

"You mean to tell me that *Devil's Hopyard* is actually good?"

"It's fucking brilliant. I can honestly say I've never read anything like William's manuscript before, and it's gonna be huge."

"Can we talk honestly, Brett? Just drop all the bullshit and stop trying to one-up each other. William is insane."

"I got him fair and square."

"I don't want him," Kyle yelled. The music had gotten louder and he had to raise his voice, the beats thumping under his feet. "He killed my cat."

"You have a cat?"

"The cat that lived in my alleyway."

"Are you on acid?"

"I am doing you a solid right now, Brett. William is dangerous and disturbed. There is a straitjacket at some asylum with his name on it."

"Well, he's a fucking good writer, and if he wants to bite his shoulder on his off time that's none of my business."

"Those first thirty pages I read made no sense!" Kyle said, gobsmacked. "It's drivel about some professor who wants to eat a girl's heart."

"No, man, the book opens up after that, it's very meta."

"You're just fucking with me."

"Kyle, I don't have the time to do that. Evidently, according to you, I spend all my energy trying to poach my colleagues' clients."

Brett started to walk away, but Kyle stopped him.

"I am *not* going crazy. *Devil's Hopyard* is a pile of shit and you're being petty."

Brett pushed Kyle out of the way and fixed his suit. "I see Front Desk Amanda standing all alone with her shaved blue head. Excuse me, but there are some pants I want to get into."

Kyle figured Brett had to be messing around, but a sliver of him actually worried that he'd misread William's opus. Had he been so shocked by its contents that he couldn't see it as art?

Impossible, he thought, making a beeline for the bar. Talking to a crazy person for long enough can make you think you've gone crazy too. He ordered a bourbon on the rocks.

Relief swelled over him once it hit his lips.

ONE MARTINI UP led to three for Sierra. She'd always thought of herself as a social person, but she'd never had to be the focal point like this. A crowd had started to fill in, and Delia yanked her from person to person: this publicist, that marketing director, this other hot new writer. It was all too overwhelming. She figured she'd be left alone at the bar so she situated herself there. Because it looked strange to be sitting without a drink, she was soon ordering a fourth martini, wondering why the barstool seemed so slippery.

She saw Jamie and Kyle intimately talking the way couples do after they already made the polite rounds and gravitated back toward each other. She had liked Jamie but got the feeling that Jamie wasn't too much of a fan. Sierra worried that maybe she'd given off the vibe that she had feelings for Kyle. Maybe Jamie had seen her look at him in a longing way? She just wanted to be cool around him, but that train had left a long time ago. Last night she'd had a rather graphic dream with Kyle as the star, and she couldn't help but wonder if he looked the same naked in real life as in her fantasy.

"I'm surprised to find you all alone," a voice said to her.

"Kyle?" she asked, licking her lips as if she could taste him. She spun around on her stool to find William.

"Sorry to disappoint," William said. He had a smaller bandage than before on his forehead and his left eye had cleared up some.

"Thanks for coming!" she said, her arms around his neck as she almost fell off the stool.

He caught her before she hit the floor and directed her back to her seat. "Watch it there."

The bartender left a fresh martini. "Maybe I shouldn't drink this." She shrugged and popped the olive in her mouth and crunched down.

"Do you need help finishing it?" William asked.

"Please, before I embarrass myself even more."

"This is your night, you should be able to do whatever you want."

Her eyes fixated on Kyle. He and Jamie seemed to be having an argument now, although maybe that was just a continuation of her fantasy.

"What I want, I can't have," she said, still staring at Kyle and Jamie.

"You like him, don't you?"

Her skin immediately got red. She could feel it spreading across her chest and up her neck. Having a pale complexion always made her emotions overly transparent.

"Can I tell you a little secret?" he asked, motioning for her to lean in closer. She complied. "Kyle and his girlfriend are about to break up."

"No way. Really?"

"He told me she suffocates him."

"Suffocates?" Sierra said, stretching out the word and making a mental note to never *ever* suffocate Kyle.

"He actually said he's developed feelings for you."

Her heartbeat sped up and a knot formed in her stomach. For a second, she thought she might puke, but she was good, *so* good.

"What did he say exactly?" she asked, her mouth dry all of a sudden. She took another gulp of the martini.

"Just that spending time with you made him realize how unhappy he is with Jamie."

She knew it! There'd been times she suspected this, like when he sat so close at the Irish bar and told her how great she was. She had chalked it up to simple, innocent flirtation, but deep down . . .

"What should I do, William?"

"Take him aside and tell him how you feel. He's been waiting so he could finally end things with Jamie. If you don't, he might never pull the trigger."

Ugh. Pressure on top of pressure on top of pressure. She coughed, and a smidge of bile tickled up her throat. She saw Jamie walking away from Kyle.

"Now's your chance, he's all alone." William took her hand and directed her off of the stool.

"I don't know if I can," she murmured, but he gave her a light push. Before she knew it, she was in front of Kyle asking if they could talk in private.

KYLE AND JAMIE'S minifight started over the dumbest thing. She wanted a breakdown of everyone at the party who might be interested in an interior designer, and he replied that she was becoming too consumed with work. He should have known that would set her off, since it was about the most hypocritical comment he could make. He didn't even mean it when he said it. He was still fuming from his interaction with Brett and hadn't meant for Jamie to get the brunt of his displaced anger. But if he'd really dissected this outburst, it stemmed from the fact that he hadn't been able to be truthful with her about what he figured William did to Capone, leaving him all alone to deal with the ramifications.

Thankfully—bourbon in hand—he was coping with it little better now.

"Can we talk in private, Kyle?" Sierra asked. She had slunk up, unnoticed.

"Of course."

They wandered over by the bathrooms to a nook with a reading bench. Bookshelves surrounded them, creating their own secluded world. He spied a few titles: *War and Peace, The Idiot, Fathers and Sons.* Clearly, they had entered Russian territory. He plucked *Crime and Punishment* and turned to a page, sitting down.

"'*Taking a new step, uttering a new word, is what people fear most,*'" Kyle read aloud.

"So true," Sierra said, her eyes glittery, but then he saw it was tears.

"Why are you crying? Don't cry."

She used the sleeve of her dress to wipe them away, but more kept coming.

"I don't think I've ever met anyone as brilliant as you," she said, her face wet. "I'm a mess."

"No, no, no." He reached into his front jacket pocket and removed a handkerchief. She cleaned herself up and placed the handkerchief to the side. "Aren't you enjoying your party?"

Before he could stop it from happening, she had nuzzled into his shoulder, her gin-laced breath warming.

"I'm ready to give all of myself to you," she said quietly. "I know you feel the same. And it will get me writing again, to touch you, to feel you, to know that you're there."

She kissed him sloppily, like a teenager on a first date. She wouldn't let him get a breath. He tried to pull away, but she was surprisingly strong, her lithe body straddling him. Her high heels slid to the floor and she tucked a bare foot into his crotch.

"Sierra . . ."

She kissed his face, his neck, grabbed him by the hair, knocked his head into the bookshelf, and dove in again. When he was finally able to peel her away, Jamie stood there, squeezing a glass of bourbon as if she was trying to make it shatter. Next to her, William's smug face revealed that he was responsible for making all of this happen.

Jamie marched over and tossed the bourbon into Sierra's face, the shock of this causing Sierra to fall to the floor.

"Jamie, it's not what you think," Kyle said, on his feet, rushing toward her.

"That's what people always say when they're caught cheating," Jamie yelled back. "I knew something was happening."

Sierra hugged her knees, beyond wasted. "B-but you two are breaking up."

Jamie towered over her. Kyle thought she might snap and beat the girl senseless.

"You can have him," Jamie said, eerily calm, then headed toward the exit.

"Jamie, wait!" Kyle shouted.

He passed by William, making sure to give a menacing sneer as he chased after Jamie.

"Baby, baby," he said, trying to grasp onto her by the stairs.

"Kyle, I know what I saw."

"I was just sitting there and she started kissing me not two seconds before you came. She's drunk, she's young. There is *nothing* between us."

But there was no chance of changing Jamie's mind. Fighting with her was always futile.

"You tell me," she began, "that you never gave that girl *any* reason to throw herself at you? You flirt with lampposts, Kyle."

"I have not nor ever would cheat on you. And especially with a writer of mine. You of all people know how much my career means to me."

"I thought we were doing better—"

"We were." And then he finally realized: "Why was William even there? He brought you over at the precise time that Sierra pounced on me."

"So it's all a big conspiracy with you as the target?"

"Yes!"

"Sad, truly sad, Kyle. Own up to your shit, fucker."

"William probably told Sierra we were having problems. Don't you see that's how he works?"

Jamie started stomping up the stairs. "Just tell me she was never in your bed. That you always fucked her in her crappy apartment so I wouldn't have to smell her on your sheets."

"I never touched her."

Jamie stopped at the top of the stairs, leering down. "If you'd just be honest . . ." She whisked her head away, tears already emerging. He thought to chase her into the street, but he knew he'd probably make it worse. He retreated down the stairs and bumped into William, who'd been waiting.

"I'm sorry Jamie had to leave so soon," William said, a soft laugh emerging from his throat.

"You goddamn son of a bitch!"

Kyle leaped at William, knocking him to the floor. People gasped and scattered out of their way as the two rolled around.

"You psychotic motherfucker!" Kyle yelled, slamming William's head into the floor.

"Kyle, stop, please," William choked out.

Kyle could feel someone trying to wrench him off of William, but he was out of control. He wrestled whoever it was away and directed a fist square into William's nose, blood gushing from the guy's nostrils, covering Kyle's knuckles as he kept pummeling, each punch giving him life. Finally enough people were able to pull him away.

"I will fucking *kill* you for this," Kyle said, aching to beat on William even more, but the group holding him back was too strong.

"What did I ever do to you, Kyle?" William asked, sounding feeble, struggling to get to his feet. Brett helped him.

"What the fuck is wrong with you?" Brett yelled, and to Kyle's surprise everyone was staring at him as if *he* was the deranged one.

"Could someone get me some water?" William asked. He was shaking now. Delia shuffled off to the bar to fulfill his request.

"This man has pushed me too far," Kyle said. "He broke into my home, he gutted my cat . . ."

Kyle stopped because the stares he received were far from sympathetic. The line had been drawn and sides had already been established. No one was on his team.

"This isn't over," he said, pointing at William, making sure the threat had been received. He tore away from his restrainers and flew up the stairs into the cold night, the wind bruising his face, the finest traces of snow flurrying in the glow of the streetlamps. His legs buckled and he collapsed to the pavement, feeling like he could melt into a puddle and wash away down the sewer drain.

In every passerby he saw William's face. He wanted to kill all of them, until the very idea of William would be erased from existence.

18

KYLE NURSED HIS bruised fist on the way to Carter's office. His boss had sent an "URGENT" e-mail that Tucker Noley would be showing up, so Kyle made sure to get to Burke & Burke before his infamous author arrived. Apparently, Tucker had resurfaced from whatever back alley brothel he'd been hiding in—Carter alluded to an opium den in Shanghai—but his boss also wanted a one-on-one before Tucker's grandiose persona hijacked the meeting. Kyle managed to avoid Brett and anyone else for fear that word had spread about his behavior at Sierra's party, but he was certain that Carter had been alerted.

"Oh, good," Carter said when Kyle entered. "We should have about ten minutes before the freight train arrives. Sit."

Carter took off his glasses and placed the frame's temple between his lips. A lecture would follow.

"Before we even discuss Tucker—"

"I want to apologize for last night," Kyle said.

"Your fist looks pretty mangled."

"You should see the other guy."

"I have." Silence. "We live in a day and age where you can't go flying off the handle like that. Brett showed me a video. Someone posted your fight on YouTube. That's a connection Burke & Burke does not want."

"Am I fired?"

"Call this a warning, but something else I've recently learned about you troubles me more." He pushed a folder across the desk. "This was faxed to me last night."

Kyle grabbed the folder, no idea what the contents could be. He opened it to find his jail record back in college and documents from a few nights in a psychiatric hospital.

"I know who sent you this," Kyle said. "I warned you this person is after me."

"That's irrelevant. What's more disturbing are the folder's contents."

"I was eighteen, I did some stupid stuff. They put me in the hospital because they were afraid of what I'd do to myself, but I was just high. I got into some bad shit and then I got it out of my system by the end of that year."

"I believe HR requires you to list any incarcerations."

"Look, I dealt some drugs my freshman year at college because I had no money, and I got caught. Didn't you do anything dumb back when you were a kid?"

Carter gave him a look that told him not to push it.

"And now Brett wants to sign my old professor just to spite me. Have you read the manuscript yet?"

"I have not, but Brett will be pitching it at the editorial meeting later today."

"Just read a few pages, it's terrible. There's no way it can be published."

"Are there any more skeletons I need to know about?"

"No, sir, that's all of them."

Carter continued chewing on his glasses, not entirely convinced. A knock on the door prevented him from prying any more.

"Come in," he said, readjusting the glasses on the tip of his nose.

Tucker Noley barged in, carrying a cane that was more like a prop. For someone of such an undetermined advanced age, he retained the sturdiness and vigor of a man who lived like Hemingway in his younger years. Four wives in the can, a week once spent in a gulag, the loss of his pinkie during a game of five-finger fillet in Moscow. He had rounded into a snowman's physique, with a beach-ball head and a larger beach-ball stomach. He took off his safari hat and pressed down the few strands of hair he had left.

"Tucker," Carter said, rising to greet him. "Looking fit as ever."

"Get a new pair of glasses," Tucker said, and wedged himself into a chair. "I just returned from drying out in this place called Fortune Nookie. Pretty girls walking all over your back to get out the kinks with their feet. Then they flip you over—"

"So I made sure Kyle came in too," Carter said, clearly not wanting to hear about any of Tucker's dalliances. Tucker came from an outdated un-PC era and could even manage to offend Carter.

"Hrmph," Tucker said, shifting in his seat.

Carter gave Kyle a confused look. "Something wrong, Tucker?"

Tucker took a moment to consider how to phrase his thoughts. White spittle collected around the edges of his mouth. Kyle pitied any of the girls at Fortune Nookie unfortunate enough to be handpicked by this beast.

"This one," Tucker said, pointing at Kyle with his cane, "has not been reachable for the past few days."

"What?" Kyle said, completely thrown off guard.

"I was ready to discuss the outline of the next Spade novel, but he wouldn't return my calls."

Kyle glanced down at his phone. Was he so distracted by everything with William that he hadn't even noticed?

"I apologize," Kyle said. "E-mail is always better."

"Hrmph! So Big Brother can monitor my every word? And now that I'm deep into ISIS research, those radicals are probably monitoring me too. As a society, we're gonna have to go back to the times of carrier pigeons if we want anything kept mum."

"I apologize for this too, Tucker," Carter said. "We're all here now if you want to go over some of the plot."

"Did you know that Random House approached me about Spade? They want to take the character into this millennium. I'm only contracted at Burke & Burke through this next book, you know."

"I assure you we can handle the Spade books best, especially since we've been doing so for thirty years."

"You pawned me off, Carter, on some young schmuck who's more concerned about getting his dick wet than my next book."

"Wait a second," Kyle said. "I was contacting you all last month and you never returned any of my—"

Carter held up his hand to stop Kyle from making things worse.

"Your father was my first editor up until '75," Tucker began. "He even edited one of my early Spade books when I was over in Nam. Threw me a party when I got back with a ton of girls all dressed like Marilyn Monroe and coke on a silver platter like it was crudité. When was the last time Burke & Burke did that for me?"

"We're in a different time than my father's era," Carter said.

Tucker put his safari hat back on with a pout. "You are gonna personally take on the Spade books, Carter. No more of your monkey boys whose mamas still need to wipe their little asses!"

Kyle heard Tucker's knees pop as he rose.

"Okay, if that's what you need to keep you on," Carter said, holding out his hand to shake. Tucker looked at it with disdain.

"Expect a call from me later this week. And I want the most primo blow you're capable of getting."

Tucker knocked into Kyle with his cane and stepped on his foot as he passed by.

"Always a pleasure, Tucker," Carter said. Tucker responded by slamming the door.

Kyle held up his hands in defense. "I swear I don't remember getting any calls from him."

Carter rubbed his forehead and patted his pocket for a cigarette. "These will be the death of me."

"I'd love one too," Kyle said.

The two of them smoked and tapped the ashes in an ashtray shaped like a bull.

"I'm sorry about these last weeks, sir."

Carter blew a smoke ring. " '*I am a man who, from his youth upwards, has been filled with a profound conviction that the easiest way of life is the best.*' Melville. '*Bartleby the Scrivener.*' "

Kyle took a final drag. "Meaning?"

"Meaning take that advice. Whatever is going on with your former mentor, *you* are the one choosing for it to continue."

"But I'm not."

Carter looked down at Kyle's right hand. "I think your bloody knuckles would disagree. Take the next week off and get your shit together."

"I'm fine. I'm ready to be here."

"This isn't a request, it's an order." He stubbed out his cigarette on the bull's snout. "How the fuck am I going to get a Scarface-size pile of cocaine to keep this blowhard happy? You don't have any contacts left from your Escobar days, do you?"

Kyle shook his head.

"Well, then, what are you good for, Kyle?" He turned around to gaze at his Rockefeller Center view. "Now give me some peace while I figure out how to open these windows so I can fling myself out one."

19

AFTER THE EDITORIAL meeting later that day, Kyle walked out confused. He'd expected Brett to try to sell Carter on *Devil's Hopyard,* but Brett had responded that he was no longer interested. Carter asked why and Brett was very vague in his answer. The next bit of business dealt with Carter taking on Tucker Noley, which left Shane Matthews's *Dead Can't Hunt You Down* available for another editor. Kyle was even more surprised when Brett suggested his name. Carter agreed to think about it while Kyle was on "vacation"—his boss actually made air quotes—and he would come to a decision when Kyle returned.

Outside the meeting, Brett cornered Kyle. "We need to talk."

"So talk."

Still in shock from what transpired at the meeting, Kyle was unsure how much to trust Brett.

"Not here," Brett said. "Let's go to Jimmy Malones. A double of whatever you want on me."

As they got to Brett's office, he popped inside and came out with a manuscript box that looked heavy in his hands.

"What's that?"

"*Devil's Hopyard* almost in its entirety," Brett said, a twitch in his eye. "Pretty much a thousand pages of madness."

Now Kyle knew why Brett was acting so strange. William had finally revealed his psychotic tendencies to someone else.

JIMMY MALONES WAS a mainstay of old New York. The place had been around since the 1800s and had a dumbwaiter and the best Buffalo wings outside of Buffalo, tongue-tingling hot and greasy as fuck. They also weren't stingy with alcohol. Brett was two drinks in and already three sheets gone.

"So after the hullabaloo last night, I offer to take William back to where he's staying," Brett said. "The guy's bleeding, since you might have broken his nose."

The bartender came over, an old guy in suspenders.

"Give me four Kick in the Balls," Brett said. "Cuervo Gold, Jack Daniel's, and Yukon Jack. Actually, just keep them coming."

The bartender poured the concoctions. Brett downed a shot without even toasting.

"So he's subletting this place on the Upper West Side. We go back there and he disappears into the bathroom. For like a half an hour. Dude has an unfurnished place, just a couch and an old TV that has fucking bunny ears. Anyway, he comes out and this gash on his forehead has opened up, like blood everywhere."

"I didn't do that to him," Kyle said, jumping in. "I punched him in the nose, man, that's it. Well, maybe the back of his head hit the floor—"

"So the door to the bathroom is open and the mirror is *covered* in blood, like it's dripping onto the sink. William sits down on the couch like nothing happened, like that was totally normal."

"What did you do?"

"I got him some paper towels. We mopped it up because it was all over his shirt. It was even on my hands. So I go to wash it in the kitchen sink, and when I come back in the living room he's holding onto *Devil's Hopyard*."

Brett hoisted the manuscript up on the bar.

"He tells me it's so close to being finished. That he stayed up for twenty-four hours straight and it has been exorcized from his body, those were the exact words he used. So he wants me to read a passage out loud."

Brett paused to down another shot and then flagged over the old bartender for a refill. He waited until it came and then continued.

"I'm like, do you want to go to the hospital, William? Because he was still bleeding. It had stopped some, but I figured he might want to check it out, right?"

Brett took a deep breath. His hand resting on the manuscript was trembling. He looked as if he might cry.

"So William shakes his head, turns to a page, and has me read it out loud." Brett slowly opens the manuscript to a marked page. "You read it." He shoved the book at Kyle, looking relieved that it was out of his hands. He slid over a shot for Kyle too. "You'll need one of these before you begin."

Kyle complied and knocked back the shot, the alcohol burning. He began to read page 774.

> And nibble on her flesh, that tattoo. And chew, chew, chew as it breaks apart in my mouth. It sinks into my molars, its taste acidic and metallic, warming and wonderful. Gnaw, gnaw, gnaw. It's not the heart yet, but it is a start, a part of her I can try without her dying. I want her to watch me devour her piece by piece till there is nothing left but my prize. And once I sink my teeth into

her precious heart, I will be complete. We will join as one in my stomach.

Kyle closed the manuscript and tossed back his second shot.

"I don't want to read any more," he said. "It's the same bullshit page after page."

"Kyle, he's writing about taking this girl into a shack, cutting out her tattoo, and then cooking it up in a fucking *frying pan*!"

Brett's eye was twitching like crazy now, fluttering as fast as a hummingbird's wing.

"But the whole manuscript is like that," Kyle said. "Why did that passage freak you out so much?"

"I told you the place he's subletting is unfurnished, right? Like I said, couch, crappy TV, and the kitchen was completely empty of anything except . . ."

"Except for what?"

"A frying pan, and I swear to motherfucking god it looked like it was corroded with dried blood, old blood, blackened blood, like he made a roux with blood once."

Brett pushed *Devil's Hopyard* back toward Kyle. "I don't want anything to do with William Lansing."

"You shouldn't have offered to sign him, then. You told me his manuscript was genius."

"I was messing with you, Kyle. You come to Burke & Burke, and everyone just falls over you with your perfect hair."

"What does that have to do with anything?"

"Do you want me to admit I was jealous? I've been at Burke & Burke since college—*yeah,* over fifteen years. I've clawed my way up from being Carter Senior's bitch boy, but I've never been able to give them something like you have with Sierra Raven. I've never been featured in a *Times* article."

Brett's face had turned red. He grappled another shot and poured it down his throat.

"I told you he was insane," Kyle said. "I've told everyone, but no one seems to want to listen. Jamie's not taking my side, Carter tells me I'm perpetuating it."

"So he makes me read this fucking filth to him and I get to the part about cooking the girl's tattooed flesh in a frying pan. I look over and the nutbar is licking his lips. He's mouthing the same words I'm saying, and he's *salivating*; I've never seen anything like it before. Blood is pouring from his forehead and he doesn't give a shit, he's lapping that up too. So I stop and . . ."

Kyle leaned closer. "And what?"

"He says that nothing gives him a bigger thrill than putting words on paper, and I'm like, dude, you know your words are kind of fucked-up, right?" Brett said, laughing now at the absurdity of it. "Then he asks me if I ever tasted human flesh? I'm flummoxed, like, I did not expect that to come out of his mouth. I tell him no, of course not. He goes, 'Shouldn't all fiction come from reality?' Of course I was like, *no,* fiction is fiction, nothing more."

"What did he say?"

Brett shook his head, sadly, as if he'd been through a war and returned to a different, unsettling world.

"He told me, 'You don't know what you're missing.' And then the guy starts chuckling, this Joker's laugh that he has. He wipes away the blood from his face and slaps me on the knee, telling me he's just kidding, that he *got me,* that I should see my face. But man, that shit was not funny. He starts talking about method actors and how they have to lose themselves to get into an intense role and how writers need to be the same, how he needs to laugh about his character to break up the seriousness of it. I'm not even listening anymore, like, I'm not publishing this fucking book, so why am I even dealing with him? I stood up and got the hell out of there."

OUTSIDE JIMMY MALONES, snow had begun to sprinkle. Kyle and Brett talked about how they never remembered it snowing this early in October. Brett had *Devil's Hopyard* tucked under his arm and it weighed that side of him down. He passed it over to Kyle.

"I don't want it," Kyle said, throwing up his hands.

"You *have* to read it."

"I don't have to do anything."

"Kyle, you're in it."

The manuscript fell from their hands to the ground.

"What do you mean, I'm in it?"

"Your name isn't used in the part I got to, but it's you. I can tell. It's like he wrote this for you."

"You're not making any sense."

Brett bent down and picked up the book.

"Just read it, you'll understand. And then show it to the fucking police if he's still bothering you."

"I talked to the police. They didn't want to help me at all."

"They will after you read what I did. Trust me."

"Do you really think he actually did all the things he wrote about?"

"Isn't it just as bad if he's fantasizing about it?"

"Uh *no,* doing it is worse."

"I don't think he actually did any of those things, but he's *very* into his character, like he's gone all method, and he clearly has some big screws loose. Someone like that is just waiting to snap."

Kyle brought the manuscript closer to his chest to get a better grip. He couldn't believe it was back in his life.

"Read it to the end, just so I know I'm not crazy," Brett said, a shriveled-up version of his former self. "After I left William's place, he called and texted me all night with ludicrous ideas, shit I couldn't even follow."

"I told you not to work with him—"

"I know, I'm sorry." He grabbed Kyle by the collar, pleading. "Please help me get rid of this albatross."

"Did you tell him Burke & Burke decided not to sign?"

"So I can become Hannibal Lecter's next victim? No thank you. Just skim it until the last part he finished. I gave you Shane Matthews, c'mon."

"Thanks so much, that's the author I originally found."

"I am a damaged fucker and have treated you like crap and you did not deserve any of it. So there is my apology, Kyle, and if you read the rest of *Devil's Hopyard* and help me get rid of this mental patient, I will be eternally grateful and make sure you are given a promotion and a raise."

Kyle couldn't stand to look at Brett anymore. Through Brett, he saw how he had appeared over this last week to everyone else. William's insanity was spreading, infecting every person he came into contact with.

He knew that the only way to help contain an outbreak was to eliminate its source. So he agreed to Brett's wishes and headed home to sink back into *Devil's Hopyard,* hopefully for the very last time.

20

"CAMDEN DESIGNS, HOW can I help you?" Jamie said, picking up her work phone. She hadn't had the chance—or the funds—to hire a secretary yet. Today she was working from home, not motivated enough to head downtown. After the fight with Kyle, she spent yesterday commiserating with her roommate, Sybil. They had finished a bottle of currant vodka, and at one point, they took to torching Kyle's pictures in a tiny garbage can. The smell of scorched photos still hung in the air.

"Jamie, this is William . . . Lansing."

The back of her neck got hot.

"William . . . ?" She was still a little tipsy from the night before. That would be the last time she'd use Sybil as a crutch.

"I got your number from your Web site," he said. "I hope it's all right that I'm calling."

"I'm sorry Kyle attacked you," she said, and then started crying. She hadn't cried yet over him this morning. "I'm sorry he's such a shit."

"Could we talk? I mean, in person. There's something I need to tell you and I'd rather not do it over the phone."

She spied Sybil dead asleep in bed through the crack in her bedroom door. The girl often dozed past noon.

"What's it about?" she asked. "I have work to do today."

"I can meet whenever is good for you. It's important, it's about Kyle. I don't think he's told you everything about what happened to him freshman year."

"Kyle is the last person I want to talk about right now," she said, but that was a lie. She was desperate for someone else to take her side.

"I don't think you know your boyfriend at all," William said, his tone urgent.

"You're telling me."

"No, I mean what he might be capable of." There was a tremor in William's voice, a note of fear that surprised her.

"I'm subletting a place on the Upper West Side now," he said. "I could come to you, or I could have you over. I'd rather not do this in public either."

"You're kinda freaking me out, William."

"I just want to protect you."

"From what?"

"There was a girl Kyle was seeing his freshman year. She went missing. Kyle was the last person she was seen with. The authorities never found her. The way Kyle acted the other night was exactly the same as when she vanished. A kind of rage that landed him in a psychiatric institution."

Jamie couldn't speak. She tried to form words, but it was too difficult. The fact that she might've never known the real Kyle was too much to grapple with. What other lies had he told? How much of him was a mirage?

"Jamie, are you there?"

"I'll come to you," she said, quietly.

"Good. I'm at 872 West 98th Street, Apartment 6F."

"Okay . . ." Her voice quivered as she hung up the phone.

Before she left, she found a swill of vodka at the bottom of the bottle and tapped it dry.

JAMIE WAS SURPRISED to see William in a Yankees cap, a T-shirt, and shorts when she arrived at his sublet. She had never seen him dressed down and almost thought she had gotten the apartment number wrong.

"Come in, come in," he said, and made his way over to the couch, the only piece of furniture in the place.

"How long have you been subletting?" she asked, holding her purse close, somehow feeling safer with it in her arms. If she rooted through it, she could find the can of pepper spray that Kyle insisted she carried when she was out late.

"Just a few days," he said. His nose had been bandaged up and a grape-colored bruise was spreading under his eyes. The cap was tipped low in an attempt to mask the damage.

"Have you seen a doctor?"

"My time in the army taught me how to fix up injuries. I think it looks worse than it feels. Can I get you a drink? I'm afraid I only have tap water and a bottle of Maker's."

"Maker's is fine," she said, and followed him into the kitchen as he poured two glasses. The kitchen was eerily empty, just a stained pan left on the counter.

"I had planned on sprucing the place up, but getting attacked has unfortunately taken the wind out of my sails. I didn't even leave the apartment all day yesterday."

He directed her over to the couch. They sat down and he put the Maker's bottle on the floor.

Jamie started welling up, hating herself for being so emotional. "I'm afraid for what you're about to tell me."

"I feel like Kyle painted me to be someone I'm not," he said. "Someone actually more like who *he* used to be."

She took a sip of the Maker's and wedged her pocketbook between her feet.

"Did people think he had anything to do with this missing girl?" she asked, after a deep breath.

"I didn't . . . at first," William said. "I was the one who advocated for him, but seeing him behave in the way he has recently, I don't know . . . it's changed my perception."

"But why would people think he was responsible?"

"How much did he tell you about that time in his life?"

Jamie filled William in on everything Kyle had confessed to her at Vinyard. William seemed to nod at the appropriate times. Finally, when she was finished, he shook his head.

"That's only half of it," he said.

She finished her Maker's and he made sure to pour her more.

"Kyle and this girl were close," he said. "Both were in my class, and I'd see them around campus, holding hands, making out. But she dated a lot of other guys too. Kyle would tell me how jealous he was. He was in love for the first time and it started to consume him."

"Was this before or after he went to jail for selling drugs?" she asked, trying to line things up chronologically.

"Afterward. You said he told you he cleaned himself up—and he did—but not before it got worse for a while. This girl made it worse. She was a user and liked to throw her hookups with other guys in his face. One time he told me, 'If I can't have her, no one can.' He swore to me he'd make sure of that, and then she vanished."

A window was open and the room got cold, a snow-laced breeze blowing in. Jamie hadn't unpacked her winter jacket yet, still dressed for fall. She was shivering.

"Are you okay to hear this?" he asked, and Jamie slowly nodded.

"The night she vanished, he showed up at my house. Laura, my wife, and the kids were all asleep. He threw a rock at my window and I met him on the back lawn. He was a wreck, babbling nonstop, talking about the fight they got into. He had a welt on his cheek from the girl's ring after she punched him; it had gotten that bad. He caught her having a threesome with some townies, these losers they used to score drugs with. He wanted to kill her."

"Is that what he said?" Jamie asked, breathless.

William nodded. "He did, but then she took off and he couldn't find her, thank God. He searched everywhere, all of her haunts. I drove him back to his dorm, calmed him down, gave him some pills to knock him out, and went home. A few days later, word began to spread that she had gone missing. Students had seen her having a knock-down, drag-out fight with Kyle the night she vanished. The police were starting to question him. They contacted me because I had vouched for him when he was in jail. But there was nothing I could do. He lost his mind because of it and had to spend a few days in a psych ward. The pressure of it all destroyed him, and I was really worried, never letting myself believe he had anything to do with this girl's disappearance. So I told the police he was with me that night. That he had a fight with her and came to me to talk about it. It wasn't a complete lie, since he did come to me that night. I just fudged the times, so they'd suspect him less. The townies soon became the police's main targets, but nothing ever came of it. I put it out of my mind, and Kyle really did start to change for the better, got himself together, even began doing well in my class. But seeing his rage at the Library—Jamie, it shook me to my core. He was out for blood—"

"I know," she said, her hands over her ears, not wanting to hear any more.

"He has a problem with obsessing over things," William said, rubbing her back in a circular motion.

"I *know*. I've told him that."

"He can hurt those he cares about the most if he thinks we've betrayed him. First that girl in college, then me. I don't want to see that happen to you."

William took the empty glass from her hands and poured more.

"Drink up, it's okay," he said.

"Oh, my God," Jamie said, grabbing the glass back, on her way to becoming wasted. She rubbed her eyes until her mascara stained her tears. "I don't know what to do."

"Don't answer his calls," William said, turning her so she faced him. "Just cut him off. Completely."

"I can't do that."

"There's something else I didn't tell you, Jamie."

"What?" she croaked.

"That night he showed up at my house. There was blood on his hands, but he didn't have any cuts or scrapes. Thinking back . . . I don't believe that blood was his own."

Jamie felt the room spin, as if she'd been placed on a tilt-a-whirl. Her body seemed to spill to the floor, broken. The cold wood massaged her cheeks as her eyes closed, and the darkness of a dream began.

WILLIAM LAY JAMIE down on the couch, her head propped up on a pillow. While he waited for her to awaken, he let his mind travel to a recent passage he'd written in *Devil's Hopyard.* His narrator had entered the shack, a slit of moonlight cutting through the wooden slats. The door shut behind him. He was all alone. Looking down, he had little-kid legs, scrawny things with knobby knees, sneakers that didn't close, since he'd been wearing them for years and the laces had become frayed. The night passed as he cried himself to sleep. In the morning he woke up starving, missing dinner. It felt like someone was digging a hole in his stomach. He had to relieve himself in the corner like an animal. The sun rose high, a beam of yellow light slicing through, the only evidence of the outside world. Once the moon rose, the door swung open quickly and a pig's heart was tossed inside. The door shut and locked. He inched over to the pig's heart, studied it. An hour later he managed to hold it in his hands, tears dripping into his lap. And finally, he took a bite, because his stomach was collapsing, and he had to survive.

BY NIGHTTIME, JAMIE began to stir. William had a glass of water ready.

"What happened?" She blinked. "I'm so thirsty."

He held the glass to her lips and helped her tip her head back.

"You fainted."

"I don't remember what was a dream and what was real."

He sat her up, pushed her hair out of her eyes.

"I was telling you that Kyle might be dangerous," he said, nodding. He counted to ten as he continued nodding.

"Yes," she said, her eyes following each nod, but then she tried to get up.

"Whoa," he said, lightly restraining her. "You were out for a few hours."

She got up anyway. "I didn't sleep last night."

"Aren't you worried Kyle might just come to your house? Aren't you afraid he's angry at you?"

She patted down her hair and checked her breath in her hand, not happy with the results.

"Honestly, I've spun my life around Kyle for too long. That's what I was dreaming about. I was an astronaut orbiting Earth but its face was Kyle, and then my spaceship crashed right into his smile."

She picked up her purse and headed toward the door. William quickly stood in her way.

"I really think you need to sit. You're not absorbing what I'm trying to say."

"William, it's late—"

He put his hands on her shoulders, staring into her eyes. The purse fell from her hands. He took her back to the couch.

"The next time you see Kyle, you'll tell him that you're through. Trust me on this."

Jamie put her hand on her heart. "I know. I have to."

He leaned in and kissed her. She pulled away, as if she'd fully awoken.

"I need to go," she said, scooping up her purse and heading toward the door.

He was on his feet, grabbing her instinctively. She let out a yelp, and he let go right away, looking at his hands as if they belonged to someone else.

"I'm sorry, I'm sorry."

She gripped the doorknob and turned it. She froze for a second as she looked back. He saw in her eyes the same disappointment he'd written about, the moment when another character realized his narrator had a switch you didn't want to flip. He knew that if his narrator were in his place, he would've slammed Jamie into the door before she could swing it open. He would've spiked the Maker's and poured it on a handkerchief, forcing her to breathe it in. That was what his character would do, so why shouldn't he act the same? But instead, he let her open the door and flee into the hall. He heard the elevator *ding* and she was gone. He retreated to the couch and took a big swig of the Maker's, surmising that the best thing he could do right now was to knock himself out stone-cold.

21

KYLE STARED AT *Devil's Hopyard.* He had positioned himself in his favorite reading chair in the bedroom, a bottle of Four Roses on the side table. The sun went down and still he stared, unable to open to the manuscript and delve back into a madman's mind. Ever since he read its first line, his life began to crumble: things with Jamie were on shaky ground, Carter had lost patience with him, and his drinking was becoming a problem. He used to swear he'd quit alcohol at forty, but if he kept it up at this rate, forty might not be reachable. His dad had passed shortly after his fortieth birthday, a pickled liver the culprit. He wondered if his destiny was to follow the same trajectory.

He decided to make a change. This bottle of Four Roses would be his last escape. He'd drain it until he finished William's perverted manuscript, and then he'd pour all the rest of his booze down the drain. He took a taste and opened to a random page in the middle.

> I was dragged to the shack like I often was if I chewed too loud or tipped over a glass of milk. She had left awhile ago, never to

return, no longer there to save me. I spent too much time waiting by the window for her to come into view. I stopped thinking that mothers existed. When he'd drag me to the shack he had no concern for my skinned knees or torn clothes. He'd get in his mind that I was bad and nothing I'd say or do could change that. I used to try. I used to beg. Now I chose to go limp. Once the door shut and locked, the shack became my home. Sometimes it felt as if I was left there for weeks, but I know at most it had been days. I'd count them through the broken slat in the wall that revealed my only source of light. I'd gotten good at ignoring my hunger. Once the moon rose, an animal's heart would be tossed inside. I became used to its sinewy taste. I'd plug my nose and pretend it was anything else: a hamburger, hot dogs, chicken fingers, mac and cheese, but it never worked. The truth of a heart cannot be duplicated.

Things became worse when I began to crave it, sometimes even when he didn't lock me in the shack. That was when I knew I had become lost. And he lorded this newfound victory over my tiny warped mind. I'd plead to be taken back to the shack so it could satisfy my needs, but he'd refuse with a devilish grin. So I stole a knife from the kitchen drawer and gutted the farm animals late at night. He'd retreat into his drug-fueled ether and never noticed me coming home with a heart in my hands. I kept this side of me concealed at school. I knew I needed to strive to appear normal, but the mask I wore hid a world of flames. Obsessions begin early in young boys, and I'd been trained to be a demon by the best of them. One time when I was in high school, when I became strong enough to retaliate, I stabbed him in the palm with a fork. He bashed my head in with a Campbell's soup can and I lost some of the hearing in my right ear. I wound up in the shack for days but never received my prize of a heart, lost the ability to move my muscles due to dehydration and hunger. I had a vision of my death and learned that there was no afterlife, just a shallow grave for my bones.

Three days later, when the door to the shack finally unlocked and he entered with some water, I summoned the only shred of energy I had and stabbed him in the heart with the slat I'd broken off from the wall. I left him writhing on the floor. I locked the door behind me, knowing no one would find him for a long time, since we lost the farm and had to sell off the animals, and all that remained was an overgrown plot of land in the middle of fucking nowhere. Then I took off and never returned to see if he'd lived. I like to think it probably took days for him to finally die.

Kyle took a break to refill his glass. It was approaching midnight, but it didn't matter since he wasn't going into the office all week and could wake up anytime he wanted. If *Devil's Hopyard* wasn't fiction, then the passage he'd just read had been a glimpse into William's past, an abusive father who forced little William to eat an animal's heart so many times that he began to crave it. While it was tough for Kyle to believe as truth, it was good backstory for the character of the professor and supported his becoming obsessed with eating the heart of the girl in his class. Kyle didn't want to admit it, but he needed to know what happened next. He'd get this feeling when he was into a manuscript he thought had potential, a desire to put everything else aside. He skimmed ahead until he reached a part about the girl again. She still hadn't been mentioned by name, but now William began to describe her. Instead of being a two-dimensional character, this time she lifted off the page for Kyle, as if he was a part of the story too.

I watch her during my Camus lecture. Teaching the same lesson for a few years has allowed me to be on autopilot. I scribble notes on the board, but she is my focus. We've met outside my classroom many times before. She has awakened me. I am asleep at home with my wife and children, but with her I am alive. One time we did it in her dorm room with a green scarf over the doorknob so her roommate wouldn't enter. The thrill of being caught made it feel electric, dangerous, a beautiful secret. But we couldn't chance it again since I could be fired if someone found out and she refused to have that on her conscience. She had a boyfriend, a skinny, forlorn guy in the back of the class, a kid I was mentoring. He would write notes to her, but she seemed disinterested. I knew she played around with other guys and girls, even men older than me. I once saw her at a bar in Mystic, her legs wrapped around a burly man in his fifties as he pecked her with kisses, her eyes high and spinning. I couldn't have her over at my house, and hotels were too expensive, but one time on a run through Devil's Hopyard I spied a shack in the distance, far enough away from civilization for anyone to notice. I set up a cot, candles, even brought a record player and some classical music LPs. She loved it the first time I took her there, said it was our secret hideaway. For months, we were drunk on each other, but I wanted more. I'd find myself listening to her heart in her sleep, its thumps like a dance party in my ear, as I wondered how it would taste. It had been years and I'd tempered my indulgence, but she made it palpable again.

And then she fizzled away.

The boyfriend became more needy. She got busier. Our days at the shack happened less and less until I could barely remember the last time they occurred. I'd see her and the boyfriend in class, their fingers entwined, a note passed between them, and then I'd see her sucking face with some drug-dealing townie on the outskirts of campus. It was as if her goal was to torture both of us, me and the boyfriend, until one of us snapped. I had desperate dreams about her heart. It was all I could think of. I could no longer have her—she made that perfectly clear with her wicked, tempting, pitying smile. But I could take that heart from her. So one day after class I pounced.

We wound up in my car on the way to Devil's Hopyard, the chloroform keeping her silent. In the shack, I tied her up tight—my Boy Scout training coming in handy—and waited with a butcher knife for her to stir. I traced an outline around her heart ready to slice. But I couldn't go through with it. One slice and she'd be gone, her heart eaten, but then what? So I envisioned going for the second best thing, a heart-shaped tattoo imprinted on her left butt cheek. Her screams would be music to my ears as I'd cut it out and observe my work in the palm of my hand. She'd inevitably pass out again, but I'd sew up the incisions and put some Hello Kitty Band-Aids I'd have taken from my daughter over the wound. Night would fall and I'd be starving, not having eaten all day. It would be similar to when I was a child, locked in the same kind of shack, waiting to be satiated. So I'd start a fire. With a frying pan I kept in the shack for a late-night snack, I'd fry up that heart-shaped tattoo and devour every last morsel, a piece of my **Mia**, a piece just for now . . .

Kyle slammed the book shut. The room slanted and righted itself again. He got to his feet only to spill over and plummet to the floor. The manuscript had opened to the page he just read, the name **Mia** in bold, loud like a crashing cymbal in his ear.

"Mia," he mumbled, a heave of vomit flowing from his lips, not having said the name of the girl he once loved and lost in many, many years.

22

KYLE WAS WITH Mia Evans when he found out his dad died. He'd known her for only a week when the call came, but it had felt like a lifetime. He hadn't fit in yet with anyone else at Bentley, most of them country club kids who summered in the Cape and had bottomless wallets. He talked to her for the first time at the Crystal Mall. He'd been eating an Arby's Beef 'n Cheddar alone when she sat down with two guys in tow who didn't look like they went to Bentley. Their pants hung below their asses without any belts. They wore doo rags and one had a blunt between his lips. Their eyes were smoked out and they talked in their own slang language.

But he recognized Mia. She sat in the front of Professor Lansing's English class. He usually knew most of the questions the professor asked, but he was too shy to answer.

"How come you never speak in class?" she asked.

He swallowed an oversize bite of Beef 'n Cheddar. "I dunno."

"Not a smart way to go through life," she said, taking out a sour apple Blow Pop and placing it between her lips. "How about the next time you want to say something in class, I'll make sure to back it up? Even if I don't agree."

She spoke with an untraceable accent that seemed to morph into a different ethnicity with each word. It started out Spanish then traversed into Eastern European terrain.

"I'm Mia. Evans."

"Kyle." *Cough.* "Broder."

"Wanna get high, Kyle Broder?" she asked, and removed a blunt tucked in the fold of her tank top.

He smoked with Mia in the parking lot, passing around a blunt with her two dudes, Rocco and Stoolie. She was a philosophy major and talked passionately about Nietzsche. Rocco and Stoolie seemed to be far from her level, both of them dropping out of high school to sell schwaggy weed. Kyle figured that was why Mia kept them around. She had doe eyes, big red lips, and multicolored hair—black on the top of her head and blondish-brown down to her shoulders. She'd finished her Blow Pop and blew a massive bubble with the leftover gum. It popped against his face, and they all laughed. An hour later he found himself on the townies' smelly couch, making out with Mia and loving the taste of her sour apple tongue.

This was what Kyle dreamed college could be. Spending a week straight with Mia, barely leaving her dorm room since her roommate dated this guy who lived off campus and was never home. He wasn't a virgin, but pretty close. She taught him things he'd only fantasized about before. By the end of the week, he told her he was in love. The next day he got a call from his mom. His father had fallen into a coma due to liver failure. His will stipulated he didn't want to be resuscitated. The funeral would be over the weekend.

Mia hadn't even heard what Kyle's mom said on the phone, but she was immediately upon him with a comforting hug. She held him for hours as he cried into her shoulder. She helped him book plane tickets.

When he returned from the worst weekend of his life, she picked him up with Rocco and Stoolie at the airport. She had a sour apple Blow Pop for him. That day he got high with them and remained in that fugue state for the next few months.

The first time he caught her cheating on him, he pretended not to care. He'd entered her dorm room to find Rocco and Stoolie having a sword fight in her mouth. She didn't apologize, just told him to either join or close the door. He found out from other students how much she liked to get around. She'd even been with girls and older men too. A rumor circulated that she was dating a professor, although no one knew which one. All of this made him want her even more. To prove himself worthy, he began selling drugs that Rocco and Stoolie procured. There was a drought for harder stuff on campus, and with his innocent blue eyes, no one would suspect him as a pusher. He kept his stash in a locked box under his bed. He had to quit his two campus jobs, since his phone was constantly ringing from students looking to score. Even his English professor caught wind of his secret life. Professor Lansing wasn't upset—in fact, he requested some sleeping aids in exchange for his silence.

Kyle liked Professor Lansing. Thanks to Mia, he began to speak more in his class, and Professor Lansing definitely took notice. He didn't get high for that class, a much-needed break from his drug-fueled reality. He confided in Professor Lansing too. It all started one night when he drank too much and was too fucked-up to figure out how to get home. Professor Lansing had given him his personal cell number and Kyle called him around midnight. Instead of being mad, Professor Lansing drove over to a bar on the outskirts of town and picked him up. He took Kyle out for coffee at a Bickford's. He asked him why he did this to himself.

"I love her," Kyle said, slurring.

"Who, Kyle?"

"Mia. Evans. She's in your spirit . . . spirituality of literature class. She sits in the front."

"I know Mia very well."

Professor Lansing was biting his cheek hard, but Kyle was too far gone to notice.

"She tells me she loves me too," Kyle whimpered, "but she sleeps with so many people. Sometimes I think she does it to be cruel."

"She does," Professor Lansing said definitively. "I know she does."

"But the thought of being without her—"

"It's too much to bear." Professor Lansing finished Kyle's thought.

"Yes. Professor, you're so cool. Like you really understand."

"I do. And you can talk to me anytime, Kyle. I'm here for you."

Selling drugs and hanging only with Mia and her townie hoodlums didn't leave Kyle much time to make other friends, so he really valued Professor Lansing's mentorship. Especially after the police raided Rocco and Stoolie's place and they narced on him. He was floored to find out that Professor Lansing not only bailed him out of jail but also got rid of any evidence in the locked box under his bed.

"Mia was involved with this too, wasn't she?" Professor Lansing asked at a Bickford's a few days after the charges were dropped.

"There's no point getting her in trouble too," Kyle said, shrugging. He wanted to put it all behind him. Now that Rocco and Stoolie were locked up, he figured that meant fewer people vying for Mia's attention. And the fact that he hadn't ratted on her should prove how much he cared.

"Girls like her use and abuse," Professor Lansing said. "She never loved you."

"She did," Kyle mumbled. "She just likes attention."

"She has no *heart,*" Professor Lansing said, slamming his fist on the table. His coffee spilled over. A waitress came over to mop it up, but Professor Lansing shooed her away.

"She deserves someone to teach her a lesson," Professor Lansing said. He was licking the coffee residue from his lips. "Don't you agree? Otherwise she'll treat everyone like this for the rest of her life."

That night, Kyle had a fight with Mia in the Commons. He got wasted and expressed exactly what Professor Lansing had said. Told her she was a user and abuser. She attacked in response, pushed him into the wall. She never liked being told what to do. He fought back, but only to protect himself. Dozens of students saw them going at each other before campus safety finally broke them up.

Later, he found himself in Professor Lansing's front yard, throwing pebbles at the bedroom window. He was hysterical when the professor came down. Professor Lansing kept asking him if he still wanted to kill her for what she had done. Kyle never remembered saying that out loud, but he guessed he had in the heat of the moment. So he took off back to the campus, wishing her dead, spending all night looking in every one of her hangout spots. But he never found her. Days passed without a word. Students began to whisper about her absence. Then the police became involved. They questioned him over and over, knowing he dated her and the two had a fight in public the night she went missing. The police were suspicious because of his record, even though his charges had been dropped.

He started to grow paranoid, since the police threatened prison unless she was found. He even wondered if he'd done something to her, having no recollection of anything that occurred that hazy night. He sometimes pumped himself with so many drugs that he believed he might be capable of the worst things imaginable. To quell his paranoia, he took a fistful of whatever he had left and wound up passing out until a family discovered him in Devil's Hopyard, naked and howling at the moon. Professor Lansing helped check him into a psychiatric ward just to monitor his behavior for a few days. He watched cartoons and slurped soup until they marked him sane and let him go. When he got out, the cops had picked up Rocco and Stoolie. Both had gotten out on bail when Mia went missing and became prime suspects. All of Bentley began searching for Mia now that more than a week had passed without a sign. News crews arrived and students were questioned. Everyone said what a sweet and beautiful girl she was. Her mother, Karen, lived nearby in Killingworth, a pill popper with a revolving round of men in her life. It was clear Mia didn't come from a happy home.

After a month without any leads, everyone figured that Mia had run away to start a new life. She no longer made the front page of the *Killingworth Gazette.* Kyle cleaned himself up, attempted to trade drugs for schoolwork, and managed to make some normal friends. He thought about Mia from time to time, even tried to talk about her with Professor Lansing, but his professor didn't want to talk about her anymore. Everyone at Bentley College had also become exhausted from hunting for a girl who didn't want to be found, and soon she was spoken about less and less. He'd see a girl on campus sucking a lollipop and he'd remember the giant bubbles that Mia used to blow; he'd hear a trace of her strange accent coming from someone else's lips and turn around thinking it was Mia, only to be disappointed.

When spring arrived, he met a girl named Cathy while sitting on the grassy quad reading *East of Eden.* She was reading it too. She was a dance major and an English minor. She made a joke that she was nothing like Cathy from *East of Eden,* the wicked temptress with the razor teeth. He watched her perform a bebop jazz dance to Miles Davis in the auditorium that night, and for the first time in a long time, he didn't think about Mia at all. They shared a malted afterward at some 1950s-inspired ice cream joint in town. She didn't drink, since dance was her drug. For the next six months with her, he didn't touch a drink, or a puff, or a snort at all.

Even after school ended, he'd let himself float back to Mia only in his dreams. He'd get a whiff of sour apple gum and start salivating. But she was always too far away for him to grasp, no longer a part of this world.

"MIA," HE SAID, stirring from sleep as a loud knock pounded against the door. Blinking the crust from his eyes, he half expected it to be her, brought back to life because he'd willed her to return.

It hurt Kyle to think that she might not have chosen to disappear—that William might have taken her away. Especially if he was somehow responsible for planting the bug in the sociopath's ear.

"I'm so sorry," he said, still trapped between his dream and reality, shaking like mad as he swung open the door and imagined her ghost in the hallway, awaiting retribution.

23

"I'M SO SORRY," Kyle said, swinging open the door to find Jamie there instead of Mia.

Jamie stepped inside, shocked by his appearance. Crusted vomit had formed on his T-shirt in a shape that resembled Europe. His hair was messed up and he wasn't wearing any pants. She checked her watch.

"Shouldn't you be getting ready for work?" she asked. She wore a professional skirt and blouse and high heels. She hung up a heavy over-coat dusted with snow.

"I'm not going in this week," he said, rubbing his eyes as a kaleido-scope of colors blinked in his line of sight.

"Because of what happened at the Library," she said, under her breath.

"Yes . . . and no."

He sat down and realized he was pretty much naked. He grabbed a pair of balled-up sweatpants and put them on.

"I know you're sorry . . ." Jamie began, but Kyle jumped up and ran into the bedroom. He returned with *Devil's Hopyard* in his hands.

"He killed her," Kyle said, waving the manuscript. "It's all in here. He's responsible!"

"What are you talking about?"

"Mia Evans!"

"I don't know who that is."

"My girlfriend," he said, and Jamie crossed her arms, looking like she was ready to stab him. "In college. She was my girlfriend freshman year, the one I told you about. We were selling drugs together and she disappeared."

Jamie grabbed his arms to calm him down. He was talking too fast for her to understand. She had never seen him like this before.

"Kyle, you're not making any sense—"

"The cops thought someone took her, but they never found any leads. Eventually they figured she ran away."

"I came here to talk about us."

He wrestled away. "You don't understand. William is the reason she disappeared. He killed her and hid her and ate her fucking heart!"

Jamie directed Kyle over to the couch and sat him down.

"You're drunk," she said evenly. "Did you sleep at all last night?"

"I had a nightmare. I'm *living* that nightmare."

He shoved *Devil's Hopyard* at her. "It's all there. The girl in William's psychotic book is named Mia too."

"It's just a name," Jamie said, talking to Kyle like the nurses did those days he spent in the psychiatric ward long ago. Like he was crazy.

"It's not just a name. Mia Evans made the papers. She was a big cold case in Connecticut, like the girl *never* turned up. Why are you defending him?"

"I'm not, he—" Jamie started welling up, dabbing the tears away before they ruined her makeup. "I went over to William's place, he's subletting in the city."

"Why would you do that?"

"It was after what happened in the Library . . ."

He clenched his fists. "Jamie, there is nothing going on with me and Sierra."

"I'm not sure I believe that."

Kyle stood up and grabbed *Devil's Hopyard* from her.

"Every problem between us over this last week was orchestrated by William. At first I thought he was plotting revenge because I didn't want to publish this . . . *thing,* but he's got a bigger plan."

Jamie shook her head. "I can't deal with this in my life right now," she said quietly.

"I'm in the book, Jamie. I'm a motherfucking character. It's me, he's described me. I'm part of the story."

"You're not listening . . ."

He smacked himself on the forehead, frustrated. "*You* are not listening. This is bigger than us right now. Look, I love you, and I would never, ever cheat on you. I promise."

"I love you too," she said, not bothering to wipe away the tears anymore. Mascara lines dripped down her cheeks. "But this isn't healthy. You're not healthy for me."

Kyle held *Devil's Hopyard* close. "The answers are in here, don't you see? What'll happen to everyone next could be in these pages, or maybe he hasn't even written it yet, maybe he's waiting to see how it'll all play out before he writes the end."

She shivered. "He told me things about you, Kyle."

"What? What things?"

"When I went over to his place. It's fuzzy, though. I had a few drinks, I was upset."

"Whatever he told you is a lie."

She rubbed her head. "It's so strange, I can barely remember that whole day, like someone carved it out of my brain. I kinda remember showing up at his place and I remember leaving, but everything else is just dark." She covered her mouth, the night at William's place slowly coming back. She opened her purse and reached inside, feeling for the pepper spray.

"William told me about a girl who went missing too," she said.

"Yes, that's Mia."

She nodded, slowly getting up, her hand still digging around in her purse.

"He said you came to his house the night she disappeared," Jamie said. "That you had blood on your hands."

"I did. It was *my* blood. I had a fight with Mia and punched the wall."

"He said your knuckles weren't scarred. That it wasn't your blood."

"This is his plan," Kyle yelled, flipping trough *Devil's Hopyard,* hoping to find the evidence that proved his accusations. He still had a good chunk of the book left to read. "He's gonna put her disappearance on me. He's already planting the seeds."

Jamie stood there, no idea how to react.

"Of course I didn't kill her, Jamie. I loved Mia. She was my first love. When my dad died, she held me for hours." He planted a hand on his forehead, just realizing. "Oh shit, William was the professor she'd been seeing. She probably wanted to end it with him and he snapped. You've seen him, he fucking snaps, right? And now this whole reunion between us, *mentor* and *protégé,* it's all been to set me up for her death with his goddamn book to prove it."

Kyle put on his sneakers and shoved his wallet and cell in his pockets.

"I need to go to Connecticut," he said, swiping Jamie's overcoat off the hanger and putting it on.

"What? Kyle, that's my coat."

He wrenched it off and took his own instead. "I need to prove that William killed Mia. Between his wife, his kids, there's a fucking town filled with secrets from ten years ago and someone knows what happened."

"Kyle, stop, this is ludicrous."

He got in her face, seething. "I can't believe you thought I could've hurt her. That I was capable of—"

"I didn't—I don't know what to think." She chucked her purse and the pepper spray to the floor. "But this is what I mean. I'm meeting another investor today and look at me. You've gotten me all *insane.* That's what you do. You get people wound up in whatever you're obsessing over."

"Wait, you still think this is just an obsession?"

"I think you are *both* obsessed, with each other. I think William has gotten caught up in his writing as if it was real, and you think you're editing the next *In Cold Blood.* And yeah, maybe he is messing with you to see how you react and then using it for his book, but you're letting him. And now *I'm* letting you both make me crazy."

She fixed her hair until the rogue strands were pressed down.

"Yes," she said, reassuring herself, "that's exactly what's happening. Your life has always revolved around fiction, both of your lives. This is your wet dream, your own twisty thriller. And you're sucking me in, you're both sucking me in . . ."

Like a zombie, Jamie walked into the kitchen, wet a paper towel, and dabbed her face. She took her time, eyeing herself in the toaster until she was presentable again.

"Elka recommended me to a friend," she said, throwing out the paper towel. "The woman is one of those Upper East Side ladies-who-lunch types. Botox parties. A little dog named Jacques in a purse. She shits money, okay? And when I woke up today, I swore she would be my priority, but my morning was free. So I got on the train to see you because I didn't like how things ended and I missed you and I missed us. And then just before I knocked on your door, I got this bad feeling, like I was making a mistake, like seeing you was the last thing I needed. It wasn't the first time I felt that way."

"Even before William entered the picture?"

"This isn't about him."

"I'm not creating all of this."

"I know you don't think you are, but trust me, Kyle, this is how you operate. You need chaos, you chase it, you're drawn to it."

"That's not true."

"These stories from your time in college are only further evidence. Drugs, jail, a psych ward, a missing girl. And as an adult, you've ended every relationship you've had after six months. When things get normal for you, you get bored. If William hadn't come along to get you manic, something else would have."

Kyle looked at her as if she was the unbalanced one. "Something bad is going to happen," he said. "And I won't be able to live with myself if I don't try to stop it."

"No, you've cast yourself in your own novel now, and all you want to do is write the next pages."

She headed back into the living room, picked up her purse, and threw in the pepper spray.

"It's why you can't commit to anything. Because actually having a lasting relationship isn't dramatic enough for you. God, you couldn't even commit to a cat."

"Yeah, well, William fucking *killed* Capone too. What do you think of that?"

"Just stop—"

"Ripped the cat's heart right out of his chest and stuffed your underpants in its place—"

She slapped him across the face. He took it, letting her get out her frustration. If she was a part of William's terrifying game, William would make sure her story came to an end—either broken up with Kyle or *way* worse. Which was why he needed to go to Connecticut and uncover the truth before Jamie became William's next gruesome plot point.

If the bastard wanted them broken up, he'd grant his old mentor that wish . . . for now.

"I need to go, Jamie."

"You're not gonna deal with what's happening between us right now? I'm angry."

He shook his head.

"Aren't you going to say anything, Kyle?"

"No."

"Asshole."

He was unable to look her in the face. He had never hurt anyone this bad, and she was the last person he ever wanted to hurt. But he had no choice. Jamie was stubborn. She'd never listen, since she didn't want to believe that fiction could be fact. But he knew he would be her undoing if she remained tethered to him. So he'd make it appear to William that he and Jamie parted ways. In reality, after all this was over, he'd explain to her why he had to do what he did. That he was the hero of this tale, and the only way to keep her out of danger was to let her go. Kyle needed William to keep thinking all his fucked-up plans were in motion, long enough to create a distraction until he could be brought down. Kyle swore he'd find a clue in Killingworth that would prove what William had done: a slipup, a crack in his mentor's intricately designed web.

He'd be the one to decide how this whole tale would end, not William, *never* William.

24

AFTER JAMIE LEFT, Kyle took a shower, packed a suitcase, and headed over to a Kinko's. He spent an hour scanning the pages of *Devil's Hopyard* onto a file, just in case it had to be e-mailed to someone. He then rented a car and set his GPS to Killingworth. Ideally, he would've taken the train so he could dig deeper into *Devil's Hopyard,* desperate to know if William was definitely pegging him for Mia's disappearance, but like most towns in Connecticut, a car was essential to get around. Halfway there on I-95, his phone rang, and he answered it on his hands-free device.

"Hello?"

"Hi, Kyle, it's . . . Sierra."

He cringed at the sound of her voice. The last time he'd seen her was at the Library, when she tried to kiss him. He hadn't had time to think about how he'd fix that mess.

"I didn't hear from you so I figured I'd call," she said, barely above a whisper. He could tell she was trying not to cry.

"It's been an insane last few days," he said, rubbing his eyes, feeling the exhaustion creeping in.

"I'm so, so sorry for what happened."

"It was a misunderstanding," he said, short with her even though he didn't mean to be. "And alcohol was involved."

She sniffed back her tears. "I just wouldn't want this to jeopardize any professional relationship we had. I'd understand if you didn't want to be my editor anymore."

"It won't, and . . . maybe I'm to blame too. Maybe I made you think—"

"It's easy to believe in something if you tell yourself over and over it's true."

He looked at the *Devil's Hopyard* manuscript, sitting in the passenger seat.

"Tell me about it."

"Are you sure you're okay?"

His eyes welled up and he wiped them with his sleeve. He was far from okay, losing himself. Would the rest of his life be dictated by what was immortalized in some novel?

"Kyle . . . ?"

"I'm headed to Connecticut," he said, wanting her comfort, needing someone on his side. "I'm afraid things with William have gotten really bad. He's trying to ruin me."

"He only had nice things to say about you. He called himself your mentor."

Mentor. Kyle never wanted to hear that word again, the very thought of it—evil.

"If he contacts you—"

"He hasn't."

"If he does, Sierra, I think he's very dangerous. He's not well. Don't be fooled by his charms."

"Okay . . ."

"Are you writing again?" he asked, finding solace in the image of her cross-legged on her bed, a laptop in front of her.

"I've been distracted since my party."

"Distraction is bad. Have you written one great thing about yourself today?"

"Don't think I can come up with one."

"You're resilient," he said, almost as if he was speaking to himself.

"Okay, I like that."

He pictured her smiling. "Now get back to *Girls Without Hope,* that's an order from your editor."

"I will. What are you planning on doing in Connecticut?"

He swallowed hard, his mouth like the Sahara. "I'm taking care of business that should've been wrapped up a long time ago."

AS KYLE PASSED the road sign for Killingworth, he felt an overwhelming sense of déjà vu. It had been a solid eight years since graduation, and he hadn't returned for his five-year reunion, but as he headed down an off-road trail, it was like he'd never left. A flood of mixed emotions made him nostalgic for the good times at Bentley, when freshman year was firmly in his rearview and he was able to tell himself it had been a blip in his life rather than a permanent penance. Of good times with Cathy, reading Steinbeck to each other naked in bed, of quiet moments when he would allow memories of Mia to invade his thoughts. Sometimes he'd trace his finger across a globe and wonder where she disappeared to, never thinking that William could have known the answer.

Was it nuts to think William had been involved in Mia's disappearance, or was this nothing more than some twisted ploy to drive Kyle to the edge of sanity? Even if that wound up being all it was, he hated to admit he could be falling right into his trap.

He passed the local package store, now with a neon sign but still as ramshackle as ever. Ethel's Edibles was still a fixture at the end of Main Street, the best crab-and-cream-cheese omelets he'd ever eaten. A wine store had sprung up next to it, new and shiny, with frequent wine tastings. An antiques store across the street had a few people milling about inside. A mailman left a package on its doorstep and waved to a woman walking a little dog. The two stopped to talk, both thoroughly engaged in the conversation. It was similar to the small Wisconsin town he'd grown up in, and his heart ached for that innocent time: when his parents were alive, when a day spent at the lake was his idea of perfection.

Off Main Street stood the Killingworth Inn. He couldn't recall it existing back in school, another sign of changed times and the town's burgeoning appeal for tourists. He parked the car and booked a room for three nights.

He always worked best if he had a deadline.

WITH A MIDTERM exam looming, William plunged into a lecture on Faulkner's classic novel *Sanctuary*. According to Faulkner, it was deliberately designed to make money and was the most horrific tale the author could imagine, full of the criminal underworld, voyeurism, rape, and murder. A fitting companion to *Devil's Hopyard,* but William thought it had less of a brutal punch.

Kelsey, sitting up front, was the first to interrupt his lecture to make a point.

"I'm sorry," she said, twirling a pen between her fingers, "but I was offended that Faulkner kept describing Temple Drake as a flirt, as if she deserved what Popeye did to her!"

Other students chimed in on the novel's antifeminist tone, even Nathaniel, who'd recently grown an opinionated backbone.

"The point is," William began, already prepared for a defense, "the way Temple acts with the boys in college is not the way she should act with criminals. And that begins her moral slide."

"It just seems outdated," Nathaniel said, after a lull from the other students. "I agree with Kelsey."

Kelsey took the compliment in stride, but it was clear she enjoyed a loyal following.

"It's not outdated," William chided. "What happened to Temple could happen to anyone on a college campus, away from home, experimenting with new things. They fall in with the wrong type of influence." He stared out the window. The leaves on the trees had crumbled and withered to the ground, sensing the onset of winter before anyone else. Branches were stark against a bone-white sky. A fine layer of snow stuck to the quad's grounds. A final winter, a time of good-byes. Would he ever see the sun again? Did he deserve to?

"Professor . . ." Kelsey hissed, her arms crossed. "We lost you . . . again."

"There was a student of mine," he responded, rather abruptly. It caught Kelsey off guard and she jumped a little in her seat. "A long time ago. She went missing, terrible tragedy. This made the papers, since she was never found."

The students all glanced at one another, not expecting this turn in the lecture.

"But maybe she met someone she shouldn't have, someone even in her class, both unaware of the way that fate would tie them together endlessly. Maybe this someone never realized the role he played in her going missing? Or maybe he had and it was easier to just forget?—"

"Professor," Kelsey said, cutting him off.

"One second, Kelsey!"

He snarled at her like a bull, and she shrank in place.

"Class is over," Kelsey said quietly.

He looked at the clock, way past when he usually let his students go. He had lost himself, like he often did when creating. So he shooed them all away but stopped Nathaniel at the door.

"I'm sorry for speaking against you," Nathaniel mumbled.

"Did you get what I asked for?"

Nathaniel gave a slow nod.

"Good. Bring it to the faculty reading later today."

Nathaniel made a move to slide out of the door. William grabbed him by the arm, staring in his eyes.

"You got *everything,* right?"

"Yes, Professor."

William eased up on his grip. Nathaniel yanked his arm away and was out the door fast. William could hear him running away down the hall. He returned his gaze to the window in the back of the classroom. The snow was teeming now, icy swirls tapping against the glass and trying to break inside.

25

KYLE DEBATED HUNKERING down in his hotel room to finish *Devil's Hopyard,* but he figured it'd be smart to pay a visit to Mia's mother first. The manuscript would have to be read in between any detective work. He found Karen Evans's address easily and drove to the outskirts of Killingworth. The place was a shambles, the house sinking into the foundation and looking like a soufflé that never rose. Paint crumbled from the façade, making it difficult to tell the difference between the real color and the primer. The screen door came off its hinges as he opened it to knock. The front door swung open just as he fit the screen back into its grooves.

"Can I help you?" a woman asked, whom he guessed to be Karen. She had a Big Gulp in hand, hair like straw, and a zoned-out gaze. A waft of alcohol blew from her lips, which explained the burst capillaries in her reddened nose.

"Are you Karen Evans?"

She answered with a nod and a slurp from her Big Gulp.

"My name is Kyle. I knew your daughter."

She froze in midslurp, as if she'd forgotten the name and he was a cruel reminder.

"Your daughter Mia," Kyle continued.

"I haven't talked to reporters in years," she said, closing the door. He wedged his foot inside.

"No, Mia was a friend of mine at Bentley. We even dated. I've thought about her all these years."

Karen had a tic that caused her right shoulder to shoot up to her ear. She seemed to apologize for it with her eyes. She pushed the door wide open and turned around, heading to her couch. She sat down as if she'd been walking for miles.

Kyle stepped inside, the stench overwhelming. A house that had never been cleaned, a hoarder's paradise. Yellowing newspapers climbed up the walls. A collection of plastic bags hid the dining room table. An old television showed some talk show, the sound muted.

Karen moved aside vials of pills on the side table and found a crumpled pack of cigarettes. She shook one between her lips, then offered Kyle. He took it to be polite. Also on the side table was a box filled with matches and lighters. She lit her cigarette and then his.

"It'll be twelve years," she said, with the faintest trace of a Southern accent. "I was young when she left, now I'm old."

He wanted to tell her she was still young, but he couldn't get the lie out fast enough.

"Mia," she said, pointing to the mantel over the fireplace. He waded over sticky magazines and picked up a framed picture. It looked as if it had been taken in high school, not quite the Mia he knew, this girl purer. She was on a beach, smiling wide, no clue of the horrors about to happen.

"She's beautiful." He made sure not to say *was* in case Karen still kept her alive in her mind.

"Oh, yes, very. That was Harkness Beach, Fourth of July. Her dad had made it to town for the weekend."

"Did he see her often?"

"That sumbitch?" She let out a wheezy laugh. "Hardly. He poked around down in Florida, swindled old ladies out of their retirement savings. Last I heard he was still locked up. But they hadn't caught him yet when that picture was taken."

Kyle placed it back on the mantel, the only part of the house kept clean and tidy.

"So why are you here now?" Karen asked, her hand shaking as she took a puff and the ashes fell everywhere. "Don't remember you bringing over any casseroles like all the rest of 'em when she vanished."

"I'm an editor now at Burke & Burke."

She shrugged her shoulders, unimpressed. He handed her his card, which didn't seem to change her opinion.

"I'm editing a book about missing girls. A lot of high-profile cases. I want to give a voice to those who aren't able to tell their story themselves. Because I knew your daughter, I wanted hers to be the final chapter."

Kyle's card fell from her hand. She blinked madly at him, her right shoulder finding her ear again.

"I really didn't come here to upset you," he said, sitting on the couch next to her.

She patted him on the cheek. "I know. You have a good face. I like your face."

"I had some questions to start, if that would be all right?"

"What about?" Karen asked, launching into a coughing attack and then settling herself.

"About your daughter. Mia."

Her eyes looped around. Whatever pills she had taken seemed to be kicking in.

"Did you see her picture over there on the mantel? It was at Harkness Beach. July Fourth weekend. We had a picnic of bologna and cheese sandwiches."

"Ms. Evans," Kyle said. "Do you believe that your daughter ran away?"

This seemed to wake her up. "Ran? *Away?* Oh, no, no. She would never. I mean they say she did. 'Cause the police did squat."

"Really?"

"Oh, they gave Mia a month of their attention. Candlelight vigils, search parties with barking dogs, combing the woods. And then something else caught their interest. Mia became nothing more than a runaway."

"Why don't you think she ran away?"

"We ain't had it perfect, mister, but we had it all right. She was pissed about her daddy going to prison, but she felt he deserved it too. I tried to snag other father figures into her life when she was a kid, but none ever stuck. Then she got a scholarship to college and she was studying . . . I don't know, philosophy or somethin', nothing I'd be able to help her with." Karen guided the cigarette to her mouth for one final, jittery suck. "But she loved me, she wouldn't just up and leave without a word all this time. I can't believe that."

"Was there anyone suspicious in her life then? Someone you didn't like?"

"Eh, she was up at school and we didn't talk as much. There were a million names she'd mention to me, tons of boyfriends, always a new boy."

"You don't remember her saying my name?"

"Sweetie, there are days I forget my own." She cocked her head over to the vials of pills.

"What about an English professor of hers? William Lansing?"

"Nope, can't say that sounds familiar."

"She never talked about any of her professors?"

Karen lit another cigarette, almost chewing on this one.

"Lansing, you say?"

"Yes, Professor William Lansing."

She flapped her hand in front of him to shut him up, as if she'd lose the thought.

"His kids own that bar on the border of town," she said. "The Royal Wee."

"His kids? You mean his twins, right?"

Her right shoulder rose up to her ear. He couldn't tell if it was a shrug or not.

"Not sure of their names, but there's something a little off about them."

"Off like how?"

Karen pressed into the couch to rise on unsteady feet. "I think it's time for my nap."

He took her by the arm to led her to the bedroom. "Ms. Evans, how are they off?"

She unstuck her eyes, mucus and tears causing them to flutter.

"Word about town is how close they are," she said with a shudder.

"Right, they're twins."

"I ain't never seen twins acting like the two of them do."

They reached her bedroom. A hurricane of clothes created a fortress as tall as the bed. The curtains were down—Kyle imagined permanently. It seemed as if light had never hit the room. Her dusty bed sighed as she rolled on top, cradling the Big Gulp. He tucked the sheets up to her neck and she appeared satisfied.

"Good night," she said.

"It's not even noon."

"The day is over for me. Yes it is. I've spent enough time in reality already."

She closed her eyes.

Kyle shook her on the shoulder. She didn't move, dead to the world.

26

ON HIS WAY to the faculty reading, William mailed a package to Brett Swenson. Brett had been avoiding all of William's e-mails and calls since Sierra's book party, and William knew that meant he probably wasn't about to be signed as a client. There'd been a fakeness about Brett that William found suspect, but he believed the guy genuinely liked *Devil's Hopyard.* He'd tossed and turned all last night guessing what Brett's motive might be for giving him a false sense of hope, and he surmised that it had to have been Brett's way of messing with Kyle. So William decided to mess with Brett.

Afterward, he headed to Rayne Auditorium to hear Brooks Jessup read from his new novel—or, rather, watch his colleague spectacularly embarrass himself in front of the whole department. Wine and cheese were being served, but he made a beeline straight to Nathaniel, who sulked by the auditorium's front doors.

"Do you have it?" William asked, smiling at the room and not looking Nathaniel's way.

Nathaniel passed him a paper bag. Inside William saw a box of ex-lax and a few containers filled with clear liquid.

"How do I know the stuff is legit?" he asked.

"It's from a dealer on campus that everyone uses for everything," Nathaniel said, devouring a fingernail.

William removed a CVS receipt from the paper bag.

"What makes you think I'd want a receipt for the laxative?" William asked, balling it up and shoving it at Nathaniel. "You didn't tell anyone about this, did you?"

The boy twisted and turned in place, a ball of nerves. "Professor, I . . ."

"What is it, Nathaniel?"

"I-I don't think I can be your research assistant anymore."

"That is disheartening to hear. You've done such a spectacular job."

"Really?"

"Solid A-plus work that will be reflected in your grade. In fact, I wanted to write you a recommendation later. There are internships I can get you into for the summer. Wouldn't that make your parents proud?"

"Yeah, but . . ."

Nathaniel had given up on his fingernail and now just gnawed on his whole finger.

"That is a disgusting habit," William said, shuddering. "You need to ask yourself how you want the world to view you."

"Who are the drugs for?" Nathaniel said, at least smart enough to whisper it.

William leaned in, causing Nathaniel to slouch. "Maybe I have an addiction, Nathaniel, one I've never been able to quell."

"But I think all that stuff does is knock you out."

"Addictions are not always easy for someone else to understand. Like the way you chew your fingernails, for example, that is an addiction I cannot understand either."

Nathaniel glanced at his fingers as if he was angry with them.

"I have one final request for you as my assistant," William said. "Then I will let you go."

"What is it?"

"I'm still figuring out the particulars. But you'll be the first to know when it's ready."

William spied Brooks over by the wine table. He was done with reassuring Nathaniel—less of a spineless wimp than when he first started molding him, but not by much. He turned on his heels and made his way over to Brooks.

WILLIAM WANTED TO get to Brooks Jessup before the guy could pick up a glass of wine. Rooting around in his paper bag, he managed to open the Ex-Lax box and grab a few pills. He squeezed until the pills were crushed up into a fine mist, took two glasses of wine from the table, and poured the overdose of laxatives into the glass he handed Brooks.

"Thanks, Bill," Brooks said, with a hearty laugh. The guy was always laughing boisterously, mostly at his own jokes. He knocked back the wine so fast there'd be no way for him to tell it was spiked.

"I'm looking forward to hearing your new novel," William said, sipping at his own glass.

"It's been a beast to write, I tell ya," Brooks said. "What with doing all the press for *Long and Winding* and trying to finish pages. Thanks for picking up my class, by the way. No way I could've taught this semester with the tour."

"My novel is at Burke & Burke now," William said, diving into this pissing contest.

"Dynamite, man!" Brooks said, slapping William on the shoulder. "This is the one you've been working on for like a decade, right?"

"I'm not one for fast prose," William said, sneering. "I read that

Junot Díaz took ten years to write *The Brief Wondrous Life of Oscar Wao.* I like to linger over each word."

"Me too, but my checkbook certainly doesn't," Brooks said. "*Long and Winding* took five years, but this new one, I'm aiming to get it done in less than a year. I got no choice, it's in my contract!"

He made a gesture at being handcuffed, and then cackled.

"So Burke & Burke, you say? Who's the editor?"

"The contract hasn't been signed yet, still doing some negotiating. But Kyle Broder will be my editor."

"He's the one who signed that debut author for a half-million-dollar deal, right? I read all about it."

"Fingers crossed I'll be his first seven-figure."

"Well, boy howdy, that is just awesome, awesome news," Brooks said, letting out a belch. "Excuse me, I feel like that one brought up last night's dinner."

The department chair, Dr. Joyce Yancey, hovered over the two of them. She loved wearing pearls, loathed any kind of humor, and ran the department with the soul-crushing grip of a tyrant.

"Brooks, we'll begin soon," Dr. Yancey said. "Looks like a packed house. I wanted to ask you about your character Anton from *Long and Winding Road* and whether you were influenced by Atticus Finch from *To Kill a Mockingbird*? We'll start the Q&A there."

"Spoiler alert," Brooks said, his laughter crowding the room. "I was!"

Dr. Yancey managed a trickle of a smile.

"Did William tell you he's signing at Burke & Burke?" Brooks asked. "It's with the editor who brokered that huge deal in the papers."

"When did this happen, Professor Lansing?" she questioned, never calling him by his first name.

"Very recently," William said. "I was going to stop by your office and tell you."

"Color me surprised," she said, although her face didn't indicate any emotion whatsoever. "And this is for that opus you've been toiling over?"

"Devil's Hopyard."

"Like the park," she said, but became distracted by the sounds emerging from Brooks's stomach. "Are you all right, Brooks?"

Sweat poured from Brooks's forehead and he scrunched up his nose. The sounds continued, as if animals were fighting inside his body. A sudden fart caused both Dr. Yancey and William to cover their noses.

"Excuse me," Brooks yelped, and dashed away.

He fled to the bathroom, where he stayed for twenty minutes. Finally, Dr. Yancey went over to knock on the door.

"Brooks," she snapped, after he refused to answer her knocks.

A sad voice came from under the crack. "Must've ate something real, real bad. Hoo boy. Don't think I can go on."

Dr. Yancey crept away from the door, as if she was afraid of being exposed to whatever Brooks was unlucky enough to have come across.

"This is a disaster," she said to William, fingering her pearls. "We've been promoting his reading all semester."

"I can go on in his place."

Dr. Yancey looked as if she wanted to slap him.

"I have pages to read from my novel, I always carry them."

She narrowed her eyes, gauging his worthiness.

"Come," she finally said, taking his arm and leading him up on the stage. The audience of hundred or so people, a healthy mix of faculty and students, settled into their seats. Dr. Yancey stood at the podium, prepped her glasses low on her nose, and tapped on the microphone.

"I want to thank everyone for coming to the first of our faculty readings this semester. I know you are all eager to hear from our very own Brooks Jessup, whose brilliant novel *The Long and Winding Road* has gotten rave reviews and made him a writer to watch. Unfortunately,

Brooks seems to have come down with a bug and will have to reschedule his reading, but in his place, we have our esteemed colleague Professor William Lansing, whose novel, *Devil's Hopyard,* is upcoming from Burke & Burke Publishing. Please give him a warm welcome."

She clapped along with the audience and motioned for him to come over. He clenched the pages in his hand and took her place at the microphone.

"Thank you, Dr. Yancey, and first, I hope that my fellow professor Brooks Jessup has a speedy recovery. I'll try to fill his boat shoes today."

A smattering of laughs came from the audience, who all knew that Brooks *only* wore boat shoes.

William looked out at the crowd, breathed in the moment, and uncrumpled his pages.

"This will be the first I'm reading it to an audience," he said quietly, as if to himself. "My novel *Devil's Hopyard,* well, let's be honest—my third child—has been a part of me for a very long time. And now I'm just a few chapters away from finishing. It's surreal. Sometimes I think about writing it forever, for the plot to keep unfolding, but I know it must end, like all things. For once I had figured out the ending, I knew I'd soon have to learn to let it go." A knot of sadness gripped William's throat, but he wasn't going to let it ruin his moment. "I'll be reading from a later chapter today, a very important one. Where one character learns that what he believed to be true from the start was far from it. And this sends him into a bout of madness. He questions his own sanity, his culpability. Could he be responsible for *murder*?" William cleared his throat, his finger on the first line of the chapter, raising his voice.

> "This morning when he woke up, he was a different man. He looked in the mirror and was no longer the man he used to be. His hair had changed color, blond now, full of waves. He was

younger, leaner, looking more like the boy who sat in the back of the classroom than the professor himself. But maybe that is who he really was all along. He realizes this as he begins the day that will define the rest of his life. The day he'll take the girl to the shack in Devil's Hopyard . . . but won't allow her to ever leave."

27

NOT HAVING EATEN lunch yet, Kyle found a spot at the bar in the Royal Wee and ordered a turkey club while he continued reading *Devil's Hopyard.* The place had a publike feel, Patriots and Red Sox paraphernalia on the walls and an empty pool table in the back, its felt eroding. A few regulars were spread out at various tables and the Pixies quietly played from the jukebox. The bartender vaguely resembled William's daughter Alicia, but Kyle had met the twins only once and that was a long time ago so he couldn't be sure. He'd question her once he finished his lunch, since he was eager to find out what happened next in the manuscript anyway and figured he could use a break from being a detective after the weird experience with Mia's mother. He opened the book to chapter 27.

> This morning when he woke up, he was a different man. He looked in the mirror and was no longer the man he used to be. His hair had changed color, blond now, full of waves. He was younger, leaner, looking more like the boy who sat in the back of

> the classroom rather than the professor himself. But maybe that is who he really was all along. He realizes this as he begins the day that will define the rest of his life. The day he'll take the girl to the shack in Devil's Hopyard . . . but won't allow her to ever leave.

There it was, evidence planted by William to make Kyle appear guilty, although he hadn't used Kyle's name yet. Evidently, this was William's plot twist three quarters into the book—the professor no longer the villain, that title taken over by his protégé. Kyle read on as the prose, strangely, switched to first person.

> Up until now, I have imagined myself to be someone I'm not, someone I aspired to be—my professor, my mentor. Who may have guided me away from a path of drugs and crime for the time being, but the truth is that our true selves never change. Those born rotten are forever waiting to spoil. The things I wrote about Mia before were just fantasies. This is REAL.
>
> I see her in class, a few feet away, no one else in the room yet. We haven't spoken since our knock-down, drag-out fight in the Commons. She will NOT look my way. I tell her I've hunted the campus all night looking for her. She asks if it was to apologize, and I tell her yes even though I know it's not true. It is she who should be apologizing to me.
>
> "Let's skip class," I say. "There is a place I want to take you to."
>
> "I think I might know where you mean," she says. "But you'll get in trouble for leaving."
>
> "So will you."
>
> "You'll be in more trouble."
>
> She's wearing a crop top and has just washed her hair, not even waiting till it dried. She procures a joint from her bra and dashes

out the door. I follow her down the hallway as another student watches us go, and we burst out on the quad into the pouring rain.

"Is this place indoors?" she asks, and I nod.

We get into my car and I'm nervous behind the wheel. I steal a kiss. I know from now on that it is the last kiss she'll give me without being forced. But this is what she deserves. She used me and every other guy she'd been with, all of us trophies, none of us real loves. I loved her with all of my heart, so now I will take hers.

We enter Devil's Hopyard as the rain ramps up. It's hard to see the trails in front of us, but I know the way. I've gone down these paths many times before in anticipation of today, and I could get there blindfolded. When we reach the shack, I see it's surrounded by briar patches and overgrown weeds, hidden by nature. Nature is working with me.

She gets out of the car and becomes swallowed by the rain, her knees knocking together as she shivers by the door to the shack. I've added locks and a dead bolt that only I have the keys to, and I open the door to her new home. Inside smells damp. There is a mattress with a blanket, a small CD player with batteries installed, and a pair of handcuffs attached to a clasp under the floorboards and tucked into the blanket out of sight.

"How romantic," she says, but she's being sarcastic. She goes over to the CD player and pushes Play. Classical music comes out from the small speakers, Bach's *The Well-Tempered Clavier.* "Not really my taste." She turns off the music and sits on the bed. She finds the handcuffs. "Kinky," she says, holding up one end. She takes off her shirt and handcuffs herself, securing it tight and doing most of the work for me.

"Come over to the bed," she says, with a curl of her finger.

I shake my head.

"Why not?" she asks, pouting.

" 'Cause you've been bad."

"So give me a spanking."

"You deserve worse than that."

"Why?"

"Because you don't love me."

"I'm too young to fall in love. And that's okay. This doesn't have to be love, it can just be for now."

"But you'll go away one day. You'll leave me. I know it."

I back up toward the door and take the CD player with me. "You didn't appreciate the music I chose anyway."

A worry line in the shape of a lightning bolt appears on her forehead.

"Where do you think you're going?" she asks.

"This is so you can see the mistake you've made, so you can learn from it. So you'll know how it feels to be rejected."

I open the door and let in a biblical-size flood of rain. She stares at me, unsure if I'm kidding but leaning toward the fact that I'm serious.

"I'll scream," she says, tears in her eyes now, her face flush with fear.

"No you won't," I tell her, whipping out a dirty cloth from my pocket. I step toward her and she puts up her free hand in defense. I grab it and cuff her with the other end of the handcuffs. She snarls and tries to bite my arm, but I stuff the cloth into her mouth and tie it behind her head. Then I kiss her on the mouth, tasting cloth. Her screams are nothing more than quiet muffles. She realizes now that this is far from a game. I will leave her to think about what she's done to me. Before I shut the door, I zero in on her rapidly beating heart and whisper, "Soon."

Then I slam the door and lock the dead bolt. I collect all the brushwood around the shack so it's camouflaged even more and drive away into a rain that is finally starting to cease.

"YOU SURE ARE into whatever it is you're reading," the bartender said. She wore a tattered Ramones T-shirt, her dyed-white hair pinned up in a bun. She cleaned a glass with disdain. "What's it about?"

Kyle glanced up, not ready to be thrust back into reality. He had entered *Devil's Hopyard* and lost all sense of place and time. He hated to admit it, but that was usually the mark of a writer with true talent.

"It's hard to explain the plot," he said, making sure to cover up the title printed in italics on the top page. He didn't know whether she had seen it or not.

"I'm always looking for a good book," she said. "My father's a writer, he's at work on his debut novel now."

"Your father wouldn't happen to be William Lansing, would he?"

She stopped cleaning the glass and poked her tongue into her cheek.

"I'm Brett Swenson," he said, choosing not to reveal who he really was in case she recognized the name Kyle Broder from years ago. "Your father is signing with me at Burke & Burke Publishing."

He extended his hand and she shook it, hers sweaty and with a powerful grip.

"Alicia, nice to meet you."

He saw elements of William in her face, mostly in her smile that struggled to stay upright. She already had faint traces of jowls from frowning.

"I'm doing a profile on Professor Lansing, it's pretty standard for new authors who we feel will have lasting careers with us. It's best if he doesn't know about it."

"And why's that?"

"I don't want the profile to be colored by his input. Do you have a few minutes?"

She gave a laugh and gestured around. "As you can see, we're booming."

A heavy-set couple sat in the back and tore into their hamburgers. At the bar, an old man sipped what looked to be milk.

"I'd like to know more about this town, since your father spent so much of his life here."

"*Killingworth?* You got about a minute, that should cover it."

"Humor me."

"How about a beer while I'll tell you?" she said. He nodded and she poured a pint. "Old Dad's about to become famous, huh?"

"Could happen. So how would you describe Killingworth?"

She tapped her chin. "Well, let's see. Typical small New England town, blue collar as opposed to wealthy, but we're changing some. Got a fancy new wine and cheese shop on Main."

"I saw it." He took out a notepad and pretended to scribble down some stuff. "Anything of note ever happen here?"

"How you mean?"

"Something that ever made the papers? Small towns like this usually have some buried secrets."

She placed her hand on her hip. "What's this gotta do with my dad?"

"It's just to give a sense of background."

She popped a piece of gum in her mouth, chewing slowly. Had he pushed things too far? Was he being obvious? He had no choice but to continue pressing.

"I heard about a girl who went missing here years ago," he said carefully. "She was a student at Bentley College, where your father teaches."

Alicia took some milk from the fridge and topped off the old man at the end of the bar, who resembled William S. Burroughs. Burroughs gave an appreciative nod.

"Her name was Mia Evans," Kyle said.

"Course I remember that. I had just started high school at the time. Whole town had a curfew for weeks. I remember sneaking out once, thinking I might be abducted."

"What happened to her?"

Alicia shrugged her shoulders. She picked up a remote and changed the TV channel to a soccer match.

"What's the point of soccer?" she asked. "Score is zero to zero and it's almost over."

"I couldn't agree more," he said, ratcheting up his flirting by extending his smile. "Give me football any day. You a Pats fan?"

"Sure am. Pats are the best team of this century, no one can argue that."

Even though Kyle was a die-hard Green Bay fan, he played along. "And Brady is by *far* the best quarterback."

She licked her teeth in agreement.

"Nothing bad probably happened to that girl back then," Alicia finally said. "She had a pill-popping mother, and she was losing her scholarship at Bentley because she was flunking out. She just ran away. It's happened before."

"How do you know that for sure?"

"She had plenty of time as the face of this town," Alicia said, her cheeks getting red. "Fliers and posters and constant sympathy for months. People crying who didn't even *know* her. And they made her into this angel. Sweet Mia Evans, what a tragedy."

"She wasn't an angel?"

"No way. By fifteen she was hanging out in truck stops, selling E, going to raves with guys she'd pick up. She went to my high school, although not when I was there. Still, she was spoken about *a lot.* A legend, but not for any good reasons."

"That doesn't mean she deserved to go missing."

Alicia snarled and rubbed at a yin-yang tattoo on the side of her neck. "I didn't say that. I just hate when someone comes off very different from who they really are."

"She was a student of your father's, wasn't she?"

Alicia rubbed the yin-yang tattoo harder. A swelling surrounded its shape, making it look as if she'd gotten a hickey right on the tattoo.

"My dad didn't know her," she mumbled.

"Oh, I thought she was in his class—"

"No!" She slapped the counter, causing Burroughs's glass of milk to wobble a bit. She rubbed her forehead. "Sorry, got a bitch of a migraine coming on. That's why a bar is a good place for me to work, barely any light all day."

"What else can you tell me about your father?" he asked. "I'm sorry we got off track. When I brought up that I was going to Killingworth to my boss, he mentioned the missing girl. Just had her on my brain—"

"S'all right," she said, waving him off and pinching the bridge of her nose. "This is a bitch of one." She closed her eyes, grimacing.

"You have a twin brother, don't you?"

One eye rose, skeptical. "Yeah, Bill. So?"

"Is he here? Can I talk to him?"

"I'm not his keeper," she said flatly. "He comes and goes. Not here now, but you're welcome to keep spending your money on beers if you want to wait for him."

She pointed to his half-empty glass. Kyle chugged it down and signaled for another.

"I'll let you get back to that book you were reading in the meantime," she said with a smirk. "What was the title again?"

"Doesn't have one," he replied. "It hasn't been published yet."

"Well, from the way you couldn't take your eyes off of it, I'm guessing it'll be a bestseller."

She poured him another beer and left it foaming in front of his nose. He took a frothy sip and left a good tip as she wet a hand towel and draped it over her forehead. She leaned back, masked by the towel, and eased into the groove between the cash register and the top shelf liquors.

Kyle plunged back into *Devil's Hopyard.* Although he wished he'd been able to get more out of William's daughter, he was satisfied by his detective abilities so far. With each subject, he was only getting better.

He was also *dying* to read farther into the manuscript, about to inch closer and closer to whatever dark fantasy William dreamed up to be its end.

28

DEVIL'S HOPYARD–CHAPTER 28

I made sure to head to the shack in Devil's Hopyard every day with her favorite foods. I know she loved sour apple Blow Pops, so I left a bag in reach, among other more nutritional items. When I got there, she wouldn't eat or drink anything. The cloth had slipped from her mouth, and her lips had become dry and started to blister and tear. She couldn't sit up straight.

"I'm killing myself so I won't give you the satisfaction of doing it," she said, a knife in my heart.

"Who says I want to kill you?" I asked, but she was right. How else could this end but in death? First hers, eventually mine. Even if I didn't want to admit that to myself.

After she passed out, I raised her skirt to get a view of her heart-shaped tattoo, no bigger than a quarter. I traced it with my finger well into the middle of the night.

Later on, I thought I remembered going to sleep in my own

bed, but when I woke up I was strapped to a different one. It smelled damp. At first I thought I might have passed out in the shack, since it had been an exhausting last few days. But this dampness felt more like I was in a basement. I could turn my neck slightly and saw a tiny, rectangular window with bars, letting in the only light.

A metal door swung open, and a massive bald man came toward me. I struggled to get out of the straps, but they were tight and made my limbs sore. The bald man removed a giant syringe and stuck me in the arm. I wanted to scream, but my voice was hoarse. A nurse walked in, metal clipboard in hand. She spoke, sounding like an echo. The drugs were coursing through my blood, but I'd set a high bar for myself ingesting everything under the sun, so whatever sedative they'd given hadn't knocked me out yet.

"What happened?" I managed to ask, the words slowly coming out. I could see them traveling through the air.

The nurse looked as if she wanted to spit on me.

"You admitted yourself," she said.

"That's . . . impossible. Why would I do that?"

She consulted her clipboard. "It says you were a harm to yourself."

"MYSELF?" I yelled. "What about her? She's waiting for me!"

The nurse gave the bald man a signal, and he jabbed the syringe into my arm again.

"She'll . . . die," I said, before a *whoosh* battered my eardrums and I was sucked down a drain.

KYLE'S PHONE BUZZED. He stopped reading the manuscript only to see if it was Jamie. As much as he knew he had to come to Connecticut, he didn't like the idea of her alone in the city, wide-open for William to possibly strike. He was surprised to see Sierra's name on his cell instead. He went to answer, but then realized it would distract him from finishing *Devil's Hopyard.* He *had* to know what happened next.

So now it looked as if William was using Kyle's time spent in an institution as a plotline. Rather clever, he thought. In reality, he wound up in one after being found naked in Devil's Hopyard, but he never knew of a shack in the park, and Mia had already been missing for a while. And yes, he'd also quit drugs and then relapsed like the character in the book—how could he not? Losing Mia on top of being questioned by the police had been too much to handle. So he took a cocktail of bad stuff. He wandered the park thinking he was werewolf and howling at the moon. This family of hikers came across him shivering in a ditch, his skin blue. But he wasn't strapped in when he woke up in the institution, at least not like William described. The straps were only around his wrists. And they had only given him a *small* sedative. Sure, there had also been an orderly who was massive and bald, but weren't most orderlies massive and bald? More important, he never would have admitted himself because he hadn't done anything crazy like handcuff and leave Mia Evans in a shack in Devil's Hopyard!

Frustrated and annoyed with the way the story was proceeding, he turned back to where he left off.

When I woke up again, a familiar face sat in the chair across from my bed. Professor Lansing, looking genuinely worried. I wasn't strapped in anymore.

"I told them that wasn't necessary," the professor said, indicating my wrists.

I sat up, my head heavy like a medicine ball.

"I can't be here."

I tried to get out of bed, my legs buckling under me. I collapsed to the floor that was filled with bugs and grime.

The professor held out a hand and helped me up.

"I have to get out of here," I said, tugging at his collar. "I left her . . . it's been days."

"Sssshhh," he said, with his finger over his lips. "I've signed your release. I told them you were having a hard time in school and with . . . what happened to Mia . . . it's was only natural you might snap."

Hearing her name made me weep, deep sobs that felt like they'd been buried for years.

"How many days have I been here?" I asked, praying that it hadn't been long enough for her to die.

He held up two fingers. "Two nights."

I counted how long it had been since I'd seen her eat. Four days. She had enough food and drink within reach to survive, but what if she was serious about killing herself? I just wanted to scare her. Show her how devoted I was. Spend time alone with her heart—not make it stop.

"I need to go," I said, taking another step. I crashed right to floor again.

"No, you need another day of rest before they'll let you go. You are pumped full of drugs."

"But then what if she dies . . . ?" I began, debating whether to tell him what I'd done. This man I looked up to, who'd never see me in the same light again. I couldn't. She had enough food. She wouldn't let herself starve. No human could do that to themselves.

"She's already gone," he said, guiding me back to the bed.

"She's gone?"

"At least for now. You being here one more day won't help bring her back if she's . . . run away. You need to focus on healing yourself."

"Thank you for helping me, Professor Lansing," I said, eating my tears.

"I hope I'm not wrong," he said.

"Wrong about what?"

He swallowed, his Adam's apple bobbing up and down. "Having you released."

In his eyes, it was as if he KNEW.

"I'm better now," I said. "I had lost myself."

"You've crossed some invisible line," the professor said. "And you feel as if you've come to a place you never thought you'd come to. And you don't know how you got here. It's a strange place that has caused you to consider death and annihilation. I'm ad-libbing a bit, but that's from Raymond Carver's 'Whoever Was Using This Bed.' "

"I was just reading that story. I skipped ahead in your syllabus."

I blinked and he was at the door.

"I hope I'm right about this," he said, his eyes downcast and saddened. Then he walked out.

KYLE LOOKED UP from the manuscript because he heard the front door to the bar open. He checked to see if it was Bill, but the mailman came in instead. He glanced at his watch and saw that it was three o'clock. He was about to return to *Devil's Hopyard* but then thought about what he'd just finished reading. The institution he'd actually wound up in was state run and a nightmare, since he lost his insurance after his father died. It had been two days of his life he never cared to think about again. The only saving grace was that he'd been too zoned out to care what was happening, the whole experience a blur. He could recall snippets of patients screaming, mutilating themselves, even going to the bathroom on the floor. After the drugs wore off, he could also remember William coming by to tell him he was being released.

"I'm vouching for you," William had said. "You don't deserve to be here."

"I had lost myself," Kyle replied, at his lowest. Life seemed pointless.

"I've always looked to literature when times were tough," William continued. "My wife found the church to fulfill her, my god is a good book."

He passed Kyle a copy of *East of Eden*. It was a brand-new edition with Oprah's seal of approval and a tree on the cover.

"Let this be your drug," William said.

Kyle held the book in his hands. The pages smelled really good.

"Read this and write an essay for me, Kyle."

Kyle rubbed his head, as if trying to erase any lingering drugs that were still clattering around inside.

"What should the essay be on?" he asked.

"Whatever you want it to be. The essay will count for any classes you've missed. That way you won't fail the semester. I'm also hoping it gives you focus."

Kyle's lip quivered. His dad dying, Mia vanishing, the cops harassing him, and now time spent in a state facility strapped to a bed—he'd taken so many wrong turns he thought it'd be impossible to find himself again. At least William cared enough to try to get him on the road back to normal.

"Thank you for helping me," Kyle said, his chin on William's shoulder as he let the tears go. William stood there patiently, allowing Kyle to grieve.

"I hope I'm not making a mistake," William said, once Kyle stopped sobbing.

"With what?"

"Having you released, Kyle."

William looked at him threateningly, but it had worked—Kyle never touched hard drugs again. He spent Pepsi-fueled hours reading *East of Eden* and writing a really good essay on spirituality in literature. He wrote about how the characters each found their own versions of God, and in his conclusion, he wrote about how he came across a feeling of a higher power while sitting on the Green with springtime finally in the air. Free of his winterish past, he'd reached the end of *East of Eden* and read the word—*timshel*—out loud. He remembered the professor saying that the word referred to man's ability to choose between good and evil. Right there he saw two divergent paths laid out before him: one dark and treacherous, full of addiction, sin, and self-loathing; the other lined with tall bookcases and a life devoted to literature. He stood up and walked into literature's welcoming arms, never swaying again.

STILL AT THE bar, Kyle reread chapter 28 because there were so many parallels to what actually happened in his life. Since there were records showing he'd spent time at a state facility, anyone reading *Devil's Hopyard* might really start to believe he'd been the guilty one and not William.

He stopped himself from thinking any more of these insane thoughts. He needed to calm down. First off, *Devil's Hopyard* hadn't been published and the likelihood it ever would be was slim. Sure, there was a chance William could self-publish it and gain an audience. Authors certainly had successes with self-publishing, but the majority didn't. There was no reason to think that William's wild accusations could get him in trouble.

Kyle looked down and saw he'd gone through three pints of beer already. He had to stay sober enough to question Bill whenever the guy finally showed up. William's wife was also on his list to interview, provided William wasn't home.

He flipped through the remaining pages William had given him, about fifty or so left. He knew there wouldn't be a resolution when he got to the end of those pages, because in real life, a resolution hadn't occurred yet. Still, he had to know where the plot went, at least if it answered what happened to Mia and whether she died or managed to escape and then kept running. He had a bad feeling that the fictionalized version of him was about to "cross some invisible line" that he could never return from, just as Raymond Carver ominously wrote.

" 'Nother one?" Alicia asked, coming over to clear the empties. She'd taken to wearing dark sunglasses indoors to survive her migraine.

"Just a club soda. Thanks."

"How's the book coming along?" she asked, and sprayed some club soda into a glass for him. "Looks like you're about to reach the end."

"I hope so," Kyle said, as she tended to another customer and he got back to *Hopyard.*

I burst out of the institution into the sunniest day Connecticut had seen in a while. When I entered the nuthouse, it'd been rainy and cold, so it almost seemed as if I'd spent an entire season stuck inside. I got in my car and drove right over to the shack in Devil's Hopyard, praying to an unknown entity that Mia would be all right.

When I reached the shack, I moved away the surrounding brushwood and listened with my ear flush against the door. No sound. I put the key in the lock, quaking, and unlatched the dead bolt. When I swung open the door, the smell hit me right away and I knew what had occurred. Flies had already taken to her body, but she seemed peaceful, as if she'd just closed her eyes and never got a chance to open them again.

I was angry and trashed the shack, flinging the mattress and trying to rip up the sheets. Mia had spilled to the floor, and I spied the heart-shaped tattoo on her ass. It was the first thing I ever noticed about her. She'd bent over in class to pick up a pen that she dropped and wasn't wearing any underwear. I was writing an answer on the board at the time, but it must have looked like chicken scratch. All I could pay attention to had been the little black heart she'd permanently etched into her left butt cheek.

And now it had revealed itself again. I think I must have vomited, but once I got myself together I whipped out my key chain with my Swiss Army knife attached to it and began to cut out that tattooed heart. Just to keep a piece of her with me because I already missed her so. I know it sounds awful, but like a surgeon, I made careful incisions, then I found a pan I'd left in the shack to cook eggs and made a fire outside. I fried up her piece of flesh, her other heart, and took little bites so it would last as long as possible. We had been reading *East of Eden* in class before this all started, and I thought of the way the novel ended, since Professor Lansing always liked to test us on the final sentences of great classics.

"*Timshel,*" I said out loud, as I swallowed the last bite of heart. I knew the word referred to man's ability to choose between good and evil. I had written an essay for the professor arguing that we were all descendants of Cain, and like Cain we had free will to decide between good and evil. But as much as we inherited Cain's curse, we also inherited the ability to redeem ourselves. In his weakness and filth, Cain made a choice and murdered his brother; but no matter how deep-rooted the sin, there was always a chance for redemption. If you improve yourself, you will be forgiven; if you don't, sin will rest at the door. I realized I had to accept my sins as well and work toward conquering them.

I'd done terrible things; there was no going back.

I could only go forward.

• • •

KYLE SLAMMED THE manuscript closed, completely freaked-out now. Here he was just thinking about the last lines of *East of Eden* and how they saved him freshman year, and now his character in *Devil's Hopyard* was going through the same revelation. He scanned the bar to see if William was watching. He pictured the bastard rubbing his hands together in delight. Just as he was about to make a mad dash for his rental car to flee Connecticut in fright, he realized that William had obviously used his essay to influence the character's angst. William was a master at fucking with someone's head, and Kyle knew he needed to stop getting so worked up over what was obviously fiction.

He was about to dive back into the final pages when the front door to the Royal Wee opened again. A wiry guy with spooked eyes entered.

Jackpot. It had been over a decade since Kyle had seen him last, but despite the receding hairline, Bill looked just as odd as he remembered.

29

BILL WENT RIGHT over to his sister. They spoke in hushed tones so Kyle couldn't hear what they were saying, but it seemed to be about her migraines. Bill felt her forehead, rather tenderly, almost like a lover would, and fixed some frazzled strands of hair escaping from her bun. She hugged him, and the two rocked together for about a minute, as if they were relieved to be reunited. Then Alicia whispered something in her brother's ear and pointed at Kyle.

Kyle quickly glanced away, pretending to be absorbed in whatever was on the TV. He could feel the energy shift in the place as Bill sidled up next to him.

"My sister says you had questions about our dad?" Bill asked. He had a ghostly pallor as if he was allergic to the sun. Purpling skin, almost translucent. Bags the size of quarters under his eyes. A ball of what Kyle guessed to be chew tucked in his bottom lip.

"Yes, I'm Brett Swenson," Kyle said, extending his hand.

Bill had one of those creepy handshakes where the person's hand felt like it melted in your palm. A chill crawled up Kyle's back.

"Bill Lansing," Bill replied, chewing away. "Come on, let's go to my office."

Bill's "office" was a room in the back about as welcoming as a sketchy van with tinted windows. Kyle sensed that something bad had transpired there, but then he wondered if that had to do with the way he viewed Bill. The one time he'd met the guy was at a charity function at Bentley. Bill must have been about fifteen or sixteen at the time, and his parents had stuffed him into a suit that he clearly wasn't comfortable in. Kyle had gone to smoke a cigarette and found him outside. Bill had trapped a wren in his hands and was slowly pulling apart the feathers of the chirping bird.

"Hey, I don't think the little guy likes that," Kyle said, trying to play it cool since he knew it was the professor's son.

"But I like it," Bill said, plucking another feather and letting it float to the ground. The wren now had a patch of raw pink skin peeking through.

"Seriously, man, that bird can't fend for himself."

"Fuck it," Bill said, and tossed the bird into the sky. The wren seemed confused and took a second before spreading its wings and fleeing the scene.

Bill rose and got in Kyle's face. "Are you happy now?"

Kyle took a drag. "I'm elated."

"Well, fuck you too."

Bill exhaled a hot spurt of air from his nostrils and took off. In the moment, Kyle recalled that people who hurt animals tended to have psychopathic tendencies. He should've realized it was an unfortunate trait that ran in the Lansing family.

"You look familiar," Bill said now, as he got comfortable on a dusty couch and picked up a pipe filled with marijuana. "Smoke?"

Kyle didn't want to, but he was game to anything that might help Bill divulge some Lansing secrets.

"Thanks." He took a hit of what was clearly schwag, its taste like tar, criminal in his lungs. He hoped it was actually pot.

"Yeah, you do look familiar. Licia said you're an editor working on my dad's book?"

"Yes and I'm here to do a profile. Where he came from, some background of Bentley and of Killingworth too."

Bill was more interested in his pipe. He tapped out the ash and packed another. "Yeah, Licia mentioned you were asking about things in this town."

"I read about a girl who went missing here years ago," Kyle said, not wanting to waste any more time.

Bill didn't answer right away. He took a bunch of hits from his pipe. Then he glided his hand through the air, finding it fascinating. He let out a chuckle, similar to his father's, soft at first until it echoed throughout the tiny office.

"Her name was Mia Evans," Kyle said, feeling a little faint from the hit. He held on to the edge of a table to make sure he stayed upright.

"Yeah, I remember that name," Bill said. "Pretty girl who just up and vanished."

"She was a student of your father's."

"My father's had a lot of students, but I'm sure you know that."

"Did it hurt him when she disappeared? Did he talk about it at all?"

Bill pointed at Kyle as he rose from the couch. It seemed like he had something important to say but then forgot it by the time he stood up.

"And why are you asking about this now?"

Bill made his way over to a small fridge in the corner and grabbed himself a beer. He opened it with his teeth and spit the bottle cap in Kyle's direction.

"Because it's very similar to what your dad wrote about in his book," Kyle said. *"Devil's Hopyard."*

This caught Bill's attention. His tell was an eyebrow raise, ever so slight.

"I'm curious to know if this girl's disappearance influenced his work," Kyle said.

"So why don't you ask him?"

"I thought I'd find out from the people who know him best."

Bill took a swig of beer that emptied half the bottle. He wiped his mouth with the back of his hand, never taking his eyes off of Kyle.

"Yeah, she was a student of his. He was real broken up when they couldn't find her. But the whole town was, even people who didn't know her."

"Did *you* know her?"

Bill killed the rest of his beer and then spit the ball of chew into the bottle. He placed it down among similar empties.

"Nope. She was just a name, nothing more."

"But she was more to your father?"

Bill started rubbing his chin, repeating the motion over and over while staring in Kyle's eyes.

"She was just his student," Bill said, nodding. "And like all his students, I'm sure he cared very deeply about her well-being. My father is a good man. He's a mentor to those lucky enough to have him as their professor. Wouldn't you say so?"

"Why would I say so?" Kyle gulped.

Bill wagged his finger, a devilish grin creeping up his face.

A knock on the door came at just the right time.

"*Entrez,*" Bill said, as Alicia entered.

"Billy," she said, with an emergence of tears, "I need you for a sec."

"You okay, Licia?" he asked, his tone of voice shifting from threatening to genuine concern.

"Just come here," she said, and turned to Kyle. "Please excuse us for a minute."

Bill didn't acknowledge Kyle as he followed her out of the office and shut the door.

Kyle could feel his heart beating rapidly. He didn't know what to make of Bill's answers except for the fact that the guy knew more than he was letting on. Alicia had been adamant that Mia wasn't a student of William's, but that had obviously been a lie. He wondered how much the twins knew about what happened and if either was complicit in her disappearance. Even kooky Karen Evans spoke about their weird bond and how something was clearly *off* about them.

He sat on the dusty couch to get his head straight, the hit of pot plus the three pints of beer already taking hold. Here he'd set out to stay sober and couldn't even follow through for one full day. He laid his head back on a pillow and stared at the small office. On the wall hung an M. C. Escher poster of two hands drawing one another, each necessary to create the other. He looked closer, as an overwhelming sense of déjà vu crowded the room. He'd come across this artwork before. He realized he'd seen it in this very spot.

He lay back down on the couch and traveled back over ten years to a moment at the Royal Wee when he'd drunk too much and had to be carried to this same couch, its smell of stale corn chips and spilled drinks overpowering. The bartender had put him there and asked whom to call. Kyle must've murmured Professor Lansing's name because an hour later, William was shaking his shoulder.

"Come," William said. "I'm taking you home."

In the car, Kyle was talking about the Escher poster. He described the two hands drawing one another in the dream he had. He wondered which hand had been drawn first if both were necessary to create each other.

"There's blood on your knuckles," William said. "I can take you to the infirmary."

Kyle shook his head. "I punched a wall. I was angry."

“You and your girlfriend had a fight?” William asked.

The night was dark with barely a sliver of moon. Kyle stared out at the endless blackened expanse.

“Mia doesn’t love me,” Kyle said.

William took out a handkerchief and handed it to Kyle. “You’re bleeding all over your clothes.” Kyle mopped up the blood pouring from his knuckles.

“Give me that, I’ll dispose of it,” William said, taking the bloody handkerchief.

“You’re bleeding too,” he said to William, and pointed at his collar painted with a splash of red.

“It’s nothing. Nicked myself while shaving.” William folded the reddened collar so it was tucked in.

“Your elbow patch is torn too.” Kyle stuck his finger through a hole in William’s elbow.

William wrenched off his blazer and threw it in the backseat. He pulled the car over to the shoulder and stopped. He took Kyle by the shoulders and turned him so the two were facing.

“You called me tonight to pick you up from the bar. I took you home to your dorm. I was with you into the night because you were puking.”

“I haven’t puked,” Kyle said, looking around to make sure that was true.

“You will. And I stayed with you. That’s what you’ll say if anyone asks.”

“Who will ask?”

“I’m trying to help you, Kyle,” William said, raising his voice. “You were underage drinking in a bar. You caused a disturbance. You already have the police on your radar. Do what I say.”

Kyle quickly rolled down the side window, stuck his head out, and vomited on the road. “Shit,” he said, wiping his mouth.

“Good, Kyle. Let it all out. Very good.”

Kyle could barely remember being taken back to his dorm room. His roommate went home every weekend so no one else was there. He was tucked into his bed, and William left a bottle of water on the side table.

"I have to go now," William said. "I have something to take care of."

"Mmmmm," Kyle replied, his head heavy on the pillow and the room spinning. The two drawing hands floated in and out of his thoughts, furiously stenciling in a race to see which would finish first.

Back on the couch at the Royal Wee, Kyle saw that the hands on the poster had been drawn to completion. He questioned how reliable memories were. Sometimes they could be fabricated simply because it made for a better narrative. This office felt so familiar: its mildewed smell, the poster on the wall of the hands. Had the night William had driven him back to his dorm been the night the guy killed Mia? Had he picked Kyle up from the bar only to use him as an alibi? Had he kept a handkerchief with Kyle's blood on it to frame him if need be? What was William's plan? It exhausted Kyle to think that he'd lost all sense of what was real and what was fiction anymore.

He lurched to the small window in the back, opened it, and threw up on the side of the building, watching his sickness drip down.

The door opened and Bill entered on a cell phone.

"Just thought I'd let you know what's going on," Bill said into the cell, and shoved it in his pocket.

"I'm not feeling so good," Kyle said, his forehead lined with sweat.

"I think it's time for you to go," Bill said with a firm nod. "Show yourself out."

Kyle got out of the office as fast as he could. By the bar, Alicia was scowling while cleaning a dirty glass with a rag.

"Billy tell you what you wanted to hear?" she asked, her eyes swollen. "Hope today gave you a good profile on my dad."

"Yeah . . . sure." He grabbed the manuscript from off the bar and tucked it under his arm. He had to wonder whether she'd flipped through the pages and told her brother what Kyle was reading. That William's editor had come here to verify how much of their father's fiction was actually the truth.

"I'll tell him you stopped by," she said. "Oh, give me your business card. I forgot your name. Kevin? Keith? Or was it . . . ?"

"I have to run," Kyle said, bolting out of the place just as heard his real name whispered from her lips. Or had he imagined that? He didn't know anymore. He tossed the manuscript into his rental car and took off without even paying attention to which way he was headed.

30

WILLIAM WAITED IN front of Jamie's apartment building, a walk-up on 110th and Central Park West. In his pants leg rattled a carefully concealed bone saw. He doubted she'd let him in if he buzzed, but he wasn't in a rush. His phone rang just as he spied an old lady making her way out. He ignored the call and held the door open for her as she passed him by, then he snuck inside. On the mailboxes he located Camden/Popplewell—1B, guessing Jamie's roommate might be British from the surname.

He knocked on the door and held on to two syringes in his pocket, ready to strike should Jamie open the door. Instead a sleepy woman in a bathrobe answered.

"Yes?" she asked in a shrill British accent. He'd been right about her last name.

"I'm looking for Jamie," he said, slouching. He gave himself a bit of a tremor for show, angling to appear as pathetic as possible.

"Oh, she's not here right now—"

"The outside door was open, I'm sorry for bothering you. I'm an investor in her design business. We had plans to meet, but I'm terribly early."

"I'm not sure when she'll be back," the woman said. She had long brown hair that went down to her waist, styled like a child would.

"Oh, you wouldn't have a glass of water? I've been walking all day."

She took a second to observe him. He clutched one of the syringes, ready for her as well if need be.

"Yes, let me get you one," she finally said, and headed inside. He closed the door behind him and locked it, releasing his grip on the syringe.

"I'm sorry to bother you," he called out. "I thought I'd walk through the park but I got so lost."

She returned with a glass that had chipped rainbow decals. The water looked like tap from the sink, slightly cloudy.

"No, it's good you woke me," she said, rubbing away her eye crust. "Sometimes my afternoon naps become a problem."

"I'm such an insomniac I'll take sleep anytime I can get it." He extended his hand. "I'm William. I really am sorry to bother you."

"Sybil," she said, with a bone-crushing grip. William thought that if he had to describe her to someone he'd say she was big boned. She could probably take him in a fight, but not if she was at a disadvantage from a needle in her neck. "What time was your meeting with Jamie?"

"In half an hour or so," he said, already sitting down in the living room area. Despite the small space, Jamie had obviously given the room her touch: prewar intricate crown moldings, antique ottomans, Manet posters in expensive frames. A room that could exist in any era. A fireplace was used as storage for books. He picked up *In Search of Lost Time.* The copy was worn and clearly read many times over. He turned to an underlined passage: *Love is a striking example of how little reality means to us.* He snapped the book shut, as if it had ripped open his mind and fumbled around inside.

"Is the Proust yours or Jamie's?" he asked, placing the book back in the fireplace.

"Oh, that's Jamie's. Her boyfriend's some big editor and she's always reading a book. Tryin' to impress him and all."

"Don't really like him, do you?"

She was taken aback but smiled.

"Is it so obvious? He's all right, real good-looking and all. The few times he's stayed over at our place he just came off like he thinks he's better than me."

She went to the refrigerator and pulled out a half-empty bottle of Chardonnay.

"Offer you a glass?" Sybil asked, shaking the remaining contents. "We can kill it."

"Kill it," he said, chuckling softly as the sound spread through the tiny apartment, folding into the nooks and crannies. "Yes, let's kill it."

WILLIAM LET SYBIL finish her glass of white before he injected her with the syringe. He had sat down next to her as she complained about her boyfriend, Erik, who didn't have a job while he was trying to get his food truck business off the ground. The problem being that she'd helped invest in it with the little savings she had two years ago and nothing had been accomplished yet.

"He's an *arse,*" Sybil said. "Cheated on me with this skank who waits tables at the diner up the block. Like, how fucked-up is it that I used to eat breakfast there all the time?"

"I abhor cheating," he said. "My wife . . . well, she had an affair."

"That's so sad," Sybil said, swaying. He assumed she'd started on the bottle of Chardonnay that morning.

"She fell in love with someone else," he said, but he was speaking about himself. "It ended as things often do, but she and I stayed together. I knew all about it the whole time, our kids too."

"Your children found out?" she asked, gulping the wine.

"Children know a lot more than you give them credit for. They sense things."

"I'm so sorry."

"I'm sorry too," he said, inserting the syringe into her thigh. One eye lightly twitched, but other than that she gave no indication that she'd been stabbed. The syringe was small. Injected the right way, it would feel like nothing more than a mosquito bite.

"This wine . . ." she said, with a yawn that never ended.

"Rest your head." He fluffed up a pillow and lay her down.

"Maybe for just for a minute."

Her eyes shut and she was still, paralyzed for the next six hours. He undid her bathrobe and pulled the neck of her shirt down until he could place his palm over her heart. It pumped with a steady beat, music to his ears. He took out a black Sharpie from his pocket and drew a perfect black heart over her real one, filling it in, making it resemble a tattoo. This had been the second black heart he'd drawn today, the owner of the first one knocked out in the trunk of his car. He had punched a hole to let in air.

It was a big trunk so there'd be room for two.

THE AFTERNOON WAS ending. Since it was mid-October, it began to get dark early. William sat watch over Sybil, poised for Jamie to return. He thought about the quote she had underlined in Proust's *In Search of Lost Time.*

Love is a striking example of how little reality means to us.

If he stood before God or the devil or whomever he might meet at the end of this life and was asked who his true love had been, he couldn't say Laura. He would say Mia without hesitation, and that was why everything from here on out had to go off without a hitch. She deserved this legacy. And he deserved to be able to give it to her . . .

His thoughts were interrupted by the sound of the front door opening and someone stepping inside. He picked up the syringe and attacked.

BRETT SWENSON HAD escaped from the office for his final cigarette of the workday. He'd told Darcy not to bother him, but sure enough, his cell was ringing with the name ASSISTANT. Darcy was his eighth assistant since he'd started at Burke & Burke. He never let himself grow attached because no one ever aspired to be an admin forever.

"I'll be back in two seconds," he snapped into the phone.

"You said to tell you if any packages came," she said, stringing the words together in one garbled spew.

"I meant if I was in the office."

"Oh—"

He hung up on her and lit a cigarette. The street was busy, people knocking into him, but he blocked them all out and focused on the beauty of a drag. He made love to that cigarette, his perfect two-minute meditation every three hours or so. He figured it was worth it to shave off a couple of years from the end of his life, having no desire to wither away in an old age home. *Make it quick and easy,* he confirmed with his higher power, the only time he'd ever prayed.

Upstairs, Darcy waited with a package in hand, manuscript-size.

"I'm sorry," she said, her head hanging low. "I just thought you'd want it because of who it's from."

He swiped it from her and saw the name on the return label: *PROF. WILLIAM LANSING.*

He dropped the package like it was full of snakes and stepped backward as if it might explode.

"What's inside?" he asked.

"I didn't look," Darcy said. The phone on her desk rang and she went to get it.

Brett was going to ask her to open it, but then changed his mind because he didn't like her thinking he was afraid. If she were always a little fearful of him, she'd work even harder.

He grabbed the package and went into his office. He shook it and felt the edges, realizing it was only paper. Unless a little anthrax had been tossed inside too.

"Ah hell." He tore it open and jammed his hand in.

Sssssnnnnaaaappppp.

He yanked away his throbbing hand that had been caught by a mousetrap. Blood dribbled down his arm as he released his swollen digits. He must've been screaming because Darcy came running inside.

"Fuck, get me some bandages," he yelled, shooing her out of the room. The manuscript had fallen to the floor. He picked it up and read the Post-it note, carefully written in calligraphy blood.

Surprise, dear editor!
There's still more Devil's Hopyard *to come.*
Just because you don't want to read any more
Does not mean that the story has ended.
Sincerely,
Your Author, W

31

KYLE DROVE TO Bentley College, just to clear his head. He had planned to question William's wife, Laura, next, but he needed to gather his thoughts first. First of all, he was clearly being framed for either the disappearance or murder of Mia Evans. William had been planning this for sometime now, and Kyle's recent success only accelerated the inevitable. Second, somehow the twins were involved. How much was uncertain since each told a very different story about William's relationship with Mia. And third, he'd have to make sure William wasn't home before he paid Laura a visit, although part of him wanted to come face-to-face with his enemy. William was baiting him and he was ready to bite. Maybe that was what brought him back to Bentley—the possibility he might run into his nemesis and surprise him with an attack.

He drove by the castle-like gray stone dorms, picturesque with a fine coating of snow. He pondered briefly on his four years there, the beginning so different from the end. *Devil's Hopyard* sat in the passenger seat, almost finished. So he parked and found a bench on the quad. He sat there with the manuscript in his lap, wondering if it had the answers to what might happen next. He turned to where he'd left off.

DEVIL'S HOPYARD—CHAPTER 31

When I woke up the next morning, I expected to see the same young man in the mirror I'd been seeing for some time: the one who'd left his girlfriend chained up in a shack while he went crazy in a nuthouse. But the mirror had been lying. Standing naked before me was the man I'd always been. Middle-aged with streaks of gray cut through his brown hair, the tiniest paunch visible despite daily runs and sparring with a boxing bag in the basement. A smile that could never fully develop no matter how hard he tried because from a very young age he knew the terrible things he was capable of: the strange desires, the fixation on hearts. He clutched his own that beat nervously, for he had aged twenty-five years overnight and turned back into the man he was most afraid of—the professor and no longer the student.

What else had he imagined? Could the girl in the shack still be alive?

Though he hated returning to his former self, the thought of Mia's beating heart enlivened him. He ran all the way to Devil's Hopyard, panting and sopping with sweat upon reaching the shack. His foot caught a rock and he fell to the ground, skinning his knee, the blood staining the rock that had taken him down. He went to unleash his anger on it, but then saw its shape, a perfectly etched heart in stone. He picked it up in awe and placed his lips on its grainy surface. He gave the rock a kiss and carried it to the shack.

Pressing his ear against the door, he heard rustling from inside. He was relieved to know it had all just been a terrible nightmare; Mia was still very much alive! But when he opened the door, she came for him. She had ripped out a chunk of flooring from the foundation to break free. Along with being handcuffed to the bedframe, she used her entire weight to charge at him. The corner of the bed knocked him in the temple, sending him to the ground. Her hands were still handcuffed, so she used her teeth as weapons. He looked up to see her lips smeared with blood, an eerie shade of red lipstick.

"I love you, I love you, I love you," he screamed, trying to fight her off. "I'm helping you! So you can see how bad you've been. So you can get your life back on track."

She spit in his face, speaking in tongues. Calling him the worst names imaginable, hating him with such a fire. This had all gone so wrong. She took a bite of his neck, and then he managed to pick up the heart-shaped rock, knowing what he had to do.

They had reached a point where only one of them would make it out of this predicament alive.

Does that sound familiar, Kyle Broder?????????????????????????????

KYLE SLAMMED THE manuscript shut. He'd been so absorbed in the tale that he hadn't noticed the snow falling at a faster pace, the manuscript frozen in his hands. He wasn't wearing gloves. Not a soul was walking around, the campus unnervingly quiet. In the distance, a shadow appeared down the path, coming closer. Because of the snow it was hard to make out a face, but he could tell it was a man about six feet tall with a normal build. *William.*

He reached into his pocket for any type of weapon, always carrying the Swiss Army knife attached to his Wisconsin Badgers key chain. He snapped the sharp knife open as the shadow drew nearer. Just as the shadow closed in, he rose to his feet, the knife in his grasp. But it was not his mentor, only another professor making his way through the flurries. Kyle excused himself and sank back to the bench, his head in his hands.

"What the fuck is your game?" he asked, quietly at first until he tipped his head back toward the bone-colored sky.

"WHAT THE FUCK IS YOUR GAME?" he shouted. Two birds on a bare branch became startled and flew away. He shouted it over and over until it echoed. He could still hear his cries after he got back in the car and drove away.

KYLE FOUND HIMSELF outside William's house. He was shaking in the car, unsure whether from the cold or shock. He now reasoned he wasn't being framed—only fucked with. But why would William want to confess what he'd done after all this time? Unless this was just another plot twist and William still intended to hang him. He looked up William's landline number on his phone and called his house.

"Hello?" a sweet voice asked.

"Yes, may I speak with William Lansing?"

"He's not here right now. Would you like to leave a message?"

"Do you know when he'll be back?"

"Probably in a few hours. He's in the city right now. Who may I ask is—"

Kyle hung up. He dialed Jamie's number, getting her voice mail. He was about to leave a message, but he had no idea what to say. She seemed so far away, almost as if she'd been a part of a different life, a better one. Could he ever return to it, to her, to what he no longer believed was a possibility? He hung up on her as well and reopened *Devil's Hopyard,* ready to see how William planned to wrap this all up.

I will spare you the gory details of how Mia's heart tasted, how it was bitter but sweet at the same time, how I'd never felt so fulfilled until I chewed the last bite. For once, a heart was no longer on my mind because it was in my stomach. I wondered if it might satiate me for good and I could work toward becoming normal again, no longer ruled by my hunger.

With dirt beneath my fingers from burying her deep in the earth, I returned home and went right to my office. Under the floorboards by my desk was a secret compartment where I kept pictures of Mia. I burned all her images and replaced them with the heart-shaped rock, stained with our blood. It was all I needed of her memory, so I locked it up and covered it with an area rug. Then I tore into my bedroom, heaving, and woke up my wife by pleasuring her. We didn't sleep all night (if you catch my drift). In the morning, she told me that last night was like it had been when we first met. I was actually present because I always seem distracted. I truly looked at her. Usually I had my eyes closed. She couldn't remember the last time I made love to her with them open.

Kyle closed the book and tossed it into the passenger seat, his heart furiously beating. He wondered if William had slipped up by pointing out that the heart-shaped rock was located beneath the floorboards in his office. But then it could also be the perfect bait to get Kyle to enter his home.

He got out of the car and headed to the front door, no other choice but to find out.

32

"YES, CAN I help you?" Laura Lansing asked as she opened the door. The snow was coming down harder, and she pinched her heavy sweater closed. Kyle thought she had kind eyes, at least upon a second impression. He remembered that about her from years ago. The one time he'd met her had been at the same charity function where Bill pried the feathers off the bird. William had introduced Kyle to her as one of his *very* promising students. This had been some time after Mia's disappearance and his two-night stint in the psych ward. Laura had acted gracious, probably having heard similar praise of a student before, but she made him feel special. She asked him what he wanted to do when he graduated.

"Something with literature," Kyle said, sticking to a club soda that night. He hadn't allowed himself anything stronger yet. That would soon change after his relationship with Cathy dissolved.

"Maybe a professor?" William chimed in. But Kyle didn't think himself smart enough. Without realizing, he said so.

"Nonsense," Laura said, a hand on his shoulder. "You're young, you still have so much knowledge left to soak up in school. My husband has a lot left to teach you."

So he thinks, Kyle thought with a smirk, now that he stood at William's door.

"I work at Burke & Burke," he said to Laura, debating whether to introduce himself as Kyle or Brett, or as an entirely made-up person. "We're publishing—"

"Oh, *yes,*" she squealed, tugging at him. "William's novel! He's not home right now. Are you the one who called earlier?"

"No," Kyle said, as she whisked him inside and shut the door.

He observed his rival's home. Typical New England décor: nautical themed, gloomy seascape paintings, blues and whites. Pictures of the family on the mantel above a roaring fireplace: vacations and arms around one another. Not a hint of the evil that lurked here beneath the surface.

"I didn't catch your name," she said. "I'm Laura. Can I get you some coffee, tea?"

"Tea would be great," Kyle said. "It's Carter. Carter Burke."

"You wouldn't be the publisher, would you?"

Kyle gave a stern nod.

"Oh, I am so honored," she said, flustered. She went over to a bookshelf and pulled out a few titles. "I've been a fan of your mystery division for some time. I love mysteries." She showed him a title, as if recommending it. "The Fairchild Series. I've read all twenty-seven—no, twenty-eight books!"

Kyle pegged her as a lonely woman stuck in this house on a weekday afternoon, eager for the thrill of the twenty-ninth book being delivered.

"Let me get your tea."

She scooted into the kitchen, leaving him out of sight. He quickly took an inventory of the first floor, no sign of William's office. Somehow he'd have to get up to the second floor. He thought to ask to use the bathroom but then spied a half bath off to the side. That wouldn't help. Laura returned with the tea.

"Orange rooibos, I hope you like," she said, handing him a cup and tucking a strand of graying hair behind her ear.

"I do, thank you for your hospitality."

She sat on the couch and he faced her on a chair, a coffee table between them.

"What brings you here?" she asked, a hint of uncertainty in her tone. Maybe she was hiding something. Maybe she was just insecure and didn't want to say the wrong thing to a man of his supposed stature.

"I have a weekend place in Connecticut, so I was in the area," Kyle said. "William's editor passed along his manuscript, and I wanted to talk to him about me taking it on personally. I edit so few books these days."

"You're so young to be the publisher," she said, burning her tongue and spilling some tea from her shaking hands. "I don't mean that as an insult."

"I'm older than you think. It was my father's company. I'm just trying to preserve his legacy."

"How grand."

"Anyway, maybe you could help me with some questions I had about the manuscript before William returns?"

She placed her hand over her heart. "Oh, no, no. Bill will want to be his own mouthpiece and I haven't read it . . . yet."

"Really? I would've assumed you had because you're obviously such a voracious reader."

"Well, yes, but Bill has never even showed me a sentence after all these years. Do you know he's been writing it for over a decade? His dedication inspires me."

Kyle couldn't believe this woman was naïve enough not to suspect her husband had psychotic tendencies, unless she was possibly just as dangerous.

"I was curious about his influences," Kyle continued.

"Again, it'd be better if he answered. I could probably come up with a few, but the obscure ones I wouldn't be able to remember."

She fingered a small silver cross hanging from her neck. In fact, before every answer she gave that Kyle didn't buy, her hand went right to that cross as a security blanket.

"I didn't mean authors who've influenced him necessarily, more how the plot came together."

"Again, Mr. Burke, I haven't read the manuscript."

"He hasn't told you what it's about?"

"I'm afraid not."

"Well, it's called *Devil's Hopyard,* which is a park close by."

"Yes," she said, squeezing the cross. "He used to go for runs there. My husband is a big runner. He's the athletic one." Her voice had developed a singsong quality to it.

"And you?"

"The chef. And I sing in my church's choir."

"That's really beautiful, Mrs. Lansing. I'm a firm believer in worshipping the Lord through song."

He didn't know where those words had come from, but they seemed to do the trick. She lit up, her blue eyes getting wide.

"What sect are you?" she asked.

"Episcopalian."

"Bill and I are Lutheran."

The conversation was going off the rails. He had to steer it back.

"There are great passages about faith in *Devil's Hopyard,*" he said, and she looked up, surprised. "But I was most curious about the book's parallels to something that happened in this town a long time ago."

Her hand went right back to her cross. She chewed on the corner of her lip. She had to know what he meant.

"Does the name Mia Evans ring a bell?"

She went to speak but then stopped herself. She seemed saddened. Her cup of tea knocked over. He couldn't tell if she'd done it on purpose.

"Oh, nuts," she said, scurrying to the kitchen. He watched the tea spread across the coffee table. She returned with paper towels.

"I'm such a clumsybum." She smiled, but it was strained, more like William's attempts at a smile. She began to mop up the spill.

"What was that name again?" she asked offhandedly.

"Mia Evans."

This time she really thought about the name, or at least pretended to.

"Oh . . . yes, the girl who went missing."

"It seems as if she's a character in William's book. And that she was a student of his?"

"Such a terrible tragedy," Laura continued. "I recall how broken up Bill was back then. You get used to burying those older than you, but not younger."

"I thought there was no conclusive evidence that she was murdered. The papers said she went missing."

"Yes, oh, yes, I meant her presence had been buried. No one ever heard from her again. And her poor, dear mother. I can't imagine outliving one's child."

"William said you have two children?" Kyle asked, because Laura seemed like she was shrinking in place. He didn't want her to clam up for good. From detective shows that he watched, he knew it was best to pepper with questions rather than go full throttle.

"We do. The twins, Alicia and Bill . . . Junior. Well, no one calls him Junior anymore. As a child he wouldn't leave his father's side."

"And as an adult?"

"Oh, children grow out of that early on. One minute they're latched onto your leg and the next . . . well, they want nothing to do with you."

"Did either of your children know Mia from school or—"

"Not at all. They were both younger, passing ships at high school, I presume. I doubt they were even there at the same time."

"Why do you think your husband wanted to write about this girl Mia?" he asked, balls to the wall, no time anymore to pussyfoot around.

Laura didn't respond right away. The fire popped and crackled, sparks flinging into the air. She rose and picked up a poker to tend to the fire. She held on to the poker, possibly to utilize it as a defense. Or a threat. He still couldn't get a good read on her.

"Pardon me for saying this, Mr. Burke, but these are awfully unsettling questions." She was lightly shaking. "I remember praying for that girl's soul so long ago. I assume Bill always felt bad about what happened to her. Maybe he wanted to keep her spirit alive?"

"He talks about eating her heart in the book."

The poker fell from her hands and clanged on the floor. She went to pick it back up and blinked wildly at him.

"Did you say . . . ?"

"We love William's book, Mrs. Lansing. Please don't think this is an inquisition."

She cupped a hand over her mouth, shaking even more.

"You've upset me."

"That's not my intention. It's just that after the book is published, people will be asking these same questions."

She was too stunned to answer. He realized there was no way she'd been complicit in Mia's disappearance. Her face radiated genuine shock—otherwise she deserved an Academy Award.

"Could I use your bathroom, Mrs. Lansing? Is there one upstairs?"

She waved toward the staircase, her other hand grasping at her cross. He headed for the stairs, watching her slowly sit back down on the couch, shell-shocked.

Upstairs, he opened doors along the hallway—Alicia and Bill's old rooms, the master bedroom, and finally at the end of the hall, William's office. Inside was a big desk surrounded by leather-bound first editions of classics: *The Great Gatsby, The Quiet American, The Moon and Sixpence,* a lifetime of collecting the greats. The literary nerd in Kyle would have loved to be able to stop and pore over these tomes, but the newly minted detective knew he had precious little time. By the desk, he moved aside an area rug. Beneath it in the floor was a tiny silver keyhole. As a kid he'd been fascinated with picking locks, using his Swiss Army knife to open many forbidden doors. He was a curious child and it had finally paid off. He picked the lock rather easily and removed a black metal box. He opened the lid to find a large heart-shaped rock covered in dried blood just like it had been described in *Devil's Hopyard.*

The phone on the desk rang, a piercing scream that nearly gave him a heart attack. It rang again and he crept toward the door, hearing Laura murmuring downstairs. He quickly whipped out his cell and took a few pictures of the rock from different angles, along with evidence of it being located in William's office. Then he heard a car pull up to the driveway, the tires crunching stones. He looked out the window and saw William exiting the car.

"Fuck." He chucked the heart-shaped rock back into the black box and returned it into the floor. He covered it with the rug and hurried down the stairs. He saw the front door unlock and slowly begin to open. He ran toward the back door that led to the garden.

"Mr. Burke? Oh, Mr. Burke?" he heard Laura asking. She was climbing up the stairs.

The front door opened and William stood at the threshold. The hairs on Kyle's arms tingled. He was at an angle where he could see William while he doubted William could see him. He slid open the glass door behind him as William entered.

"Laura?" William asked, closing the front door. "Whose car is that?"

Laura scooted back down the stairs. Their conversation became muted because Kyle backed up out of their home, squashing the remnants of vegetables that struggled to grow in the snow. He left footprints of his escape, but there was nothing he could do about that. Then he ran around to the front, jumped in the rental car, and took off. In the rear-view mirror, he could see William stepping outside and watching him flee with a fully developed smirk stamped on his face.

33

SHERIFF PEALEY'S DAY had been pretty uneventful for the most part. Got out of bed at four in the morning to pee and couldn't fall back asleep, so he drank two black coffees with a bran muffin and watched the sun rise with his black Lab, Champ. There'd been a motorcycle accident late morning on an off road, but the driver was all right, just a little shook up. He had a crab-and-cream-cheese omelet at Ethel's Edibles and had to eat and run since Ms. Tooley's cat got stuck in her white oak tree. When he arrived, the volunteer fire department had already saved Buttons. Ms. Tooley gave him a slice of pineapple pie and a few nips of whiskey anyway. He'd been napping at his desk ever since until Loretta hesitantly knocked on the door.

"I'm sorry to bother your nap," Loretta said. She had worked for him ever since she finished high school twenty-five years ago. She knew his rhythms. She had brought him dinners to freeze after his wife, Ann-Marie, passed. She did that for a year. She made sure he never sat too long because blood clots ran high in his family. She was a good face for him to wake up to.

"No bother, Loretta, what is it?"

"There's a man outside who says he needs to see you. Says it's urgent but he wouldn't go into it."

"Don't recognize him?"

Loretta shook her head. Pealey looked at the wall clock and saw that it was about leaving time. Still, he told Loretta to send the man in.

A blond guy in his late twenties, maybe early thirties came inside. He had a giant bound manuscript under his arm. He seemed frazzled.

"Sheriff, I'm Kyle Broder. Detective Tomás Ruiz contacted you a week or so ago about a cat that had been killed."

"Uh-huh. Go on."

Kyle launched into a long and complicated story. It involved some professor of his who was writing some book, and when Kyle wouldn't publish the book, the professor snapped. The sheriff half listened. He had learned from almost fifty years on the force to strip away anything extraneous because people tended to babble.

"He lives in this town," Kyle said. "His name is William Lansing."

Now Pealey remembered the whole tale. William Lansing had spoken of a former student who'd become a little obsessive. And lo and behold, the crazy showed up at the sheriff's door.

"Son, why don't you take a seat?" he said, in the most calming tone he could muster. "You're pacing all around."

Kyle obeyed. He placed *Devil's Hopyard* on the desk.

"Like the park," Pealey said, tracing a thumb across the letters.

"Were you sheriff here when Mia Evans went missing?"

Like he'd been gutted, Pealey felt a sharp jab to his stomach. Mia Evans had been the one true blight on a solid career. He didn't like puzzles—or rather, he didn't like not solving them. Mia's disappearance remained a haunting enigma.

"William is writing about her," Kyle said, turning to a dog-eared page.

Pealey put on his glasses and read a sick and disturbing paragraph about a professor who wanted to eat Mia's heart.

"Is this some kind of joke?"

Kyle turned to another passage, this one where the professor chains her up in a shack. Pealey closed the book after getting through a few sentences.

"I can't read this filth."

Kyle took out his cell. For a split second, the sheriff reacted as if it was a weapon—hearing about Mia had put him on edge—but then Kyle showed him a picture of a rock shaped like a heart and covered with blood.

"William writes about killing Mia with a heart-shaped rock and *this* was hidden in his office."

From the angle the picture had been taken, Pealey could clearly see it was William Lansing's office. The rock was held up next to a framed diploma with Lansing's name.

Kyle reopened the manuscript to where Mia was bludgeoned in a shack in Devil's Hopyard.

"Mia was my girlfriend at Bentley."

Pealey recalled hearing that from a few boys his team had questioned years ago. All of them had alibis for that night. They questioned each student and faculty member at Bentley, and even when the papers stopped printing about Mia, Pealey still poked his nose around. For a while, he thought that Karen Evans was involved, since she had a string of bad news ex-boyfriends. One was a crank dealer who came back to town right before Mia disappeared. Pealey had been certain the guy took her and he'd even got a warrant to search the guy's trailer, but the ex had gone clean and was staying at a Motel 6 up in Lewiston, Maine, the day Mia vanished. Her mother also seemed too high on opiates to be the master of any plot. Everyone soon moved on from the case, but Mia became the sheriff's own private obsession, a distraction from Ann-Marie's cancer. After Ann-Marie died, the missing girl preoccupied his lonely nights. And then one night, he passed out on a knocked-over bottle of Jim Beam and a sea of newspaper clippings with Mia's face. He had dreamt that he saw her lips moving on the clippings. Then she spoke. She told him to forget about her. She said whatever happened to her no longer mattered. She wanted peace, and more than that, she wanted him to have peace. She told him to find a companion other than her. So he put her clippings in boxes up in the attic. He drove out to a kennel and got a black Lab puppy. He stopped drinking so much, only a nip here and there, and rose early for the sunrise. He found the best kind of happy he could.

"William was just getting home if you go question him now," Kyle said. "I think he killed Mia and she's buried somewhere in Devil's Hopyard. I haven't finished the manuscript yet, but the end might reveal where—"

Pealey tugged at his mustache, his habit when plunging into deep thought. He'd brought Professor Lansing into the station after Mia's disappearance—all her teachers were questioned. The professor had a strong alibi from both his wife and a student and actually accused the police of not doing enough to find the girl. This soon became the town's sentiment until an unseasonably frigid winter blew in and their focus switched to their own issues. The ice for the next three months also made it impossible to do any real searching. The professor had never been on his radar, and Pealey doubted the guy was the missing puzzle piece.

"Son, there are three sides to every story," Pealey said. "Yours, his, and the truth."

"I know the truth of what happened. That son of a bitch fucking *killed* Mia. He was having an affair with her, she tried to end it, and he went psycho."

"I understand how someone can love a pet very much," Pealey said.

"What the fuck does that mean?"

"Obviously, you're heartbroken over your cat that was killed. I have a dog at home who I talk to as if he's human. He saved my life. But I don't think this man killed your cat and I don't think he killed—"

Kyle leaped from his seat and pushed the manuscript at the sheriff. "The proof is all here!"

"Now, this is what a *book* told you, that don't mean it's a fact. And how do I know you weren't the one who wrote it?"

"His children are involved in Mia's death too," Kyle insisted. "Somehow. Either they knew or helped. I'm not sure about his wife, but I don't think so. She seemed genuinely surprised when I told her what William was writing about."

"I know his children," the sheriff said, running through his mind any interactions he'd had with them. This was becoming increasingly more difficult to do than it used to be now that he was pushing seventy and holes started appearing in his memories. "They took over the Royal Wee."

"The son, Bill Jr., is a little off," Kyle said. "Psychopathic tendencies, and his relationship with his sister is weirdly close. The whole family is hiding secrets."

Pealey recalled a time when the daughter must have been in junior high or high school and was caught shoplifting at the Crystal Mall. She'd stolen a pair of leggings after already paying for a sweater. She had stuffed the leggings in her waistband and they'd beeped when she tried to go through security. He'd given her a stern lecture.

"The one time I met Bill," Kyle said, "he was picking the feathers off a living bird. Really hurting it."

"How long ago was that?" Pealey asked, sitting up straight for the first time since Kyle entered.

"Ten years. College."

About a decade ago, an ornithologist connected to Bentley had come to the station complaining about a rash of injuries to some of his birds. Evidently, he believed someone had broken into his research facility and plucked the feathers off of a good number of them. He'd suspected fraternity activity, or some cruel dare, but whoever picked the facility's lock had done so with the utmost care not to arouse suspicion—not likely a wasted frat guy. These mutilations continued for some time, the culprit moving on from the ornithologist's birds and attacking ones in the wild. People suspected an out-of-control animal, but the ornithologist said a rabid animal would go after nonavian species too and wouldn't be so specific with its prey.

"Plucking off the bird's feathers?" Pealey said, tugging at his mustache some more. "You don't say."

Kyle looked exhausted, like he'd been running nonstop and didn't know what to do with himself now that he'd become still. He removed a jump drive from his pocket and picked up the large manuscript from the desk.

"The manuscript is on the drive for you to read. I don't know why William's deciding to do this now, but he is *confessing* his crimes in it. Please . . . could you just look it over and talk to him again?"

Maybe it was the desperation Pealey could hear in the young guy's voice or the coincidence of the mysterious bird mauler who might just be Bill that made him not brush off Broder's claims anymore. If William Lansing's son had a penchant for harming birds, maybe the father *did* kill Kyle's cat, and even worse—Mia.

He looked over at a picture of Ann-Marie on his desk. He hadn't kept any from the cancer years, wanting her to remain robust in his eyes. She was in a baby blue dress up at her sister's place in Vermont, giving him a Mona Lisa smile with a string of mountains as a backdrop. He could've sworn he saw her lips moving. Possibly the nips of whiskey he'd had were still fogging his brain, but he could hear Ann-Marie's serene voice. She whispered: *Follow this lead.*

He had adored her for thirty-five years and never once ignored any of her requests. He wasn't about to start now.

34

NATHANIEL WAITED FOR Professor Lansing on the side of the road past the college's entrance. The professor had sent a text asking Nathaniel to deliver a note. So Nathaniel bundled up in a heavy winter coat and scarf, not sure how far he'd have to travel. He watched the road for Professor Lansing's car to emerge. The sun was setting and cars had turned on their lights to cut through the snow. He wrapped the scarf around his mouth so only his eyes were visible. He decided this would be the last favor he'd do for the professor. He was glad that he'd be getting a good grade in class, but he was also becoming increasingly weirded out by the professor's demands. The trip all the way to Brooklyn to leave a fruit basket had been a strange request, but the professor swore how much his friend loved surprises. Then the Ex-Lax and drugs gave Nathaniel too much of a glimpse into the professor's life of constipation and sleepless nights. If this final demand wouldn't be the end of his duties, he'd have to tell his mentor that he was done for good.

Heavy brights lit up the distance and a car screeched to a stop by his feet. The window rolled down and Professor Lansing stuck his head out.

He had an envelope, sealed with a *W* in fine calligraphy. A large bandage covered his arm, blood leaking out.

"Deliver this to the motel on Pine Road, room twelve," Professor Lansing said. "Knock on the door, leave it, and make sure you're not seen."

Nathaniel took the envelope. "Okay."

"This will be the last thing I ask of you," the professor said. "This is good-bye."

"Good-bye?" Nathaniel asked, but Professor Lansing rolled up the window. Nathaniel heard classical music pumping from the speakers as the car took off. He stared at the blank envelope, curious as to what was inside, but he tucked it in his inside pocket and zipped his coat closed, making his way to Pine Road.

KYLE RETURNED TO his motel and crawled into bed with *Devil's Hopyard.* It had been a long day and he craved a nap more than anything, but he *had* to know how the manuscript ended. There was no guarantee that the sheriff took him seriously and would go question William again. If Kyle wanted answers, he'd have to rely on himself to discover them. With only a few pages to go, he flipped to where he'd left off.

> I return to our shack, our home. The floorboards had all been removed and you are buried beneath. At first I'd done a crude job, the thrill of the taste of your heart distracted me, and I could tell upon entering that a crime had been committed here. So I lied to my wife and told her I had a faraway conference and spent the entire weekend perfecting your eternal resting spot. I removed the bedframe and mattress; all I kept was the blackened pan I used to cook you, hoping a sliver might have remained for a later bite. I burned the wooden bedframe and mattress outside along with

any of evidence of what transpired in this shack. Afterward it was like when I'd found it, wholly pure again.

I spent the weekend sleeping on its bare floor, my ear flush and listening to you a few feet under. I could say it didn't have to end this way, that if you hadn't rejected me we could've been good together for much longer, possibly forever, but I knew that was a lie. From the very moment you walked into my classroom, I saw our true future. What beats inside of me is not a heart; it is pure rot and sin. I challenge anyone who grew up the way I did to turn out any differently. I knew cruelty before I could even form words. My father punched my mother in the stomach upon learning there was a life inside. I watched her exist with busted lips and broken bones, and maybe she loved me, but not as much as she loved herself. She left me to suffer, knowing that if one of us remained, my father wouldn't attempt to come after the one who got away.

The shack that he tortured me in was not very different from this one. That was what drew me to it. I'll never forget the day I went running in Devil's Hopyard and saw its beacon of light, its calling arms. It told me what to do and just how to do it, much like the shack from my past that said it was okay to feed on a heart as opposed to starving. And I'd been starving for so long before I met Mia. I had built up so much rage I had no idea how to release it. I worried that the brunt of it might go toward my wife, my children. That I might turn into my father. I needed someone else to absorb my evil, someone I loved so the act of her murder had weight. I want to make it clear how much she meant to me. The two of us will be larger in death than in life once our story is shared with the world.

Kyle rubbed his eyes, sleep yanking at his consciousness. There were only a few pages left to go. He slapped his face to keep himself awake. A loud knock on the door did the trick even better. He swung off the bed and crept to the door. The knocking got louder and louder, a desperate pounding. Was it William? Would this be the place of their final battle? He opened the door ready to fight, but saw a shivering Mia instead of his enemy, not even wearing a coat, practically naked in the snow.

With quivering purple lips, Mia asked, “C-c-can I come in?”

35

MIA APPEARED OTHERWORLDLY, the fallen snow creating a lush backdrop for this angel's return to Earth. She wore only a bra and underwear, her toes frostbitten, a shade of blue. She had barely aged at all, still looking nineteen but no longer wide-eyed. She had seen the worst of humankind and would never find her way back to innocence. These thoughts flooded Kyle's mind as she stood before him at his motel door.

"C-c-can I come in?" she asked, and he took her by the hand and carefully brought her inside. She felt real, and he had a genuine spark upon touching her wrist. He ran over to the closet and took out a bathrobe to warm her up. She sat on the bed and he stood as far away from her as possible, his lips shivering just as much as hers.

"Aren't you dead?" he said, after a moment of silence, of disbelief.

"'*Die at the right time: thus teaches Zarathustra,*'" she said. "Nietzsche. My time wasn't meant to be ten years ago in Devil's Hopyard."

"You escaped from William?" Kyle asked, no longer knowing what might have truly occurred in that shack. The scenario he had created was now blown to bits.

"I didn't escape," she said. "I found a different hell. I wandered for a long time and finally came back here. Because I saw you were looking."

"But how did you know?"

She rose and came toward him. He backed up until he banged into the wall. Her breath was so sweet, a hint of sour apple.

"I've followed you through the years," she said. "I was with you after I vanished. I held your hand those two nights in the psych ward, you just couldn't feel me yet."

"I don't understand."

"And when your mom passed, I was there too. I may have just been a whisper, but I told you that she loved you even though she never really said it because she was difficult and prone to fits and numbed herself with any medication that could quiet the noises in her head, just like my own mom. I told you to finish up your master's and move to New York City. I knew you could accomplish whatever you set your mind to."

"You *are* dead," Kyle said, tears filling his eyes.

"I don't think of myself that way. Like Nietzsche said, '*Many die too late, and few die too early.*' There's a tombstone with my name in a graveyard, but it doesn't have a corpse in it, so I'm not dead, just gone. My death will be at the age of ninety-three, not early at all." She looked into the distance, this future materializing. "I will be a great-grandparent. I will have many true loves. I will have seen the world. I will close my eyes one night and won't wake from my dream. That's how it should be."

But Kyle knew this wouldn't happen. The girl before him was nothing more than an apparition.

"I wish I could have done something to save you," he said, the tears flowing. They blurred his vision and made her appear even hazier.

"I played with danger because I liked doing it, because I thought I was just flirting and not destroying myself. Because I thought boredom was the worst sin imaginable. I learned the truth the hard way."

"Did you know who William was?" Kyle asked. "The kind of person capable of doing the things he did?"

She nodded. "Everyone close to him knew who he was. Even you."

"That's not true. I never saw this coming."

"You didn't want to believe it so you made him into something he isn't. He has that kind of charm. He's done it to many people before, even me. But we both recognized his sadness and his evil heart too. We just chose to look the other way."

"No, I didn't. I swear I never would've—"

She placed her finger over his lips, shook her head. "You saw us together that one time. It was outside the Royal Wee. He had hoisted me up against a wall, and I'd wrapped my legs around his waist. You watched the entire thing. You told yourself I was the seductress, the one to blame. He was a god who could do no wrong. You forced yourself to forget what was true."

The memory beat in Kyle's skull, brought him to his knees. Mia half naked in the chill night, his mentor thrusting into her in the alleyway.

"You told him the kind of person you thought I was," she continued. "A cheat, a whore. And you were right. I know you loved me, but I wasn't ready to feel so strongly about anyone, you or him. That is why I'm bones and dust now. If I'd truly loved you both, I might still be here."

Kyle hugged his legs to his chest. "I caused this."

"No, no, no." She crouched down and took his head in her hands. "He would've done this to me no matter what. The only difference is you would've never been involved."

The scent of sour apples tickled his nose. She had moved in for a kiss and he accepted, her soft lips just like he remembered. A knock at the door made him pull away.

She seemed frightened. She removed the bathrobe and crept toward the window. The knocks grew louder and louder, pounding to get inside. He covered his ears. She opened the window, letting in swirls of cold air, and climbed out into the night. He got to his feet and thrust open the door, but the knocking continued, a plague between his ears.

Knock. Knock. *KNOCK.*

KYLE WOKE UP sweating under the comforter. *Devil's Hopyard* had been tossed to the floor. Loud knocking continued at the door and then it suddenly went silent. He got out of bed and flung open the door, desperate to ask Mia a thousand more questions.

Perched in the snow was an envelope sealed with a *W.* He glanced around to see who had left it, but the parking lot was empty. He grabbed the envelope and closed the door. The window had been left open and he shut that too. He ripped open the envelope and discovered a note written in blood.

You've toyed with something of mine
Now I'm going to toy with something of yours.
But you'll have to finish the book
To know where to find her.
For in the end is a map of a gruesome literary scavenger hunt through Devil's Hopyard
That will lead you back to her pretty little hands
(should they still have life in them if you don't take too long).
Your mentor, W

The note spiraled to the floor, his worst fear come true. He grabbed his phone and called Jamie, getting her voice mail. He left a frantic message, begging her to call him back, praying she was all right. He told her how much he loved her, that he never meant to hurt her, that she was his everything.

Lying on the floor, the manuscript seemed to stare up at him. He cursed at it as he tucked it under his arm and threw on a pair of shoes without even remembering a coat. Then he headed to the car to drive to Devil's Hopyard, his mind racing about how he would end this tale if he were the writer, knowing that for the most dramatic impact, Jamie had to die, that every great novel ends in some kind of death so the other characters can learn and grow from that experience.

One question remained: Who would survive the last page, and who—like Mia—would become bones and dust?

36

SHERIFF PEALEY HAD Loretta figure out how to use the jump drive with the manuscript from Kyle Broder. He didn't trust technology, still using a rotary phone and a typewriter; Loretta handled all his e-mails. A psychologist once told him he was stuck in the year Ann-Marie passed, but he'd been a technophobe long before—even though a part of him blamed all the Wi-Fi/radio frequencies in the air for her sickness.

When he finally sat down in front of Loretta's computer with a jelly donut and a coffee, he wasn't prepared for the horrors on the screen. After not thinking about Mia for some time, William Lansing had brought her back to life. She became tangible again. He had never met her before, and he realized from reading *Devil's Hopyard* that he never really knew her—nor did he want to know her in this way. When Loretta knocked on the door after an hour to ask if he wanted a coffee refill, she found him hunched over her desk, his face red with tears.

"Sheriff Pealey?" she said, running in and placing her hand on his back.

"Can you print the end part for me? I need to go."

He put on his cap and grabbed his holster with the loaded gun already in it.

"Sheriff, are you okay? You're crying. I haven't seen you like this since—"

"Print these last pages, Loretta. C'mon!"

She jumped in place, not used to him speaking to her like that. He maintained a laconic manner in the office. "*Let the world fall to pieces around you, but never let it shake you up.*" Sheriff Lee Mucken, the toughest son of a bitch he knew and the prior sheriff of this county, told him that when they came across his first dead body.

Loretta printed out the forty or so pages he asked for and handed them over. He knew she wanted an explanation of what was going on, but that would take too much time.

"I gotta go, Loretta."

He was out the door before she could say anything more. He *couldn't* explain what he'd just read. The depravity of the writer's mind, the details that felt so eerily true. Mia's bones and dust buried somewhere in Devil's Hopyard. He thought of past interactions with William Lansing. Once at Gussie's General Store, he'd witnessed William being very rude to old Gussie. William needed lye to raise the soil pH in Laura's garden and Gussie was out of it. William got very angry and Pealey had to come between them. Gussie didn't like being talked to in a certain way, and even at her elderly age could be provoked into a fight. The sheriff managed to deescalate the situation. Eventually, William simmered down and apologized. He said something about having problems with his kids recently, but Pealey couldn't remember what exactly. One of those holes in his memory, lost forever.

With the last pages of *Devil's Hopyard,* he drove to the Lansings' house. He never made night calls unless it was an emergency, so they would clearly know something was up. He rang the doorbell, Bach's *Well-Tempered Clavier* the only sound on the quiet block. He recognized the piece well. Ann-Marie had been a classical-music nut and broadened his musical tastes beyond country.

Laura Lansing opened the door, a slight tremor in her hands that became more pronounced when she saw him. Always a tiny, fragile woman, she seemed to have shrunk since he'd seen her last, her nervous energy whittling her down to practically nothing.

"Sheriff Pealey?" she said, looking him in the eye and then looking away. "What brings you here?"

"Is your husband home, Mrs. Lansing?"

He peered inside, viewing the house from an entirely new perspective. Anything could be evidence.

"No. I believe he's at Bentley, writing," she said. "But he could be anywhere at the college. Sometimes in his office, sometimes the library, there's also a coffee klatch on campus—"

"Does he have an office at home, as well?" he interrupted. Pealey had always been suspicious of babblers who thought that talking a lot might cover up their guilt.

"Yes, it's right up the stairs," she said. "What's this about, Sheriff?"

He knew the truth wouldn't work, especially if she was involved at all.

"It seems like there's some trouble with that student of William's I was here about last week . . ."

"Yes, what about him?"

"It appears things have taken a turn for the worse. May I come in?"

"Yes . . . of course."

She held the door open and he entered. A spotless house, always a sign of something hiding beneath the surface. Just another show this family had put on for years if everything he read was true.

"No tea, thank you," he said, because she always offered it upon entering. "So, Kyle Broder has made a formal threat against William."

Laura fingered her cross. "Oh, Lord."

"Now sometimes these threats stay idle and then die away, but we do have to look into them."

"Well, yes, of course."

"Has Broder been at this house?"

She thought for a moment. "No, I don't believe he has."

"He said he was here today in William's office."

"What?" she said, and then stopped herself, genuinely shocked. "There was another man here today . . . my husband's publisher. And I did think he looked too young to be at such a high-up level."

"Was he in your husband's office?"

"Why?"

"I think he may have left something there. May I check?"

Pealey made a move for the staircase, but Laura grabbed his arm.

"Bill *really* doesn't like people going in his office."

"Laura, there could be evidence there I need."

"It's just . . . he keeps everything just so. It's an environment he's created that allows him access into the world of his book, that's what he said. Any bit of interruption—"

"I promise, Laura, I'll keep everything how it is."

"O-okay," she said, but he was already marching up the stairs, his hand on his gun belt. When he was out of earshot, he made a call to his deputy for backup just in case.

He got out his gun and pointed it at the office door. He'd been so spooked from reading *Devil's Hopyard,* he half expected William to come charging out with a syringe. He pushed open the office door with his gun. No William inside. He'd spied the framed diploma, which let him know that Kyle Broder *had* really been here. He reholstered the gun and moved aside the area rug. He got out a knife and picked the silver keyhole. He took out the black box and lifted the handle to find a heart-shaped rock covered in dried blood.

"Well, fuck me sideways and call me Sally."

He heard a crash, the sound ringing in his ears. He tipped over and hit his face on the floor. Liquid covered his eyes that he realized was blood. He turned onto his back, groaning as if someone had ripped open his skull.

Laura Lansing stood over him with a candlestick in hand.

"I said *not* to go into in Bill's office."

MERCIFULLY, LAURA DIDN'T hit Sheriff Pealey twice with the candlestick, but she was holding it out threatening to strike him again.

"You don't want to do this," he said.

She was shaking madly. The candlestick fell to the floor and clanged. The tears came. She crouched down and got to her knees, wobbly on her feet.

Pealey clamped a hand over his wound to keep the blood from spilling out. He reached into his holster and pointed the gun at her. This made her cry even more. She started babbling, sounding like it was in a different language until she finally got herself under control.

"What . . . what has he done?" she said, fearful.

"Damn, you really hit me," Pealey said, as if he just realized. "Got a bit of my brains on the floor."

He helped her up and she felt weightless in his arms. He hated to do it but had to aim the gun at her again.

"Now where is your husband, Mrs. Lansing? Is he in the park—Devil's Hopyard?"

"He's on a walkabout," Laura said. "He said he's on the final chapter of his novel and has to wander around for it all to come to him. He's a great writer."

"That is true, ma'am. Wouldn't argue with that."

"What did he do, Sheriff?"

Her eyes told the sheriff that she was expecting the worst. He guessed she'd been waiting for this moment for so long that it had become a part of her life, a nagging reminder of how easily everything could fall apart.

"Where is the shack that he goes to in Devil's Hopyard?"

"The shack?" Laura said, disappointed. More tears came. "That was where he'd take her."

"Take who, Mrs. Lansing? Mia Evans?"

Her mouth dropped wide open.

"How did you know?" She steeled herself to continue. "That's where they would go. Just the two of them. It was their spot. To make love."

"Do you know where it is?"

"I followed them once. He knew I knew about her, and we coexisted like that for some time. I have my own issues. Back then, I was agoraphobic, didn't go outside for a year except for my garden. Don't know why. I just wanted to stay in my home. So I should have known he'd stray. She was beautiful, I'll give him that, but rather tawdry. I don't know—I wouldn't have expected her type to catch his eye, but there she was, the two of them holding hands as they got out of his car—our car, what I am saying? They were in that shack for hours, and when he stepped out, he seemed . . . alive. It was as if the man I knew had actually been dead up until that moment, and . . . well, my heart broke. But I hid instead of confronting him. I couldn't be the one to take away his happiness, isn't that foolish? It seems foolish now. And then she disappeared."

"Do you think William had something to do with that?"

Laura stared at him as if she'd left reality and returned to it in a crash landing. She gave one sad nod.

"Where is the shack located, Laura?"

"In its heart," she said.

"What does that mean?"

"If you look at a map of the park, the shack is located right where the heart would be. The park is kind of shaped like a human body. I know this because he told it to her when I saw them. He said he found a place for them to make love that was located right in the heart of Devil's Hopyard. And it was perfect because she was his heart. He couldn't live without her. That was what he said."

BACK IN HIS car, Sheriff Pealey got out a map of Killingworth and found Devil's Hopyard. He hadn't noticed it before, but it was sort of shaped like a human body just like Mrs. Lansing described. He circled right where the heart would be. Then he made a call to his deputy to come and take Mrs. Lansing into custody for more questions. He had handcuffed her to the couch's leg—after she had tended to his wound with a bandage. Both wound up apologizing to each other. His deputy would be there in ten minutes to get her. Then he put up his siren and floored it to Devil's Hopyard, thinking the last time he'd used his siren for such an emergency was probably when Mia went missing.

37

WHILE DRIVING TO Devil's Hopyard, Kyle got out a map of the park that William had inserted toward the end of the manuscript. On the next page was the first clue. All it said was, *As I Lay Dying at the entrance.* He feared seeing Jamie's dead body upon pulling up to the park and was relieved to find nothing at the entrance when he arrived. The gates were still open since the park closed around ten at night. He was about to head inside when he spotted a copy of William Faulkner's *As I Lay Dying* perched against the gate.

He got out of the car into the heavy snow and realized that he'd forgotten a coat. At least he'd remembered shoes. With frozen fingers he picked up the book—the story of the death of Addie Bundren and her poor rural family's quest to honor her wish to be buried in her Mississippi hometown. Faulkner wrote the novel over the span of six weeks from midnight to four in the morning and didn't change one word. Kyle tried to think of what clue it might offer and flipped through the text until a dollar bill fell out into the snow. On the bill had been written, *It hadn't bothered me much.*

Kyle wondered about the significance of the sentence. Was William saying he hadn't been bothered much about something? Possibly, but Kyle didn't know what that had to do with finding where he'd taken Jamie. Then he thought it was a quote from George Washington, but he couldn't figure out how that related to *As I Lay Dying* either. He got back in the car, quieted his shivers, and flipped through the book again. Faulkner had written it from the perspective of multiple characters, and he recalled the character of Cash—the oldest sibling who was a carpenter and built the coffin for his mother, Addie. While crossing a river, Cash fell and broke his leg. After enduring the pain of a cement cast, Cash said, "It never bothered me much." Kyle knew Cash represented the Christ-like figure of the novel who sacrifices his own pain to push forward so Addie can be buried.

Feeling like he was getting closer to deciphering the clue, Kyle spread out the map of Devil's Hopyard on the dashboard. The different parts of the park all had various names, and he searched for one referencing Christ. No dice. At the bottom of the map was a spot called Phantom Limb. He wondered if William had chosen that because of Cash's wounded leg. If he had any chance of saving Jamie, he needed to go with his gut and not second-guess himself, so he took off.

It was a circuitous journey to Phantom Limb, since he had to take many of the side roads. Obviously, this was a destination no one traveled to and he could see why. At the edge of the park, a solitary cliff thrust out, the river lapping beneath. He left his brights on and exited the car, two yellow beams creating the only paths of light in the dark expanse. The snow was coming down harder now, and he had to shield his eyes. A book was propped up in the center of a white mound, practically covered. When he got closer, he wiped away the snow and saw it was George Orwell's *1984,* the dystopian novel that takes place in a world of perpetual war, omnipresent government surveillance, and public manipulation.

Kyle picked up the book and turned through the pages. In angry black marker William had written *Big Brother is watching, Big Brother is watching, Big Brother is watching,* over and over. Kyle glanced around, as if he were being spied on. Only a hooting owl seemed to have eyes on him. It took off into the night. He stared at the mound of snow that *1984* had been stuck into. Upon closer inspection, it resembled the shape of a leg. Though his hands were numb from the frigid temperature, he moved aside the coating of snow until he discovered a severed leg, hacked off at the thigh.

He doubled back, tripping over himself, screaming and hearing his echo rustle through the trees. He threw up to his side, unable to look away from the severed leg. *Was it Jamie's?* He crept closer and saw that it had slightly decomposed, making it impossible to tell if it belonged to her. Jamie had no identifiable marks on either of her legs. He grabbed the copy of *1984* and locked himself in the car, the beams of yellow light illuminating the gruesome scene.

He was past tears, his throat sore. He got out his phone to try and call Jamie again, but there was no cell reception. A sadistic fuck like William might want to mutilate her but ultimately keep her alive. *Right?* he wondered. There was a chance he hadn't lost Jamie completely. He reached for the map and looked for any part of the park with *big* or *brother* in its name but couldn't locate any. There was, however, a place called Lookout Point at the other end. The cover of *1984* showed an eye, watching. It was worth a shot.

Lookout Point was a hill at the edge of the park, which jutted out over a different river. When he reached it, he found a copy of Shakespeare's *Titus Andronicus.* He steeled himself for the next body part he might find, knowing that the leg was only the beginning. He flipped through the pages and came across an eyeball as a bookmark. It fell to the snow, staring back at him. Now he cried. He sank to his knees, bellowing "I'm sorry" into the wind. He'd been responsible for Mia dying at William's hands, and now he'd caused Jamie's death too. He thought of the time he and Jamie crashed a wedding in Brooklyn on a whim and made up crazy backstories and danced all night to Jewish klezmer music. And once when they went back to their hometowns in Wisconsin and went skinny-dipping in a lake, Jamie emerged with a leech on her ass, and instead of freaking out, she started laughing. He thought of early-morning cuddling sessions before their workdays began. It destroyed him that he'd never be able to feel her touch again. He was a harbinger of bad luck—all who came across his path perished. And he knew his final punishment would be to watch William dismember the second girl he'd truly loved, ten years after murdering the first.

He sat in the snow with *Titus Andronicus,* unaware that hypothermia was setting in. His ice-ridden brain managed to recall plot points from Shakespeare's minor classic. The character of Aaron persuaded Titus to cut off his own hand to use as ransom for the return of Titus's son, even though Aaron tricked him and his sons were already dead. Now William would take Jamie's hands next. Soon there'd be nothing left of her.

He trudged to the car and read the map for any place with *hands* in its name. Hold Lane was a thruway in the park, so he headed there, obliterated, no longer human because he wasn't dealing with a human anymore, only the devil at his most wicked. He almost missed the turn-off for Hold Lane because a note had been nailed to its sign, covering the lettering. He got out of the car to read it.

Now this is the point. You fancy me mad.
Madmen know nothing.
I admit the deed!
Tear up the planks!
Here, here!—it is the beating of . . .

Kyle immediately recognized the lines from Edgar Allan Poe's "The Tell-tale Heart." He'd taken a Poe class his junior year with William, loving the writer's gory, chilling humor. He never wanted to look at a Poe tale again.

A thumping sound beat from the ground below. He could feel it in what little sensation he had left in his toes. He frantically dug up a mound of snow to find a black box buried beneath. With bile lurching up his throat, he opened the box to find a speaker that mimicked a heart-beat sound along with a pair of cut-off hands holding a bleeding heart. He knew even before he picked up the box that Jamie was gone. He'd been too late. He launched the box with its dreadful contents and watched as it disappeared into the black sky. He yelled loud enough for the echoes to give him chills.

After he became too hoarse to scream anymore, he wandered back to the car, out for blood. He looked around for the shack, but he could barely see a few feet ahead thanks to the snow cover. He studied the map of the park again and considered the clues he'd been given. A leg. An eye. Hands holding a heart. He stared at the map even more closely until the park revealed itself to be the shape of a human body.

He knew precisely where to go next.

Right into its heart.

CLOSING IN ON the heart, Kyle's cell phone buzzed. He almost didn't answer it, too focused on what he'd do to William once they'd reunited for their final battle. He saw the call was coming from Jamie and expected to hear William's voice on the other end.

"What did you do to her, you evil motherfucker?" Kyle shouted into the phone. "She wasn't a part of any of this. She didn't deserve—"

"Kyle?"

The voice was decidedly female. Definitely not William.

"Jamie?"

The steering wheel spun through his fingers as the car shot off the road. It crashed into a small tree, the air bag deploying. He fumbled for the phone, hearing a murmur of a voice on the other end.

"Jamie? Jamie, where did he take you?"

Blood gushed from his forehead, but he didn't care.

"Kyle, I'm in the hospital."

"But you're alive," he said, able to breathe again. "You're alive?"

Jamie didn't answer right away. A flash of Mia's ghost exploded in his mind, and he worried he could be hallucinating again.

"It's Sybil and her boyfriend, Erik," Jamie said, frantic. He could hear it in her voice. Pure fear.

"What about them?"

"It's William!" Jamie cried. "He was in my apartment. He was waiting for me but I was away all day. He drugged Sybil and Erik. And when Sybil woke up . . ."

Jamie let out a cry that gave him chills.

"Jamie, what? Tell me."

"When she woke up, Erik was lying next to her. His heart had been cut out, his hands, his leg, even an eye."

"Jesus *Christ* . . . I thought William had done that to *you*. That I'd lost you. I love you so much. I'm so sorry for everything."

"Kyle, where are you now?"

"I'm in Connecticut. I'm going after him."

"No, the police are on their way. Let them handle it."

The reception started to break up. It was hard to tell what she was saying from the escalating winds. He held the phone close to his ear.

"Jamie, are you there?"

"You're . . . breaking . . ."

"Stay in the hospital. Don't go back to your apartment in case William has some trap waiting for you there."

"Kyle, do *not* go after him."

"This has to end now," Kyle said.

"I'm sorry I didn't believe you . . . about William," Jamie said. "You tried to warn me—"

"I love you," he said, clutching himself, pretending she was actually there soothing him.

"Oh, God, I can't believe Erik is dead," she sniffed.

"Wait. Then who's in the shack?" Kyle asked.

"What?"

"If you aren't there, who did he take to the shack?"

"Kyle, I can barely hear you. Please be safe—"

The phone went dead.

He tried to call her again, but there was no reception. He tipped his head back to the sky and murmured "Thank you," even though he'd never believed in God before. Jamie was still alive, which meant that someone was fully looking out for him. Hopefully, they would keep watch over his safety too.

With the map from *Devil's Hopyard* tucked under his arm, he made his way toward the heart of the park. When he saw the shack in the distance tilting to the west, it seemed less ominous than he imagined it would be. A rather ordinary wooden lean-to that no one would ever look twice at. He left the map by its entrance and picked up a heavy branch as a weapon. Slowly, he opened the creaky door.

It was dark inside. A sliver of moonlight cut through a hole in the roof. Someone or something was moving in the back, a moan escaping from the prisoner's lips. He stepped in farther and saw it was Sierra chained to the floor, the tips of her fingers sliced off as she bled out.

"Help . . . me . . ." she croaked, her irises traveling up into her sockets, only the whites visible.

"Sierra?"

He dropped the heavy branch and took another step as the door shut and locked. William appeared from behind as a syringe stabbed into Kyle's neck. He fell into William's arms.

"Ssssshhh, sssssshhh," William whispered, placing Kyle down gently on the floor.

Kyle stared at the devil in front of him, hovering, having patiently planned this endgame. A smile spread across William's lips along with a laugh that began softly at first until it made the shack quake, and then unconsciousness took hold.

38

THE MOUSETRAP HAD broken three of Brett's fingers. He spent the day at Lenox Hill Hospital, where a doctor put splints on them and then taped them all together. He returned to the office to read *Devil's Hopyard,* hopped up on pain meds. He was surprised to find Darcy still at her desk. She was nibbling on a halved avocado in a Tupperware container and sprinkling it with salt from a shaker shaped like a book.

"What are you still doing here?" he asked, seeing two of her before they finally merged into one.

"I wanted to see how you were doing," she mumbled into her avocado. She brushed a strand of long hair over one eye.

"I'm in fucking pain," he said. "But I'm also flying high from the meds they gave me so it's all evening out."

"I should've felt the package to make sure it was safe."

"Where's the manuscript now?"

She pointed toward his office as if she was afraid. He barreled inside and found it on his desk. He went to pick it up, forgetting his broken fingers, and it slipped from his hands.

"Goddamn it!"

Darcy came in with an ice packet. She held it to his fingers. Maybe it was the pain meds, but he had never found her so statuesque up until that moment. She usually worked in silence, saying little, easy to overlook. The most he knew about her was that she was from Colorado and had a little dog named Jane Austen that she liked to dress up in period garb. Her cubicle wall held evidence of that. She had been with him two—*wait, no, three*—years, longer than any other assistant.

"How's your family in Colorado doing?" he asked.

"My family?" She brushed away her long hair until it wasn't covering her eye anymore. "Mom and Dad are good. They're thinking of retiring. Selling the ski lodge."

"They own a ski lodge?"

She gave a sad nod, which told him this was something he should've already known.

"You wanna pick up that manuscript for me?" he asked, indicating his busted hand.

"Sure, Mr. Swenson."

She used both hands, struggling to get a grip, and managed to get it back on the desk.

"Am I fucking mental for wanting to finish the rest?" he asked with a laugh. "William certainly thought it was worth getting my attention again."

She tapped at her chin. "How important is an ending for you?"

"Meaning?"

"Can you really assess a novel without completing the whole thing?"

This was why he kept Darcy around. She was a mute ninety percent of the time but a fantastic fucking reader. She was his first eye on anything crossing his desk. She rarely called them wrong.

"Have you read any of it, Darcy?"

She gulped. "Yes. All day since you went to the hospital."

"And what do you think?"

She took a moment to compose herself, clearly having rehearsed this since he'd left.

"It's really badly written in parts," she began. "But I think that's the author's point. To show William unraveling. And soon the line between the author and the professor disappears. I started to forget about the word choice and sentence structure, it just felt as if I'd entered a madman's mind. I believed his ravings."

"You think it's true? That he actually killed this girl Mia Evans who went missing?"

Darcy seemed short of breath, as if it was hard for her to continue.

"Mr. Swenson . . . that's not the only person he kills."

"Who else?"

"First, this guy Erik Lassen. He dismembers him and leaves his body parts all over Devil's Hopyard as clues."

"How far did you get in the book?"

"To the end."

Her voice became hushed. He realized they were the only two left in the office. It was late at night, later than he'd ever been at work. The place had an eerie hum to it that he found disconcerting.

"Who else does he kill?" Brett asked, tugging at his collar.

"Let me read it to you," Darcy said, and sat at his desk.

Her bottom lip was quivering. She took a deep breath and turned to the final chapter.

> "Devil's Hopyard. Chapter 38. 'Good night,' William says, laying a kiss on the top of Kyle's head. William waited for Kyle to wake up after injecting him with a heavy dose of GHB. He had bandaged up Sierra's fingers to stop them from bleeding out. The police would come for him eventually. He'd either be dragged out of the shack dead or carted off to jail, but death would be a more dramatic end, so that was what he'd aim for. This would

be all over the headlines tomorrow, his name trending. With the final manuscript in Brett Swenson's hands, Burke & Burke would be foolish not to publish his masterpiece. Sensationalism sells!

"The world will always wonder: What came first, the idea for his modern classic or the egg??? Meaning, did he set out to write this novel to cope with killing Mia, OR did he murder her to have fodder for a surefire bestseller?

"But an even bigger question remained. Would its hero, Kyle Broder, live to tell the story?

"Readers are inclined to think that the hero MUST make it to the end. We hold our trust in this setup. It is an agreement between the author and the reader. But I think I've shown that my book zigs when you expect it to zag. I let the girlfriend, Jamie, live, dear readers, when you thought she had died. I kidnapped Kyle's star protégée instead, for there can be only one true mentor and I am he. Kyle will watch as young Sierra pays the price for his mistakes. If he had trusted how good *Devil's Hopyard* was and agreed to have it published, he wouldn't be receiving a syringe with something way more sinister than a tranquilizer. But sometimes greatness comes from our biggest mistakes, right, Alexander Fleming? For the best way *Devil's Hopyard* can end is with its so-called hero's heart stopping. What could be more SHOCKING THAN THAT?

"Ah, I look over and see that Kyle's eyes have finally opened!

"He stares at me. I creep over to Sierra and unravel her bandages until her blood coats the shack's floor. She begins to convulse. Kyle tries to shut his eyes, but I keep them open. I make him watch. After a few minutes there is no way she can still be alive.

"'Why?' Kyle asks me, barely making a sound. I read his lips that look like a dead fish's.

"And now we've reached the moment in the book where the villain normally reveals his diabolical plans, but not in this one. I won't give Kyle or you readers the satisfaction. Soon the local police will show up. Since they are untrained dealing with a crime on this level, they will shoot before questioning. A shot would land right in my brain. This is the optimal ending, Kyle closing his eyes for good and then mine will shut too. I will return into the ground, to her, to Mia. And we'll watch from below as our names unite the world in rapt horror.

"I have written a note for my wife, Laura, and my children. It has been left in Mia's skeleton hands. I wrote it ten years ago on paper I made sure would never disintegrate. All my affairs are in order and I am ready to go.

" 'The truth is, Kyle, you are not the hero of this story,' I tell him.

" 'Why?' he manages to ask. This takes a great deal of struggle because I have loaded the syringe with pure strychnine and injected it in his shoulder.

" 'Because the hero is whoever wins at the end. Solves his quest. Realizes his full potential. A shelf in Barnes & Noble with *Devil's Hopyard* front and center will prove who is the hero.'

"Kyle's eyes flutter before closing.

" 'You were always my favorite pupil.'

"A loud knocking soon beats the door down. There is yelling and men in blue. One bullet in the chest brings me to the ground. Another gets me right between my eyes. In that second before the lights go out, I envision Mia Evans walking into my class for the first time. I'm scribbling on the chalkboard and my fingers go numb. I foresee what our future holds—this vision all too real—as I speed through the next decade until that final bullet spirals toward my fate in Devil's Hopyard.

"But in darkness, we ascend. In death, she and I become more alive than we ever were in life. We will be reincarnated and read my novel for the first time, again and again through the ages, each time clutching our hearts through its twists and turns, unaware that we are viewing our past lives, but completely enthralled by the tale."

39

KYLE MANAGED TO open one gummy eye. The other lay flush against the shack's floor. A metallic taste sat under his tongue. His hands had been tied tight with a chain around his wrists. A silver line of moonlight found its way through a broken slat, the only source of light. He parted the cobwebs in his brain, slowly circling back to reality. This was exactly how Mia met her end. He thought of her lying in the ground beneath him, waiting.

In the corner, William was bandaging up Sierra's fingers. A large pool of blood had collected by her feet. She was unconscious, a limp doll in his arms. He noticed Kyle waking up and came closer.

"Ah," William said. "You've opened your eyes."

He carefully lifted Kyle's head and propped it against the wall. It started to slip but he caught it.

"Why are you doing this?" Kyle managed to say.

From the way Kyle was positioned, he was able to see that a third person had entered the shack. Mia—just bones and dust, a handwritten note clasped in her skeleton fingers. With the soil flung around her, it looked like she'd erupted from the earth.

"I've dug up her body to make it as easy as possible for them," William said, filling his syringe from a small brown bottle labeled STRYCHNINE.

"For who?" Kyle coughed, the words drooling from his mouth.

"The police."

"Whatever you have planned won't work out in the end. I'll make sure of that."

William slapped Kyle across the face. It stung at first, but seconds later it woke Kyle up. William held the syringe to his neck.

"The only reason this isn't flowing through your veins right now is that I want you to watch Sierra die. I've taped her fingers to slow down her death, but it's inevitable."

"Why . . . does she have to be involved?"

"The *why* isn't important because it isn't in my manuscript. I can tell you my reasons, but no one else will know them, so it doesn't matter. The two of you will be found dead at the hands of a deeply disturbed soul. Let them speculate for ages *why.*"

"And what will happen to you?"

"The police will write the narrative for how this goes. Will they kill me here in the shack, or do they risk sparing my life and giving me a chance to rage?"

"I've told the town's sheriff about you," Kyle said. "He has the final draft of *Devil's Hopyard.* He'll find this place."

"I know he will. I know him well. How he moves. His motivations, what Mia had meant to him all these years. You and I are not the only ones who had been spellbound. And Brett Swenson has the book too. I guarantee once he finishes and reads tomorrow's headlines, *Devil's Hopyard* will be sent right off to the presses."

"So that's what this was all about, just to write a bestseller?"

William chuckled his signature laugh. "A bestseller means nothing these days. Morons have written bestsellers. I've created something that's never been done in literature before."

Kyle figured his best chance was to keep talking. Whatever he could do to keep William preoccupied.

"You haven't created anything, only destroyed. Mia was nineteen years old—"

"*She* made promises she couldn't keep."

"You loved her, I know." Kyle pushed through the cobwebs in his mind as hard as he could. He had to take control of this ending. In his pants pocket was a Wisconsin Badger's key chain with a Swiss Army knife attached. Even with his hands chained, he could try to maneuver it out of his pocket.

"We had made plans," William said. He bent down and picked up what was left of her jaw. "Did she ever make big plans with you?"

"No," Kyle said.

William nodded smugly. "That's the difference between your relationship with her and mine."

Kyle managed to get his pinkie looped inside his pocket. He shifted in place to try to dig deeper.

"You were a child," William said. "She wasn't interested in a child."

"So you killed her so I couldn't have her?"

"*No,* Kyle, despite your belief that the world revolves around you, you did not factor into that decision. You were a toy to her just like all the rest. And lamentably, so was I. She rejected me because I was her chance at happiness, but she didn't feel like she deserved it. That's what made us so close, made us into the same person. We came from poison, we knew rot, me in a faraway shack like this one, and her disintegrating just a mile from here, with a cranked-out stepdad slipping into her bed each night."

"I didn't know that," Kyle said, but he did. Mia had told him all about her past. He'd been complaining about his mom because she was always a little whackadoo depending on whatever meds she was on. Mia had the same situation with hers, but things were far worse at her home.

"Imagine having a doped-up mother along with a rapey stepdad," Mia told him. She had said it so nonchalantly.

Kyle never complained about his family to her again. It made him try to reach out to his dad to mend things, even though his attempt was too late. He and his dad had never been close. Wally Broder didn't like books or see the point in them. He wanted a son to hunt with and watch NASCAR. He was a mechanic and spent the day working on cars, coming home smelling of grease and oil and a different scent of perfume each night. One day he just stopped coming home, not a word for a year until a letter floated into their mailbox telling of another family he had out in Eau Claire. Kyle's mother was a challenge, high-strung and a pill addict; it was one of the first things he and Mia bonded over—but Wally never laid a hand on him, just lost interest.

Kyle had gotten his ring finger inside the pocket now, his middle finger so close. The chains sliced into his wrists. They were slick with his blood. He prayed they wouldn't saw into an artery.

"Mia was badly abused," William continued. His voice had dropped in vibrato, the tone slower, more practiced. He'd let the conversation become untethered, but now he was bringing it back, seizing control. He knew exactly what he wanted to reveal. Kyle could see a flicker of excitement in the fucker's eyes.

"Mia's mother had her boyfriend move back in," William said. "The crank dealer. Mia couldn't afford dorm dues so she was living at home. He started forcing himself on her again."

Mia had never told this to Kyle, which made him question whether or not it was true. He knew only what her stepdad did when she was in high school. He didn't know it had continued.

"This shack became her hideout. A place she could go to when things got bad. That's why I found it for her. She came to me one afternoon drenched in tears. She asked me to take her away. We had plans."

"You were going to leave your wife?"

Kyle finally tucked his middle finger into his pocket.

"I was, I really thought I was. Whether I would have actually gone through with it, who knows? But Mia had inspired me then. I started writing again. Having children . . . well, it had sucked up all my time for many years. I wrote nothing, and it made me angry. I am capable of terrible things, and that foulness festered inside me. I'm aware of the many faces I have. I have to find ways to release these demons. So sometimes I'd drive to an animal farm at night. I'd get out a blade and leave behind a slaughter. I'd sit in their blood, paint my eyes, howl at the moon. You don't know where I've come from, Kyle. The evil that I've seen."

"I know, I've read your book."

"And do you believe it?"

"I do."

"Yet you still think it's not good enough to be published?"

Kyle wrenched his index finger into the pocket, only his thumb dangling off the side. He tried to grasp for his knife. He tapped against cold metal, but it was still too far away.

"Who am I to say if your novel's good or not if I still haven't seen how it ends?"

"It ends in death, just like all great endings. Yours and mine."

"Actually," Kyle said, managing a grin, "my favorite kinds of books don't have a definitive ending. They leave the reader hanging a bit. So the story continues on in their minds."

Now Kyle got his thumb jammed into the pocket. He planned to grab the knife and fall on top of William so the knife would plunge into his stomach. It was a crazy idea, but it was all he could think of trying.

"You don't see that as a cop-out?" William asked.

"No, it's more realistic. Nothing in life ever ends completely anyway. People die, but their loved ones live on after them, keep their memories alive."

William nodded frantically, tears in his eyes.

"*Yes,* that's what I *wanted.* To keep Mia's memory alive. In life, what would she have become? She would've dropped out of Bentley, strung out around the country, looking for any way to pay for a needle."

"What do you mean pay for a needle?"

"She was doing heroin, Kyle. He injected her one night while she was sleeping—the fucking crankhead her mom was dating. He got her hooked. And then she was like a puppy at his feet. He went from scum to hero, and I took his place as scum. I got in the way of her high. So you bet I fucking chained her up in the shack, I was weaning her off smack. I was going to get her clean, and then we were going to disappear—just for a while—and I was going to write our tale, our story."

Kyle reached down even farther, feeling the shape of the Bucky Badger key chain in his fist. He started to pull it out.

"And I was going to tell Laura all about us," William continued. "I would have come back for my kids too. I wasn't going to lose my position at Bentley; this would just be my sabbatical. I had it all planned, even got that bitch Dr. Yancey to approve a proposal."

"But Mia didn't want to go?"

"I only kept her chained up for one night . . . the first time. When I came to get her, she wouldn't even look at me. I unchained her, drove her home, but . . . she never truly looked at me again. Then she used you to make me jealous, Kyle. All of a sudden you two were inseparable, but junkies are erratic and you wouldn't last. I begged her to give me another chance, told her I did it to save her life so *we* could start ours, but she became a wall I couldn't penetrate. I began to think of her in a different way."

"You mean you thought about her heart?"

William gave a solitary nod, unashamed.

"It's not to say I never thought about her heart before. It teased the back of my mind. I'd dream about it. I'd wake up in the middle of night and write these long passages about its beat, its . . . perfect muscle. I had these long scrolls penned in calligraphy, rather Jack Kerouac–like. Anyway, the final draft I did of *Hopyard* will lead its editor to where I've kept those scrolls. I imagine it could be a follow-up of some sort."

"How did she die?" Kyle asked, struggling to get the key chain out of his pocket. It had caught on a loose thread.

William stared at an imaginary point just beyond Kyle's head. Kyle wondered if he was looking at Mia's ghost. If she had visited Kyle earlier, why not William as well? Was she telling him it was time to fully confess?

William bit into his tongue, drawing blood. He chewed it for a while, contemplating.

"Weeks went by after Mia spent the night in the shack," he continued. "She had completely cut me off, treated me as if I were invisible. She stopped coming to class. You were probably too high to notice anything was wrong, but I knew. I'd stalk her every move, watch her descend into a daylong heroin high in her bedroom. Then I was in the Commons one night when I heard the two of you fighting, a drugged-out, nonsensical screaming match. The whole school watched. You went your separate ways and I followed her. She headed off campus down a trail that would eventually lead to her mom's house. I pulled up beside her in my car."

Kyle yanked the key chain from where it had caught, but it slid from his fingers. He felt this loss in the pit of his stomach and had no choice but to try for it again.

"When she saw me, she became possessed, spouting a stream of hate so dark . . . I . . . it took me back to being a child chained up in our farm's shack as my father reasoned why he needed to hurt me, and I'd . . . I'd shut him off, just pretend I couldn't hear, but with Mia . . . I loved her and so her hate was like bullets. She took off, running down the road, and I put my foot on the gas, plowed right into her. It was just an impulsive reaction, but the impact threw her a few feet, knocked her out. So I carried her to my car and we returned to her . . . final home."

Kyle was almost able to grab the key chain again, his fingers so close.

"I handcuffed her to the bed in the shack. I stayed with her all night. I woke her with a kiss, but more hate spewed from her mouth. I'd return with all her favorite things, but it didn't matter. I told her I loved her and that this was what I needed to do to help her. But she couldn't see. She was so blind. So I began to use force, and then . . ."

Kyle's thumb and pinkie grasped the key chain, straining to get it out.

"I left her for a few days. I went on a walkabout in the woods, and the whole book came to me in an instant. A confession of what I was about to do. I knew it would take me a long time to write, since I'd never finished a novel before, but I was patient. It would be our love story—as demented as our relationship was—and it would begin with her in the ground and her heart inside me. And once it was finished and on its way to the masses, I would expose the secret I buried—her bones—and engineer an ending in real life more haunting than I could ever write."

Kyle finally wrenched the key chain from his pocket. He spun it around in his hands, searching for the attached Swiss Army knife.

"Looking for this?" William was holding up the knife. He slashed Kyle across the face, cutting deep enough for the wounds to possibly never heal. "I am the *master,* not you. And now to pay for your insolence, your little pet will die."

William went over to Sierra and unraveled her bandages, the blood flowing out an alarming rate.

"Please . . . don't," Kyle said as Sierra turned pale.

"Both of our novels could've been such a success for you. You didn't have to *just choose hers.* You would've been the biggest editor in the biz with your literary darling and the madman. I was writing you a goddamn ticket, Kyle. And I was ready to sacrifice myself at the end for my art, to give *Devil's Hopyard* a stellar ending. I would have made you the hero. You always were my favorite student."

"Even though you were trying to frame me for Mia's murder?"

William wagged his finger. "That was only a backup plan. Insurance. Stick it on the crazy kid who'd just been arrested in case Sheriff Pealey came sniffing too close. But he never did. He never wanted to find the truth because the truth would've forced him to deal with reality. Hunting for Mia's killer kept him alive."

"You're forgetting something," Kyle managed to say. The blood from William cutting his face had clouded his eyes, everything painted in red, making the scene appear even more macabre. "*Devil's Hopyard* will never be published. Burke & Burke would never—"

"I think you sorely underestimate your colleague Brett and even your boss. The publishing business isn't what it used to be. Overhead is high and sales have declined. All the big houses are looking for that next breakout hit. With the national press I'll receive for what I've done, the book will be rushed into production. Although you'll never see that happen because you'll be dead. You could've had your name in lights, but—"

Outside, the sound of a car crept toward the shack. They both could hear tires crunching in the dirt. William tilted his head toward the sound, distracting himself long enough for Kyle to thrust his head into William's stomach, knocking him to the ground. William snapped back, slamming Kyle's face into Mia's skeleton, which broke into pieces. Kyle leaped up and bashed his head into William's. Both reeled from the pain, but Kyle kept going. Neither knew whose blood was being flung into the air.

At the door to the shack, a voice echoed, too far away for either Kyle or William to make out who it was. Both had entered into a surreal tussle, a fight between animals for dominance. They had left their souls, rolled around in the blood and bones, ready to die.

A shot rang out, flinging the door off its hinges. Sheriff Pealey stood with his gun raised, face flushed with horror at the swirling nightmare before him. He tried to aim at his target, but William and Kyle had merged into one terrifying organism.

"*You're* fucking dead, *you're* fucking dead," Kyle screamed. He managed to wrap his fingers around William's throat. He could feel William laughing, softly at first until it was causing his palms to shake.

"Son, let go of him," the sheriff yelled, but Kyle wouldn't relent. "Son, we'll take him in, we'll make him pay. You don't want this to be on your hands. You don't want that on you."

But Kyle couldn't hear. He was squeezing William's neck so hard. He imagined the bastard's head just popping off and then planting it on a pike.

"*Timshel,*" William gasped.

"Son, don't make me shoot you," Sheriff Pealey yelled. He fired a warning shot that seemed to jar Kyle from his state. Kyle looked over to the scattered bones of a girl he once loved. It made him think about the girl he still did—Jamie. He hadn't gone insane enough yet that he wouldn't be able to return to her. Throughout this ordeal, he hadn't done anything so awful that might plague his dreams forever. He began to ease his grip on William's neck. William wheezed in relief as Kyle's trembling fingers slid away. He rolled off William's body as the sheriff descended, twisting William's hands behind his back and throwing on handcuffs. Then he called his radio for backup and an ambulance.

Kyle ran over to Sierra and fixed the bandages over her fingers until she stopped bleeding. Sheriff Pealey restrained William, who was silent now. William had his rights read to him and seemed creepily calm, relishing this moment, this utter chaos. He smacked his lips, and Kyle didn't want to think what he might be tasting in his mind—one last tangy thrill: the heart of a girl he had obliterated.

40

WITH A DETACHED cool, William watched Kyle and Sierra being loaded into an ambulance. The sheriff's deputy, a boy named Hawker, had arrived along with the FBI. William was escorted into the backseat of the sheriff's car, with Deputy Hawker sitting shotgun. They took off, sandwiched between a chorus of FBI cars, their sirens wailing. He listened to Bach's *Well-Tempered Clavier,* the notes floating through the squad car, putting his soul at ease. The true ending of this tale would now begin.

Sheriff Pealey and Deputy Hawker were trying to get him to speak. They were mystified by it all, as they should be. Pealey was more shell-shocked, having known William for years. Despite being the size of a mountain, it was apparent Hawker was green to the job—a young kid with ears that stuck out and a bad teenage mustache.

"I just don't see how this can be," Pealey said, overcome by tears.

William guessed that someone who made it to seventy years of age thought that he'd already seen the worst things imaginable, but he had caused Pealey to become demoralized.

"Your kids, Bill!" Pealey wailed. "And Laura? What are they gonna think? What's everyone gonna think?"

William sat patiently until they passed by Eldridge Cliff. It was a precarious turn on Route 10, one that people under the influence had misjudged before and shot right over the fencing. The FBI whizzed through the turns like they were race cars on a track. Sheriff Pealey wouldn't be so lucky.

William bashed his face—once, twice—into the grate that separated him from the front seat. He used all his might, as if he were a mother lifting up a car that had fallen on her baby. He wiggled through the partition and lunged at Deputy Hawker with his teeth bared, chewed off a piece of the young rookie's ear. He spat the deputy's mangled ear in Sheriff Pealey's face and chomped down on the sheriff's nose. Cartilage crushed with each bite as the sensation of flying coursed through William's veins. He swiveled around and saw only the night before him through the front window, the moon close enough to kiss, but other than that only a black void, nothing, as the car plunged a thousand feet below into trees that lit up instantly upon impact, their nuclear leaves dotting the skyline.

From far away across Long Island Sound, spectators later said that they thought someone had been launching fireworks.

41

THE NEXT DAY, Kyle woke in the hospital from a dream where he was running but going nowhere, chased by some monstrous being. His legs still moved even after he opened his eyes. The doctors had stitched up his face when he was brought in, the sewn scars making him feel like a busted piece of furniture. The doctors gave the scars a fifty percent chance of healing. He had made a joke about it that he couldn't remember because of the pain meds. He did, however, remember that it hurt to smile.

Two FBI agents spent the morning grilling him. He went through every detail, tripping up a few times over what really happened versus the plot of William's novel. A few bits, especially from ten years ago, were difficult to place in a time frame.

"You saved Sierra Raven's life," one of the agents said. Kyle wondered why Sheriff Pealey wasn't the one questioning him.

The FBI found all of Erik Lassen's body parts that William had strewn throughout the park. As for William's body, it had incinerated in a fiery blaze. All that remained were a few teeth as identification.

"And the sheriff?" Kyle asked. "He's the real hero."

The two agents gave each other a stern look.

"Sheriff Morris Pealey and Deputy Jesse Hawker were unfortunately killed too. Looks like Lansing caused their car to go off the cliff. The road was icy."

"But William is *absolutely* dead, right?" Kyle asked, knowing the answer but wanting to hear it verbalized.

"Yeah, that son of a bitch is deader than dead."

Later, as Kyle ate his lunch of soup and Jell-O, he tortured himself by reliving the last few weeks. How much had William planned? Was everything orchestrated to create this ending? Had there been a decade of careful moves to reach this destination?

A nurse entered after what must have been an hour of steady concentration.

"Mr. Broder, your girlfriend called to say she's on the way. We thought you were sleeping so we didn't want to disturb you."

"Thank you."

Thinking of Jamie momentarily quieted his obsessive mind. He longed to hold her. The nurse went to leave.

"Wait. How is Sierra Raven doing?"

"She's gonna to be okay," the nurse said. "Come on, I'll take you to see her."

He found Sierra sitting up in bed. The doctors had affixed metal tips that resembled thimbles to all of her fingertips. She was attached to machines by various tubes. Her laptop glowed at her side, displaying a blank Word page.

"Doing some writing?" A sharp pain stabbed into his cheek. He'd have to mumble when he talked for a while.

Sierra pushed at her laptop until it fell off the bed, crashing to the floor.

"Hey, hey," he said, picking up the laptop and putting it on the side table. It had a crack down its center but still looked like it worked.

Sierra stared straight ahead, a zombie.

"The nurse said you're gonna be all right. Me too, except for the slashes—" He ran his fingers across a sewn-up scar. "Are your folks coming? From Missouri?"

"I told them to leave," she said. Her voice sounded like every word was a chore. "They're checking into a hotel."

"I can't believe you were dragged into this, Sierra." It was all he could think of saying.

"When I came home, William was already inside my house," she said in a monotone. "I don't know how he got in. He was sitting on my couch, and I had grocery bags in my hands. I told myself to run, but I didn't have the energy because I knew he'd catch up. So I gave in. I woke up paralyzed in darkness, trapped in his trunk."

She began to cry. Kyle had never seen anyone appear so wounded. He hugged her, both of them bawling, squeezing out every last tear until there were none left.

"You're gonna be okay," he said, echoing the advice to himself. "We're gonna get over this."

She shook her head.

"Never." Her face became frozen in horror. "Never, never, never."

"*No,* we will. It'll just take time—"

"Part of me will always be in that shack, as he sliced off my fingers."

She curled into a fetal position with her back to him. He put a careful palm on her shoulder.

"He wins if you act like this," Kyle said sternly. "Don't you see? We beat him and survived. That's what matters."

"Nothing matters," she said, a chill in the room, the hospital cold. Kyle became aware he was wearing only a gown and slippers.

"This will make you a better writer," Kyle said.

Sierra turned over, disappointed. "What does that mean?"

"I know you can't see this right now," he said, his words half a step ahead of his brain. "But you'll use what happened to you. It'll seep into *Girls Without Hope.* It'll make the pain of the girls more palpable for the reader."

"I have no plans of ever writing again."

He laughed in shock and then winced from the pain. It felt like a stitch had torn.

"Sure you will."

"I'll pay back my advance if I can, or give it all away to a charity that works to end violence against women and girls, or sue me, I don't care . . . I don't care," she repeated, turning over and bringing the sheets up to her neck. "Like, what's the point?" She coughed from choking on her tears. "What's the fucking point? What's the *fucking* point?"

She rocked herself into a fit. A nurse came in to calm her down. She glared at Kyle as if he was responsible.

"I'm sorry," he said to both of them. Once Sierra settled, the nurse exited with a warning not to agitate her again.

"This is what William wanted, Sierra. He was jealous of your book and that's why he did this to you. You have to keep writing to prove him—"

"He is *dead,* and I don't give a flying fuck what he wanted. All I know is that my fingers feel like they are on fire. The doctors said that if we were rescued five minutes later I would have lost too much blood." Her mouth was gaping, one bloodshot eye throbbing. "I want to crawl into a hole and never come out."

"That'll pass, all it takes is time . . ."

But he didn't know what time would bring. It was just one of those clichés people said when there was nothing sensible to say. He imagined waking up every night with his heart slamming into his chest. He felt woozy.

"We will *never* be okay," she said, her whole body shaking before she sank back into a fetal position.

He had the desire to back out of the room, rationalizing that he would be fine again. He'd give Jamie a key to his place and have her move in. He'd get right back into editing books like Shane Matthews's *The Dead Can't Hunt You Down* and even *Girls Without Hope* once Sierra was ready. He wouldn't wake from a nightmare with his heart exploding from his chest. He had defeated William and would win in the end.

As he was about to leave her room, he spied a Post-it pad with a pencil on the bedside table. He took a moment to compose his thoughts and scribbled YOU HAVE A BEAUTIFUL VOICE THAT NEEDS TO BE PUT TO PAPER. He went to tap Sierra on the back to show her, but then just left it on her pillow.

42

BACK IN HIS hospital room, the nurse asked Kyle if there was anything he needed. Since Jamie hadn't arrived yet, he requested every major paper in the newsstand with William Lansing in the headlines. She seemed hesitant but came back with a stack. She told him that reporters were waiting outside but the hospital wouldn't allow them in. He went to the window and saw a crowd of vultures below. The nurse left and he spread out all the papers on his bed. *Newsday*: "Editor Lured to a Deadly Shack." *The Wall Street Journal*: "The Manuscript That Helped Solve a 10-Year-Old Cold Case." New York *Daily News*: "Grieving Mother of Missing Girl Gets Devastating Closure." *New York Post*: "Did the Lansing Family Aid in Mia Evans's Death?" *The New York Times*: "The Murdering Mentor's Last Words."

He picked up the *Times,* which had a picture of the note William left in Mia's skeleton fist a decade ago:

To Laura and the twins.
And to the one who got away.
La Vita Nuova.

Kyle recognized the dedication from *Devil's Hopyard*. This meant that when he murdered Mia, he had already started on his novel. He'd killed her for fodder so he could write a bestseller. But he also loved her, as proved by the additional reference to Dante's book of prose and poetry *La Vita Nuova*—The New Life. When Kyle had first read the dedication, he'd glossed over the Italian words, but now he recalled a Dante seminar William had taught the semester after Mia went missing. The professor began with the author's first sonnet, which alluded to a tale of infatuation Dante had with a girl named Beatrice.

The newspaper article went on to dissect Dante's sonnet as a clue for a possible motive to William's barbaric acts. Although Dante barely knew Beatrice, she became his muse. In their final meeting, Dante wrote of a heart being consumed:

Joyfully Love seemed to me to hold
My heart in his hand, and held in his arms
My lady wrapped in a cloth sleeping.
Then he woke her, and that burning heart
He fed to her reverently, she fearing,
Afterwards he went not to be seen weeping.

After Beatrice's death, Dante's love for her only grew. Beatrice became more alive to him than in the flesh. Dante called her *"La gloriosa donna della mia mente,"* the glorious lady of my mind, a muse that he was free to imagine as he wished. It was clear that Mia became William's Beatrice.

Kyle's head hurt. How much of the truth had William confessed in the shack? Would he ever truly know the whole story? Everyone would keep trying to fit together the parts of a puzzle the psychopath laid out, but a few pieces would always remain missing. The air in the hospital room became colder, nipped at Kyle's skin. He tried not to shiver but was unsuccessful.

Kyle picked up the *Post* and read the article, "Did the Lansing Family Aid in Mia Evans's Death?" The reporter stated that Laura Lansing was being held for questioning after she was found handcuffed to her sofa. A call had come into the sheriff's office requesting backup at the Lansing house. The sheriff's secretary, Loretta Samuels, replayed the phone message, which stated that Laura Lansing had attacked Sheriff Pealey. Mrs. Lansing was brought in for questioning along with her children, Alicia and Bill Jr. At the moment, it was still uncertain whether Alicia and Bill were involved too.

A thousand theories spiraled in Kyle's brain. Had William contacted Bill to help him bring Mia's body to the shack? Did Alicia find out that her brother aided in Mia's death and choose to remain silent?

The article continued with the FBI discovering a rock covered with blood in William's office along with boxes of journals outlining *Devil's Hopyard.* The reporter stated that it would take days to comb through everything William wrote.

Kyle turned to *The Wall Street Journal*'s article: "The Manuscript That Helped Solve a 10-Year-Old Cold Case." The FBI found Kyle's copy of *Devil's Hopyard* left in the rental car and posted a photo of the manuscript's cover. Kyle had never noticed it before, but the *D* in *Devil's* had been drawn in the shape of a devil's tail with an arrowhead. The journalist went on to discuss the origin of the arrowhead on the devil's tail. Whenever a soldier was shot by an arrow to the chest, often the arrowhead was dangerously close to the heart. The wooden arrow and the head would be covered in blood. As Satan was frequently depicted in artwork as red, the red arrow and arrowhead became the devil's tail.

A knock on the door disrupted his concentration, but he ignored it.

The desire to read through the rest of the newspapers was too great. Theory upon theory of how William could be hiding such a horrible secret for so long. Kyle was desperate to know more and spied a final headline, "The Real Hannibal Lecter," with a picture of William staring back, his eyes black like marbles.

"Kyle?"

Jamie stood at the door.

"Jamie!" He pushed William aside and opened his arms. She ran into them and buried her head in his shoulder. She felt his face hesitantly.

"Oh, God, what did he do to you?" she asked. Heavy circles weighed down her eyes; it looked like she hadn't slept in weeks.

"I'm okay, I'm okay," he said, even though it hurt when she touched his scars.

"I should have listened to you," she said. "You warned me—"

"It all sounded too crazy to be true."

"The things he did," she whispered. "How could anyone . . . ?"

"He was sick, disturbed."

"I just want to pretend like it all never happened."

He reached into his pocket and pulled out his Badgers key chain.

"Bucky Badger saved my life."

She laughed at the absurdity of it, but then started crying.

"It's true," he said, collecting her tears with his thumbs. "I thought my Swiss Army knife had been attached so I tried to get it out of my pocket to stab William. He had removed the knife, but it distracted him for a moment until the sheriff finally shot down the door."

He took off the key and placed it in her palm.

"I want you to move in with me, Jamie. I want you to be there when I get home, always."

She stared at the key, and then her eyes shifted over to all of the newspapers.

"I need to know that you can let William go."

"Of course I will. He's dead."

"Kyle, this will follow you for the rest of your life. It's national news. There are a ton of reporters outside."

"Yeah, we'll have to give our statements, answer their questions . . ."

"I know," Jamie said sadly, as if that was not the response she wanted to hear. "And we will, but then . . . I worry . . ."

He brushed a strand of blond hair from her eyes. "What, baby, what?"

"I know you, Kyle, how you operate. *Why* William did this will become your new obsession."

"It was all plot for his novel."

She gestured to the newspapers on the bed. "How come you even bought these papers? Why would you do that to yourself after what you went through?"

"I was just trying to find a way to make sense of it all. But you're right, it's unhealthy."

He kissed her. Her lips were dry and she hadn't brushed her teeth. But he didn't care. He imagined she'd been woken from sleep and rushed to the hospital when she found out what happened, no time for morning rituals. That was love. That was what Dante had wanted from Beatrice. What William wanted from Mia.

"Kyle? *Kyle!*" Jamie snapped.

"What?" He circled back to Earth.

"You went away for a moment. Were you thinking about him?"

Kyle gave a solitary nod.

"I need to know if I move into your place that his name is never to be repeated in our house. We each give our statements to the press when you leave the hospital, and *HE* is never brought up again."

Kyle looked around at the sea of newspapers with William's evil face. Could he really let William go, or would that madman always be there in some form, tucked away in a fold of his brain, a soft laugh that he would barely hear at first until it became deafening? He held Jamie tight, attempting to drive William out of his psyche. He kicked away all the newspapers until they were scattered about the floor. She was right about William's presence still sinking in. Kyle needed to quit him cold turkey.

"I promise you," he said. He slid the Bucky Badger key chain on her ring finger as if he was proposing. "Please say yes."

She observed the cartoon badger as if it was an actual diamond ring. He could tell she liked the way it looked.

"Okay, I do."

"I love you so much, baby."

They kissed again, passionately, losing themselves in it. He had shut his eyes, but through a tiny slit he could see William's face on a newspaper that remained on the bed. The photo was from Bentley's Web site, a formal head shot. His silvery hair neatly combed, wearing neither a smile nor a frown, gazing out at a world that was starting to fear his name.

Kyle pictured himself strolling through the shelves of Barnes & Noble, cracking open the spine of a prominently placed book, and finding the same picture used as the author's photo.

He stopped kissing Jamie only because he was about to throw up.

43

TO ESCAPE THE media deluge that didn't seem like it was going away, Kyle and Jamie headed to her aunt's house in Wisconsin on Three Stepping Stones Lake.

Since it was far into October, her aunt had already closed up the place for the summer with no plans to return until Memorial Day. The two of them would have complete idyllic isolation.

A wall of snow banked the house. The Midwest was having the same early freezing temperatures as the Northeast. The inside had been set up with a prairie trail kind of vibe: wood everything and mounted deer antlers on the walls. Kyle had been ordered by Carter to take the next two weeks for pure vacation, so he shut off his phone and he and Jamie didn't even bother setting up the Wi-Fi. They bought provisions from the local general store along with a dozen bottles of red wine and wrapped themselves in bearskin throws and made a fire. They listened to her aunt's old Harry Belafonte and Simon and Garfunkel records, and they woke up at sunrise every morning to make love. They orbited back toward one another after having drifted apart. After a few days, Kyle felt the urge to do some work and started editing Shane Matthews's *The Dead Can't Hunt You Down.* He read passages out loud to Jamie and could see she was thrilled at the tale of an ex–hit man hunted down by his former organization. He realized how much he missed fiction after being sucked into his real-life thriller. Only once did he wake up with a pain in his heart.

A swirling blizzard had fallen that night he was awakened, scraping against the windows like it wanted to come inside. Jamie had gone to red wine dreamland so Kyle got up to tend the fire that still popped and crackled. The scraping sound became louder and louder so he went to the window to see what was up. Outside, a strange silhouette had left footprints in the backyard. Kyle huddled in a bearskin throw and put on a pair of boots to investigate.

By a snowcapped swing set, William sat munching on a heart, his mouth red with sinew and blood. At his feet was a body. Kyle expected to see that it was Mia, but Kyle's own body lay mangled on the frozen ground.

"William is immortal," Dead Kyle said to his live self, and then he woke up.

In the morning, Jamie was making pancakes and said he seemed distant. He blamed it on too much red wine.

That night would be their last at Three Stepping Stones Lake. Since it was Halloween, they dressed up as Ugly Sweater People from her aunt's bountiful collection and headed into town. The blizzard had let up and children were all in costume: vampires, witches, ghosts, and even a tiny devil with a pitchfork that weaved through the crowd. A band played spooky music. They got themselves some hot cider from a kiosk and sat on the benches.

"I feel whole again," he said.

"Will you still be when we get back?" she asked, leaving an apple-scented kiss on his cheek. "It won't be easy."

"It will be because I have you."

They laced their fingers together. This would be the woman he'd marry. They'd have children and eventually grandkids. They'd keep the torment they went through locked up in a tiny box never to be opened.

"Could you get me another cider, Monkey?" Jamie asked, pointing to a happy monkey swinging from a vine on his ugly sweater.

He kissed her nose and made his way to the apple kiosk. In front of him on line was a little boy no more than three feet tall. The boy wore khaki pants and a blazer with elbow patches. He was wearing a mask, but Kyle couldn't see what it was until the boy fully turned around. He was startled to find William staring back at him, a cheap plastic version of his former mentor. The mask was an exact duplicate of the photo all the newspapers had used, probably rushed into production for the Halloween season. Plastic William had cutouts for eyes and a hole in his mouth that a tiny tongue slithered through.

When he got back to Jamie, he was perspiring from a panic attack. He couldn't catch his breath. She kept asking what was wrong, but how could he tell her what had happened? He'd been doing so well at blocking out William, but the man couldn't be forgotten. Out of the corner of Kyle's eye, he watched the little boy dressed as William leaving the kiosk with a red candied apple in his hands, devouring his sweet prize.

KYLE RETURNED TO Burke & Burke a few days later. He wormed his way past the press hunkered outside the office, all of them looking wet and miserable. Upstairs, Amanda sat at the front desk. She ended a call when she saw him.

"Did you make it by those parasites in one piece?" she asked. "The other day, I literally threw my coffee on one of them who wanted a scoop."

She leaned over the desk to observe his face. The cuts had begun to heal but not completely. She touched one with a fingernail painted royal blue.

"So deep," she said. "I have some non-Western remedies that could help. I'll bring them to work tomorrow."

"Thank you, Amanda."

"Mr. Burke wants to see you in his office," she said, and slid back into her seat. "So brave, Kyle. You're America's hero right now."

"Don't think I'm really comfortable with that title."

"I can tell," she said, nibbling at her lip ring. "Inside of you, a storm is brewing."

"Come again?"

"Have you let out a scream yet, a guttural one from the pit of your stomach? You need to do that so you can really begin to heal."

"I'm fine, Amanda."

"Trust me, I'm an old soul," she said. "I've had many difficult past lives. I've screamed so much that my throat is eternally sore."

He hurried away from her, not wanting to be exposed anymore. Down the hallway, he walked briskly past Brett's office, no interest in dealing with him yet. In his office, Carter had a glass of twenty-five-year-old Macallan waiting for Kyle.

"It's twenty-five hundred a bottle," Carter said.

Kyle took a whiff, robust with hints of peach and wood.

"Sit down, son."

Kyle warmed his tongue with a sip and sat across from Carter, who seemed unsure how to begin.

"Feeling rested?" Carter asked.

"The lake house was just what I needed, what Jamie and I needed."

Carter rapped his desk with his knuckles. "Good . . . good."

Silence filled the room. Kyle looked out the window and saw that the Rockefeller Center Christmas tree had gone up, ready to astound thousands of tourists.

"I don't need to tell you how much attention this all has gotten," Carter began. "For Burke & Burke as well. Getting work done lately has been . . . a challenge."

"I'm sorry, sir, I never meant—"

"Of course you didn't," Carter said, and took an indulging sip. "I heard from Sierra Raven recently."

"Is she all right?" Kyle asked. "I haven't had a chance to be in touch with her since I've been back."

"She's severing her contract, no interest in writing the book anymore. In fact, her lawyer was the one who contacted me, claims excessive distress, blah, blah, wah, wah."

"She told me in the hospital that she never wanted to write again. She's been through a lot."

"I'm not fighting her in the courts," he said. "She's giving her advance to some women's antiviolence charity anyway, and I have more important business to discuss."

"I've been editing *The Dead Can't Hunt You Down,*" Kyle said.

"The what?"

"Shane Matthews's novel about the ex–hit man—"

Carter shook his head. "No, no, no. I have more pressing business. Take another sip first."

Kyle obliged and luxuriated in a long, slow sip.

Carter pulled *Devil's Hopyard* from a drawer and placed it on the desk between them.

"I've read the entire thing," Carter said.

"I'm sorry."

Carter gave a bark of a laugh. "Still haven't lost that sense of humor, I see."

Kyle felt himself inching away from the manuscript, wanting to be as far away from it as possible.

"I want to publish it," Carter said.

Kyle shook his head. "But it's garbage."

"Garbage that will make our shareholders very, very happy. This is how I see it . . ."

Kyle could tell that his boss had already planned this speech, probably practiced it in the mirror this morning.

"One of the big houses will publish this manuscript if we don't, so bemoaning any ethical reservations is pointless."

"But this is what William . . . what he wanted all along."

It gave Kyle chills to even say William's name. He hadn't mentioned him at all since he and Jamie left for the lake house.

Carter wasn't listening, caught up in his own spiel. "Publishers wait for this kind of gold mine their whole lives, and I want to give you the honor of editing it, Kyle . . . after all you've been through, of course."

"But—"

"I know Brett was technically William's editor since you passed on it, but it feels right to have it your hands. Go on."

Carter kept pushing the manuscript across the desk until it sat under Kyle's nose.

"This was what he *planned,*" Kyle said, raising his voice.

"None of the money will go to his estate. The family is up to their neck in legal troubles. The son and the wife are out on bail right now after some new evidence came through. They *want* us to publish it."

"He wins," Kyle said, softly, a dying man's final peep.

"This will take your career into the stratosphere. And I'll be giving you a promotion to executive editor."

Kyle turned to the first page, seeing the opening lines.

> This is my story about the secret to immortality. Read carefully and let me teach you. Take notes, my friend. Welcome to DEVIL'S HOPYARD.

"So what do you say?" Carter asked, giving a sharklike grin.

From deep down, Kyle let out a never-ending silent scream.

ACKNOWLEDGMENTS

I am exceedingly grateful to all the people who helped this book come to life.

First and foremost, my awesome editor, Brendan Deneen, who came up with the concept of *Cape Fear* set in the publishing world, and not only gave me the opportunity to write his stellar idea but also allowed me the freedom to make it into the twisty thriller I'd always dreamed of writing, and then pruned away anything unnecessary. I am truly indebted.

To my fantastic agent, Sam Hiyate, who's also a great friend and never gave up on me in the early years. Working with Sam has been like getting a second MFA degree, and I've become a better writer because of everything I've learned from him. Also, to all the other agents at The Rights Factory, who care for and build up their clients and are a blast to go out with when in town.

To my super-supportive readers and all their edits and words of encouragement. Vicky Forsberg and Erin Conroy for their judicious eyes on the early chapters when the book was an infant, and Jennifer Close,

Michael Soussan, Vincent Zandri, Margot Berwin, and Dad for their comments when the book had grown. Also to Lila Cecil, for letting me work at an ideal desk in her home where some of the first pages were crafted. And to David Muller and Johanna Bartha, for another great author photo.

To everyone at Thomas Dunne Books and St. Martin's Press, for making my first book at a big press such a pleasurable experience. Nicole Sohl was very helpful with every question I had, and Jimmy Iacobelli created an amazingly kick-ass cover. And a huge thanks to Elizabeth Curione and Cynthia Merman for their sharp eyes and careful copyedits.

To Jon Bassoff and Jonathan Woods, for editing and publishing my first novel, *Slow Down,* at New Pulp Press and giving a start to a career that I've fantasized about having since I was a kid.

To all my friends and family who were soundboards during this last year and half. Being a novelist is pretty much as solitary a profession as one can choose, so I'm lucky to have so many wonderful people in my life.

To the authors I read between drafts, especially Stephen King and Lou Berney, whose books were valuable guides while creating my own. And to Thomas Berger's *Arthur Rex,* for being responsible for the initial spark.

Finally, a good chunk of *The Mentor* was written outside, so thanks to nature! Specifically, Gramercy Park, Tudor City Park, Santa Monica Beach, and always, my tree in Central Park that perfectly contours to the groove of my back. You rock, tree.